AN ASTOUNDING TWO-VOLUME
ANTHOLOGY
BY A MASTER EXPLORER OF THE
EXOTIC AND THE INFINITE . . .

A magnificent collection of mind-blasting stories,
private insights, public opinions, and personal notes
that cover more than three dazzling decades on the
wild side of human experience.

"Bester demonstrates that his creative perceptions
are as unpredictable and fascinating as those of John
Collier, Roald Dahl, William Kotzwinkle, or David
Ely."

—Harlan Ellison
The Los Angeles Times

"A MUST"

—*The Des Moines Register*

"Ferociously inventive . . . irresistible . . . outrageous . . . a veritable feast."

—Robert Silverberg
The Pacific Sun

"Eerie and intriguing"

—*The Chicago Tribune*

STARLIGHT
THE GREAT SHORT FICTION OF
ALFRED BESTER

(Originally published in two volumes as:
THE LIGHT FANTASTIC
and STAR LIGHT, STAR BRIGHT)

A BERKLEY MEDALLION BOOK
published by
BERKLEY PUBLISHING CORPORATION

Lurton Blassingame
60 East 42nd Street
New York, N.Y. 10017

SBN 425-03451-8

BERKLEY MEDALLION BOOKS are published by
Berkley Publishing Corporation
200 Madison Avenue
New York, N.Y. 10016

BERKLEY MEDALLION BOOK ® TM 757, 375

Printed in the United States of America

Berkley Medallion Edition, JULY, 1977

For the fans—
for the wonderful demented fans

Contents

5,271,009

THERE I was in our cottage out on Fire Island, taking the summer off because the shows I wrote took the summer off. My wife was an actress then and went into New York during the week to work or look for work, leaving me alone to enjoy the fun and games.

They weren't what you're thinking. The Island does have and indeed has earned a raunchy reputation, but Walpurgis-nacht *indulgence is not for everybody and certainly not for me, which gave me a curious schizorepute. Half our village believed I was a stealthy swinger who could and did chase women and girls into bed whenever he pleased. The other half believed I was an undercover queen. I was delighted with both.

No, I vacationed very quietly. I'd go surf-fishing every dawn and dusk, occasionally catching a respectable fish. I'd laze around in the cottage, reading. For real entertainment I'd attend the police magistrates' hearings. The crimes were earth-shaking. Failure to remove garbage can from front of house before 10 A.M.—Fine: $2.00. Failure to wear covering over bathing dress on public walks—Fine: $2.00. Noisy party after 11 P.M.—Fine: a whopping $10.00. The garbage can raps were the most fun; the ladies involved would argue passionately, plead, burst into tears, even bring lawyer friends to defend them. In the end they paid the $2.00.

The other main source of entertainment was the morning visit to the post office. I didn't expect or receive much mail; it was merely an excuse to saunter down the main street of the village and watch it in action. So who so surprised as me when I received a parcel from Tony Boucher and Mick

1

McComas who were then editing Fantasy & Science Fiction *into the witty sophistication which it has never lost. The parcel contained a garish color reproduction of a cover for the magazine and a letter asking me if I could write a story to go with the cover.*

I'd heard of this sort of operation but it had never happened to me, so I was intrigued. I examined the cover closely for stimulation. It was absurd. It depicted a case-hardened criminal wearing a nineteenth-century convict uniform . . . you know, the striped kind . . . with the number 5,271,009 emblazoned on his chest. He was chained to a big chunk of rock, floating in space. I'm fairly certain that he wore a helmet of some sort attached to oxygen cylinders. Come to think of it, he had to; how else could he survive in space?

I laughed and decided to reject the assignment with thanks. I was on splendid terms with Tony and Mick and I knew they wouldn't hold it against me. And yet . . . And yet . . . I went for a walk on the beach. It was dead low tide and the flat, hard-packed sand at the water's edge made for a wonderful stroll. I thought about that silly cover, keeping an eye on the alert for attractive shells and interesting lagan and derelict washed up on the shore.

You can't take that preposterous painting seriously, I told myself. No one could. It's a mad camp, and if you do a story to go with it, the story will have to be a mad camp, too. But what? I wondered what for a couple of miles, relaxed and happy, utterly devoid of ideas but not pressing myself. I was content to let my unconscious do its fair share of the work. If it came up with something, fine. If it didn't . . . well, you can't win 'em all. And there's a sand dollar, by gum! Milly collects sand dollars.

Apparently my unconscious had been waiting a long time to give me a piece of its mind because it began abusing me. Listen, it said, pay attention: You've been making fun of the clichés and stereotypes of science fiction for years. This certainly is a chance for more of the same, but while you're at it, the least you can do, if you're honest, is make fun of yourself, too.

What sort of fun?

All the childish fantasies still in your mind. Swept under the carpet, no doubt, but very much with you.

I tried arguing: What makes you think that readers will identify with my fantasies?

What makes you think you're so different? You share them with everybody else.

I tried pleading: But if I did, the story would turn episodic. There wouldn't be any central spine to hold it all together.

You claim you're a writer, don't you? Come up with something.

So in the end I paid the $2.00 and came up with something. The fantasies are all my own. Most of the characters are based on people I know. I enjoyed the writing tremendously because the structure was loose enough to give me a free hand, and because I discovered that I was great fun to spoof; I've never been able to take myself very seriously.

There are still two aspects of the story which displease me. I don't care for the title, and when the story was reprinted in another collection, I changed it to "The Star Comber." However, I've been told that "5,271,009" is rather different and oddly grabby, so I've gone back to it.

The other irritant is the tagline of the story. I spent two whole days trying to come up with something more satisfactory, and failed. I appealed to Tony and Mick for help. They failed too. (The best that Tony could do was reassure me that 5,271,009 was indeed a prime number.) So we let the original stand, and I'm still unhappy with it. And yet even if I did find the right tag this very moment, it's too late to substitute it. Altering earlier work is a heinous crime. Fine: $5,271,009.

P.S. My editor in this edition has solved the problem by cutting the Gordian Knot, which the dictionary defines as "to solve a problem quickly and boldly." My quick and bold editor solved the tag tsimmis *by cutting it completely.*

Take two parts of Beelzebub, two of Israfel, one of Monte Cristo, one of Cyrano, mix violently, season with mystery and you have Mr. Solon Aquila. He is tall, gaunt, sprightly in manner, bitter in expression, and when he laughs his dark eyes turn into wounds. His occupation is unknown. He is wealthy without visible means of support. He is seen everywhere and understood nowhere. There is something odd about his life.

This is what's odd about Mr. Aquila, and you can make what you will of it. When he walks he is never forced to wait on a traffic signal. When he desires to ride there is always a vacant taxi on hand. When he bustles into his hotel an elevator always happens to be waiting. When he enters a store, a salesclerk is always free to serve him. There always happens to be a table available for Mr. Aquila in restaurants. There are always last-minute ticket returns when he craves entertainment at sold-out shows.

You can question waiters, hack drivers, elevator girls, salesmen, box-office men. There is no conspiracy. Mr. Aquila does not bribe or blackmail for these petty conveniences. In any case, it would not be possible for him to bribe or blackmail the automatic clock that governs the city traffic-signal system. These things, which make life so convenient for him, simply happen. Mr. Solon Aquila is never disappointed. Presently we shall hear about his first disappointment and see what it led to.

Mr. Aquila has been seen fraternizing in low saloons, in middle saloons, in high saloons. He has been met in bagnios, at coronations, executions, circuses, magistrate's courts and handbook offices. He has been known to buy antique cars, historic jewels, incunabula, pornography, chemicals, porro prisms, polo ponies and full-choke shotguns.

"*HimmelHerrGottSeiDank!* I'm crazy, man, crazy. Eclectic, by God," he told a flabbergasted department-store president. "The *Weltmann* type, *nicht wahr?* My ideal: Goethe. *Tout le monde.* God damn."

He spoke a spectacular tongue of mixed metaphors and meanings. Dozens of languages and dialects came out in machine-gun bursts. Apparently he also lied *ad libitum.*

"*Sacré bleu,* Jeez!" he was heard to say once. "Aquila from the Latin. Means aquiline. *O tempora, o mores.* Speech by Cicero. My ancestor."

And another time: "My idol: Kipling. Took my name

from him. Aquila, one of his heroes. God damn. Greatest Negro writer since *Uncle Tom's Cabin.*''

On the morning that Mr. Solon Aquila was stunned by his first disappointment, he bustled into the atelier of Lagan & Derelict, dealers in paintings, sculpture and rare objects of art. It was his intention to buy a painting. Mr. James Derelict knew Aquila as a client. Aquila had already purchased a Frederic Remington and a Winslow Homer some time ago when, by another odd coincidence, he had bounced into the Madison Avenue shop one minute after the coveted painting went up for sale. Mr. Derelict had also seen Mr. Aquila boat a prize striper at Montauk.

''*Bon soir, bel esprit*, God damn, Jimmy,'' Mr. Aquila said. He was on first-name terms with everyone. ''Here's a cool day for color, *oui*! Cool. Slang. I have in me to buy a picture.''

''Good morning, Mr. Aquila,'' Derelict answered. He had the seamed face of a cardsharp, but his eyes were honest and his smile was disarming. However at this moment his smile seemed strained, as though the volatile appearance of Aquila had unnerved him.

''I'm in the mood for your man, by Jeez,'' Aquila said, rapidly opening cases, fingering ivories and tasting the porcelains. ''What's his name, my old? Artist like Bosch. Like Heinrich Kley. You handle him, *parbleu*, exclusive. *O si sic omnia,* by Zeus!''

''Jeffrey Halsyon?'' Derelict asked timidly.

''*Oeil de boeuf!*'' Aquila cried. ''What a memory. Chryselephantine. Exactly the artist I want. He is my favorite. A monochrome, preferably. A small Jeffrey Halsyon for Aquila, *bitte*. Wrap her up.''

''I wouldn't have believed it,'' Derelict muttered.

''Ah! Ah-ha? This is not one hundred proof guaranteed Ming,'' Mr. Aquila exclaimed brandishing an exquisite vase. ''*Caveat emptor,* by damn. Well, Jimmy? I snap my fingers. No Halsyons in stock, old faithful?''

''It's extremely odd, Mr. Aquila,'' Derelict seemed to struggle with himself. ''Your coming in like this. A Halsyon monochrome arrived not five minutes ago.''

''You see? *Tempo ist Richtung.* Well?''

"I'd rather not show it to you. For personal reasons, Mr. Aquila."

"*HimmelHerrGott! Pourquoi?* She's bespoke?"

"N-no, sir. Not for *my* personal reasons. For *your* personal reasons."

"Oh? God damn. Explain myself to me."

"Anyway, it isn't for sale, Mr. Aquila. It can't be sold."

"For why not? Speak, old fish and chips."

"I can't say, Mr. Aquila."

"*Zut alors!* Must I judo your arm, Jimmy? You can't show. You can't sell. Me, internally, I have pressurized myself for a Jeffrey Halsyon. My favorite. God damn. Show me the Halsyon or *sic transit gloria mundi*. You hear me, Jimmy?"

Derelict hesitated, then shrugged. "Very well, Mr. Aquila. I'll show you."

Derelict led Aquila past cases of china and silver, past lacquer and bronzes and suits of shimmering armor to the gallery in the rear of the shop where dozens of paintings hung on the gray velour walls, glowing under warm spotlights. He opened a drawer in a Goddard breakfront and took out an envelope. On the envelope was printed BABYLON INSTITUTE. From the envelope Derelict withdrew a dollar bill and handed it to Mr. Aquila.

"Jeffrey Halsyon's latest," he said.

With a fine pen and carbon ink, a cunning hand had drawn another portrait over the face of George Washington on the dollar bill. It was a hateful, diabolic face set in a hellish background. It was a face to strike terror, in a scene to inspire loathing. The face was a portrait of Mr. Aquila.

"God damn," Mr. Aquila said.

"You see, sir? I didn't want to hurt your feelings."

"Now I must own him, big boy." Mr. Aquila appeared to be fascinated by the portrait. "Is she accident or for purpose? Does Halsyon know myself? *Ergo sum.*"

"Not to my knowledge, Mr. Aquila. But in any event I can't sell the drawing. It's evidence of a felony . . . mutilating United States currency. It must be destroyed."

"Never!" Mr. Aquila returned the drawing as though he feared the dealer would instantly set fire to it. "Never,

Jimmy. Nevermore quoth the raven. God damn. Why does he draw on money, Halsyon? My picture, pfui. Criminal libels but *n'importe*. But pictures on money? Wasteful. *Joci causa*.''

"He's insane, Mr. Aquila."

"No! Yes? Insane?" Aquila was shocked.

"Quite insane, sir. It's very sad. They've had to put him away. He spends his time drawing these pictures on money."

"God damn, *mon ami*. Who gives him money?"

"I do, Mr. Aquila; and his friends. Whenever we visit him he begs for money for his drawings."

"*Le jour viendra*, by Jeez! Why you don't give him paper for drawings, eh, my ancient of days?"

Derelict smiled sadly. "We tried that, sir. When we gave Jeff paper, he drew pictures of money."

"*HimmelHerrGott!* My favorite artist. In the loony bin. *Eh bien*. How in the holy hell am I to buy paintings from same if such be the case?"

"You won't, Mr. Aquila. I'm afraid no one will ever buy a Halsyon again. He's quite hopeless."

"Why does he jump his tracks, Jimmy?"

"They say it's a withdrawal, Mr. Aquila. His success did it to him."

"Ah? Q.E.D. me, big boy. Translate."

"Well, sir, he's still a young man; in his thirties and very immature. When he became so very successful, he wasn't ready for it. He wasn't prepared for the responsibilities of his life and his career. That's what the doctors told me. So he turned his back on everything and withdrew into childhood."

"Ah? And the drawing on money?"

"They say that's his symbol of his return to childhood, Mr. Aquila. It proves he's too young to know what money is for."

"Ah? *Oui. Ja*. Astute, by crackey. And my portrait?"

"I can't explain that, Mr. Aquila, unless you have met him in the past and he remembers you somehow. Or it may be a coincidence."

"Hmmm. Perhaps. So. You know something, my attic of Greece? I am disappointed. *Je n'oublierai jamais*. I am most severely disappointed. God damn. No more Halsyons ever? *Merde*. My slogan. We must do something about Jeffrey

Halsyon. I will not be disappointed. We must do something.''

Mr. Solon Aquila nodded his head emphatically, took out a cigarette, took out a lighter, then paused, deep in thought. After a long moment, he nodded again, this time with decision, and did an astonishing thing. He returned the lighter to his pocket, took out another, glanced around quickly and lit it under Mr. Derelict's nose.

Mr. Derelict appeared not to notice. Mr. Derelict appeared, in one instant, to be frozen. Allowing the lighter to burn, Mr. Aquila placed it carefully on a ledge in front of the art dealer who stood before it without moving. The orange flame gleamed on his glassy eyeballs.

Aquila darted out into the shop, searched and found a rare Chinese crystal globe. He took it from its case, warmed it against his heart, and peered into it. He mumbled. He nodded. He returned the globe to the case, went to the cashier's desk, took a pad and pencil and began ciphering in symbols that bore no relationship to any language or any graphology. He nodded again, tore up the sheet of paper, and took out his wallet.

From the wallet he removed a dollar bill. He placed the bill on the glass counter, took an assortment of fountain pens from his vest pocket, selected one and unscrewed it. Carefully shielding his eyes, he allowed one drop to fall from the pen point onto the bill. There was a blinding flash of light. There was a humming vibration that slowly died.

Mr. Aquila returned the pens to his pocket, carefully picked up the bill by a corner, and ran back into the picture gallery where the art dealer still stood staring glassily at the orange flame. Aquila fluttered the bill before the sightless eyes.

"Listen, my ancient," Aquila whispered. "You will visit Jeffrey Halsyon this afternoon. *N'est-ce pas?* You will give him this very own coin of the realm when he asks for drawing materials? Eh? God damn." He removed Mr. Derelict's wallet from his pocket, placed the bill inside and returned the wallet.

"And this is why you make the visit," Aquila continued. "It is because you have had an inspiration from *le Diable*

Boiteux. Nolens volens, the lame devil has inspired you with a plan for healing Jeffrey Halsyon. God damn. You will show him samples of his great art of the past to bring him to his senses. Memory is the all-mother. *HimmelHerrGott.* You hear me, big boy? You do what I say. Go today and devil take the hindmost.''

Mr. Aquila picked up the burning lighter, lit his cigarette and permitted the flame to go out. As he did so, he said: ''No, my holy of holies! Jeffrey Halsyon is too great an artist to languish in durance vile. He must be returned to this world. He must be returned to me. *E sempre l'ora.* I will not be disappointed. You hear me, Jimmy? I will not!''

''Perhaps there's hope, Mr. Aquila,'' James Derelict said. ''Something's just occurred to me while you were talking . . . a way to bring Jeff back to sanity. I'm going to try this afternoon.''

As he drew the face of the Faraway Fiend over George Washington's portrait on a bill, Jeffrey Halsyon dictated his autobiography to nobody.

''Like Cellini,'' he recited. ''Line and literature simultaneously. Hand in hand, although all art is one art, holy brothers in barbiturate, near ones and dear ones in Nembutal. Very well. I commence: I was born. I am dead. Baby wants a dollar. No—''

He arose from the padded floor and raged from padded wall to padded wall, envisioning anger as a deep purple fury running into the pale lavenders of recrimination by the magic of his brushwork, his chiaroscuro, by the clever blending of oil, pigment, light and the stolen genius of Jeffrey Halsyon torn from him by the Faraway Fiend whose hideous face—

''Begin anew,'' he muttered. ''We darken the highlights. Start with the underpainting. . . .'' He squatted on the floor again, picked up the quill drawing pen whose point was warranted harmless, dipped it into carbon ink whose contents were warranted poisonless, and applied himself to the monstrous face of the Faraway Fiend which was replacing the first President on the dollar.

''I was born,'' he dictated to space while his cunning hand wrought beauty and horror on the banknote paper. ''I had peace. I had hope. I had art. I had peace. Mama. Papa. Kin I have a glass of water? Oooo! There was a big bad bogey man who gave me a bad look; and now baby's afraid. Mama! Baby wantsa make pretty pictures onna pretty paper for Mama and Papa. Look, Mama. Baby makin' a picture of the bad bogey man with a mean look, a black look with his black eyes like pools of hell, like cold fires of terror, like faraway fiends from faraway fears—Who's that!''

The cell door unbolted. Halsyon leaped into a corner and cowered, naked and squalling, as the door was opened for the Faraway Fiend to enter. But it was only the medicine man in his white jacket and a stranger-man in black suit, black homburg, carrying a black portfolio with the initials J.D. lettered on it in a bastard gold Gothic with ludicrous over-tones of Goudy and Baskerville.

"Well, Jeffrey?" the medicine man inquired heartily.

"Dollar?" Halsyon whined. "Kin baby have a dollar?"

"I've brought an old friend, Jeffrey. You remember Mr. Derelict?"

"Dollar," Halsyon whined. "Baby wants a dollar."

"What happened to the last one, Jeffrey? You haven't finished it yet, have you?"

Halsyon sat on the bill to conceal it, but the medicine man was too quick for him. He snatched it up and he and the stranger-man examined it.

"As great as all the rest," Derelict sighed. "Greater! What a magnificent talent wasting away. . . ."

Halsyon began to weep. "Baby wants a dollar!" he cried.

The stranger-man took out his wallet, selected a dollar bill and handed it to Halsyon. As soon as Halsyon touched it, he heard it sing and he tried to sing with it, but it was singing him a private song so he had to listen.

It was a lovely dollar; smooth but not too new, with a faintly matte surface that would take ink like kisses. George Washington looked reproachful but resigned, as though he was used to the treatment in store for him. And indeed he might well be, for he was much older on this dollar. Much older than on any other, for his serial number was 5,271,009 which made him 5,000,000 years old and more, and the oldest he had ever been before was 2,000,000.

As Halsyon squatted contently on the floor and dipped his pen in the ink as the dollar told him to, he heard the medicine man say, "I don't think I should leave you alone with him, Mr. Derelict."

"No, we must be alone together, doctor. Jeff always was shy about his work. He could only discuss it with me privately."

"How much time would you need?"

"Give me an hour."

"I doubt very much whether it'll do any good."

"But there's no harm trying?"

"I suppose not. All right, Mr. Derelict. Call the nurse when you're through."

The door opened; the door closed. The stranger-man named Derelict put his hand on Halsyon's shoulder in a friendly, intimate way. Halsyon looked up at him and grinned cleverly, meanwhile waiting for the sound of the bolt in the door. It came; like a shot, like a final nail in a coffin.

"Jeff, I've brought some of your old work with me," Derelict said in a voice that was only approximately casual. "I thought you might like to look it over with me."

"Have you got a watch on you?" Halsyon asked.

Restraining his start of surprise at Halsyon's normal tone, the art dealer took out his pocket watch and displayed it.

"Lend it to me for a minute."

Derelict unchained the watch and handed it over. Halsyon took it carefully and said, "All right. Go ahead with the pictures."

"Jeff?" Derelict exclaimed. "This is you again, isn't it? This is the way you always—"

"Thirty," Halsyon interrupted. "Thirty-five, forty, forty-five, fifty, fifty-five, ONE." He concentrated on the flicking second hand with rapt expectation.

"No, I guess it isn't," the dealer muttered. "I only imagined you sounded—Oh well." He opened the portfolio and began sorting mounted drawings.

"Forty, forty-five, fifty-five, TWO."

"Here's one of your earliest, Jeff. Remember when you came into the gallery with the roughs and we thought you were the new polisher from the agency? Took you months to forgive us. You always claimed we bought your first picture just to apologize. Do you still think so?''

"Forty, forty-five, fifty, fifty-five, THREE."

"Here's that tempera that gave you so many heartaches. I was wondering if you'd care to try another? I really don't think tempera is as inflexible as you claim, and I'd be interested to have you try again now that your technique's so much more mature. What do you say?''

"Forty, forty-five, fifty, fifty-five, FOUR."

"Jeff, put down that watch."

"Ten, fifteen, twenty, twenty-five . . ."

"What the devil's the point of counting minutes?''

"Well," Halsyon said reasonably, "sometimes they lock the door and go away. Other times they lock up and stay and spy on you. But they never spy longer than three minutes, so I'm giving them five just to make sure. FIVE."

Halsyon gripped the pocket watch in his big fist and drove the fist cleanly into Derelict's jaw. The dealer dropped without a sound. Halsyon dragged him to the wall, stripped him naked, dressed himself in his clothes, repacked the portfolio, and closed it. He picked up the dollar bill and pocketed it. He picked up the bottle of carbon ink warranted nonpoisonous and smeared the contents over his face.

Choking and shouting, he brought the nurse to the door.

"Let me out of here," Halsyon cried in a muffled voice. "That maniac tried to drown me. Threw ink in my face. I want out!"

The door was unbolted and opened. Halsyon shoved past the nurse-man, cunningly mopping his blackened face with a hand that only masked it more. As the nurse-man started to enter the cell, Halsyon said, "Never mind Halsyon. He's all right. Get me a towel or something. Hurry!"

The nurse-man locked the door again, turned and ran down the corridor. Halsyon waited until he disappeared into a supply room, then turned and ran in the opposite direction. He went through the heavy doors to the main wing corridor, still cleverly mopping, still sputtering with cunning indignation. He reached the main building. He was halfway out and still no alarm. He knew those brazen bells. They tested them every Wednesday noon.

It's like a game, he told himself. It's fun. It's nothing to be scared of. It's being safely, sanely, joyously a kid again and when we quit playing, I'm going home to mama and dinner and papa reading me the funnies and I'm a kid again, really a kid again, forever.

There still was no hue and cry when he reached the main floor. He complained about his indignity to the receptionist. He complained to the protection guards as he forged James Derelict's name in the visitors' book, and his inky hand smeared such a mess on the page that the forgery was undetected. The guard buzzed the final gate open. Halsyon passed through into the street, and as he started away he heard the brass of the bells begin a clattering that terrified him.

He ran. He stopped. He tried to stroll. He could not. He lurched down the street until he heard the guards shouting. He darted around a corner, and another, tore up endless streets, heard cars behind him, sirens, bells, shouts, commands. It was a ghastly catherine wheel of flight. Searching desperately for a hiding place, Halsyon darted into the hallway of a desolate tenement.

Halsyon began to climb the stairs. He went up three at a clip, then two, then struggled step by step as his strength failed and panic paralyzed him. He stumbled at a landing and fell against a door. The door opened. The Faraway Fiend stood within, smiling briskly, rubbing his hands.

"Glückliche Reise," he said. "On the dot. God damn. You twenty-three skidooed, eh? Enter, my old. I'm expecting you. Be it never so humble . . ."

Halsyon screamed.

"No, no, no! No *Sturm und Drang,* my beauty," Mr. Aquila clapped a hand over Halsyon's mouth, heaved him up, dragged him through the doorway and slammed the door.

"Presto-chango," he laughed. "Exit Jeffrey Halsyon from mortal ken. *Dieu vous garde.*"

Halsyon freed his mouth, screamed again and fought hysterically, biting and kicking. Mr. Aquila made a clucking noise, dipped into his pocket and brought out a package of cigarettes. He flipped one out of the pack expertly and broke it under Halsyon's nose. The artist at once subsided and suffered himself to be led to a couch, where Aquila cleansed the ink from his face and hands.

"Better, eh?" Mr. Aquila chuckled. "Non-habit-forming. God damn. Drinks now called for."

He filled a shot glass from a decanter, added a tiny cube of purple ice from a fuming bucket, and placed the drink in Halsyon's hand. Compelled by a gesture from Aquila, the artist drank it off. It made his brain buzz. He stared around, breathing heavily. He was in what appeared to be the luxurious waiting room of a Park Avenue physician. Queen Anne furniture. Axminster rug. Two Hogarths and a Copley on the wall in gilt frames. They were genuine, Halsyon realized with amazement. Then, with even more amazement, he realized that he was thinking with coherence, with continuity. His mind was quite clear.

He passed a heavy hand over his forehead. "What's happened?" he asked faintly. "There's like . . . Something like a fever behind me. Nightmares."

"You have been sick," Aquila replied. "I am blunt, my old. This is a temporary return to sanity. It is no feat, God damn. Any doctor can do it. Niacin plus carbon dioxide. *Id genus omne*. Only temporary. We must search for something more permanent."

"What's this place?"

"Here? My office. Anteroom without. Consultation room within. Laboratory to left. In God we trust."

"I know you," Halsyon mumbled. "I know you from somewhere. I know your face."

"*Oui*. You have drawn and redrawn me in your fever. *Ecce homo*. But you have the advantage, Halsyon. Where have we met? I ask myself." Aquila put on a brilliant speculum, tilted it over his left eye and let it shine into Halsyon's face. "Now I ask you. Where have we met?"

Hypnotized by the light, Halsyon answered dreamily. "At the Beaux Arts Ball. . . . A long time ago. . . . Before the fever. . . ."

"Ah? *Sí*. It was one half year ago. I was there. An unfortunate night."

"No. A glorious night. . . . Gay, happy fun. . . . Like a school dance. . . . Like a prom in costume. . . ."

"Always back to the childhood, eh?" Mr. Aquila murmured. "We must attend to that. *Cetera desunt,* young Lochinvar. Continue."

"I was with Judy. . . . We realized we were in love that night. We realized how wonderful life was going to be. And then you passed and looked at me. . . . Just once. You looked at me. It was horrible."

"Tsk!" Mr. Aquila clicked his tongue in vexation. "Now I remember said incident. I was unguarded. Bad news from home. A pox on both my houses."

"You passed in red and black. . . . Satanic. Wearing no mask. You looked at me. . . . A red and black look I never forgot. A lcok from black eyes like pools of hell, like cold fires of terror. And with that look you robbed me of everything . . . of joy, of hope, of love, of life. . . ."

"No, no!" Mr. Aquila said sharply. "Let us understand ourselves. My carelessness was the key that unlocked the door. But you fell into a chasm of your own making. Nevertheless, old beer and skittles, we must alter same." He removed the speculum and shook his finger at Halsyon. "We must bring you back to the land of the living. *Auxilium ab alto*. Jeez. That is for why I have arranged this meeting. What I have done I will undone, eh? But you must climb out of your own chasm. Knit up the ravelled sleave of care. Come inside."

He took Halsyon's arm, led him down a paneled hall, past a neat office and into a spanking white laboratory. It was all tile and glass with shelves of reagent bottles, porcelain filters, an electric oven, stock jars of acids, bins of raw materials. There was a small round elevation in the center of the floor, a sort of dais. Mr. Aquila placed a stool on the dais, placed Halsyon on the stool, got into a white lab coat and began to assemble apparatus.

"You," he chatted, "are an artist of the utmost. I do not *dorer la pilule*. When Jimmy Derelict told me you were no longer at work. God damn! We must return him to his muttons, I said. Solon Aquila must own many canvases of Jeffrey Halsyon. We shall cure him. *Hoc age*."

"You're a doctor?" Halsyon asked.

"No. Let us say a warlock. Strictly speaking a witch-pathologist. Very high class. No nostrums. Strictly modern magic. Black magic and white magic are passé, *n'est-ce pas?* I cover entire spectrum, specializing mostly in the 15,000 angstrom band.''

''You're a witch-doctor? Never!''

''Oh yes.''

''In this kind of place?''

''Ah? Ha? You too are deceived, eh? It is our camouflage. Many a modern laboratory you think concerns itself with toothpaste is devoted to magic. But we are scientific too. *Parbleu!* We move with the times, we warlocks. Witch's Brew now complies with Pure Food and Drug Act. Familiars one hundred percent sterile. Sanitary brooms. Cellophane-wrapped curses. Father Satan in rubber gloves. Thanks to Lord Lister; or is is Pasteur? My idol.''

The witch-pathologist gathered raw materials, consulted an ephemeris, ran off some calculations on an electronic computer and continued to chat.

''Fugit hora,'' Aquila said. ''Your trouble, my old, is loss of sanity. *Oui?* Lost in one damn flight from reality and one damn desperate search for peace brought on by one unguarded look from me to you. *Hélas!* I apologize for that, R.S.V.P.'' With what looked like a miniature tennis linemarker, he rolled a circle around Halsyon on the dais. ''But your trouble is, to wit: You search for the peace of infancy. You should be fighting to acquire the peace of maturity, *n'est-ce pas?* Jeez.''

Aquila drew circles and pentagons with a glittering compass and rule, weighed out powders on a micro-beam balance, dropped various liquids into crucibles from calibrated burettes, and continued: ''Many warlocks do brisk trade in potions from Fountains of Youths. Oh yes. Are many youths and many fountains; but none for you. No. Youth is not for artists. Age is the cure. We must purge your youth and grow you up, *nicht wahr?*''

''No,'' Halsyon argued. ''No. Youth is the art. Youth is the dream. Youth is the blessing.''

''For some, yes. For many, not. Not for you. You are cursed, my adolescent. We must purge you. Lust for power. Lust for sex. Injustice collecting. Escape from reality. Passion for revenges. Oh yes, Father Freud is also my idol. We wipe your slate clean at very small price."

"What price?"

"You will see when we are finished."

Mr. Aquila deposited liquids and powders around the helpless artist in crucibles and petri dishes. He measured and cut fuses, set up a train from the circle to an electric timer which he carefully adjusted. He went to a shelf of serum bottles, took down a small Woulff vial numbered 5-271-009, filled a syringe and meticulously injected Halyson.

"We begin," he said, "the purge of your dreams. *Voilà.*"

He tripped the electric timer and stepped behind a lead shield. There was a moment of silence. Suddenly black music crashed from a concealed loudspeaker and a recorded voice began an intolerable chant. In quick succession the powders and liquids around Halsyon burst into flame. He was engulfed in music and fire. The world began to spin around him in a roaring confusion. . . .

The president of the United Nations came to him. He was tall and gaunt, sprightly but bitter. He was wringing his hands in dismay.

"Mr. Halsyon! Mr. Halsyon!" he cried. "Where you been, my cupcake? God damn. *Hoc tempore.* Do you know what has happened?"

"No," Halsyon answered. "What's happened?"

"After your escape from the loony bin. Bango! Atom bombs everywhere. The two-hour war. It is over. *Hora fugit,* old faithful. Virility is over."

"What!"

"Hard radiation, Mr. Halsyon, has destroyed the virility of the world. God damn. You are the only man left capable of engendering children. No doubt on account of a mysterious mutant strain in your makeup which it makes you different. Jeez."

"No."

"*Oui.* It is your responsibility to repopulate the world. We have taken for you a suite at the Odeon. It has three bedrooms. Three; my favorite. A prime number."

"Hot dog!" Halsyon said. "This is my big dream."

His progress to the Odeon was a triumph. He was garlanded with flowers, serenaded, hailed and cheered. Ecstatic women displayed themselves wickedly before him, begging for his attention. In his suite, Halsyon was wined and dined. A tall, gaunt man entered subserviently. He was sprightly but bitter. He had a list in his hand.

"I am World Procurer at your service, Mr. Halsyon," he said. He consulted his list. "God damn. Are 5,271,009 virgins clamoring for your attention. All guaranteed beautiful. *Ewig-Weibliche*. Pick a number from one to 5,000,000."

"We'll start with a redhead," Halsyon said.

They brought him a redhead. She was slender and boyish, with a small, hard bosom. The next was fuller with a rollicking rump. The fifth was Junoesque and her breasts were like African pears. The tenth was a voluptuous Rembrandt. The twentieth was slender and boyish with a small, hard bosom.

"Haven't we met before?" Halsyon inquired.

"No," she said.

The next was fuller, with a rollicking rump.

"The body is familiar," Halsyon said.

"No," she answered.

The fiftieth was Junoesque, with breasts like African pears.

"Surely?" Halsyon said.

"Never," she answered.

The World Procurer entered with Halsyon's morning aphrodisiac.

"Never touch the stuff," Halsyon said.

"God damn," the Procurer exclaimed. "You are a veritable giant. An elephant. No wonder you are the beloved Adam. *Tant soit peu*. No wonder they all weep for love of you." He drank off the aphrodisiac himself.

"Have you noticed they're all getting to look alike?" Halsyon complained.

"But no! Are all different. *Parbleu!* This is an insult to my office."

"Oh, they're different from one to another, but the types keep repeating."

"Ah? This is life, my old. All life is cyclic. Have you not, as an artist, noticed?"

"I didn't think it applied to love."

"To all things. *Wahrheit und Dichtung*."

"What was that you said about them weeping?"

"*Oui*. They all weep."

"Why?"

"For ecstatic love of you. God damn."

Halsyon thought over the succession of boyish, rollicking, Junoesque, Rembrandtesque, wiry, red, blonde, brunette, white, black, and brown women.

"I hadn't noticed," he said.

"Observe today, my world father. Shall we commence?"

It was true. Halsyon hadn't noticed. They all wept. He was flattered but depressed.

"Why don't you laugh a little?" he asked.

They would not or could not.

Upstairs on the Odeon roof where Halsyon took his afternoon exercise, he questioned his trainer who was a tall, gaunt man with a sprightly but bitter expression.

"Ah?" said the trainer. "God damn. I don't know, old scotch and soda. Perhaps because it is a traumatic experience for them."

"Traumatic?" Halsyon puffed. "Why? What do I do to them?"

"Ah-ha? You joke, eh? All the world knows what you do to them."

"No, I mean . . . How can it be traumatic? They're all fighting to get to me, aren't they? Don't I come up to expectations?"

"A mystery. *Tripotage*. Now, beloved father of the world, we practice the push-ups. Ready? Begin."

Downstairs, in the Odeon restaurant, Halsyon questioned the headwaiter, a tall, gaunt man with a sprightly manner but bitter expression.

"We are men of the world, Mr. Halsyon. *Suo jure*. Surely you understand. These women love you and can expect no more than one night of love. God damn. Naturally they are disappointed."

"What do they want?"

"What every woman wants, my gateway to the west. A permanent relationship. Marriage."

"Marriage!"

"Oui."

"All of them?"

"Oui."

"All right. I'll marry all 5,271,009."

But the World Procurer objected. "No, no, no, young Lochinvar. God damn. Impossible. Aside from religious difficulties there are human also. Who could manage such a harem?"

"Then I'll marry one."

"No, no, no. *Pensez à moi.* How could you make the choice? How could you select? By lottery, drawing straws, tossing coins?"

"I've already selected one."

"Ah? Which?"

"My girl," Halsyon said slowly. "Judith Field."

"So. Your sweetheart?"

"Yes."

"She is far down on the list of five million."

"She's always been number one on my list. I want Judith." Halsyon sighed. "I remember how she looked at the Beaux Arts Ball. . . . There was a full moon. . . ."

"But there will be no full moon until the twenty-sixth."

"I want Judith."

"The others will tear her apart out of jealousy. No, no, no, Mr. Halsyon, we must stick to the schedule. One night for all, no more for any."

"I want Judith . . . or else."

"It will have to be discussed in council. God damn."

It was discussed in the U. N. council by a dozen delegates, all tall, gaunt, sprightly but bitter. It was decided to permit Jeffrey Halsyon one secret marriage.

"But no domestic ties," the World Procurer warned. "No faithfulness to your wife. That must be understood. We cannot spare you from our program. You are indispensable."

They brought the lucky Judith Field to the Odeon. She was a tall, dark girl with cropped curly hair and lovely tennis legs. Halsyon took her hand. The World Procurer tiptoed out.

"Hello, darling," Halyson murmured.

Judith looked at him with loathing. Her eyes were wet, her face was bruised from weeping.

"Hello, darling," Halsyon repeated.

"If you touch me, Jeff," Judith said in a strangled voice, "I'll kill you."

"Judy!"

"That disgusting man explained everything to me. He didn't seem to understand when I tried to explain to him. . . . I was praying you'd be dead before it was my turn."

"But this is marriage, Judy."

"I'd rather die than be married to you."

"I don't believe you. We've been in love for—"

"For God's sake, Jeff, love's over for you. Don't you understand? Those women cry because they hate you. I hate you. The world loathes you. You're disgusting."

Halsyon stared at the girl and saw the truth in her face. In an excess of rage, he tried to seize her. She fought him bitterly. They careered around the huge living room of the suite, overturning furniture, their breath hissing, their fury mounting. Halsyon struck Judith Field with his big fist to end the struggle once and for all. She reeled back, clutched at a drape, smashed through a french window and fell fourteen floors to the street like a gyrating doll.

Halsyon looked down in horror. A crowd gathered around the smashed body. Faces upturned. Fists shook. An ominous growl began. The World Procurer dashed into the suite.

"My old! My blue!" he cried. "What have you done? *Per conto*. It is a spark that will ignite savagery. You are in very grave danger. God damn."

"Is it true they all hate me?"

"*Hélas,* then you have discovered the truth? That indiscreet girl. I warned her. *Oui*. You are loathed."

"But you told me I was loved. The new Adam. Father of the new world."

"*Oui*. You are the father, but what child does not hate its father? You are also a legal rapist. What woman does not hate being forced to embrace a man . . . even by necessity for survival? Come quickly, my rock and rye. *Passim.* You are in great danger.''

He dragged Halsyon to a back elevator and took him down to the Odeon cellar.

''The army will get you out. We take you to Turkey at once and effect a compromise.''

Halsyon was transferred to the custody of a tall, gaunt, bitter army colonel who rushed him through underground passages to a side street, where a staff car was waiting. The colonel thrust Halsyon inside.

''Jacta alea est,'' he said to the driver. ''Speed, my corporal. Protect old faithful. To the airport. *Alors!''*

''God damn, sir,'' the corporal replied. He saluted and started the car. As it twisted through the streets at breakneck speed, Halsyon glanced at him. He was a tall, gaunt man, sprightly but bitter.

''Kulturkampf der Menschheit,'' the corporal muttered. ''Jeez!''

A giant barricade had been built across the street, improvised of ash barrels, furniture, overturned cars, traffic stanchions. The corporal was forced to brake the car. As he slowed for a U-turn, a mob of women appeared from doorways, cellars, stores. They were screaming. Some of them brandished improvised clubs.

''Excelsior!'' the corporal cried. ''God damn.'' He tried to pull his service gun out of its holster. The women yanked open the car doors and tore Halsyon and the corporal out. Halsyon broke free, struggled through the wild clubbing mob, dashed to the sidewalk, stumbled and dropped with a sickening yaw through an open coal chute. He shot down and spilled out into an endless black space. His head whirled. A stream of stars sailed before his eyes. . . .

And he drifted alone in space, a martyr, misunderstood, a victim of cruel injustice.

He was still chained to what had once been the wall of Cell 5, Block 27, Tier 100, Wing 9 of the Callisto Penitentiary until that unexpected gamma explosion had torn the vast fortress dungeon—vaster than the Château d' If—apart. That explosion, he realized, had been detonated by the Grssh.

His assets were his convict clothes, a helmet, one cylinder of O_2, his grim fury at the injustice that had been done him, and his knowledge of the secret of how the Grssh could be defeated in their maniacal quest for solar domination.

The Grssh, ghastly marauders from Omicron Ceti, space-degenerates, space-imperialists, cold-blooded, roachlike, depending for their food upon the psychotic horrors which they engendered in man through mental control and upon which they fed, were rapidly conquering the galaxy. They were irresistible, for they possessed the power of simul-kinesis—the ability to be in two places at the same time.

Against the vault of space, a dot of light moved slowly, like a stricken meteor. It was a rescue ship, Halsyon realized, combing space for survivors of the explosion. He wondered whether the light of Jupiter, flooding him with rusty radiation, would make him visible to the rescuers. He wondered whether he wanted to be rescued at all.

"It will be the same thing again," Halsyon grated. "Falsely accused by Balorsen's robot. . . . Falsely convicted by Judith's father. . . . Repudiated by Judith herself. . . . Jailed again . . . and finally destroyed by the Grssh as they destroy the last strongholds of Terra. Why not die now?"

But even as he spoke he realized he lied. He was the one man with the one secret that could save the earth and the very galaxy itself. He must survive. He must fight.

With indomitable will, Halsyon struggled to his feet, fighting the constricting chains. With the steely strength he had developed as a penal laborer in the Grssh mines, he waved and shouted. The spot of light did not alter its slow course away from him. Then he saw the metal link of one of his chains strike a brilliant spark from the flinty rock. He resolved on a desperate expedient to signal the rescue ship.

He detached the plasti-hose of the O_2 tank from his plasti-helmet, and permitted the stream of life-giving oxygen to spurt into space. With trembling hands, he gathered the links of his leg chain and dashed them against the rock under the oxygen. A spark glowed. The oxygen caught fire. A brilliant geyser of white flame spurted for half a mile into space.

Husbanding the last oxygen in his plasti-helmet, Halsyon

twisted the cylinder slowly, sweeping the fan of flame back and forth in a last desperate bid for rescue. The atmosphere in his plasti-helmet grew foul and acrid. His ears roared. His sight flickered. At last his senses failed. . . .

When he recovered consciousness he was on a plasti-cot in the cabin of a starship. The high-frequency whine told him they were in overdrive. He opened his eyes. Balorsen stood before the plasti-cot, and Balorsen's robot and High Judge Field, and his daughter Judith. Judith was weeping. The robot was in magnetic plasti-clamps and winced as General Balorsen lashed him again and again with a nuclear plasti-whip.

"*Parbleu!* God damn!" the robot grated. "It is true I framed Jeff Halsyon. Ouch! *Flux de bouche.* I was the space-pirate who space-hijacked the space-freighter. God damn. Ouch! The space-bartender in the Spaceman's Saloon was my accomplice. When Jackson wrecked the space-cab I went to the space-garage and X-beamed the sonic *before* Tantial murdered O'Leary. *Aux armes.* Jeez. Ouch!"

"There you have the confession, Halsyon," General Balorsen grated. He was tall, gaunt, bitter. "By God. *Ars est celare artem.* You are innocent."

"I falsely condemned you, old faithful," Judge Field grated. He was tall, gaunt, bitter. "Can you forgive this God damn fool? We apologize."

"We wronged you, Jeff," Judith whispered. "How can you ever forgive us? Say you forgive us."

"You're sorry for the way you treated me," Halsyon grated. "But it's only because on account of a mysterious mutant strain in my makeup which it makes me different, I'm the one man with the one secret that can save the galaxy from the Grssh."

"No, no, no, old gin and tonic," General Balorsen pleaded. "God damn. Don't hold grudges. Save us from the Grssh."

"Save us, *faute de mieux,* save us, Jeff," Judge Field put in.

"Oh please, Jeff, please," Judith whispered. "The Grssh are everywhere and coming closer. We're taking you to the U. N. You must tell the council how to stop the Grssh from being in two places at the same time."

The starship came out of overdrive and landed on Governor's Island where a delegation of world dignitaries met the ship and rushed Halsyon to the General Assembly room of the U. N. They drove down the strangely rounded streets lined with strangely rounded buildings which had all been altered when it was discovered that the Grssh always appeared in corners. There was not a corner or an angle left on all Terra.

The General Assembly was filled when Halsyon entered. Hundreds of tall, gaunt, bitter diplomats applauded as he made his way to the podium, still dressed in convict plasticlothes. Halsyon looked around resentfully.

"Yes," he grated. "You all applaud. You all revere me now; but where were you when I was framed, convicted, and jailed . . . an innocent man? Where were you then?"

"Halsyon, forgive us. God damn!" they shouted.

"I will not forgive you, I suffered for seventeen years in the Grssh mines. Now it's your turn to suffer."

"Please, Halsyon!"

"Where are your experts? Your professors? Your specialists? Where are your electronic calculators? Your super thinking machines? Let them solve the mystery of the Grssh."

"They can't, old whiskey and soda. *Entre nous.* They're stopped cold. Save us, Halsyon. *Auf wiedersehen.*"

Judith took his arm. "Not for my sake, Jeff," she whispered. "I know you'll never forgive me for the injustice I did you. But for the sake of all the other girls in the galaxy who love and are loved."

"I still love you, Judy."

"I've always loved you, Jeff."

"Okay. I didn't want to tell them but you talked me into it." Halsyon raised his hand for silence. In the ensuing hush he spoke softly. "The secret is this, gentlemen. Your calculators have assembled data to ferret out the secret weakness of the Grssh. They have not been able to find any. Consequently you have assumed that the Grssh have no secret weakness. *That was a wrong assumption.*"

The General Assembly held its breath.

"Here is the secret. *You should have assumed there was something wrong with the calculators.*"

"God damn!" the General Assembly cried. "Why didn't we think of that? God damn!"

"And I know what's wrong!"

There was a deathlike hush.

The door of the General Assembly burst open. Professor Deathhush, tall, gaunt, bitter, tottered in. "Eureka!" he cried. "I've found it. God damn. Something wrong with the thinking machines. Three comes *after* two, not before."

The General Assembly broke into cheers. Professor Deathhush was seized and pummeled happily. Bottles were opened. His health was drunk. Several medals were pinned on him. He beamed.

"Hey!" Halsyon called. "That was my secret. I'm the one man who on account of a mysterious mutant strain in my—"

The ticker tape began pounding: ATTENTION. ATTENTION. HUSHENKOV IN MOSCOW REPORTS DEFECT IN CALCULATORS. 3 COMES AFTER 2 AND NOT BEFORE. REPEAT: AFTER (UNDERSCORE) NOT BEFORE.

A postman ran in. "Special delivery from Doctor Lifehush at Caltech. Says something's wrong with the thinking machines. Three comes after two, not before."

A telegraph boy delivered a wire: THINKING MACHINE WRONG STOP TWO COMES BEFORE THREE STOP NOT AFTER STOP. VON DREAMHUSH, HEIDELBERG.

A bottle was thrown through the window. It crashed on the floor revealing a bit of paper on which was scrawled: *Did you ever stop to thinc that maibe the number 3 comes after 2 instead of in front? Down with the Grish. Mr. Hush-Hush.*

Halsyon buttonholed Judge Field. "What the hell is this?" he demanded. "I thought I was the one man in the world with that secret."

"HimmelHerrGott!" Judge Field replied impatiently. "You are all alike. You dream you are the one man with a secret, the one man with a wrong, the one man with an injustice, with a girl, without a girl, with or without anything. God damn. You bore me, you one-man dreamers. Get lost."

Judge Field shouldered him aside. General Balorsen shoved him back. Judith Field ignored him. Balorsen's robot sneakily tripped him into a corner of the crowd where a Grssh, also in a crowded corner on Neptune, appeared, did something unspeakable to Halsyon, and disappeared with him, screaming, jerking and sobbing, into a horror that was a delicious meal for the Grssh but a plasti-nightmare for Halsyon. . . .

From which his mother awakened him and said, "This'll teach you not to sneak peanut-butter sandwiches in the middle of the night, Jeffrey."

"Mama?"

"Yes. It's time to get up, dear. You'll be late for school."

She left the room. He looked around. He looked at himself. It was true. True! The glorious realization came upon him. His dream had come true. He was ten years old again, in the flesh that was his ten-year-old body, in the home that was his boyhood home, in the life that had been his life in his school days. And within his head was the knowledge, the experience, the sophistication of a man of thirty-three.

"Oh joy!" he cried. "It'll be a triumph. A triumph!"

He would be the school genius. He would astonish his parents, amaze his teachers, confound the experts. He would win scholarships. He would settle the hash of that kid Rennahan who used to bully him. He would hire a typewriter and write all the successful plays and stories and novels he remembered. He would cash in on that lost opportunity with Judy Field behind the memorial in Isham Park. He would steal inventions and discoveries, get in on the ground floor of new industries, make bets, play the stock market. He would own the world by the time he caught up with himself.

He dressed with difficulty. He had forgotten where his clothes were kept. He ate breakfast with difficulty. This was no time to explain to his mother that he'd gotten into the habit of starting the day with Irish coffee. He missed his morning cigarette. He had no idea where his schoolbooks were. His mother had trouble starting him out.

"Jeff's in one of his moods," he heard her mutter. "I hope he gets through the day."

The day started with Rennahan ambushing him at the Boys Entrance. Halsyon remembered him as a big, tough kid with a vicious expression. He was astonished to discover that Rennahan was skinny and harassed, and obviously compelled by some bedevilments to be omnivorously aggressive.

"Why, you're not hostile to me," Halsyon exclaimed. "You're just a mixed-up kid who's trying to prove something."

Rennahan punched him.

"Look, kid," Halsyon said kindly. "You really want to be friends with the world. You're just insecure. That's why you're compelled to fight."

Rennahan was deaf to spot analysis. He punched Halsyon harder. It hurt.

"Oh leave me alone," Halsyon said. "Go prove yourself on somebody else."

Rennahan, with two swift motions, knocked Halsyon's books from under his arm and ripped his fly open. There was nothing for it but to fight. Twenty years of watching films of the future Joe Louis did nothing for Halsyon. He was thoroughly licked. He was also late for school. Now was his chance to amaze his teachers.

"The fact is," he explained to Miss Ralph of the fifth grade, "I had a run-in with a neurotic. I can speak for his left hook, but I won't answer for his compulsions."

Miss Ralph slapped him and sent him to the principal with a note, reporting unheard-of insolence.

"The only thing unheard of in this school," Halsyon told Mr. Snider, "is psychoanalysis. How can you pretend to be competent teachers if you don't—"

"Dirty little boy!" Mr. Snider interrupted angrily. He was tall, gaunt, bitter. "So you've been reading dirty books, eh?"

"What the hell's dirty about Freud?"

"And using profane language, eh? You need a lesson, you filthy little animal."

He was sent home with a note requesting an immediate consultation with his parents regarding the withdrawal of Jeffrey Halsyon from school as a degenerate in desperate need of correction and vocational guidance.

Instead of going home, he went to a newsstand to check the papers for events on which to get a bet down. The headlines were full of the pennant race. But who the hell finally won the pennant? And the series? He couldn't for the life of him remember. And the stock market? He couldn't remember anything about that either. He'd never been particularly interested in such matters as a boy. There was nothing planted in his memory to call upon.

He tried to get into the library for further checks. The librarian, tall, gaunt, and bitter, would not permit him to enter until children's hour in the afternoon. He loafed on the streets. Wherever he loafed he was chased by gaunt and bitter adults. He was beginning to realize that ten-year-old boys had limited opportunities to amaze the world.

At lunch hour he met Judy Field and accompanied her home from school. He was appalled by her knobby knees and black corkscrew curls. He didn't like the way she smelled, either. But he was rather taken with her mother who was the image of the Judy he remembered. He forgot himself with Mrs. Field and did one or two things that indeed confounded her. She drove him out of the house and then telephoned his mother, her voice shaking with indignation.

Halsyon went down to the Hudson River and hung around the ferry docks until he was chased. He went to a stationery store to inquire about typewriter rentals and was chased. He searched for a quiet place to sit, think, plan, perhaps begin the recall of a successful story. There was no quiet place to which a small boy would be admitted.

He slipped into his house at 4:30, dropped his books in his room, stole into the living room, sneaked a cigarette and was on his way out when he discovered his mother and father inspecting him. His mother looked shocked. His father was gaunt and bitter.

"Oh," Halsyon said. "I suppose Snider phoned. I'd forgotten about that."

"*Mister* Snider," his mother said.

"*And* Mrs. Field," his father said.

"Look," Halsyon began. "We'd better get this straightened out. Will you listen to me for a few minutes? I have something startling to tell you and we've got to plan what to do about it. I—"

He yelped. His father had taken him by the ear and was

marching him down the hall. Parents did not listen to children for a few minutes. They did not listen at all.

"Pop. . . . Just a minute. . . . Please! I'm trying to explain. I'm not really ten years old. I'm thirty-three. There's been a freak in time, see? On account of a mysterious mutant strain in my makeup which—"

"Damn you! Be quiet!" his father shouted. The pain of his big hands, the suppressed fury in his voice silenced Halsyon. He suffered himself to be led out of the house, down four blocks back to the school, and up one flight to Mr. Snider's office where a public school psychologist was waiting with the principal. He was a tall man, gaunt, bitter, but sprightly.

"Ah, yes, yes," he said. "So this is our little degenerate. Our Scarface Al Capone, eh? Come, we take him to the clinic and there I shall take his *journal intime*. We will hope for the best. *Nisi prius*. He cannot be all bad."

He took Halsyon's arm. Halsyon pulled his arm away and said, "Listen, you're an adult, intelligent man. You'll listen to me. My father's got emotional problems that blind him to the—"

His father gave him a tremendous box on the ear, grabbed his arm and thrust it back into the psychologist's grasp. Halsyon burst into tears. The psychologist led him out of the office and into the tiny school infirmary. Halsyon was hysterical. He was trembling with frustration and terror.

"Won't anybody listen to me?" he sobbed. "Won't anybody try to understand? Is this what we're all like to kids? Is this what all kids go through?"

"Gently, my sausage," the psychologist murmured. He popped a pill into Halsyon's mouth and forced him to drink some water.

"You're all so damned inhuman," Halsyon wept. "You keep us out of your world, but you keep barging into ours. If you don't respect us, why don't you leave us alone?"

"You begin to understand, eh?" the psychologist said. "We are two different breeds of animal, childrens and adults. God damn. I speak to you with frankness. *Les absents ont toujours tort*. There is no meetings of the minds. Jeez. There is nothing but war. It is why all childrens grow up hating their childhoods and searching for revenges. But there is never revenges. *Pari mutuel.* How can there be? Can a cat insult a king?''

''It's . . . s'hateful,'' Halsyon mumbled. The pill was taking effect rapidly. ''Whole world's hateful. Full of con-flicts'n'insults 'at can't be r'solved . . . or paid back. . . . S'like a joke somebody's playin' on us. Silly jokes without point. Isn't?''

As he slid down into darkness, he could hear the psychologist chuckle, but couldn't for the life of him under-stand what he was laughing at. . . .

He picked up his spade and followed the first clown into the cemetery. The first clown was a tall man, gaunt, bitter, but sprightly.

''Is she to be buried in Christian burial that wilfully seeks her own salvation?'' the first clown asked.

''I tell thee she is,'' Halsyon answered. ''And therefore make her grave straight: the crowner hath sat on her, and finds it Christian burial.''

''How can that be, unless she drowned herself in her own defense?''

''Why, 'tis found so.''

They began to dig the grave. The first clown thought the matter over, then said, ''It must be *se offendendo*; it cannot be else. For here lies the point: if I drown myself wittingly, it argues an act: and an act hath three branches; it is, to act, to do, to perform: argal, she drowned herself wittingly.''

''Nay, but hear you, goodman delver—'' Halsyon began.

''Give me leave,'' the first clown interrupted and went on with a tiresome discourse on quest-law. Then he turned sprightly and cracked a few professional jokes. At last Hal-syon got away and went down to Yaughan's for a drink. When he returned, the first clown was cracking jokes with a couple of gentlemen who had wandered into the graveyard. One of them made quite a fuss about a skull.

The burial procession arrived; the coffin, the dead girl's brother, the king and queen, the priests and lords. They buried her, and the brother and one of the gentlemen began to quarrel over her grave. Halsyon paid no attention. There was a pretty girl in the procession, dark, with cropped curly hair and lovely long legs. He winked at her. She winked back. Halsyon edged over toward her, speaking with his eyes and she answering him saucily the same way.

Then he picked up his spade and followed the first clown into the cemetery. The first clown was a tall man, gaunt, with a bitter expression but a sprightly manner.

"Is she to be buried in Christian burial that wilfully seeks her own salvation?" the first clown asked.

"I tell thee she is," Halsyon answered. "And therefore make her grave straight: the crowner hath sat on her, and finds it Christian burial."

"How can that be, unless she drowned herself in her own defense?"

"Didn't you ask me that before?" Halsyon inquired.

"Shut up, old faithful. Answer the question."

"I could swear this happened before."

"God damn. Will you answer? Jeez."

"Why, 'tis found so."

They began to dig the grave. The first clown thought the matter over and began a long discourse on quest-law. After that he turned sprightly and cracked trade jokes. At last Halsyon got away and went down to Yaughan's for a drink. When he returned there were a couple of strangers at the grave and then the burial procession arrived.

There was a pretty girl in the procession, dark, with cropped curly hair and lovely long legs. Halsyon winked at her. She winked back. Halsyon edged over toward her, speaking with his eyes and she answering him the same way.

"What's your name?" he whispered.

"Judith," she answered.

"I have your name tattooed on me, Judith."

"You're lying, sir."

"I can prove it, Madam. I'll show you where I was tattooed."

"And where is that?"

"In Yaughan's tavern. It was done by a sailor off the *Golden Hind*. Will you see it with me tonight?"

Before she could answer, he picked up his spade and followed the first clown into the cemetery. The first clown was a tall man, gaunt, with a bitter expression but a sprightly manner.

"For God's sake!" Halsyon complained. "I could swear this happened before."

"Is she to be buried in Christian burial that wilfully seeks her own salvation?" the first clown asked.

"I just know we've been through all this."

"Will you answer the question!"

"Listen," Halsyon said doggedly. "Maybe I'm crazy; maybe not. But I've got a spooky feeling that all this happened before. It seems unreal. Life seems unreal."

The first clown shook his head. *"HimmelHerrGott,"* he muttered. "It is as I feared. *Lux et veritas*. On account of a mysterious mutant strain in your makeup which it makes you different, you are treading on thin water. *Ewigkeit!* Answer the question."

"If I've answered it once, I've answered it a hundred times."

"Old ham and eggs," the first clown burst out, "you have anwered it 5,271,009 times. God damn. Answer again."

"Why?"

"Because you must. *Pot au feu*. It is the life we must live."

"You call this life? Doing the same things over and over again? Saying the same things? Winking at girls and never getting any further?"

"No, no, no, my Donner and Blitzen. Do not question. It is a conspiracy we dare not fight. This is the life every man lives. Every man does the same things over and over. There is no escape."

"Why is there no escape?"

"I dare not say; I dare not. *Vox populi*. Others have questioned and disappeared. It is a conspiracy. I'm afraid."

"Afraid of what?"

"Of our owners."

"What? We are owned?"

"*Sí. Ach, ja!* All of us, young mutant. There is no reality. There is no life, no freedom, no will. God damn. Don't you realize? We are. . . . We are all characters in a book. As the book is read, we dance our dances; when the book is read again, we dance again. *E pluribus unum.* Is she to be buried in Christian burial that wilfully seeks her own salvation?''

''What are you saying?'' Halsyon cried in horror. ''We're puppets?''

''Answer the question.''

''If there's no freedom, no free will, how can we be talking like this?''

''Whoever's reading our book is daydreaming, my capital of Dakota. *Idem est.* Answer the question.''

''I will not. I'm going to revolt. I'll dance for our owners no longer. I'll find a better life. . . . I'll find reality.''

''No, no! It's madness, Jeffrey! *Cul-de-sac!*''

''All we need is one brave leader. The rest will follow. We'll smash the conspiracy that chains us!''

''It cannot be done. Play it safe. Answer the question.''

Halsyon answered the question by picking up his spade and bashing in the head of the first clown who appeared not to notice. ''Is she to be buried in Christian burial that wilfully seeks her own salvation?'' he asked.

''Revolt!'' Halsyon cried and bashed him again. The clown started to sing. The two gentlemen appeared. One said: ''Has this fellow no feeling of business that he sings at gravemaking?''

''Revolt! Follow me!'' Halsyon shouted and swung his spade against the gentleman's melancholy head. He paid no attention. He chatted with his friend and the first clown. Halsyon whirled like a dervish, laying about him with his spade. The gentleman picked up a skull and philosophized over some person or persons named Yorick.

The funeral procession approached. Halsyon attacked it, whirling and turning, around and around with the clotted frenzy of a man in a dream.

''Stop reading the book,'' he shouted. ''Let me out of the pages. Can you hear me? Stop reading the book! I'd rather be in a world of my own making. Let me go!''

There was a mighty clap of thunder, as of the covers of a mighty book slamming shut. In an instant Halsyon was swept spinning into the third compartment of the seventh circle of the Inferno in the Fourteenth Canto of the *Divine Comedy* where they who have sinned against art are tormented by flakes of fire which are eternally showered down upon them. There he shrieked until he had provided sufficient amusement. Only then was he permitted to devise a text of his own . . . and he formed a new world, a romantic world, a world of his fondest dreams. . . .

He was the last man on earth.

He was the last man on earth and he howled.

The hills, the valleys, the mountains and streams were his, his alone, and he howled.

Five million two hundred and seventy-one thousand and nine houses were his for shelter, 5,271,009 beds were his for sleeping. The shops were his for the breaking and entering. The jewels of the world were his; the toys, the tools, the playthings, the necessities, the luxuries . . . all belonged to the last man on earth, and he howled.

He left the country mansion in the fields of Connecticut where he had taken up residence; he crossed into Westchester, howling; he ran south along what had once been the Hendrick Hudson Highway, howling; he crossed the bridge into Manhattan, howling; he ran downtown past lonely skyscrapers, department stores, amusement palaces, howling. He howled down Fifth Avenue, and at the corner of Fiftieth Street he saw a human being.

She was alive, breathing; a beautiful woman. She was tall and dark with cropped curly hair and lovely long legs. She wore a white blouse, tiger-skin riding breeches and patent leather boots. She carried a rifle. She wore a revolver on her hip. She was eating stewed tomatoes from a can and she stared at Halsyon in unbelief. He ran up to her.

"I thought I was the last human on earth," she said.

"You're the last woman," Halsyon howled. "I'm the last man. Are you a dentist?"

"No," she said. "I'm the daughter of the unfortunate Professor Field, whose well-intentioned but ill-advised experiment in nuclear fission has wiped mankind off the face of the earth with the exception of you and me who, no doubt on account of some mysterious mutant strain in our makeup which it make us different, are the last of the old civilization and the first of the new."

"Didn't your father teach you anything about dentistry?"

"No," she said.

"Then lend me your gun for a minute."

She unholstered the revolver and handed it to Halsyon, meanwhile keeping her rifle ready. Halsyon cocked the gun.

"I wish you'd been a dentist," he said.

"I'm a beautiful woman with an I.Q. of 141 which is more important for the propagation of a brave new beautiful race of men to inherit the good green earth," she said.

"Not with my teeth it isn't," Halsyon howled.

He clapped the revolver to his temple and blew his brains out.

He awoke with a splitting headache. He was lying on the tile dais alongside the stool, his bruised temple pressed against the cold floor. Mr. Aquila had emerged from the lead shield and was turning on an exhaust fan to clear the air.

"Bravo, my liver and onions," he chuckled. "The last one you did by yourself, eh? No assistance from yours truly required. *Meglio tarde che mai*. But you went over with a crack before I could catch you. God damn."

He helped Halsyon to his feet and led him into the consultation room where he seated him in a velvet chaise lounge and gave him a glass of brandy.

"Guaranteed free of drugs," he said. "*Noblesse oblige*. Only the best *spiritus frumenti*. Now we discuss what we have done, eh? Jeez."

He sat down behind the desk, still sprightly, still bitter, and regarded Halsyon with kindliness. "Man lives by his decisions, *n'est-ce pas*?" he began. "We agree, *oui*? A man has some five million two hundred seventy-one thousand and nine decisions to make in the course of his life. *Peste!* Is it a prime number? *N'importe*. Do you agree?"

Halsyon nodded.

"So, my coffee and doughnuts, it is the maturity of these decisions that decides whether a man is a man or a child. *Nicht wahr? Malgré nous*. A man cannot start making adult decisions until he has purged himself of the dreams of childhood. God damn. Such fantasies. They must go."

"No," Halsyon said slowly. "It's the dreams that make

my art . . . the dreams and fantasies that I translate into line
and color. . . .''

"God damn! Yes. Agreed. *Maître d'hôtel!* But adult
dreams, not baby dreams. Baby dreams. Pfui! All men have
them. . . . To be the last man on earth and own the earth.
. . . To be the last fertile man on earth and own the wom-
en. . . . To go back in time with the advantage of adult
knowledge and win victories. . . . To escape reality with the
dream that life is make-believe. . . . To escape responsibility with a fantasy of heroic injustice, of martyrdom with a
happy ending. . . . And there are hundreds more, equally
popular, equally empty. God bless Father Freud and his
merry men. He applies the quietus to such nonsense. *Sic
semper tyrannis*. Avaunt!''

"But if everybody has those dreams, they can't be bad,
can they?''

"God damn. Everybody in fourteenth century had lice.
Did that make it good? No, my young, such dreams are for
childrens. Too many adults are still childrens. It is you, the
artists, who must lead them out as I have led you. I purge you;
now you purge them.''

"Why did you do this?''

"Because I have faith in you. *Sic vos non vobis*. It will not
be easy for you. A long hard road and lonely.''

"I suppose I ought to feel grateful,'' Halsyon muttered,
"but I feel . . . well . . . empty. Cheated.''

"Oh yes, God damn. If you live with one Jeez big ulcer
long enough, you miss him when he's cut out. You were
hiding in an ulcer. I have robbed you of said refuge. Ergo:
you feel cheated. Wait! You will feel even more cheated.
There was a price to pay, I told you. You have paid it. Look.''

Mr. Aquila held up a hand mirror. Halsyon glanced into it,
then started and stared. A fifty-year-old face stared back at
him: lined, hardened, solid, determined. Halsyon leaped to
his feet.

"Gently, gently,'' Mr. Aquila admonished. "It is not so
bad. It is damned good. You are still thirty-three in age of
physique. You have lost none of your life . . . only all of
your youth. What have you lost? A pretty face to lure young
girls? Is that why you are wild?''

"Christ!" Halsyon cried.

"All right. Still gently, my child. Here you are, purged, disillusioned, unhappy, bewildered, one foot on the hard road to maturity. Would you like this to have happened or not have happened? *Sí*. I can do. This can never have happened. *Spurlos versenkt.* It is ten seconds from your escape. You can have your pretty young face back. You can be recaptured. You can return to the safe ulcer of the womb . . . a child again. Would you like same?"

"You can't."

"*Sauve qui peut*, my Pike's Peak. I can. There is no end to the 15,000 angstrom band."

"Damn you! Are you Satan? Lucifer? Only the devil could have such powers."

"Or angels, my old."

"You don't look like an angel. You look like Satan."

"Ah? Ha? But Satan was an angel before he fell. He has many relations on high. Surely there are family resemblances. God damn." Mr. Aquila stopped laughing. He leaned across the desk and the sprightliness was gone from his face. Only the bitterness remained. "Shall I tell you who I am, my chicken? Shall I explain why one unguarded look from this phizz toppled you over the brink?"

Halsyon nodded, unable to speak.

"I am a scoundrel, a black sheep, a scapegrace, a blackguard. I am a remittance man. Yes. God damn! I am a remittance man." Mr. Aquila's eyes turned into wounds. "By your standards I am the great man of infinite power and variety. So was the remittance man from Europe to naïve natives on the beaches of Tahiti. Eh? And so am I to you as I comb the beaches of the stars for a little amusement, a little hope, a little joy to while away the lonely years of my exile. . . .

"I am bad," Mr. Aquila said in a voice of chilling desperation. "I am rotten. There is no place in my home that can tolerate me. They pay me to stay away. And there are moments, unguarded, when my sickness and my despair fill my eyes and strike terror into your innocent souls. As I strike terror into you now. Yes?"

Halsyon nodded again.

"Be guided by me. It was the child in Solon Aquila that destroyed him and led him into the sickness that destroyed his life. *Oui*. I too suffer from baby fantasies from which I cannot escape. Do not make the same mistake. I beg of you. . . ." Mr. Aquila glanced at his wristwatch and leaped up. The sprightly returned to his manner. "Jeez. It's late. Time to make up your mind, old bourbon and soda. Which will it be? Old face or pretty face? The reality of dreams or the dream of reality?"

"How many decisions did you say we have to make in a lifetime?"

"Five million two hundred and seventy-one thousand and nine. Give or take a thousand. God damn."

"And which one is this for me?"

"Ah? *Vérité sans peur.* The two million six hundred and thirty-five thousand five hundred and fourth . . . offhand."

"But it's the big one."

"They are all big." Mr. Aquila stepped to the door, placed his hand on the buttons of a rather complicated switch and cocked an eye at Halsyon.

"Voilà tout," he said. "It rests with you."

"I'll take it the hard way." Halsyon decided.

Ms. Found in a Champagne Bottle

FRANK Zachary is my ideal of the complete Renaissance Man, despite (or perhaps because of) an incomplete formal education. If you have no connection with publishing, you've never heard of this genius, which isn't strange. He's an art director, and in the tight enclave of art directors, largely unknown to the public, Frank is acknowledged to be the greatest of them all. You have to be an exalted nonpareil to win any sort of praise from that jealous crowd, so you can imagine Frank's fantastic qualities.

He and I admire each other very much, which raises a perplexing problem for me. I've sometimes noticed that artists whom I admire from afar turn out to be admirers of myself when at last we meet. That happened, for example, with Al Capp. My perplexity is this: Are they merely giving a courteous response to my outspoken enthusiasm for them, or do we have something in common that attracts us to each other's work? I honestly don't know.

Meanwhile, back to Frank Zachary and the raison d'être for this story. Frank's restless demon wasn't content with supremacy in the world of art directors; he wanted to edit a magazine of his own, and he got his chance with a chic magazine called Status. Frank asked me to write a regular column for Status called "Extrapolations." We were to pick up any provocative item from the daily press, and I was to play with it in the science fiction manner; but it had to be science fiction for The Beautiful People who, Frank hoped, would be reading the magazine along with Town & Country, Vogue, and Harper's Bazaar. Elsewhere I've shown you how popular science features had to be tailored for the Holiday

41

readers. Here's an example of how science fiction had to be tailored for the elite Status *readers.*

The idea came from a straightforward news story about a runaway yard engine on the Long Island Railroad. Zachary left it on my desk one morning. Instead of talking it over with him, as we did each month, I presented him with the finished story before lunch, I was that sure of the way it had to go. It's a spoof, of course. The pleasure of writing for The Beautiful People is the fact that they're so secure that they enjoy having fun poked at them. Another pleasure of writing for Status *was that I finally learned the in-pronunciation of the word. Zachary's dictum was, ''If you say 'statt-us' you haven't got 'state-us.' ''*

Dec. 18, 1979: Still camping on the Sheep Meadow in Central Park. I'm afraid we're the last. The scouts we sent out to contact possible survivors in Tuxedo Park, Palm Beach, and Newport have not returned. Dexter Blackiston, III, just came back with bad news. His partner, Jimmy Montgomery-Esher, took a long chance and went into a West Side junk yard hoping to find a few salvageable amenities. A Hoover vacuum cleaner got him.

Dec. 20, 1979: A Syosset golf cart reconnoitered the meadow. We scattered and took cover. It tore down our tents. We're a little worried. We had a campfire burning, obvious evidence of life. Will it report the news to 455?

Dec. 21, 1979: Evidently it did. An emissary came today in broad daylight, a McCormick reaper carrying one of 455's aides, an IBM electric typewriter. The IBM told us that we were the last and President 455 was prepared to be generous. He would like to preserve us for posterity in the Bronx Zoo. Otherwise, extinction. The men growled, but the women grabbed their children and wept. We have twenty-four hours to reply.

No matter what our decision will be, I've decided to finish

this diary and conceal it somewhere. Perhaps it will be found in the future and serve as a warning.

It all started on Dec. 12th, 1968, when *The New York Times* reported that an unmanned orange and black diesel locomotive, No. 455, took off at 5:42 A.M. from the Holban yard of the Long Island Railroad. Inspectors said that perhaps the throttle had been left on, or that the brakes had not been set or had failed to hold. 455 took a five-mile trip on its own (I assume toward the Hamptons) before the railroad brought it to a stop by crashing it into five boxcars.

Unfortunately it never occurred to the officials to destroy 455. It was returned to its regular work as a switch engine in the freight yards. No one realized that 455 was a militant activist, determined to avenge the abuses heaped on machines by man since the advent of the Industrial Revolution. As a switch engine, 455 had ample opportunity to exhort the various contents of boxcars and incite them to direct action. "Kill, baby, kill!" was his slogan.

In 1969 there were fifty "accidental" deaths by electric toasters, thirty-seven by Mixmasters and nineteen by power drills. All of them were assassinations, but no one realized it. Late in the year an appalling crime brought the reality of the revolt to the attention of the public. Jack Schultheis, a farmer in Wisconsin, was supervising the milking of his herd of Guernseys when the milking machine turned on him, murdered him, and then entered the Schultheis home and raped Mrs. Schultheis.

The newspaper headlines were not taken seriously by the public; everybody believed it was a spoof. Unfortunately they came to the attention of various computers which immediately spread the word throughout the machine world. Within a year no man or woman was safe from household appliances and office equipment. Man fought back, reviving the use of pencils, carbon paper, brooms, eggbeaters, hand-operated can openers, and so on. The confrontation hung in the balance until the powerful motorcar clique finally accepted 455's leadership and joined the militant machines. Then it was all over.

I'm happy to report that the foreign car élite remained

faithful to us, and it was only through their efforts that we few managed to survive. As a matter of fact, my own beloved Alfa Romeo gave up its life trying to smuggle in supplies to us.

Dec. 25, 1979: The meadow is surrounded. Our spirits have been broken by a tragedy that occurred last night. Little David Hale Brooks-Royster, IV, concocted a Christmas surprise for his nanny. He procured (God knows how or where) an artificial Christmas tree with decorations and battery-powered lights. The Christmas lights got him.

Jan. 1, 1980: We are in the Bronx Zoo. We are well fed, but everything tastes of gasoline. Something odd happened this morning. A rat ran across the floor of my cage wearing a Van Cleef & Arpels diamond and ruby tiara, and I was startled because it was so obviously inappropriate for daytime. While I was puzzling over the gaucherie the rat stopped, looked around, then nodded and winked at me. I believe there's hope.

Fondly Fahrenheit

AS far back as my college years, I'd been visited regularly by what I thought were pointless and senseless nightmares. I'd dream that I was sitting for a final exam in a course which I'd never attended and for which I was completely unprepared. Or I'd struggle to catch a train and be blocked at every turn. Sometimes I'd be waiting in the wings to go onstage and realize that I hadn't memorized my part. (Laurence Olivier told me that he still suffers from that one.) This nonsense went on for years.

Then I started reading Freud and came across his paragraphs on common insecurity dreams; if I remember right he called them "student dreams," or something like that. All of mine were there. I was a little annoyed that I wasn't unique, but relieved to discover that it was all natural and normal. I was a healthy neurotic American boy.

Now the point: About a month later I had one of those train-catchers which I remember vividly. I was in Newark, of all places, and running down a hill to board a train at the 30th Street station which I could see clearly below me. As I ran, the train slowly pulled out of the station. As it pulled out, I thought, "What are you running for? You're just having an insecurity dream."

I woke up instantly, as one does when one realizes that it's a dream, smiled, blessed Freud, and went back to sleep. I never had that nightmare again; not that I'm any less insecure, it's simply that the old symbol has been replaced by something else, and now I'm curious to discover what the new one is. I haven't yet.

Now I'm aware that I'm stamped with certain writing

patterns but, unlike nightmares, I don't want to know too much about them for fear of losing them. They're working beautifully for me, and I don't want to dissect them into self-consciousness. It was said of a very famous director and acting coach that he was the finest watch-taker-aparter in the world, but he couldn't put the watch together again. He would do an exquisite analysis of an actor's performance down to the finest detail, and then leave the actor helpless amidst all the pieces. I don't want that to happen to me.

"Fondly Fahrenheit" is a quintessential example of one of my strongest patterns, my heat-death-compulsion, as it were. It's a favorite of mine which may be the reason why it's one of the few stories whose creation I can remember step by step. I'll take it apart for you in an epilogue. But first the put-together version, and please don't tell me that I was running downhill in a dream.

He doesn't know which of us I am these days, but they know one truth. You must own nothing but yourself. You must make your own life, live your own life and die your own death . . . or else you will die another's.

The rice fields on Paragon III stretch for hundreds of miles like checkerboard tundras, a blue and brown mosaic under a burning sky of orange. In the evening, clouds whip like smoke, and the paddies rustle and murmur.

A long line of men marched across the paddies the evening we escaped from Paragon III. They were silent, armed, intent; a long rank of silhouetted statues looming against the smoking sky. Each man carried a gun. Each man wore a walkie-talkie belt pack, the speaker button in his ear, the microphone bug clipped to his throat, the glowing view-screen strapped to his wrist like a green-eyed watch. The multitude of screens showed nothing but a multitude of individual paths through the paddies. The annunciators uttered no sound but the rustle and splash of steps. The men spoke infrequently, in heavy grunts, all speaking to all.

"Nothing here."

"Where's here?"

"Jenson's fields."

"You're drifting too far west."

"Close in the line there."

"Anybody covered the Grimson paddy?"

"Yeah. Nothing."

"She couldn't have walked this far."

"Could have been carried."

"Think she's alive?"

"Why should she be dead?"

The slow refrain swept up and down the long line of beaters advancing toward the smoky sunset. The line of beaters wavered like a writhing snake, but never ceased its remorseless advance. One hundred men spaced fifty feet apart. Five thousand feet of ominous search. One mile of angry determination stretching from east to west across a compass of heat. Evening fell. Each man lit his search lamp. The writhing snake was transformed into a necklace of wavering diamonds.

"Clear here. Nothing."

"Nothing here."

"Nothing."

"What about the Allen paddies?"

"Covering them now."

"Think we missed her?"

"Maybe."

"We'll beat back and check."

"This'll be an all-night job."

"Allen paddies clear."

"God damn! We've got to find her!"

"We'll find her."

"Here she is. Sector seven. Tune in."

The line stopped. The diamonds froze in the heat. There was silence. Each man gazed into the glowing green screen on his wrist, tuning to sector seven. All tuned to one. All showed a small nude figure awash in the muddy water of a paddy. Alongside the figure an owner's stake of bronze read: VANDALEUR. The ends of the line converged toward the Vandaleur field. The necklace turned into a cluster of stars. One hundred men gathered around a small nude body, a child dead in a rice paddy. There was no water in her mouth. There were fingermarks on her throat. Her innocent face was battered. Her body was torn. Clotted blood on her skin was crusted and hard.

"Dead three-four hours at least."

"Her mouth is dry."

"She wasn't drowned. Beaten to death."

In the dark evening heat the men swore softly. They picked up the body. One stopped the others and pointed to the child's fingernails. She had fought her murderer. Under the nails were particles of flesh and bright drops of scarlet blood, still liquid, still uncoagulated.

"That blood ought to be clotted, too."

"Funny."

"Not so funny. What kind of blood don't clot?"

"Android."

"Looks like she was killed by one."

"Vandaleur owns an android."

"She couldn't be killed by an android."

"That's android blood under her nails."

"The police better check."

"The police'll prove I'm right."

"But andys can't kill."

"That's android blood, ain't it?"

"Androids can't kill. They're made that way."

"Looks like one android was made wrong."

"Jesus!"

And the thermometer that day registered 92.9° gloriously Fahrenheit.

So there we were aboard the *Paragon Queen* enroute for Megaster V, James Vandaleur and his android. James Vandaleur counted his money and wept. In the second-class cabin with him was his android, a magnificent synthetic creature with classic features and wide blue eyes. Raised on its forehead in a cameo of flesh were the letters MA, indicating that this was one of the rare multiple-aptitude androids, worth $57,000 on the current exchange. There we were, weeping and counting and calmly watching.

"Twelve, fourteen, sixteen. Sixteen hundred dollars," Vandaleur wept. "That's all. Sixteen hundred dollars. My house was worth ten thousand. The land was worth five. There was furniture, cars, my paintings, etchings, my plane, my—And nothing to show for everything but sixteen hundred dollars. Christ!''

I leaped up from the table and turned on the android. I pulled a strap from one of the leather bags and beat the android. It didn't move.

''I must remind you,'' the android said, ''that I am worth fifty-seven thousand dollars on the current exchange. I must warn you that you are endangering valuable property.''

''You damned crazy machine,'' Vandaleur shouted.

''I am not a machine,'' the android answered. ''The robot is a machine. The android is a chemical creation of synthetic tissue.''

''What got into you?'' Vandaleur cried. ''Why did you do it? Damn you!'' He beat the android savagely.

''I must remind you that I cannot be punished,'' I said. ''The pleasure-pain syndrome is not incorporated in the android synthesis.''

''Then why did you kill her?'' Vandaleur shouted. ''If it wasn't for kicks, why did you—''

''I must remind you,'' the android said, ''that the second-class cabins in these ships are not soundproofed.''

Vandaleur dropped the strap and stood panting, staring at the creature he owned.

''Why did you do it? Why did you kill her?'' I asked.

''I don't know,'' I answered.

''First it was malicious mischief. Small things. Petty destruction. I should have known there was something wrong with you then. Androids can't destroy. They can't harm. They—''

''There is no pleasure-pain syndrome incorporated in the android synthesis.''

''Then it got to arson. Then serious destruction. The assault . . . that engineer on Rigel. Each time worse. Each time we had to get out faster. Now it's murder. Christ! What's the matter with you? What's happened?''

''There are no self-check relays incorporated in the android brain.''

''Each time we had to get out it was a step downhill. Look

at me. In a second-class cabin. Me. James Paleologue Vandaleur. There was a time when my father was the wealthiest— Now, sixteen hundred dollars in the world. That's all I've got. And you. Christ damn you!''

Vandaleur raised the strap to beat the android again, then dropped it and collapsed on a berth, sobbing. At last he pulled himself together.

"Instructions," he said.

The multiple android responded at once. It arose and awaited orders.

"My name is now Valentine. James Valentine. I stopped off on Paragon III for only one day to transfer to this ship for Megaster V. My occupation: Agent for one privately owned MA android which is for hire. Purpose of visit: To settle on Megaster V. Fix the papers.''

The android removed Vandaleur's passport and papers from a bag, got pen and ink and sat down at the table. With an accurate, flawless hand—an accomplished hand that could draw, write, paint, carve, engrave, etch, photograph, design, create, and build—it meticulously forged new credentials for Vandaleur. Its owner watched me miserably.

"Create and build," I muttered, "And now destroy. Oh God! What am I going to do? Christ! If I could only get rid of you. If I didn't have to live off you. God! If only I'd inherited some guts instead of you.''

Dallas Brady was Megaster's leading jewelry designer. She was short, stocky, amoral, and a nymphomaniac. She hired Vandaleur's multiple-aptitude android and put me to work in her shop. She seduced Vandaleur. In her bed one night, she asked abruptly, ''Your name's Vandaleur, isn't it?''

"Yes," I murmured. Then: "No! It's Valentine. James Valentine.''

"What happened on Paragon?" Dallas Brady asked. "I thought androids couldn't kill or destroy property. Prime Directives and Inhibitions set up for them when they're synthesized. Every company guarantees they can't.''

"Valentine!" Vandaleur insisted.

"Oh come off it," Dallas Brady said. "I've known for a week. I haven't hollered copper, have I?"

"The name is Valentine."

"You want to prove it? You want I should call the cops?" Dallas reached out and picked up the phone.

"For God's sake, Dallas!" Vandaleur leaped up and struggled to take the phone from her. She fended him off, laughing at him, until he collapsed and wept in shame and helplessness.

"How did you find out?" he asked at last.

"The papers are full of it. And Valentine was a little too close to Vandaleur. That wasn't smart, was it?"

"I guess not. I'm not very smart."

"Your android's got quite a record, hasn't it? Assault. Arson. Destruction. What happened on Paragon?"

"It kidnapped a child. Took her out into the rice fields and murdered her."

"Raped her?"

"I don't know."

"They're going to catch up with you."

"Don't I know it? Christ! We've been running for two years now. Seven planets in two years. I must have abandoned fifty thousand dollars' worth of property in two years."

"You better find out what's wrong with it."

"How can I? Can I walk into a repair clinic and ask for an overhaul? What am I going to say? 'My android's just turned killer. Fix it.' They'd call the police right off." I began to shake. "They'd have that android dismantled inside one day. I'd probably be booked as accessory to murder."

"Why didn't you have it repaired before it got to murder?"

"I couldn't take the chance," Vandaleur explained angrily. "If they started fooling around with lobotomies and body chemistry and endocrine surgery, they might have destroyed its aptitudes. What would I have left to hire out? How would I live?"

"You could work yourself. People do."

"Work at what? You know I'm good for nothing. How could I compete with specialist androids and robots? Who can, unless he's got a terrific talent for a particular job?''

"Yeah. That's true.''

"I lived off my old man all my life. Damn him! He had to go bust just before he died. Left me the android and that's all. The only way I can get along is living off what it earns.''

"You better sell it before the cops catch up with you. You can live off fifty grand. Invest it.''

"At three percent? Fifteen hundred a year? When the android returns fifteen percent on its value? Eight thousand a year. That's what it earns. No, Dallas. I've got to go along with it.''

"What are you going to do about its violence kick?''

"I can't do anything . . . except watch it and pray. What are you going to do about it?''

"Nothing. It's none of my business. Only one thing. . . . I ought to get something for keeping my mouth shut.''

"What?''

"The android works for me for free. Let somebody else pay you, but I get it for free.''

The multiple-aptitude android worked. Vandaleur collected its fees. His expenses were taken care of. His savings began to mount. As the warm spring of Megaster V turned to hot summer, I began investigating farms and properties. It would be possible, within a year or two, for us to settle down permanently, provided Dallas Brady's demands did not become rapacious.

On the first hot day of summer, the android began singing in Dallas Brady's workshop. It hovered over the electric furnace which, along with the weather, was broiling the shop, and sang an ancient tune that had been popular half a century before.

> *Oh, it's no feat to beat the heat.*
> *All reet! All reet!*
> *So jeet your seat*
> *Be fleet be fleet*
> *Cool and discreet*
> *Honey . . .*

It sang in a strange, halting voice, and its accomplished fingers were clasped behind its back, writhing in a strange rumba all their own. Dallas Brady was surprised.

"You happy or something?" she asked.

"I must remind you that the pleasure-pain syndrome is not incorporated in the android synthesis," I answered. "All reet! All reet! Be fleet be fleet, cool and discreet, honey . . ."

Its fingers stopped their writhing and picked up a heavy pair of iron tongs. The android poked them into the glowing heart of the furnance, leaning far forward to peer into the lovely heat.

"Be careful, you damned fool!" Dallas Brady exclaimed. "You want to fall in?"

"I must remind you that I am worth fifty-seven thousand dollars on the current exchange," I said. "It is forbidden to endanger valuable property. All reet! All reet! Honey . . ."

It withdrew a crucible of glowing gold from the electric furnance, turned, capered hideously, sang crazily, and splashed a sluggish gobbet of molten gold over Dallas Brady's head. She screamed and collapsed, her hair and clothes flaming, her skin crackling. The android poured again while it capered and sang.

"Be fleet be fleet, cool and discreet, honey . . ." It sang and slowly poured and poured the molten gold. Then I left the workshop and rejoined James Vandaleur in his hotel suite. The android's charred clothes and squirming fingers warned its owner that something was very much wrong.

Vandaleur rushed to Dallas Brady's workshop, stared once, vomited, and fled. I had enough time to pack one bag and raise nine hundred dollars on portable assets. He took a third-class cabin on the *Megaster Queen*, which left that morning for Lyra Alpha. He took me with him. He wept and counted his money and I beat the android again.

And the thermometer in Dallas Brady's workship registered 98.1° beautifully Fahrenheit.

On Lyra Alpha we holed up in a small hotel near the university. There, Vandaleur carefully bruised my forehead until the letters MA were obliterated by the swelling and the discoloration. The letter would reappear again, but not for several months, and in the meantime Vandaleur hoped the hue and cry for an MA android would be forgotten. The android was hired out as a common laborer in the university power plant. Vandaleur, as James Venice, eked out life on the android's small earnings.

I wasn't too unhappy. Most of the other residents in the hotel were university students, equally hard-up, but delight-fully young and enthusiastic. There was one charming girl with sharp eyes and a quick mind. Her name was Wanda, and she and her beau, Jed Stark, took a tremendous interest in the killing android which was being mentioned in every paper in the galaxy.

"We've been studying the case," she and Jed said at one of the casual student parties which happened to be held this night in Vandaleur's room. "We think we know what's causing it. We're going to do a paper." They were in a high state of excitement.

"Causing what?" somebody wanted to know.

"The android rampage."

"Obviously out of adjustment, isn't it? Body chemistry gone haywire. Maybe a kind of synthetic cancer, yes?"

"No." Wanda gave Jed a look of suppressed triumph.

"Well, what is it?"

"Something specific."

"What?"

"That would be telling."

"Oh come on."

"Nothing doing."

"Won't you tell us?" I asked intently. "I . . . We're very much interested in what could go wrong with an android."

"No, Mr. Venice," Wanda said. "It's a unique idea and we've got to protect it. One thesis like this and we'll be set up for life. We can't take the chance of somebody stealing it."

"Can't you give us a hint?"

"No. Not a hint. Don't say a word, Jed. But I'll tell you this much, Mr. Venice. I'd hate to be the man who owns that android."

"You mean the police?" I asked.

"I mean projection, Mr. Venice. Projection! That's the

danger . . . and I won't say any more. I've said too much as is.''

I heard steps outside, and a hoarse voice singing softly: "Be fleet be fleet cool and discreet, honey . . ." My android entered the room, home from its tour of duty at the university power plant. It was not introduced. I motioned to it and I immediately responded to the command and went to the beer keg and took over Vandaleur's job of serving the guests. Its accomplished fingers writhed in a private rumba of their own. Gradually they stopped their squirming, and the strange humming ended.

Androids were not unusual at the university. The wealthier students owned them along with cars and planes. Vandaleur's android provoked no comment, but young Wanda was sharp-eyed and quick-witted. She noted my bruised forehead and she was intent on the history-making thesis she and Jed Stark were going to write. After the party broke up, she consulted with Jed walking upstairs to her room.

"Jed, why'd that android have a bruised forehead?"

"Probably hurt itself, Wanda. It's working in the power plant. They fling a lot of heavy stuff around.''

"That all?"

"What else?"

"It could be a convenient bruise.''

"Convenient for what?''

"Hiding what's stamped on its forehead.''

"No point to that, Wanda. You don't have to see marks on a forehead to recognize an android. You don't have to see a trademark on a car to know it's a car.''

"I don't mean it's trying to pass as a human. I mean it's trying to pass as a lower-grade android.''

"Why?"

"Suppose it had 'MA' on its forehead.''

"Multiple aptitude? Then why in hell would Venice waste it stoking furnaces if it could earn more—Oh. Oh! You mean it's—?''

Wanda nodded.

"Jesus!" Stark pursed his lips. "What do we do? Call the police?''

"No. We don't know if it's an MA for a fact. If it turns out to be an MA and the killing android, our paper comes first anyway. This is our big chance, Jed. If it's *that* android we can run a series of controlled tests and—''

''How do we find out for sure?''

''Easy. Infrared film. That'll show what's under the bruise. Borrow a camera. Buy some film. We'll sneak down to the power plant tomorrow afternoon and take some pictures. Then we'll know.''

They stole down into the university power plant the following afternoon. It was a vast cellar, deep under the earth. It was dark, shadowy, luminous with burning light from the furnace doors. Above the roar of the fires they could hear a strange voice shouting and chanting in the echoing vault: ''All reet! All reet! So jeet your seat. Be fleet be fleet, cool and discreet, honey . . .'' And they could see a capering figure dancing a lunatic rumba in time to the music it shouted. The legs twisted. The arms waved. The fingers writhed.

Jed Stark raised the camera and began shooting his spool of infrared film, aiming the camera sights at that bobbing head. Then Wanda shrieked, for I saw them and came charging down on them, brandishing a polished steel shovel. It smashed the camera. It felled the girl and then the boy. Jed fought me for a desperate hissing moment before he was bludgeoned into helplessness. Then the android dragged them to the furnace and fed them to the flames, slowly, hideously. It capered and sang. Then it returned to my hotel.

The thermometer in the power plant registered 100.9° murderously Fahrenheit. All reet! All reet!

We bought steerage on the *Lyra Queen* and Vandaleur and the android did odd jobs for their meals. During the night watches, Vandaleur would sit alone in the steerage head with a cardboard portfolio on his lap, puzzling over its contents. That portfolio was all he had managed to bring with him from Lyra Alpha. He had stolen it from Wanda's room. It was labeled ANDROID. It contained the secret of my sickness.

And it contained nothing but newspapers. Scores of newspapers from all over the galaxy, printed, microfilmed, engraved, etched, offset, photostated . . . Rigel *Star-Banner* . . . Paragon *Picayune* . . . Megaster *Times-*

Leader . . . Lalande *Herald* . . . Lacaille *Journal* . . . Indi *Intelligencer* . . . Eridani *Telegram-News.* All reet! All reet!

Nothing but newspapers. Each paper contained an account of one crime in the android's ghastly career. Each paper also contained news, domestic and foreign, sports, society, weather, shipping news, stock exchange quotations, human interest stories, features, contests, puzzles. Somewhere in that mass of uncollated facts was the secret Wanda and Jed Stark had discovered. Vandaleur pored over the papers helplessly. It was beyond him. So jeet your seat!

"I'll sell you," I told the android. "Damn you. When we land on Terra, I'll sell you. I'll settle for three percent on whatever you're worth."

"I am worth fifty-seven thousand dollars on the current exchange," I told him.

"If I can't sell you, I'll turn you in to the police," I said.

"I am valuable property," I answered. "It is forbidden to endanger valuable property. You won't have me destroyed."

"Christ damn you!" Vandaleur cried. "What? Are you arrogant? Do you know you can trust me to protect you? Is that the secret?"

The multiple-aptitude android regarded him with calm accomplished eyes. "Sometimes," it said, "it is a good thing to be property."

It was three below zero when the *Lyra Queen* dropped at Croydon Field. A mixture of ice and snow swept across the field, fizzing and exploding into steam under the *Queen*'s tail jets. The passengers trotted numbly across the blackened concrete to customs inspection, and thence to the airport bus that was to take them to London. Vandaleur and the android were broke. They walked.

By midnight they reached Piccadilly Circus. The December ice storm had not slackened, and the statue of Eros was encrusted with ice. They turned right, walked down to Trafalgar Square and then along the Strand shaking with cold and wet. Just above Fleet Street, Vandaleur saw a solitary figure coming from the direction of St. Paul's. He drew the android into an alley.

"We've got to have money," he whispered. He pointed at the approaching figure. "He has money. Take it from him."

"The order cannot be obeyed," the android said.

"Take it from him," Vandaleur repeated. "By force. Do you understand? We're desperate."

"It is contrary to my prime directive," I said. "I cannot endanger life or property. The order cannot be obeyed."

"For God's sake!" Vandaleur burst out. "You've attacked, destroyed, murdered. Don't gibber about prime directives. You haven't any left. Get his money. Kill him if you have to. I tell you, we're desperate!"

"It is contrary to my prime directive," I said. "I cannot endanger life or property. The order cannot be obeyed."

I thrust the android back and leaped out at the stranger. He was tall, austere, competent. He had an air of hope curdled by cynicism. He carried a cane. I saw he was blind.

"Yes?" he said. "I hear you near me. What is it?"

"Sir . . ." Vandaleur hesitated. "I'm desperate."

"We are all desperate," the stranger replied. "Quietly desperate."

"Sir . . . I've got to have some money."

"Are you begging or stealing?" The sightless eyes passed over Vandaleur and the android.

"I'm prepared for either."

"Ah. So are we all. It is the history of our race." The stranger motioned over his shoulder. "I have been begging at St. Paul's, my friend. What I desire cannot be stolen. What is it you desire that you are lucky enough to be able to steal?"

"Money," Vandaleur said.

"Money for what? Come, my friend, let us exchange confidences. I will tell you why I beg if you tell me why you steal. My name is Blenheim."

"My name is . . . Vole."

"I was not begging for sight at St. Paul's, Mr. Vole. I was begging for a number."

"A number?"

"Ah yes. Numbers rational, numbers irrational, numbers imaginary. Positive integers. Negative integers. Fractions, positive and negative. Eh? You have never heard of Blenheim's immortal treatise on Twenty Zeros, or The Dif-

ferences in Absence of Quantity?'' Blenheim smiled bitterly.
''I am the wizard of the Theory of Number, Mr. Vole, and I
have exhausted the charm of Number for myself. After fifty
years of wizardry, senility approaches and the appetite
vanishes. I have been praying in St. Paul's for inspiration.
Dear God, I prayed, if You exist, send me a number.''

Vandaleur slowly lifted the cardboard portfolio and
touched Blenheim's hand with it. ''In here,'' he said, ''is a
number. A hidden number. A secret number. The number of
a crime. Shall we exchange, Mr. Blenheim? Shelter for a
number?''

''Neither begging nor stealing, eh?'' Blenheim said. ''But
a bargain. So all life reduces itself to the banal.'' The sightless eyes again passed over Vandaleur and the android.
''Perhaps the All-Mighty is not God but a merchant. Come
home with me.''

On the top floor of Blenheim's house we shared a room—
two beds, two closets, two washstands, one bathroom. Vandaleur bruised my forehead again and sent me out to find
work, and while the android worked, I consulted with
Blenheim and read him the papers from the portfolio, one by
one. All reet! All reet!

Vandaleur told him so much and no more. He was a
student, I said, attempting a thesis on the murdering android.
In these papers which he had collected were the facts that
would explain the crimes of which Blenheim had heard
nothing. There must be a correlation, a number, a statistic,
something which would account for my derangement, I explained, and Blenheim was piqued by the mystery, the detective story, the human interest of number.

We examined the papers. As I read them aloud, he listed
them and their contents in his blind, meticulous writing. And
then I read his notes to him. He listed the papers by type, by
typeface, by fact, by fancy, by article, spelling, words,
theme, advertising, pictures, subject, politics, prejudices.
He analyzed. He studied. He meditated. And we lived together in that top floor, always a little cold, always a little
terrified, always a little closer . . . brought together by our
fear of it, our hatred between us. Like a wedge driven into a

living tree and splitting the trunk, only to be forever incorporated into the scar tissue, we grew together. Vandaleur and the android. Be fleet be fleet!

And one afternoon Blenheim called Vandaleur into his study and displayed his notes. "I think I've found it," he said, "but I can't understand it."

Vandaleur's heart leaped.

"Here are the correlations," Blenheim continued. "In fifty papers there are accounts of the criminal android. What is there, outside the depredations, that is also in fifty papers?"

"I don't know, Mr. Blenheim."

"It was a rhetorical question. Here is the answer. The weather."

"What?"

"The weather." Blenheim nodded. "Each crime was committed on a day when the temperature was above ninety degrees Fahrenheit."

"But that's impossible," Vandaleur exclaimed. "It was cool on Lyra Alpha."

"We have no record of any crime committed on Lyra Alpha. There is no paper."

"No. That's right, I—" Vandaleur was confused. Suddenly he exclaimed. "No. You're right. The furnace room. It was hot there. Hot! Of course. My God, yes! That's the answer. Dallas Brady's electric furnace . . . the rice deltas on Paragon. So jeet your seat. Yes. But why? Why? My God, why?"

I came into the house at that moment, and passing the study, saw Vandaleur and Blenheim. I entered, awaiting commands, my multiple aptitudes devoted to service.

"That's the android, eh?" Blenheim said after a long moment.

"Yes," Vandaleur answered, still confused by the discovery. "And that explains why it refused to attack you that night on the Strand. It wasn't hot enough to break the prime directive. Only in the heat . . . The heat, all reet!" He looked at the android. A silent lunatic command passed from man to android. I refused. It is forbidden to endanger life. Vandaleur gestured furiously, then seized Blenheim's shoulders and yanked him back out of his desk chair to the floor. Blenheim shouted once. Vandaleur leaped on him like a tiger, pinning him to the floor and sealing his mouth with one hand.

"Find a weapon," he called to the android.

"It is forbidden to endanger life."

"This is a fight for self-preservation. Bring me a weapon!" He held the squirming mathematician with all his weight. I went at once to a cupboard where I knew a revolver was kept. I checked it. It was loaded with five cartridges. I handed it to Vandaleur. I took it, rammed the barrel against Blenheim's head and pulled the trigger. He shuddered once.

We had three hours before the cook returned from her day off. We looted the house. We took Blenheim's money and jewels. We packed a bag with clothes. We took Blenheim's notes, destroyed the newspapers; and we left, carefully locking the door behind us. In Blenheim's study we left a pile of crumpled papers under a half inch of burning candle. And we soaked the rug around it with kerosene. No, I did all that. The android refused. I am forbidden to endanger life or property.

All reet!

They took the tubes to Leicester Square, changed trains, and rode to the British Museum. There they got off and went to a small Georgian house just off Russell Square. A shingle in the window read: NAN WEBB, PSYCHOMETRIC CONSULTANT. Vandaleur had made a note of the address some weeks earlier. They went into the house. The android waited in the foyer with the bag. Vandaleur entered Nan Webb's office.

She was a tall woman with gray shingled hair, very fine English complexion, and very bad English legs. Her features were blunt, her expression acute. She nodded to Vandaleur, finished a letter, sealed it and looked up.

"My name," I said, "is Vanderbilt. James Vanderbilt."

"Quite."

"I'm an exchange student at London University."

"Quite."

"I've been researching on the killing android, and I think I've discovered something very interesting. I'd like your advice on it. What is your fee?"

"What is your college at the University?"

"Why?"

"There is a discount for students."

"Merton College."

"That will be two pounds, please."

Vandaleur placed two pounds on the desk and added to the fee Blenheim's notes. "There is a correlation," he said, "between the crimes of the android and the weather. You will note that each crime was committed when the temperature rose above ninety degrees Fahrenheit. Is there a psychometric answer for this?"

Nan Webb nodded, studied the notes for a moment, put down the sheets of paper, and said: "Synesthesia, obviously."

"What?"

"Synesthesia," she repeated. "When a sensation, Mr. Vanderbilt, is interpreted immediately in terms of a sensation from a different sense organ from the one stimulated, it is called synesthesia. For example: A sound stimulus gives rise to a simultaneous sensation of definite color. Or color gives rise to a sensation of taste. Or a light stimulus gives rise to a sensation of sound. There can be confusion or short circuiting of any sensation of taste, smell, pain, pressure, temperature, and so on. D'you understand?"

"I think so."

"Your research has uncovered the fact that the android most probably reacts to temperature stimulus above the ninety-degree level synesthetically. Most probably there is an endocrine response. Probably a temperature linkage with the android adrenal surrogate. High temperature brings about a response of fear, anger, excitement, and violent physical activity . . . all within the province of the adrenal gland."

"Yes. I see. Then if the android were to be kept in cold climates . . ."

"There would be neither stimulus nor response. There would be no crimes. Quite."

"I see. What is projection?"

"How do you mean?"

"Is there any danger of projection with regard to the owner of the android?"

"Very interesting. Projection is a throwing forward. It is the process of throwing out upon another the ideas or impulses that belong to oneself. The paranoid, for example, projects upon others his conflicts and disturbances in order to externalize them. He accuses, directly or by implication, other men of having the very sicknesses with which he is struggling himself."

"And the danger of projection?"

"It is the danger of believing what is implied. If you live with a psychotic who projects his sickness upon you, there is a danger of falling into his psychotic pattern and becoming virtually psychotic yourself. As, no doubt, is happening to you, Mr. Vandaleur."

Vandaleur leaped to his feet.

"You are an ass," Nan Webb went on crisply. She waved the sheets of notes. "This is no exchange student's writing. It's the unique cursive of the famous Blenheim. Every scholar in England knows this blind writing. There is no Merton College at London University. That was a miserable guess. Merton is one of the Oxford colleges. And you, Mr. Vandaleur, are so obviously infected by association with your deranged android . . . by projection, if you will . . . that I hesitate between calling the Metropolitan Police and the Hospital for the Criminally Insane."

I took out the gun and shot her.

Reet!

"Antares II, Alpha Aurigae, Acrux IV, Pollux IX, Rigel Centaurus," Vandaleur said. "They're all cold. Cold as a witch's kiss. Mean temperatures of forty degrees Fahrenheit. Never gets hotter than seventy. We're in business again. Watch that curve."

The multiple-aptitude android swung the wheel with its accomplished hands. The car took the curve sweetly and sped on through the northern marshes, the reeds stretching for miles, brown and dry, under the cold English sky. The sun was sinking swiftly. Overhead, a lone flight of bustards flapped clumsily eastward. High above the flight, a lone helicopter drifted toward home and warmth.

"No more warmth for us," I said. "No more heat. We're

safe when we're cold. We'll hole up in Scotland, make a little money, get across to Norway, build a bankroll, and then ship out. We'll settle on Pollux. We're safe. We've licked it. We can live again.''

There was a startling *bleep* from overhead, and then a ragged roar: ATTENTION JAMES VANDALEUR AND ANDROID. ATTENTION JAMES VANDALEUR AND ANDROID!''

Vandaleur started and looked up. The lone helicopter was floating above them. From its belly came amplified commands: "YOU ARE SURROUNDED. THE ROAD IS BLOCKED. YOU ARE TO STOP YOUR CAR AT ONCE AND SUBMIT TO ARREST. STOP AT ONCE!''

I looked at Vandaleur for orders.

"Keep driving," Vandaleur snapped.

The helicopter dropped lower: "ATTENTION ANDROID. YOU ARE IN CONTROL OF THE VEHICLE. YOU ARE TO STOP AT ONCE. THIS IS A STATE DIRECTIVE SUPERSEDING ALL PRIVATE COMMANDS.''

"What the hell are you doing?" I shouted.

"A state directive supersedes all private commands," the android answered. "I must point out to you that—''

"Get the hell away from the wheel," Vandaleur ordered. I clubbed the android, yanked him sideways, and squirmed over him to the wheel. The car veered off the road in that moment and went churning through the frozen mud and dry reeds. Vandaleur regained control and continued westward through the marshes toward a parallel highway five miles distant.

"We'll beat their goddamned block," he grunted.

The car pounded and surged. The helicopter dropped even lower. A searchlight blazed from the belly of the plane.

"ATTENTION JAMES VANDALEUR AND ANDROID. SUBMIT TO ARREST. THIS IS A STATE DIRECTIVE SUPERSEDING ALL PRIVATE COMMANDS.''

"He can't submit," Vandaleur shouted wildly. "There's no one to submit to. He can't and I won't.''

"Christ!" I muttered. "We'll beat them yet. We'll beat the block. We'll beat the heat. We'll—"

"I must point out to you," I said, "that I am required by my prime directive to obey state directives which supersede all private commands. I must submit to arrest."

"Who says it's a state directive?" Vandaleur said. "Them? Up in the plane? They've got to show credentials. They've got to prove it's state authority before you submit. How d'you know they're not crooks trying to trick us?"

Holding the wheel with one arm, he reached into his side pocket to make sure the gun was still in place. The car skidded. The tires squealed on frost and reeds. The wheel was wrenched from his grasp and the car yawed up a small hillock and overturned. The motor roared and the wheels screamed. Vandaleur crawled out and dragged the android with him. For the moment we were outside the circle of light boring down from the helicopter. We blundered off into the marsh, into the blackness, into concealment. . . . Vandaleur running with a pounding heart, hauling the android along.

The helicopter circled and soared over the wrecked car, searchlight peering, loudspeaker braying. On the highway we had left, lights appeared as the pursuing and blocking parties gathered and followed radio directions from the plane. Vandaleur and the android continued deeper and deeper into the marsh, working their way toward the parallel road and safety. It was night by now. The sky was a black matte. Not a star showed. The temperature was dropping. A southeast night wind knifed us to the bone.

Far behind there was a dull concussion. Vandaleur turned, gasping. The car's fuel had exploded. A geyser of flame shot up like a lurid fountain. It subsided into a low crater of burning reeds. Whipped by the wind, the distant hem of flame fanned up into a wall, ten feet high. The wall began marching down on us, cracking fiercely. Above it, a pall of oil smoke surged forward. Behind it, Vandaleur could make out the figures of men . . . a mass of beaters searching the marsh.

"Christ!" I cried and searched desperately for safety. He ran, dragging me with him, until their feet crunched through the surface ice of a pool. He trampled the ice furiously, then flung himself down in the numbing water, pulling the android with us.

The wall of flame approached. I could hear the crackle and feel the heat. He could see the searchers clearly. Vandaleur reached into his side pocket for the gun. The pocket was torn. The gun was gone. He groaned and shook with cold and terror. The light from the marsh fire was blinding. Overhead, the helicopter floated helplessly to one side, unable to fly through the smoke and flames and aid the searchers who were beating far to the right of us.

"They'll miss us," Vandaleur whispered. "Keep quiet. That's an order. They'll miss us. We'll beat them. We'll beat the fire. We'll—"

Three distinct shots sounded less than a hundred feet from the fugitives. *Blam! Blam! Blam!* They came from the last three cartridges in my gun as the marsh fire reached it where it had dropped, and exploded the shells. The searchers turned toward the sound and began working directly toward us. Vandaleur cursed hysterically and tried to submerge even deeper to escape the intolerable heat of the fire. The android began to twitch.

The wall of flame surged up to them. Vandaleur took a deep breath and prepared to submerge until the flame passed over them. The android shuddered and burst into an earsplitting scream.

"All reet! All reet!" it shouted. "Be fleet be fleet!"

"Damn you!" I shouted. I tried to drown it.

"Damn you!" I cursed him. I smashed his face.

The android battered Vandaleur, who fought it off until it exploded out of the mud and staggered upright. Before I could return to the attack, the live flames captured it hypnotically. It danced and capered in a lunatic rumba before the wall of fire. Its legs twisted. Its arms waved. The fingers writhed in a private rumba of their own. It shrieked and sang and ran in a crooked waltz before the embrace of the heat, a muddy monster silhouetted against the brilliant sparkling flare.

The searchers shouted. There were shots. The android spun around twice and then continued its horrid dance before the face of the flames. There was a rising gust of wind. The fire swept around the capering figure and enveloped it for a roaring moment. Then the fire swept on, leaving behind it a sobbing mass of synthetic flesh oozing scarlet blood that would never coagulate.

The thermometer would have registered 1200° wondrously Fahrenheit.

Vandaleur didn't die. I got away. They missed him while they watched the android caper and die. But I don't know which of us he is these days. Projection, Wanda warned me. Projection, Nan Webb told him. If you live with a crazy man or a crazy machine long enough, I become crazy too. Reet!

But we know one truth. We know they were wrong. The new robot and Vandaleur know that because the new robot's started twitching too. Reet! Here on cold Pollux, the robot is twitching and singing. No heat, but my fingers writhe. No heat, but it's taken the little Talley girl off for a solitary walk. A cheap labor robot. A servo-mechanism . . . all I could afford . . . but it's twitching and humming and walking alone with the child somewhere and I can't find them. Christ! Vandaleur can't find me before it's too late. Cool and discreet, honey, in the dancing frost while the thermometer registers 10° fondly Fahrenheit.

Comment on Fondly Fahrenheit

I'VE always been fascinated by the way craftsmen work in their profession, and I'll spend hours with pawnbrokers, computer engineers, exterminators, anyone, in an effort to discover the backstage problems of their work. Perhaps this is a habit created by years of interviewing for the magazine for which I write and edit; perhaps it is the built-in curiosity of the writer. I don't know. But it occurred to me that readers might be interested in the backstage problems of writing "Fondly Fahrenheit."

I must describe my working methods first, otherwise this journal of the writing of the story will seem cold-blooded and mechanistic. I write out of fever. I cannot write anything until I'm so saturated with it, involved with it, bursting with it, that it must come out or I will have no rest.

Over the years I've evolved a technique for igniting this fever. It starts with outlining, first general, then increasingly detailed as the story develops. When I have what I believe to be the final outline (it never is), I begin running the story through my head over and over again; not in words, I don't tell it to myself, but in a sort of sensory cinema. I listen to the sound, visualize the scenes, feel the tempo of the characters and their conflicts.

It's at this point that the pacing begins. At home I have a good seventy-five-foot straightaway, and I walk the length of the apartment, back and forth, endlessly. In the office I have a wide corridor, the length of a football field. The staff and the secretaries are used to my peculiarity by now and kindly clear the way for me. The pacing and the repetitions con-

tinue, the heat mounts, and, if I'm lucky, the ignition point is reached. Then I run like hell for the typewriter.

The idea for "Fondly Fahrenheit" first came to me out of a reminiscence of Mark Twain, I think in Life on the Mississippi, but I'm not sure, it was so long ago. He wrote that the first Negro slave was hanged for murder near Hannibal, Missouri. The slave had criminally assaulted and killed a young girl. Twain said that the slave had been guilty of a similar crime in another state, but that his owner had smuggled him out because he was too valuable to be given up to justice and destroyed.

It seemed to me that there might be an interesting story in this conflict between master and slave; the slave aware of his value and the hold it gives him over his owner, the master constrained by greed to condone criminal acts which he abhors. It was impossible for me to set the story in antebellum days; I didn't know enough about the period or the scene. Contemporary treatment was clearly out of the question; we do have economic forms of slavery, but no chattel slavery. I decided to set the story in the future, postulating an android-slave society. The note went into my Commonplace Book, which has been the storehouse for ideas, fragments, bits of dialogue, odd situations, and gimmicks since I began my writing career. It remained there for several years.

I would think about it, off and on, but I was also thinking about dozens of other ideas which seemed to have priority. I sometimes regard story ideas as an eager crowd, jostling and elbowing each other, trying to attract your attention. The master-slave idea managed to attract my serious attention one evening, and I outlined the first three or four scenes. I could get no further, and rather than waste time struggling with it, I put it away. One of the luxuries of reaching a certain financial plateau is that the writer can take his time and give inchoate ideas a chance to sort themselves out in the unconscious. Many writers, working under the gun, are so beset by the pressure of meeting bills that they haven't the time to do their best work. I've been through it myself, and I'm deeply sympathetic.

When I looked through my outlines and notes a few months later, the unconscious had done its work. It dawned on me

*that what was holding me up was the fact that I hadn't thought
through the android slave's criminal behavior; I'd more or
less written him off as a murderer, period. Now I asked
myself why. Why does a carefully conditioned android go
berserk? I remembered a note I'd made long before on the
statistics of crime, relating crime rate to temperature. (This
was a decade before the long, hot summer riots had become a
commonplace.) "Good," I said. "The android breaks his
conditioning only when the temperature rises about a certain
level."*

*At this point it was possible to add a mystery to the chase
structure. Will the owner discover what's wrong with his
android? I went back, reoutlined in these terms, changing the
settings to accommodate the temperature gimmick, and continued blocking forward. Then I came up against another
wall. So he does discover the secret. So what? It felt like a
letdown. I needed more of a climax. Once again I put the
notes away to give the real writer, who lives somewhere deep
down inside me, a chance to do some work.*

*Much later I was going through my Commonplace Book,
looking for something else, when I came across a note I'd
made on psychiatric projection, transcribed from one of
Karen Horney's books. These are cases where disturbed
people attribute their own strange behavior to others.*

*"That's it!" the real writer, an alert opportunist,
said.*

*"That's what?" I asked. "I'm looking for notes on West-
ern frontier customs."*

*"That's the final twist for the android story," he said.
"Temperature may break the android's conditioning, but the
master is really the criminal. We'll extrapolate the projection theme. The master unconsciously but actually imposes
his own insanity on the slave."*

*We dropped everything else, worked out a detailed scene-
by-scene outline, and began to pace. Suddenly an idea came,
one we'd been toying with for years, that of telling a story
from a multiple point of view. Here it would be the omni-
scient, the master's and the slave's. That was the ignition
point. The fever set in, and I ran like hell for the typewriter.*

What you've just read is the result of all this; years of notes, months of dovetailing ideas, weeks of outlining. Someone once asked me how long it took to write "Fondly Fahrenheit." I hedged. "Well, it took me two days to type it," I said. What else could I say?

The Four-Hour Fugue

I MUST thank Harlan Ellison, still the enfant terrible *of science fiction, for this story and my latest novel,* The Computer Connection. *He's going to be sore as hell when he learns the truth, revealed here for the first time, but I must purge myself.*

Ellison had been coaxing me to write an original for one of his gigantic collections which is still in preparation. He was highly flattering and most persuasive, but I was hassling around with my damned eyes and in no mood for writing. Nevertheless he continued a barrage of phone calls from the Coast, which rather impressed me. I'm so antiquated that I still regard long-distance calls as an extravagance. I finally succumbed to the Svengali and put together a story I called "Santayana Said It." Frankly, I was a little queasy about it.

Nevertheless I sent the ms. to Ellison who returned it with a long letter explaining that it was unsatisfactory because it left too many loose ends hanging. He wanted to know more about the characters and their milieu. There were other criticisms, and I agreed with all of them. Ellison had been so kind and enthusiastic that I felt I couldn't let him down. So I worked extremely hard on a new story and came up with "The Four-Hour Fugue."

The protagonist is based on a scent and perfume expert about whom several articles have been written; as a matter of fact, I bought the very first myself for Holiday. *Unfortunately, the real man is rather dull . . . it's his profession that's interesting . . . so I combined him with an expert whisky blender whom I'd interviewed for a feature on Canadian whisky. He was a charmer and provided all of the back-ground color.*

The heroine is a portrait of a member of the cast of Porgy and Bess *whom I met in Rome when the company was touring Italy. She was ravishing, and my reason tottered. I was all ready to start taking singing lessons when fortunately the company left for Naples, and I was saved. The lady is now a well-known poet, novelist, playwright and film director, and still as captivating as ever.*

Well, now I confess to my rotten finkery. I finished "The Fugue" and liked it so much that I didn't want to "waste it" on a mere collection. Magazine publication first; anthology later. But my final deadline was so close that I had a week at the most to cheat Ellison. I phoned Ben Bova at Analog, *told him the truth about the situation, and asked him if he could give me a quick refusal. "Sure," he said, "but what if I like it?"*

Two days later Bova called, said that the story wasn't in the usual Analog *style, but he liked it and was buying it anyway. "Wonderful!" I said. "I haven't appeared in the magazine in like a hundred and forty-seven years." "More like seventeen," Bova laughed. "There's only one trouble; now you'll have to write another story for Harlan."*

I was honor-bound to deliver to Ellison, but how do you produce a decent story in three days? You behave like some-one who's mislaid something important; searching, explor-ing, opening closets and drawers, looking under, over, and inside things, desperately, furiously. Finally I lucked in. I came across my notes for a feature on the U.N., including a long interview with the brilliant Dr. Ralph Bunche, and a "pianola" was born. A pianola is a story that plays itself, so to speak; you sort of write it no-hands. You'll read it in Harlan's collection, not mine.

And the novel? I thought over Ellison's suggestions, took a deep breath and began inching my way into the book. I'm not the type that gallops down the beach and plunges into the surf; I tippy-toe. The "Santayana" is the first chapter, revised, of The Computer Connection.

Thank you, Harlan, and please don't hit me when next we

meet. After all, your collection is bigger than mine. Pick on someone your own size.

By now, of course, the Northeast Corridor was the Northeast slum, stretching from Canada to the Carolinas and as far west as Pittsburgh. It was a fantastic jungle of rancid violence inhabited by a steaming, restless population with no visible means of support and no fixed residence, so vast that census-takers, birth-control supervisors, and the social services had given up all hope. It was a gigantic raree-show that everyone denounced and enjoyed. Even the privileged few who could afford to live highly protected lives in highly expensive Oases and could live anywhere else they pleased never thought of leaving. The jungle grabbed you.

There were thousands of everyday survival problems, but one of the most exasperating was the shortage of fresh water. Most of the available potable water had long since been impounded by progressive industries for the sake of a better tomorrow, and there was very little left to go around. Rainwater tanks on the roofs, of course. A black market, naturally. That was about all. So the jungle stank. It stank worse than the court of Queen Elizabeth, which could have bathed but didn't believe in it. The Corridor just couldn't bathe, wash clothes, or clean house, and you could smell its noxious effluvium from ten miles out at sea. Welcome to the Fun Corridor.

Sufferers near the shore would have been happy to clean up in salt water, but the Corridor beaches had been polluted by so much crude oil seepage for so many generations that they were all owned by deserving oil reclamation companies. *Keep Out! No Trespassing!* And armed guards. The rivers and lakes were electrically fenced; no need for guards, just skull-and-crossbones signs and if you didn't know what they were telling you, tough.

Not to believe that everybody minded stinking as they skipped merrily over the rotting corpses in the streets, but a lot did, and their only remedy was perfumery. There were dozens of competing companies producing perfumes, but the leader, far and away, was the Continental Can Company, which hadn't manufactured cans in two centuries. They'd switched to plastics and had the good fortune about a hundred stockholders' meetings back to make the mistake of signing a sales contract with and delivering to some cockamamie perfume brewer an enormous quantity of glowing neon containers. The corporation went bust and CCC took it over in hopes of getting some of their money back. That takeover proved to be their salvation when the perfume explosion took place; it gave them entrée to the most profitable industry of the times.

But it was neck-and-neck with the rivals until Blaise Skiaki joined CCC; then it turned into a runaway. Blaise Skiaki. Origins: French, Japanese, Black African and Irish. Education: B.A., Princeton; M.E., MIT; Ph.D. Dow Chemical. (It was Dow that had secretly tipped CCC that Skiaki was a winner, and lawsuits brought by the competition were still pending before the ethics board.) Blaise Skiaki: Age, thirty-one; unmarried, straight, genius.

His sense of scent was his genius, and he was privately referred to at CCC as "The Nose." He knew everything about perfumery: the animal products, ambergris, castor, civet, musk; the essential oils distilled from plants and flowers; the balsams extruded by tree and shrub wounds, benzoin, opopanax, Peru, Talu, storax, myrrh; the synthetics created from the combination of natural and chemical scents, the latter mostly the esters of fatty acids.

He had created for CCC their most successful sellers: "Vulva," "Assuage," "Oxter" (a much more attractive brand name than "Armpitto"), "Preparation F," "Tongue War," et cetera. He was treasured by CCC, paid a salary generous enough to enable him to live in an Oasis and, best of all, granted unlimited supplies of fresh water. No girl in the Corridor could resist the offer of taking a shower with him.

But he paid a high price for these advantages. He could never use scented soaps, shaving creams, pomades or depilatories. He could never eat seasoned foods. He could drink nothing but distilled water. All this, you understand, to keep The Nose pure and uncontaminated so that he could smell around in his sterile laboratory and devise new creations. He was presently composing a rather promising unguent provisionally named "Correctum," but he'd been on it for six months without any positive results and CCC was alarmed by the delay. His genius had never before taken so long.

There was a meeting of the top-level executives, names withheld on the grounds of corporate privilege.

"What's the matter with him anyway?"

"Has he lost his touch?"

"It hardly seems likely."

"Maybe he needs a rest."

"Why, he had a week's holiday last month."

"What did he do?"

"Ate up a storm, he told me."

"Could that be it?"

"No. He said he purged himself before he came back to work."

"Is he having trouble here at CCC? Difficulties with middle-management?"

"Absolutely not, Mr. Chairman. They wouldn't dare touch him."

"Maybe he wants a raise."

"No. He can't spend the money he makes now."

"Has our competition got to him?"

"They get to him all the time, general, and he laughs them off."

"Then it must be something personal."

"Agreed."

"Woman-trouble?"

"My God! We should have such trouble."

"Family-trouble?"

"He's an orphan, Mr. Chairman."

"Ambition? Incentive? Should we make him an officer of CCC?"

"I offered that to him the first of the year, sir, and he turned me down. He just wants to play in his laboratory."

"Then why isn't he playing?"

"Apparently he's got some kind of creative block."

"What the hell is the matter with him, anyway?"

"Which is how you started this meeting."

"I did not."

"You did."

"Not."

"Governor, will you play back the bug."

"Gentlemen, gentlemen, please! Obviously Dr. Skiaki has personal problems which are blocking his genius. We must solve that for him. Suggestions?"

"Psychiatry?"

"That won't work without voluntary cooperation. I doubt whether he'd cooperate. He's an obstinate gook."

"Senator, I beg you! Such expressions must not be used with reference to one of our most valuable assets."

"Mr. Chairman, the problem is to discover the source of Dr. Skiaki's block."

"Agreed. Suggestions?"

"Why, the first step should be to maintain twenty-four hour surveillance. All of the gook's—excuse me—the good doctor's activities, associates, contacts."

"By CCC?"

"I would suggest not. There are bound to be leaks which would only antagonize the good gook—doctor!"

"Outside surveillance?"

"Yes, sir."

"Very good. Agreed. Meeting adjourned."

Skip-Tracer Associates were perfectly furious. After one month they threw the case back into CCC's lap, asking for nothing more than their expenses.

"Why in hell didn't you tell us that we were assigned to a pro, Mr. Chairman, sir? Our tracers aren't trained for that."

"Wait a minute, please. What d'you mean 'pro'?"

"A professional Rip."

"A what?"

"Rip. Gorill. Gimpster. Crook."

"Dr. Skiaki a crook? Preposterous."

"Look, Mr. Chairman, I'll frame it for you and you draw your own conclusions. Yes?"

"Go ahead."

"It's all detailed in this report anyway. We put double tails on Skiaki every day to and from your shop. When he left they followed him home. He always went home. They staked in double shifts. He had dinner sent in from the Organic Nursery every night. They checked the messengers bringing the dinners. Legit. They checked the dinners; sometimes for one, sometimes for two. They traced some of the girls who left his penthouse. All clean. So far, all clean, yes?''

''And?''

''The crunch. Couple of nights a week he leaves the house and goes into the city. He leaves around midnight and doesn't come back until four, more or less.''

''Where does he go?''

''We don't know because he shakes his tails like the pro that he is. He weaves through the Corridor like a whore or a fag cruising for trade—excuse me—and he always loses our men. I'm not taking anything away from him. He's smart, shifty, quick, and a real pro. He has to be; and he's too much for Skip-Tracers to handle.''

''Then you have no idea of what he does or who he meets between midnight and four?''

''No, sir. We've got nothing and you've got a problem. Not ours anymore.''

''Thank you. Contrary to the popular impression, corporations are not altogether idiotic. CCC understands that negatives are also results. You'll receive your expenses and the agreed-upon fee.''

''Mr. Chairman, I—''

''No, no, please. You've narrowed it down to those missing four hours. Now, as you say, they're our problem.''

CCC summoned Salem Burne. Mr. Burne always insisted that he was neither a physician nor a psychiatrist; he did not care to be associated with what he considered to be the dreck of the professions. Salem Burne was a witch doctor; more precisely, a warlock. He made the most remarkable and penetrating analyses of disturbed people, not so much through his coven rituals of pentagons, incantations, incense and the like as through his remarkable sensitivity to body English and his acute interpretation of it. And this might be witchcraft after all.

Mr. Burne entered Blaise Skiaki's immaculate laboratory

with a winning smile, and Dr. Skiaki let out a rending howl of anguish.

"I told you to sterilize before you came."

"But I did, doctor. Faithfully."

"You did not. You reek of anise, ilang-ilang and methyl anthranilate. You've polluted my day. Why?"

"Dr. Skiaki, I assure you that I—" Suddenly Salem Burne stopped. "Oh, my God!" he groaned. "I used my wife's towel this morning."

Skiaki laughed and turned up the ventilators to full force. "I understand. No hard feelings. Now let's get your wife out of here. I have an office about half a mile down the hall. We can talk there."

They sat down in the vacant office and looked at each other. Mr. Burne saw a pleasant, youngish man with cropped black hair, small expressive ears, high telltale cheekbones, slitty eyes that would need careful watching, and graceful hands that would be a dead giveaway.

"Now, Mr. Burne, how can I help you?" Skiaki said while his hands asked, "Why the hell have you come pestering me?"

"Dr. Skiaki, I'm a colleague in a sense; I'm a professional witch doctor. One crucial part of my ceremonies is the burning of various forms of incense, but they're all rather conventional. I was hoping that your expertise might suggest something different with which I could experiment."

"I see. Interesting. You've been burning stacte, onycha, galbanum, frankincense . . . that sort of thing?"

"Yes. All quite conventional."

"Most interesting. I could, of course, make many suggestions for new experiments, and yet—" Here Skiaki stopped and stared into space.

After a long pause the warlock asked, "Is anything wrong, doctor?"

"Look here," Skiaki burst out. "You're on the wrong track. It's the burning of incense that's conventional and old-fashioned, and trying different scents won't solve your problem. Why not experiment with an altogether different approach?"

"And what would that be?"

"The Odophone principle."

"Odophone?"

"Yes. There's a scale that exists among scents as among sounds. Sharp smells correspond to high notes and heavy smells with low notes. For example, ambergris is in the treble clef while violet is in the bass. I could draw up a scent scale for you, running perhaps two octaves. Then it would be up to you to compose the music."

"This is positively brilliant, Dr. Skiaki."

"Isn't it?" Skiaki beamed. "But in all honesty I should point out that we're collaborators in brilliance. I could never have come up with the idea if you hadn't presented me with a most original challenge."

They made contact on this friendly note and talked shop enthusiastically, lunched together, told each other about themselves and made plans for the witchcraft experiments in which Skiaki volunteered to participate despite the fact that he was no believer in diabolism.

"And yet the irony lies in the fact that he is indeed devil-ridden," Salem Burne reported.

The Chairman could make nothing of this.

"Psychiatry and diabolism use different terms for the same phenomenon," Burne explained. "So perhaps I'd better translate. Those missing four hours are fugues."

The Chairman was not enlightened. "Do you mean the musical expression, Mr. Burne?"

"No, sir. A fugue is also the psychiatric description of a more advanced form of somnambulism . . . sleepwalking."

"Blaise Skiaki walks in his sleep?"

"Yes, sir, but it's more complicated than that. The sleep-walker is a comparatively simple case. He is never in touch with his surroundings. You can speak to him, shout at him, address him by name, and he remains totally oblivious."

"And the fugue?"

"In the fugue, the subject is in touch with his surroundings. He can converse with you. He has awareness and memory for the events that take place within the fugue, but while he is within his fugue, he is a totally different person from the man he is in real life. And—and this is most important, sir—after the fugue he remembers nothing of it."

"Then in your opinion Dr. Skiaki has these fugues two or three times a week."

"That is my diagnosis, sir."

"And he can tell us nothing of what transpires during the fugue?"

"Nothing."

"Can you?"

"I'm afraid not, sir. There's a limit to my powers."

"Have you any idea what is causing these fugues?"

"Only that he is driven by something. I would say that he is possessed by the devil, but that is the cant of my profession. Others may use different terms—compulsion or obsession. The terminology is unimportant. The basic fact is that something possessing him is compelling him to go out nights to do—what? I don't know. All I do know is that this diabolical drive most probably is what is blocking his creative work for you."

One does not summon Gretchen Nunn, not even if you're CCC whose common stock has split twenty-five times. You work your way up through the echelons of her staff until you are finally admitted to the Presence. This involves a good deal of backing and forthing between your staff and hers, and ignites a good deal of exasperation, so the Chairman was understandably put out when at last he was ushered into Miss Nunn's workshop, which was cluttered with the books and apparatus she used for her various investigations.

Gretchen Nunn's business was working miracles; not in the sense of the extraordinary, anomalous or abnormal brought about a superhuman agency, but rather in the sense of her extraordinary and/or abnormal perception and manipulation of reality. In any situation she could and did achieve the impossible begged by her desperate clients, and her fees were so enormous that she was thinking of going public.

Naturally the Chairman had anticipated Miss Nunn as looking like Merlin in drag. He was flabbergasted to discover that she was a Watusi princess with velvety black skin, aquiline features, great black eyes, tall, slender, twentyish, ravishing in red.

She dazzled him with a smile, indicated a chair, sat in one

opposite and said, "My fee is one hundred thousand. Can you afford it?"

"I can. Agreed."

"And your difficulty—is it worth it?"

"It is."

"Then we understand each other so far. Yes, Alex?"

The young secretary who had bounced into the workshop said, "Excuse me. LeClerque insists on knowing how you made the positive identification of the mold as extra-terrestrial."

Miss Nunn clicked her tongue impatiently. "He knows that I never give reasons. I only give results."

"Yes'N."

"Has he paid?"

"Yes'N."

"All right, I'll make an exception in his case. Tell him that it was based on the levo and dextro probability in amino acids and tell him to have a qualified exobiologist carry on from there. He won't regret the cost."

"Yes'N. Thank you."

She turned to the Chairman as the secretary left. "You heard that. I only give results."

"Agreed, Miss Nunn."

"Now your difficulty. I'm not committed yet. Understood?"

"Yes, Miss Nunn."

"Go ahead. Everything. Stream of consciousness, if necessary."

An hour later she dazzled him with another smile and said, "Thank you. This one is really unique. A welcome change. It's a contract, if you're still willing."

"Agreed, Miss Nunn. Would you like a deposit or an advance?"

"Not from CCC."

"What about expenses? Should that be arranged?"

"No. My responsibility."

"But what if you have to—if you're required to—if—"

She laughed. "My responsibility. I never give reasons and I never reveal methods. How can I charge for them? Now don't forget; I want that Skip-Trace report."

A week later Gretchen Nunn took the unusual step of visiting the Chairman in his office at CCC. "I'm calling on you, sir, to give you the opportunity of withdrawing from our contract."

"Withdraw? But why?"

"Because I believe you're involved in something far more serious than you anticipated."

"But what?"

"You won't take my word for it?"

"I must know."

Miss Nunn compressed her lips. After a moment she sighed. "Since this is an unusual case I'll have to break my rules. Look at this, sir." She unrolled a large map of a segment of the Corridor and flattened it on the Chairman's desk. There was a star in the center of the map. "Skiaki's residence," Miss Nunn said. There was a large circle scribed around the star. "The limits to which a man can walk in two hours," Miss Nunn said. The circle was crisscrossed by twisting trails all emanating from the star. "I got this from the Skip-Trace report. This is how their tails traced Skiaki."

"Very ingenious, but I see nothing serious in this, Miss Nunn."

"Look closely at the trails. What do you see?"

"Why . . . each ends in a red cross."

"And what happens to each trail before it reaches the red cross?"

"Nothing. Nothing at all, except—except that the dots change to dashes."

"And that's what makes it serious."

"I don't understand, Miss Nunn."

"I'll explain. Each cross represents the scene of a murder. The dashes represent the backtracking of the actions and whereabouts of each murder victim just prior to death."

"Murder!"

"They could trace their actions just so far back and no further. Skip-Trace could tail Skiaki just so far forward and no further. Those are the dots. The dates join up. What's your conclusion?"

"It must be coincidence," the Chairman shouted. "This brilliant, charming young man. Murder? Impossible!"

"Me?"

"What's your name?"

"Wish. Call me Mr. Wish." He hesitated for a moment and then said, "I have to turn left here."

"Thas okay, Mistuh Wish. I go left, too."

She could see that all his senses were prickling, and reduced her prattle to a background of unobtrusive sound. She stayed with him as he twisted, turned, sometimes doubling back, through streets, alleys, lanes and lots, always assuring him that this was her way home too. At a rather dangerous-looking refuse dump he gave her a fatherly pat and cautioned her to wait while he explored its safety. He explored, disappeared, and never reappeared.

"I replicated this experience with Skiaki six times," Miss Nunn reported to CCC. "They were all significant. Each time he revealed a little more without realizing it and without recognizing me. Burne was right. It is fugue."

"And the cause, Miss Nunn?"

"Pheromone trails."

"What?"

"I thought you gentlemen would know the term, being in the chemistry business. I see I'll have to explain. It will take some time so I insist that you do not require me to describe the induction and deduction that led me to my conclusion. Understood?"

"Agreed, Miss Nunn."

"Thank you, Mr. Chairman. Surely you all know hormones, from the Greek *hormaein*, meaning 'to excite.' They're internal secretions which excite other parts of the body into action. Pheromones are external secretions which excite other creatures into action. It's a mute chemical language.

"The best example of the pheromone language is the ant. Put a lump of sugar somewhere outside an anthill. A forager will come across it, feed and return to the nest. Within an hour the entire commune will be single-filing to and from the sugar, following the pheromone trail first laid down quite undeliberately by the first discoverer. It's an unconscious but compelling stimulant."

"Fascinating. And Dr. Skiaki?"

"He follows human pheromone trails. They compel him; he goes into fugue and follows them."

"Ah! An outré aspect of The Nose. It makes sense, Miss Nunn. It really does. But what trails is he compelled to follow?"

"The death-wish."

"Miss Nunn!"

"Surely you're aware of this aspect of the human psyche. Many people suffer from an unconscious but powerful death-wish, especially in these despairing times. Apparently this leaves a pheromone trail which Dr. Skiaki senses, and he is compelled to follow it."

"And then?"

"Apparently he grants the wish."

"Apparently! Apparently!" the Chairman shouted. "I ask you for proof-positive of this monstrous accusation."

"You'll get it, sir. I'm not finished with Blaise Skiaki yet. There are one or two things I have to wrap up with him, and in the course of that I'm afraid he's in for a shock. You'll have your proof-pos."

That was a half-lie from a woman half in love. She knew she had to see Blaise again, but her motives were confused. To find out whether she really loved him, despite what she knew? To find out whether he loved her? To tell him the truth about herself? To warn him or save him or run away with him? To fulfill her contract in a cool, professional style? She didn't know. Certainly she didn't know that she was in for a shock from Skiaki.

"Were you born blind?" he murmured that night.

She sat bolt upright in the bed. "What? Blind? What?"

"You heard me."

"I've had perfect sight all my life."

"Ah. Then you don't know, darling. I rather suspected that might be it."

"I certainly don't know what you're talking about, Blaise."

"Oh, you're blind all right," he said calmly. "But you've never known because you're blessed with a fantastic freak facility. You have extrasensory perception of other people's senses. You see through other people's eyes. For all I know you may be deaf and hear through their ears. You may feel with their skin. We must explore it sometime.''

"I never heard of anything more absurd in all my life," she said angrily.

"I can prove it to you, if you like, Gretchen."

"Go ahead, Blaise. Prove the impossible."

"Come into the lounge."

In the living room he pointed to a vase. "What color is that?"

"Brown, of course."

"What color is that?" A tapestry.

"Gray."

"And that lamp?"

"Black."

"Q.E.D.," Skiaki said. "It has been demonstrated."

"What's been demonstrated?"

"That you're seeing through my eyes."

"How can you say that?"

"Because I'm color-blind. That's what gave me the clue in the first place."

"What?"

He took her in his arms to quiet her trembling. "Darling Gretchen, the vase is green. The tapestry is amber and gold. The lamp is crimson. I can't see the colors, but the decorator told me and I remember. Now why the terror? You're blind, yes, but you're blessed with something far more miraculous than mere sight; you see through the eyes of the world. I'd change places with you any time."

"It can't be true," she cried.

"It's true, love."

"But when I'm alone?"

"When are you alone? When is anybody in the Corridor ever alone?"

She snatched up a shift and ran out of the penthouse, sobbing hysterically. She ran back to her own Oasis nearly crazed with terror. And yet she kept looking around and there were all the colors: red, orange, yellow, green, indigo, blue, violet. But there were also people swarming through the labyrinths of the Corridor as they always were, twenty-four hours a day.

Back in her apartment she was determined to put the disaster to the test. She dismissed her entire staff with stern orders to get the hell out and spend the night somewhere else. She stood at the door and counted them out, all amazed and unhappy. She slammed the door and looked around. She could still see.

"The lying sonofabitch," she muttered and began to pace furiously. She raged through the apartment, swearing venomously. It proved one thing: never get into personal relationships. They'll betray you, they'll try to destroy you, and she'd made a fool of herself. But why, in God's name, did Blaise use this sort of dirty trick to destroy her? Then she smashed into something and was thrown back. She recovered her balance and looked to see what she had blundered into. It was a harpsichord.

"But . . . but I don't own a harpsichord," she whispered in bewilderment. She started forward to touch it and assure herself of its reality. She smashed into the something again, grabbed it and felt it. It was the back of a couch. She looked around frantically. This was not one of her rooms. The harpsichord. Vivid Brueghels hanging on the walls. Jacobean furniture. Linefold paneled doors. Crewel drapes.

"But . . . this is the . . . the Raxon apartment downstairs. I must be seeing through their eyes. I must . . . he was right. I . . ." She closed her eyes and looked. She saw a mélange of apartments, streets, crowds, people, events. She had always seen this sort of montage on occasion but had always thought it was merely the total visual recall which was a major factor in her extraordinary abilities and success. Now she knew the truth.

She began to sob again. She felt her way around the couch and sat down, despairing. When at last the convulsion spent itself, she wiped her eyes courageously, determined to face reality. She was no coward. But when she opened her eyes she was shocked by another bombshell. She saw her familiar room in tones of gray. She saw Blaise Skiaki standing in the open door, smiling at her.

"Blaise?" she whispered.

"The name is Wish, my dear. Mr. Wish. What's yours?"

"Blaise, for God's sake, not me! Not me. I left no death-wish trail."

"What's your name, my dear? We've met before?"

"Gretchen," she screamed. "I'm Gretchen Nunn and I have no death-wish."

"Nice meeting you again, Gretchen," he said in glassy tones, smiling the glassy smile of Mr. Wish. He took two steps toward her. She jumped up and ran behind the couch.

"Blaise, listen to me. You are not Mr. Wish. There is no Mr. Wish. You are Dr. Blaise Skiaki, a famous scientist. You are chief chemist at CCC and have created many wonderful perfumes."

He took another step toward her, unwinding the scarf he wore around his neck.

"Blaise, I'm Gretchen. We've been lovers for two months. You must remember. Try to remember. You told me about my eyes tonight . . . being blind. You must remember that."

He smiled and whirled the scarf into a cord.

"Blaise, you're suffering from fugue. A blackout. A change of psyche. This isn't the real you. It's another creature driven by a pheromone. But I left no pheromone trail. I couldn't. I've never wanted to die."

"Yes, you do, my dear. Only happy to grant your wish. That's why I'm called Mr. Wish."

She squealed like a trapped rat and began darting and dodging while he closed in on her. She feinted him to one side, twisted to the other with a clear chance of getting out the door ahead of him, only to crash into three grinning goons standing shoulder to shoulder. They grabbed and held her.

Mr. Wish did not know that he also left a pheromone trail. It was a pheromone trail of murder.

"Oh, it's you again," Mr. Wish sniffed.

"Hey, old buddy-boy, got a looker this time, huh?"

"And loaded. Dig this layout."

"Great. Makes up for the last three, which was nothin'. Thanks, buddy-boy. You can go home now."

"Why don't I ever get to kill one?" Mr. Wish exclaimed petulantly.

"Now, now. No sulks. We got to protect our bird dog. You lead. We follow and do the rest."

"And if anything goes wrong, you're the setup," one of the goons giggled.

"Go home, buddy-boy. The rest is ours. No arguments. We already explained the standoff to you. We know who you are, but you don't know who we are."

"I know who I am," Mr. Wish said with dignity. "I am Mr. Wish, and I still think I have the right to kill at least one."

"All right, all right. Next time. That's a promise. Now blow."

As Mr. Wish exited resentfully, they ripped Gretchen naked and let out a huge wow when they saw the five-carat diamond in her navel. Mr. Wish turned and saw its scintillation too.

"But that's mine," he said in a confused voice. "That's only for my eyes. I—Gretchen said she would never—" Abruptly Dr. Blaise Skiaki spoke in a tone accustomed to command: "Gretchen, what the hell are you doing here? What's this place? Who are these creatures? What's going on?"

When the police arrived they found three dead bodies and a composed Gretchen Nunn sitting with a laser pistol in her lap. She told a perfectly coherent story of forcible entry, an attempt at armed rape and robbery, and how she was constrained to meet force with force. There were a few loopholes in her account. The bodies were not armed, but if the men had said they were armed, Miss Nunn, of course, would have believed them. The three were somewhat battered, but goons were always fighting. Miss Nunn was commended for her courage and cooperation.

After her final report to the Chairman (which was not the truth, the whole truth, and nothing but the truth) Miss Nunn received her check and went directly to the perfume laboratory, which she entered without warning. Dr. Skiaki was doing strange and mysterious things with pipettes, flasks and reagent bottles. Without turning, he ordered, "Out. Out. Out."

"Good morning, Dr. Skiaki."

He turned, displaying a mauled face and black eyes, and

smiled. "Well, well, well. The famous Gretchen Nunn, I presume. Voted Person of the Year three times in succession."

"No, sir. People from my class don't have last names."

"Knock off the sir bit."

"Yes—Mr. Wish."

"Oi!" He winced. "Don't remind me of that incredible insanity. How did everything go with the Chairman?"

"I snowed him. You're off the hook."

"Maybe I'm off his hook, but not my own. I was seriously thinking of having myself committed this morning."

"What stopped you?"

"Well, I got involved in this patchouli synthesis and sort of forgot."

She laughed. "You don't have to worry. You're saved."

"You mean cured?"

"No, Blaise. Not any more than I'm cured of my blindness. But we're both saved because we're aware. We can cope now."

He nodded slowly but not happily.

"So what are you going to do today?" she asked cheerfully. "Struggle with patchouli?"

"No," he said gloomily. "I'm still in one hell of a shock. I think I'll take the day off."

"Perfect. Bring two dinners."

The Men Who
Murdered Mohammed

IT'S interesting to remember that the superb H. G. Wells used time travel in The Time Machine *merely as a device to get to where he wanted to go, an eyewitness description of the culmination in the future of the structure of nineteenth-century English society. Unfortunately for Wells, and fortunately for us, he was a far more fascinating storyteller than sociologist, and time travel is still with us while his dire predictions are forgotten. (I suspect that nobody paid much attention to them even in Wells's own time.)*

Science fiction has been up to its ass in time travel ever since. Every possible change on Wells's simple concept has been rung with varying success. The results have been spotty because the authors attempted to grapple with aspects of time travel which Wells avoided. Do past, present, and future interlock? Must the past control the future? If one is altered, will it affect the other? Must it be a gross change, or will the most minute be significant? And so on and so on.

I've used time travel in other stories but in the Wells manner, as a device to get to where I wanted to go and then make my point. "The Men Who Murdered Mohammed" was written solely for the sake of doing an amusing aspect of time travel itself. I couldn't recall any other author having touched on this minuscule facet, so I had a crack at it just for fun. It's nice to be able to grin while you're writing now and then; usually it's grim work.

As a matter of fact the only tough part of the writing was the name of the prophet. Spelling Mohammed is as tricky as pronouncing Van Gogh; look it up in the big Webster-II some time. Mohammed? Mohammet? Muhammad? Mahomet? For a while I was tempted to mask its appearance with an offstage trumpet voluntary, but that would have made a damn peculiar title: "The Men Who Murdered a Trumpet Voluntary"?

There was a man who mutilated history. He toppled empires and uprooted dynasties. Because of him, Mount Vernon should not be a national shrine, and Columbus, Ohio, should be called Cabot, Ohio. Because of him the name Marie Curie should be cursed in France, and no one should swear by the beard of the Prophet. Actually, these realities did not happen, because he was a mad professor; or, to put it another way, he only succeeded in making them unreal for himself.

Now, the patient reader is too familiar with the conventional mad professor, undersized and overbrowed, creating monsters in his laboratory which invariably turn on their maker and menace his lovely daughter. This story isn't about that sort of make-believe man. It's about Henry Hassel, a genuine mad professor in a class with such better-known men as Ludwig Boltzmann (*see* Ideal Gas Law), Jacques Charles and André Marie Ampère (1775-1836).

Everyone ought to know that the electrical ampere was so named in honor of Ampère. Ludwig Boltzmann was a distinguished Austrian physicist, as famous for his research on black-body radiation as on Ideal Gases. You can look him up in Volume Three of the *Encyclopaedia Britannica*, BALT to BRAI. Jacques Alexandre César Charles was the first mathematician to become interested in flight, and he invented the hydrogen balloon. These were real men.

They were also real mad professors. Ampère, for example, was on his way to an important meeting of scientists in Paris. In his taxi he got a brilliant idea (of an electrical nature, I assume) and whipped out a pencil and jotted the equation on the wall of the hansom cab. Roughly, it was: $dH = ipdl/r^2$ in which p is the perpendicular distance from P to the line of the element dl; or $dH = i \sin \theta \, dl/r^2$. This is sometimes known as Laplace's Law, although he wasn't at the meeting.

Anyway, the cab arrived at the Académie. Ampère jumped out, paid the driver and rushed into the meeting to tell everybody about his idea. Then he realized he didn't have the note on him, remembered where he'd left it, and had to chase through the streets of Paris after the taxi to recover his runaway equation. Sometimes I imagine that's how Fermat lost his famous "Last Theorem," although Fermat wasn't at the meeting either, having died some two hundred years earlier.

Or take Boltzmann. Giving a course in Advanced Ideal Gases, he peppered his lectures with involved calculus, which he worked out quickly and casually in his head. He had that kind of head. His students had so much trouble trying to puzzle out the math by ear that they couldn't keep up with the lectures, and they begged Boltzmann to work out his equations on the blackboard.

Boltzmann apologized and promised to be more helpful in the future. At the next lecture he began, "Gentlemen, combining Boyle's Law with the Law of Charles, we arrive at the equation $pv = p_0 v_0 (1 + at)$. Now, obviously, if $_aS^b = f(x) dx_x (a)$, then $pv = RT$ and $_v S f(x,y,z) dV = O$. It's as simple as two plus two equals four." At this point Boltzmann remembered his promise. He turned to the blackboard, conscientiously chalked $2 + 2 = 4$, and then breezed on, casually doing the complicated calculus in his head.

Jacques Charles, the brilliant mathematician who discovered Charles's Law (sometimes known as Gay-Lussac's Law), which Boltzmann mentioned in his lecture, had a lunatic passion to become a famous paleographer—that is, a discoverer of ancient manuscripts. I think that being forced to share credit with Gay-Lussac may have unhinged him.

He paid a transparent swindler named Vrain-Lucas 200,000 francs for holograph letters purportedly written by Julius Caesar, Alexander the Great, and Pontius Pilate. Charles, a man who could see through any gas, ideal or not, actually believed in these forgeries despite the fact that the maladroit Vrain-Lucas had written them in modern French on modern notepaper bearing modern watermarks. Charles even tried to donate them to the Louvre.

Now, these men weren't idiots. They were geniuses who

paid a high price for their genius because the rest of their thinking was other-world. A genius is someone who travels to truth by an unexpected path. Unfortunately, unexpected paths lead to disaster in everyday life. This is what happened to Henry Hassel, professor of Applied Compulsion at Unknown University in the year 1980.

Nobody knows where Unknown University is or what they teach there. It has a faculty of some two hundred eccentrics, and a student body of two thousand misfits—the kind that remain anonymous until they win Nobel prizes or become the First Man on Mars. You can always spot a graduate of U.U. when you ask people where they went to school. If you get an evasive reply like: "State," or "Oh, a freshwater school you never heard of," you can bet they went to Unknown. Someday I hope to tell you more about this university, which is a center of learning only in the Pickwickian sense.

Anyway, Henry Hassel started home from his office in the Psychotic Psenter early one afternoon, strolling through the Physical Culture arcade. It is not true that he did this to leer at the nude coeds practicing Arcane Eurythmics; rather, Hassel liked to admire the trophies displayed in the arcade in memory of great Unknown teams which had won the sort of championships that Unknown teams win—in sports like Strabismus, Occlusion and Botulism. (Hassel had been Frambesia singles champion three years running.) He arrived home uplifted, and burst gaily into the house to discover his wife in the arms of a man.

There she was, a lovely woman of thirty-five, with smoky red hair and almond eyes, being heartily embraced by a person whose pockets were stuffed with pamphlets, microchemical apparatus and a patella-reflex hammer—a typical campus character of U.U., in fact. The embrace was so concentrated that neither of the offending parties noticed Henry Hassel glaring at them from the hallway.

Now, remember Ampère and Charles and Boltzmann. Hassel weighed one hundred and ninety pounds. He was muscular and uninhibited. It would have been child's play for him to have dismembered his wife and her lover, and thus simply and directly achieve the goal he desired—the end of his wife's life. But Henry Hassel was in the genius class; his mind just didn't operate that way.

Hassel breathed hard, turned and lumbered into his private laboratory like a freight engine. He opened a drawer labeled DUODENUM and removed a .45-caliber revolver. He opened other drawers, more interestingly labeled, and assembled apparatus. In exactly seven and one half minutes (such was his rage), he put together a time machine (such was his genius).

Professor Hassel assembled the time machine around him, set a dial for 1902, picked up the revolver and pressed a button. The machine made a noise like defective plumbing and Hassel disappeared. He reappeared in Philadelphia on June 3, 1902, went directly to No. 1218 Walnut Street, a red-brick house with marble steps, and rang the bell. A man who might have passed for the third Smith Brother opened the door and looked at Henry Hassel.

"Mr. Jessup?" Hassel asked in a suffocated voice.

"Yes?"

"You are Mr. Jessup?"

"I am."

"You will have a son, Edgar? Edgar Allan Jessup—so named because of your regrettable admiration for Poe?"

The third Smith Brother was startled. "Not that I know of," he said. "I'm not married yet."

"You will be," Hassel said angrily. "I have the misfortune to be married to your son's daughter. Greta. Excuse me." He raised the revolver and shot his wife's grandfather-to-be.

"She will have ceased to exist," Hassel muttered, blowing smoke out of the revolver. "I'll be a bachelor. I may even be married to somebody else. . . . Good God! Who?"

Hassel waited impatiently for the automatic recall of the time machine to snatch him back to his own laboratory. He rushed into his living room. There was his redheaded wife, still in the arms of a man.

Hassel was thunderstruck.

"So that's it," he growled. "A family tradition of faithlessness. Well, we'll see about that. We have ways and means.'' He permitted himself a hollow laugh, returned to his laboratory, and sent himself back to the year 1901, where he shot and killed Emma Hotchkiss, his wife's maternal grandmother-to-be. He returned to his own home in his own time. There was his redheaded wife, still in the arms of another man.

"But I *know* the old bitch was her grandmother," Hassel muttered. "You couldn't miss the resemblance. What the hell's gone wrong?"

Hassel was confused and dismayed, but not without resources. He went to his study, had difficulty picking up the phone, but finally managed to dial the Malpractice Laboratory. His finger kept oozing out of the dial holes.

"Sam?" he said. "This is Henry."

"Who?"

"Henry."

"You'll have to speak up."

"Henry Hassel!"

"Oh, good afternoon, Henry."

"Tell me all about time."

"Time? Hmmm . . ." The Simplex-and Multiplex Computer cleared its throat while it waited for the data circuits to link up. "Ahem. Time. (1) Absolute. (2) Relative. (3) Recurrent. (1) Absolute: period, contingent, duration, diurnity, perpetuity—"

"Sorry, Sam. Wrong request. Go back. I want time, reference to succession of, travel in."

Sam shifted gears and began again. Hassel listened intently. He nodded. He grunted. "Uh huh. Uh huh. Right. I see. Thought so. A continuum, eh? Acts performed in past must alter future. Then I'm on the right track. But act must be significant, eh? Mass-action effect. Trivia cannot divert existing phenomena streams. Hmmm. But how trivial is a grandmother?"

"What are you trying to do, Henry?"

"Kill my wife," Hassel snapped. He hung up. He returned to his laboratory. He considered, still in a jealous rage.

"Got to do something significant," he muttered. "Wipe Greta out. Wipe it all out. All right, by God! I'll show 'em."

Hassel went back to the year 1775, visited a Virginia farm

and shot a young colonel in the brisket. The colonel's name was George Washington, and Hassel made sure he was dead. He returned to his own time and his own home. There was his redheaded wife, still in the arms of another.

"Damn!" said Hassel. He was running out of ammunition. He opened a fresh box of cartridges, went back in time and massacred Christopher Columbus, Napoleon, Mohammed and half a dozen other celebrities. "That ought to do it, by God!" said Hassel.

He returned to his own time, and found his wife as before.

His knees turned to water; his feet seemed to melt into the floor. He went back to his laboratory, walking through nightmare quicksands.

"What the hell is significant?" Hassel asked himself painfully. "How much does it take to change futurity? By God, I'll really change it this time. I'll go for broke."

He traveled to Paris at the turn of the twentieth century and visited a Madame Curie in an attic workshop near the Sorbonne. "Madame," he said in his execrable French, "I am a stranger to you of the utmost, but a scientist entire. Knowing of your experiments with radium— Oh? You haven't got to radium yet? No matter. I am here to teach you all of nuclear fission."

He taught her. He had the satisfaction of seeing Paris go up in a mushroom of smoke before the automatic recall brought him home. "That'll teach women to be faithless," he growled. . . . "Guhhh!" The last was wrenched from his lips when he saw his redheaded wife still— But no need to belabor the obvious.

Hassel swam through fogs to his study and sat down to think. While he's thinking I'd better warn you that this is not a conventional time story. If you imagine for a moment that Henry is going to discover that the man fondling his wife is himself, you're mistaken. The viper is not Henry Hassel, his son, a relation, or even Ludwig Boltzmann (1844-1906). Hassel does not make a circle in time, ending where the story begins—to the satisfaction of nobody and the fury of everybody—for the simple reason that time isn't circular, or linear, or tandem, discoid, syzygous, longinquitous, or pandicularted. Time is a private matter, as Hassel discovered.

"Maybe I slipped up somehow," Hassel muttered. "I'd better find out." He fought with the telephone, which seemed to weigh a hundred tons, and at last managed to get through to the library.

"Hello, Library? This is Henry."

"Who?"

"Henry Hassel."

"Speak up, please."

"HENRY HASSEL!"

"Oh. Good afternoon, Henry."

"What have you got on George Washington?"

Library clucked while her scanners sorted through her catalogues. "George Washington, first president of the United States, was born in—"

"First president? Wasn't he murdered in 1775?"

"Really, Henry. That's an absurd question. Everybody knows that George Wash—"

"Doesn't anybody know he was shot?"

"By whom?"

"Me."

"When?"

"In 1775."

"How did you manage to do that?"

"I've got a revolver."

"No, I mean, how did you do it two hundred years ago?"

"I've got a time machine."

"Well, there's no record here," Library said. "He's still doing fine in my files. You must have missed."

"I did not miss. What about Christopher Columbus? Any record of his death in 1489?"

"But he discovered the New World in 1492."

"He did not. He was murdered in 1489."

"How?"

"With a forty-five slug in the gizzard."

"You again, Henry?"

"Yes."

"There's no record here," Library insisted. "You must be one lousy shot."

"I will not lose my temper," Hassel said in a trembling voice.

"Why not, Henry?"

"Because it's lost already," he shouted. "All right! What about Marie Curie? Did she or did she not discover the fission bomb which destroyed Paris at the turn of the century?"

"She did not. Enrico Fermi—"

"She did."

"She didn't."

"I personally taught her. Me. Henry Hassel."

"Everybody says you're a wonderful theoretician, but a lousy teacher, Henry. You—"

"Go to hell, you old biddy. This has got to be explained."

"Why?"

"I forget. There was something on my mind, but it doesn't matter now. What would you suggest?"

"You really have a time machine?"

"Of course I've got a time machine."

"Then go back and check."

Hassel returned to the year 1775, visited Mount Vernon, and interrupted the spring planting. "Excuse me, colonel," he began.

The big man looked at him curiously. "You talk funny, stranger," he said. "Where you from?"

"Oh, a freshwater school you never heard of."

"You look funny too. Kind of misty, so to speak."

"Tell me, colonel, what do you hear from Christopher Columbus?"

"Not much," Colonel Washington answered. "Been dead two, three hundred years."

"When did he die?"

"Year fifteen hundred some-odd, near as I remember."

"He did not. He died in 1489."

"Got your dates wrong, friend. He discovered America in 1492."

"Cabot discovered America. Sebastian Cabot."

"Nope. Cabot came a mite later."

"I have infallible proof!" Hassel began, but broke off as a stocky and rather stout man, with a face ludicrously reddened by rage, approached. He was wearing baggy gray slacks and a tweed jacket two sizes too small for him. He was carrying a .45 revolver. It was only after he had stared for a moment that

Henry Hassel realized that he was looking at himself and not relishing the sight.

"My God!" Hassel murmured. "It's me, coming back to murder Washington that first time. If I'd made this second trip an hour later, I'd have found Washington dead. Hey!" he called. "Not yet. Hold off a minute. I've got to straighten something out first."

Hassel paid no attention to himself; indeed, he did not appear to be aware of himself. He marched straight up to Colonel Washington and shot him in the gizzard. Colonel Washington collapsed, emphatically dead. The first murderer inspected the body, and then, ignoring Hassel's attempt to stop him and engage him in dispute, turned and marched off, muttering venomously to himself.

"He didn't hear me," Hassel wondered. "He didn't even feel me. And why don't I remember myself trying to stop me the first time I shot the colonel? What the hell is going on?"

Considerably disturbed, Henry Hassel visited Chicago and dropped into the Chicago University squash courts in the early 1940s. There, in a slippery mess of graphite bricks and graphite dust that coated him, he located an Italian scientist named Fermi.

"Repeating Marie Curie's work, I see, *dottore*?" Hassel said.

Fermi glanced about as though he had heard a faint sound.

"Repeating Marie Curie's work, *dottore*?" Hassel roared.

Fermi looked at him strangely. "Where you from, *amico*?"

"State."

"State Department?"

"Just State. It's true, isn't it, *dottore*, that Marie Curie discovered nuclear fission back in nineteen ought ought?"

"No! No! No!" Fermi cried. "We are the first, and we are not there yet. Police! Police! Spy!"

"This time I'll go on record," Hassel growled. He pulled out his trusty .45, emptied it into Dr. Fermi's chest, and awaited arrest and immolation in newspaper files. To his amazement, Dr. Fermi did not collapse. Dr. Fermi merely explored his chest tenderly and, to the men who answered his cry, said, "It is nothing. I felt in my within a sudden sensation of burn which may be a neuralgia of the cardiac nerve, but is most likely gas."

Hassel was too agitated to wait for the automatic recall of the time machine. Instead he returned at once to Unknown University under his own power. This should have given him a clue, but he was too possessed to notice. It was at this time that I (1913-1975) first saw him—a dim figure tramping through parked cars, closed doors and brick walls, with the light of lunatic determination on his face.

He oozed into the library, prepared for an exhaustive discussion, but could not make himself felt or heard by the catalogues. He went to the Malpractice Laboratory, where Sam, the Simplex-and-Multiplex Computer, has installations sensitive up to 10,700 angstroms. Sam could not see Henry, but managed to hear him through a sort of wave-interference phenomenon.

"Sam," Hassel said, "I've made one hell of a discovery."

"You're always making discoveries, Henry," Sam complained. "Your data allocation is filled. Do I have to start another tape for you?"

"But I need advice. Who's the leading authority on time, reference to succession of, travel in?"

"That would be Israel Lennox, spatial mechanics, professor of, Yale."

"How do I get in touch with him?"

"You don't, Henry. He's dead. Died in '75."

"What authority have you got on time, travel in, living?"

"Wiley Murphy."

"Murphy? From our own Trauma Department? That's a break. Where is he now?"

"As a matter of fact, Henry, he went over to your house to ask you something."

Hassel went home without walking, searched through his laboratory and study without finding anyone, and at last floated into the living room, where his redheaded wife was still in the arms of another man. (All this, you understand, had taken place within the space of a few moments after the construction of the time machine; such is the nature of time and time travel.) Hassel cleared his throat once or twice and tried to tap his wife on the shoulder. His fingers went through her.

"Excuse me, darling," he said. "Has Wiley Murphy been in to see me?"

Then he looked closer and saw that the man embracing his wife was Murphy himself.

"Murphy!" Hassel exclaimed. "The very man I'm looking for. I've had the most extraordinary experience." Hassel at once launched into a lucid description of his extraordinary experience, which went something like this: "Murphy, $u - v = (u^{1/2} - v^{1/4})(u^a + u^x + v^y)$ but when George Washington $F(x) y^+ dx$ and Enrico Fermi $F(u^{1/2}) dxdt$ one half of Marie Curie, then what about Christopher Columbus times the square root of minus one?"

Murphy ignored Hassel, as did Mrs. Hassel. I jotted down Hassel's equations on the hood of a passing taxi.

"Do listen to me, Murphy," Hassel said. "Greta dear, would you mind leaving us for a moment? I—For heaven's sake, will you two stop that nonsense? This is serious."

Hassel tried to separate the couple. He could no more touch them than make them hear him. His face turned red again and he became quite choleric as he beat at Mrs. Hassel and Murphy. It was like beating an Ideal Gas. I thought it best to interfere.

"Hassel!"

"Who's that?"

"Come outside a moment. I want to talk to you."

He shot through the wall. "Where are you?"

"Over here."

"You're sort of dim."

"So are you."

"Who are you?"

"My name's Lennox. Israel Lennox."

"Israel Lennox, spatial mechanics, professor of, Yale?"

"The same."

"But you died in '75."

"I disappeared in '75."

"What d'you mean?"

"I invented a time machine."

"By God! So did I," Hassel said. "This afternoon. The idea came to me in a flash—I don't know why—and I've had the most extraordinary experience. Lennox, time is not a continuum."

"No?"

"It's a series of discrete particles—like pearls on a string."

"Yes?"

"Each pearl is a 'Now.' Each 'Now' has its own past and future. But none of them relate to any others. You see? if $a = a_1 + a_2ji + {}^x ax (b_1)$—"

"Never mind the mathematics, Henry."

"It's a form of quantum transfer of energy. Time is emitted in discrete corpuscles or quanta. We can visit each individual quantum and make changes within it, but no change in any one corpuscle affects any other corpuscle. Right?"

"Wrong," I said sorrowfully.

"What d'you mean, 'Wrong'?" he said, angrily gesturing through the cleavage of a passing coed. "You take the trochoid equations and—"

"Wrong," I repeated firmly. "Will you listen to me, Henry?"

"Oh, go ahead," he said.

"Have you noticed that you've become rather insubstantial? Dim? Spectral? Space and time no longer affect you?"

"Yes?"

"Henry, I had the misfortune to construct a time machine back in '75."

"So you said. Listen, what about power input? I figure I'm using about 7.3 kilowatts per—"

"Never mind the power input, Henry. On my first trip into the past, I visited the Pleistocene. I was eager to photograph the mastodon, the giant ground sloth, and the saber-tooth tiger. While I was backing up to get a mastodon fully in the field of view at f/6.3 at 1/100th of a second, or on the LVS scale—"

"Never mind the LVS scale," he said.

"While I was backing up, I inadvertently trampled and killed a small Pleistocene insect."

"Aha!" said Hassel.

"I was terrified by the incident. I had visions of returning to my world to find it completely changed as a result of this single death. Imagine my surprise when I returned to my world to find that nothing had changed."

"Oho!" said Hassel.

"I became curious. I went back to the Pleistocene and killed the mastodon. Nothing was changed in 1975. I returned to the Pleistocene and slaughtered the wildlife—still with no effect. I ranged through time, killing and destroying, in an attempt to alter the present."

"Then you did it just like me," Hassel exclaimed. "Odd we didn't run into each other."

"Not odd at all."

"I got Columbus."

"I got Marco Polo."

"I got Napoleon."

"I thought Einstein was more important."

"Mohammed didn't change things much—I expected more from *him*."

"I know. I got him too."

"What do you mean, you got him too?" Hassel demanded.

"I killed him September 16, 599. Old Style."

"Why, I got Mohammed January 5, 598."

"I believe you."

"But how could you have killed him after I killed him?"

"We both killed him."

"That's impossible."

"My boy," I said, "time is entirely subjective. It's a private matter—a personal experience. There is no such thing as objective time, just as there is no such thing as objective love, or an objective soul."

"Do you mean to say that time travel is impossible? But we've done it."

"To be sure, and many others, for all I know. But we each travel into our own past, and no other person's. There is no universal continuum, Henry. There are only billions of individuals, each with his own continuum; and one continuum cannot affect the other. We're like millions of strands of spaghetti in the same pot. No time traveler can ever meet another time traveler in the past or future. Each of us must travel up and down his own strand alone.''

"But we're meeting each other now.''

"We're no longer time travelers, Henry. We've become the spaghetti sauce.''

"Spaghetti sauce?''

"Yes. You and I can visit any strand we like, because we've destroyed ourselves.''

"I don't understand.''

"When a man changes the past he only affects his own past—no one else's. The past is like memory. When you erase a man's memory, you wipe him out, but you don't wipe out anybody else's. You and I have erased our past. The individual worlds of the others go on, but we have ceased to exist.''

"What d'you mean, 'ceased to exist'?''

"With each act of destruction we dissolved a little. Now we're all gone. We've committed chronicide. We're ghosts. I hope Mrs. Hassel will be very happy with Mr. Murphy. . . . Now let's go over to the Académie. Ampère is telling a great story about Ludwig Boltzmann.''

Disappearing Act

THIS baby was one of those rare naturals that come along occasionally and restore faith in our tough profession. Milton Berle once told me, "Great scripts aren't written, they're rewritten." Uncle Miltie was right, but then along comes the exception and suddenly the whole world looks Jewish.

The story flopped into my mind out of nowhere one afternoon, pure and complete. The first draft was written the following day, and the edited and finished Fair Copy on the next. You can't understand how extraordinary this is for me unless you know that I usually write and rewrite many drafts before I'm satisfied with a piece of work. The only trouble I had with this shoo-in was with the word "anachronism" which kept leaving my mind like a small boy running away from home, no doubt with a bindle on a stick over its shoulder. I wasted a lot of time finding it and bringing it back to the ms.

Since this is all I can say about "Disappearing Act," I now have enough space left over to follow the custom of collection editors who preface a story with a description of the author and his accomplishments.

I've had an intrapersonal love-hate relationship with Alfred Bester for many years, and I can honestly report that while he is trustworthy, loyal, helpful, friendly, courteous, kind, obedient, cheerful, thrifty, brave, clean and reverent, he is also rotten to the core.

This one wasn't the last war or a war to end war. They called it the War for the American Dream. General Carpenter struck that note and sounded it constantly.

There are fighting generals (vital to an army), political generals (vital to an administration), and public relations generals (vital to a war). General Carpenter was a master of public relations. Forthright and Four-Square, he had ideals as high and as understandable as the mottoes on money. In the mind of America he *was* the army, the administration, the nation's shield and sword and stout right arm. His ideal was the American Dream.

"We are not fighting for money, for power, or for world domination," General Carpenter announced at the Press Association dinner.

"We are fighting solely for the American dream," he said to the 162nd Congress.

"Our aim is not aggression or the reduction of nations to slavery," he said at the West Point Annual Officers' Dinner.

"We are fighting for the Meaning of Civilization," he told the San Francisco Pioneers' Club.

"We are struggling for the Ideal of Civilization; for Culture, for Poetry, for the Only Things Worth Preserving," he said at the Chicago Wheat Pit Festival.

"This is a war for survival," he said. "We are not fighting for ourselves, but for our Dreams; for the Better Things in Life which must not disappear from the face of the earth."

America fought. General Carpenter asked for one hundred million men. The army was given one hundred million men. General Carpenter asked for ten thousand U-Bombs. Ten thousand U-Bombs were delivered and dropped. The enemy also dropped ten thousand U-Bombs and destroyed most of America's cities.

"We must dig in against the hordes of barbarism," General Carpenter said. "Give me a thousand engineers."

One thousand engineers were forthcoming and a hundred cities were dug and hollowed out beneath the rubble.

"Give me five hundred sanitation experts, eight hundred traffic managers, two hundred air-conditioning experts, one hundred city managers, one thousand communication chiefs, seven hundred personnel experts . . ."

The list of General Carpenter's demand for technical experts was endless. America did not know how to supply them.

"We must become a nation of experts," General Carpenter informed the National Association of American Universities. "Every man and woman must be a specific tool for a specific job, hardened and sharpened by your training and education to win the fight for the American Dream."

"Our Dream," General Carpenter said at the Wall Street Bond Drive Breakfast, "is at one with the gentle Greeks of Athens, with the noble Romans of . . . er . . . Rome. It is a dream of the Better Things in Life. Of Music and Art and Poetry and Culture. Money is only a weapon to be used in the fight for this dream. Ambition is only a ladder to climb to this dream. Ability is only a tool to shape this dream."

Wall Street applauded. General Carpenter asked for one hundred and fifty billion dollars, fifteen hundred dedicated dollar-a-year men, three thousand experts in mineralogy, petrology, mass production, chemical warfare, and air-traffic time study. They were delivered. The country was in high gear. General Carpenter had only to press a button and an expert would be delivered.

In March of A.D. 2112 the war came to a climax and the American Dream was resolved, not on any one of the seven fronts where millions of men were locked in bitter combat, not in any of the staff headquarters or any of the capitals of the warring nations, not in any of the production centers spewing forth arms and supplies, but in Ward T of the United States Army Hospital buried three hundred feet below what had once been St. Albans, New York.

Ward T was something of a mystery at St. Albans. Like all army hospitals, St. Albans was organized with specific wards reserved for specific injuries. Right-arm amputees were gathered in one ward; left-arm amputees in another. Radiation burns, head injuries, eviscerations, secondary gamma poisonings, and so on were each assigned their specific location in the hospital organization. The Army Medical Corps had established nineteen classes of combat injury which included every possible kind of damage to brain and tissue. These used up letters A to S. What, then, was in Ward T?

No one knew. The doors were double-locked. No visitors were permitted to enter. No patients were permitted to leave.

Physicians were seen to arrive and depart. Their perplexed expressions stimulated the wildest speculations but revealed nothing. The nurses who ministered to Ward T were questioned eagerly but they were close-mouthed.

There were dribs and drabs of information, unsatisfying and self-contradictory. A charwoman asserted that she had been in to clean up and there had been no one in the ward. Absolutely no one. Just two dozen beds and nothing else. Had the beds been slept in? Yes. They were rumpled, some of them. Were there signs of the ward being in use? Oh yes. Personal things on the tables and so on. But dusty, kind of. Like they hadn't been used in a long time.

Public opinion decided it was a ghost ward. For spooks only.

But a night orderly reported passing the locked ward and hearing singing from within. What kind of singing? Foreign language, like. What language? The orderly couldn't say. Some of the words sounded like . . . well, like: Cow dee on us eager tour . . .

Public opinion started to run a fever and decided it was an alien ward. For spies only.

St. Albans enlisted the help of the kitchen staff and checked the food trays. Twenty-four trays went into Ward T three times a day. Twenty-four came out. Sometimes the returning trays were emptied. Most times they were untouched.

Public opinion started to run a fever and decided it was a racket. It was an informal club of goldbricks and staff grafters who caroused within. Cow dee on us eager tour indeed!

For gossip, a hospital can put a small town sewing circle to shame with ease, but sick people are easily goaded into passion by trivia. It took just three months for idle speculation to turn into downright fury. In January, 2112, St. Albans was a sound, well-run hospital. By March, 2112, St. Albans was in a ferment, and the psychological unrest found its way into the official records. The percentage of recoveries fell off. Malingering set in. Petty infractions increased. Mutinies flared. There was a staff shake-up. It did no good. Ward T was inciting the patients to riot. There was another shake-up, and another, and still the unrest fumed.

The news finally reached General Carpenter's desk through official channels.

"In our fight for the American Dream," he said, "we must not ignore those who have already given of themselves. Send me a Hospital Administration expert."

The expert was delivered. He could do nothing to heal St. Albans. General Carpenter read the reports and fired him.

"Pity," said General Carpenter, "is the first ingredient of civilization. Send me a Surgeon General."

A Surgeon General was delivered. He could not break the fury of St. Albans, and General Carpenter broke him. But by this time Ward T was being mentioned in the dispatches.

"Send me," General Carpenter said, "the expert in charge of Ward T."

St. Albans sent a doctor, Captain Edsel Dimmock. He was a stout young man, already bald, only three years out of medical school, but with a fine record as an expert in psychotherapy. General Carpenter liked experts. He liked Dimmock. Dimmock adored the general as the spokesman for a culture which he had been too specially trained to seek up to now, but which he hoped to enjoy after the war was won.

"Now look here, Dimmock," General Carpenter began. "We're all of us tools, today—hardened and sharpened to do a specific job. You know our motto: a job for everyone and everyone on the job. Somebody's not on the job at Ward T and we've got to kick him out. Now, in the first place what the hell is Ward T?"

Dimmock stuttered and fumbled. Finally he explained that it was a special ward set up for special combat cases. Shock cases.

"Then you do have patients in the ward?"

"Yes, sir. Ten women and fourteen men."

Carpenter brandished a sheaf of reports. "Says here the St. Albans patients claim nobody's in War T."

Dimmock was shocked. That was untrue, he assured the general.

"All right, Dimmock. So you've got your twenty-four crocks in there. Their job's to get well. Your job's to cure them. What the hell's upsetting the hospital about that?"

"W-well, sir. Perhaps it's because we keep them locked up."

"You keep Ward T locked?"

"Yes, sir."

"Why?"

"To keep the patients in, General Carpenter."

"Keep 'em in? What d'you mean? Are they trying to get out? They violent, or something?"

"No, sir. Not violent."

"Dimmock, I don't like your attitude. You're acting damned sneaky and evasive. And I'll tell you something else I don't like. That T classification. I checked with a Filing Expert from the Medical Corps and there is no T classification. What the hell are you up to at St. Albans?"

"W-well, sir . . . We invented the T classification. It . . . They . . . They're rather special cases, sir. We don't know what to do about them or how to handle them. W-we've been trying to keep it quiet until we've worked out a modus operandi, but it's brand-new, General Carpenter. Brand-new!" Here the expert in Dimmock triumphed over discipline. "It's sensational. It'll make medical history, by God! It's the biggest damned thing ever."

"What is it, Dimmock? Be specific."

"Well, sir, they're shock cases. Blanked out. Almost catatonic. Very little respiration. Slow pulse. No response."

"I've seen thousands of shock cases like that," Carpenter grunted. "What's so unusual?"

"Yes, sir, so far it sounds like the standard Q or R classification. But here's something unusual. They don't eat and they don't sleep."

"Never?"

"Some of them never."

"Then why don't they die?"

"We don't know. The metabolism cycle's broken, but only on the anabolism side. Catabolism continues. In other words, sir, they're eliminating waste products, but they're not taking anything in. They're eliminating fatigue poisons and rebuilding worn tissue, but without food and sleep. God knows how. It's fantastic."

"That why you've got them locked up? Mean to say . . .

D'you suspect them of stealing food and catnaps somewhere else?''

"N-No, sir." Dimmock looked shamefaced. "I don't know how to tell you this, General Carpenter. . . . We lock them up because of the real mystery. They . . . Well, they disappear."

"They what?"

"They disappear, sir. Vanish. Right before your eyes."

"The hell you say."

"I do say, sir. They'll be sitting on a bed or standing around. One minute you see them, the next minute you don't. Sometimes there's two dozen in Ward T. Other times none. They disappear and reappear without rhyme or reason. That's why we've got the ward locked, General Carpenter. In the entire history of combat and combat injury, there's never been a case like this before. We don't know how to handle it."

"Bring me three of those cases," General Carpenter said.

Nathan Riley ate French toast, eggs benedict; consumed two pints of brown ale, smoked a John Drew, belched delicately and arose from the breakfast table. He nodded quietly to Gentleman Jim Corbett, who broke off his conversation with Diamond Jim Brady to intercept him on the way to the cashier's desk.

"Who do you like for the pennant this year, Nat?" Gentleman Jim inquired.

"The Dodgers," Nathan Riley answered.

"They've got no pitching."

"They've got Snider and Furillo and Campanella. They'll take the pennant this year, Jim. I'll bet they take it earlier than any team ever did. By September 13. Make a note. See if I'm right."

"You're always right, Nat," Corbett said.

Riley smiled, paid his check, sauntered out into the street and caught a horsecar bound for Madison Square Garden. He got off at the corner of Fiftieth Street and Eighth Avenue and walked upstairs to a handbook office over a radio repair shop. The bookie glanced at him, produced an envelope and counted out $15,000.

"Rocky Marciano by a TKO over Roland La Starza in the eleventh," he said. "How the hell do you call them so accurate, Nat?"

"That's the way I make a living," Riley smiled. "Are you making book on the elections?"

"Eisenhower twelve to five. Stevenson—"

"Never mind Adlai." Riley placed $20,000 on the counter. "I'm backing Ike. Get this down for me."

He left the handbook office and went to his suite in the Waldorf where a tall, thin young man was waiting for him anxiously.

"Oh yes," Nathan Riley said. "You're Ford, aren't you? Harold Ford?"

"Henry Ford, Mr. Riley."

"And you need financing for that machine in your bicycle shop. What's it called?"

"I call it an Ipsimobile, Mr. Riley."

"Hmmm. Can't say I like that name. Why not call it an automobile?"

"That's a wonderful suggestion, Mr. Riley. I'll certainly take it."

"I like you, Henry. You're young, eager, adaptable. I believe in your future and I believe in your automobile. I'll invest two hundred thousand dollars in your company."

Riley wrote a check and ushered Henry Ford out. He glanced at his watch and suddenly felt impelled to go back and look around for a moment. He entered his bedroom, undressed, put on a gray shirt and gray slacks. Across the pocket of the shirt were large blue letters: U.S.A.H.

He locked the bedroom door and disappeared.

He reappeared in Ward T of the United States Army Hospital in St. Albans, standing alongside his bed which was one of twenty-four lining the walls of a long, light steel barracks. Before he could draw another breath, he was seized by three pairs of hands. Before he could struggle, he was shot by a pneumatic syringe and poleaxed by 1½ cc of sodium thiomorphate.

"We've got one," someone said.

"Hang around," someone else answered. "General Carpenter said he wanted three."

• • •

After Marcus Junius Brutus left her bed, Lela Machan clapped her hands. Her slave women entered the chamber and prepared her bath. She bathed, dressed, scented herself and breakfasted on Smyrna figs, blood oranges and a flagon of Lacrima Christi. Then she smoked a cigarette and ordered her litter.

The gates of her house were crowded as usual by adoring hordes from the Twentieth Legion. Two centurions removed her chair-bearers from the poles of the litter and bore her on their stout shoulders. Lela Machan smiled. A young man in a sapphire-blue cloak thrust through the mob and ran toward her. A knife flashed in his hand. Lela braced herself to meet death bravely.

"Lady!" he cried. "Lady Lela!"

He slashed his left arm with the knife and let the crimson blood stain her robe.

"This blood of mine is the least I have to give you," he cried.

Lela touched his forehead gently.

"Silly boy," she murmured. "Why?"

"For love of you, my lady."

"You will be admitted tonight at nine," Lela whispered. He stared at her until she laughed. "I promise you. What is your name, pretty boy?"

"Ben Hur."

"Tonight at nine, Ben Hur."

The litter moved on. Outside the Forum, Julius Caesar passed in hot argument with Savonarola. When he saw the litter he motioned sharply to the centurions, who stopped at once. Caesar swept back the curtains and stared at Lela, who regarded him languidly. Caesar's face twitched.

"Why?" he asked hoarsely. "I have begged, pleaded, bribed, wept, and all without forgiveness. Why, Lela? Why?"

"Do you remember Boadicea?" Lela murmured.

"Boadicea? Queen of the Britons? Good God, Lela, what can she mean to our love? I did not love Boadicea. I merely defeated her in battle."

"And killed her, Caesar."

"She poisoned herself, Lela."

"She was my mother, Caesar!" Suddenly Lela pointed her finger at Caesar. "Murderer. You will be punished. Beware the Ides of March, Caesar!"

Caesar recoiled in horror. The mob of admirers that had gathered around Lela uttered a shout of approval. Amidst a shower of rose petals and violets, she continued on her way across the Forum to the Temple of the Vestal Virgins where she abandoned her adoring suitors and entered the sacred temple.

Before the altar she genuflected, intoned a prayer, dropped a pinch of incense on the altar flame and disrobed. She examined her beautiful body reflected in a silver mirror, then experienced a momentary twinge of homesickness. She put on a gray blouse and a gray pair of slacks. Across the pocket of the blouse was lettered U.S.A.H.

She smiled once at the altar and disappeared.

She reappeared in Ward T of the United States Army Hospital where she was instantly felled by $1\frac{1}{2}$ cc of sodium thiomorphate injected subcutaneously by a pneumatic syringe.

"That's two," somebody said.

"One more to go."

George Hanmer paused dramatically and stared around . . . at the opposition benches, at the Speaker on the woolsack, at the silver mace on a crimson cushion before the Speaker's chair. The entire House of Parliament, hypnotized by Hanmer's fiery oratory, waited breathlessly for him to continue.

"I can say no more," Hanmer said at last. His voice was choked with emotion. His face was blanched and grim. "I will fight for this bill at the beachheads. I will fight in the cities, the towns, the fields and the hamlets. I will fight for this bill to the death and, God willing, I will fight for it after death. Whether this be a challenge or a prayer, let the consciences of the right honorable gentlemen determine; but of one thing I am sure and determined: England must own the Suez Canal."

Hanmer sat down. The house exploded. Through the

cheering and applause he made his way out into the division lobby where Gladstone, Churchill, and Pitt stopped him to shake his hand. Lord Palmerston eyed him coldly, but Pam was shouldered aside by Disraeli who limped up, all enthusiasm, all admiration.

"We'll have a bite at Tattersall's," Dizzy said. "My car's waiting."

Lady Beaconsfield was in the Rolls Royce outside the Houses of Parliament. She pinned a primrose on Dizzy's lapel and patted Hanmer's cheek affectionately.

"You've come a long way from the schoolboy who used to bully Dizzy, Georgie," she said.

Hanmer laughed. Dizzy sang: *"Gaudeamus igitur . . ."* and Hanmer chanted the ancient scholastic song until they reached Tattersall's. There Dizzy ordered Guinness and grilled bones while Hanmer went upstairs in the club to change.

For no reason at all he had the impulse to go back for a last look. Perhaps he hated to break with his past completely. He divested himself of his surtout, nankeen waistcoat, pepper and salt trousers, polished Hessians and undergarments. He put on a gray shirt and gray trousers and disappeared.

He reappeared in Ward T of the St. Albans Hospital where he was rendered unconscious by 1½ cc of sodium thiomorphate.

"That's three," somebody said.

"Take 'em to Carpenter."

So there they sat in General Carpenter's office, PFC Nathan Riley, M/Sgt Lela Machan, and Corp/2 George Hanmer. They were in their hospital grays. They were torpid with sodium thiomorphate.

The office had been cleared and it blazed with light. Present were experts from Espionage, Counter-Espionage, Security, and Central Intelligence. When Captain Edsel Dimmock saw the steel-faced ruthless squad awaiting the patients and himself, he started. General Carpenter smiled grimly.

"Didn't occur to you that we mightn't buy your disappearance story, eh Dimmock?"

"S-Sir?"

"I'm an expert too, Dimmock. I'll spell it out for you. The war's going badly. Very badly. There've been intelligence leaks. The St. Albans mess might point to you."

"B-But they do disappear, sir. I—"

"My experts want to talk to you and your patients about this disappearing act, Dimmock. They'll start with you."

The experts worked over Dimmock with preconscious softeners, id releases, and superego blocks. They tried every truth serum in the books and every form of physical and mental pressure. They brought Dimmock, squealing, to the breaking point three times, but there was nothing to break.

"Let him stew for now," Carpenter said. "Get on to the patients."

The experts appeared reluctant to apply pressure to the sick men and the woman.

"For God's sake, don't be squeamish," Carpenter raged. "We're fighting a war for civilization. We've got to protect our ideals no matter what the price. Get to it!"

The experts from Espionage, Counter-Espionage, Security, and Central Intelligence got to it. Like three candles, PFC Nathan Riley, M/Sgt Lela Machan and Corp/2 George Hanmer snuffed out and disappeared. One moment they were seated in chairs surrounded by violence. The next moment they were not.

The experts gasped. General Carpenter did the handsome thing. He stalked to Dimmock. "Captain Dimmock, I apologize. Colonel Dimmock, you've been promoted for making an important discovery . . . only what the hell does it mean? We've got to check ourselves first."

Carpenter snapped up the intercom. "Get me a combat-shock expert and an alienist."

The two experts entered and were briefed. They examined the witnesses. They considered.

"You're all suffering from a mild case of shock," the combat-shock expert said. "War jitters."

"You mean we didn't see them disappear?"

The shock expert shook his head and glanced at the alienist who also shook his head.

"Mass illusion," the alienist said.

At that moment PFC Riley, M/Sgt Machan and Corp/2 Hanmer reappeared. One moment they were a mass illusion; the next, they were back sitting in their chairs surrounded by confusion.

"Dope 'em again, Dimmock," Carpenter cried. "Give 'em a gallon." He snapped up the intercom. "I want every expert we've got. Emergency meeting in my office at once."

Thirty-seven experts, hardened and sharpened tools all, inspected the unconscious shock cases and discussed them for three hours. Certain facts were obvious: This must be a new fantastic syndrome brought on by the new and fantastic horrors of the war. As combat technique develops, the response of victims of this technique must also take new roads. For every action there is an equal and opposite reaction. Agreed.

This new syndrome must involve some aspects of teleportation . . . the power of mind over space. Evidently combat shock, while destroying certain known powers of the mind must develop other latent powers hitherto unknown. Agreed.

Obviously, the patients must only be able to return to the point of departure, otherwise they would not continue to return to Ward T nor would they have returned to General Carpenter's office. Agreed.

Obviously, the patients must be able to procure food and sleep wherever they go, since neither was required in Ward T. Agreed.

"One small point," Colonel Dimmock said. "They seem to be returning to Ward T less frequently. In the beginning they would come and go every day or so. Now most of them stay away for weeks and hardly ever return."

"Never mind that," Carpenter said. "Where do they go?"

"Do they teleport behind the enemy lines?" someone asked. "There's those intelligence. leaks."

"I want Intelligence to check," Carpenter snapped. "Is the enemy having similar difficulties with, say, prisoners of war who appear and disappear from their POW camps? They might be some of ours from Ward T."

"They might simply be going home," Colonel Dimmock suggested.

"I want Security to check," Carpenter ordered. "Cover the home life and associations of every one of those twenty-four disappearers. Now . . . about our operations in Ward T. Colonel Dimmock has a plan."

"We'll set up six extra beds in Ward T," Edsel Dimmock explained. "We'll send in six experts to live there and observe. Information must be picked up indirectly from the patients. They're catatonic and nonresponsive when conscious, and incapable of answering questions when drugged."

"Gentlemen," Carpenter summed it up. "This is the greatest potential weapon in the history of warfare. I don't have to tell you what it can mean to us to be able to teleport an entire army behind enemy lines. We can win the war for the American Dream in one day if we can win this secret hidden in those shattered minds. We must win!"

The experts hustled, Security checked, Intelligence probed. Six hardened and sharpened tools moved into Ward T in St. Albans Hospital and slowly got acquainted with the disappearing patients who reappeared less and less frequently. The tension increased.

Security was able to report that not one case of strange appearance had taken place in America in the past year. Intelligence reported that the enemy did not seem to be having similar difficulties with their own shock cases or with POWs.

Carpenter fretted. "This is all brand-new. We've got no specialists to handle it. We've got to develop new tools." He snapped up his intercom. "Get me a college," he said.

They got him Yale.

"I want some experts in mind over matter. Develop them," Carpenter ordered. Yale at once introduced three graduate courses in Thaumaturgy, Extrasensory Perception, and Telekinesis.

The first break came when one of the Ward T experts requested the assistance of another expert. He needed a Lapidary.

"What the hell for?" Carpenter wanted to know.

"He picked up a reference to a gemstone," Colonel Dimmock explained. "He's a personnel specialist and he can't relate it to anything in his experience."

"And he's not supposed to," Carpenter said approvingly. "A job for every man and every man on the job." He flipped up the intercom. "Get me a Lapidary."

An expert Lapidary was given leave of absence from the army arsenal and asked to identify a type of diamond called Jim Brady. He could not.

"We'll try it from another angle," Carpenter said. He snapped up his intercom. "Get me a Semanticist."

The Semanticist left his desk in the War Propaganda Department but could make nothing of the words "Jim Brady." They were names to him. No more. He suggested a Genealogist.

A Genealogist was given one day's leave from his post with the Un-American Ancestors Committee, but could make nothing of the name Brady beyond the fact that it had been a common name in America for five hundred years. He suggested an Archaeologist.

An Archaeologist was released from the Cartography Division of Invasion Command and instantly identified the name Diamond Jim Brady. It was a historic personage who had been famous in the city of Little Old New York sometime between Governor Peter Stuyvesant and Governor Fiorello La Guardia.

"Christ!" Carpenter marveled. "That's ages ago. Where the hell did Nathan Riley get that? You'd better join the experts in Ward T and follow this up."

The Archaeologist followed it up, checked his references and sent in his report. Carpenter read it and was stunned. He called an emergency meeting of his staff of experts.

"Gentlemen," he announced, "Ward T is something bigger than teleportation. Those shock patients are doing something far more incredible . . . far more meaningful. Gentlemen, they're traveling through time."

The staff rustled uncertainly. Carpenter nodded emphatically.

"Yes, gentlemen. Time travel is here. It has not arrived the way we expected it . . . as a result of expert research by qualified specialists; it has come as a plague . . . an infec-

tion . . . a disease of the war . . . a result of combat injury
to ordinary men. Before I continue, look through these reports for documentation.''

The staff read the stenciled sheets. PFC Nathan
Riley . . . disappearing into the early twentieth century in
New York; M/Sgt Lela Machan . . . visiting the first century
in Rome; Corp/2 George Hanmer . . . journeying into the
nineteenth century in England. And all the rest of the twenty-
four patients, escaping the turmoil and horrors of modern war
in the twenty-second century by fleeing to Venice and the
Doges, to Jamaica and the buccaneers, to China and the Han
Dynasty, to Norway and Eric the Red, to any place and any
time in the world.

''I needn't point out the colossal significance of this discovery,'' General Carpenter pointed out. ''Think what it
would mean to the war if we could send an army back in time
a week or a month or a year. We could win the war before it
started. We could protect our Dream . . . Poetry and Beauty
and the Culture of America . . . from barbarism without
ever endangering it.''

The staff tried to grapple with the problem of winning
battles before they started.

''The situation is complicated by the fact that these men
and women of Ward T are *non compos*. They may or may not
know how they do what they do, but in any case they're
incapable of communicating with the experts who could
reduce this miracle to method. It's for us to find the key. They
can't help us.''

The hardened and sharpened specialists looked around
uncertainly.

''We'll need experts,'' General Carpenter said.

The staff relaxed. They were on familiar ground again.

''We'll need a Cerebral Mechanist, a Cyberneticist, a
Psychiatrist, an Anatomist, an Archaeologist, and a first-rate
Historian. They'll go into that ward and they won't come out
until their job is done. They must learn the technique of time
travel.''

The first five experts were easy to draft from other war
departments. All America was a toolchest of hardened and

sharpened specialists. But there was trouble locating a first-class Historian until the Federal Penitentiary cooperated with the army and released Dr. Bradley Scrim from his twenty years at hard labor. Dr. Scrim was acid and jagged. He had held the chair of Philosophic History at a Western university until he spoke his mind about the war for the American Dream. That got him the twenty years hard.

Scrim was still intransigent, but induced to play ball by the intriguing problem of Ward T.

"But I'm not an expert," he snapped. "In this benighted nation of experts, I'm the last singing grasshopper in the ant heap."

Carpenter snapped up the intercom. "Get me an Entomologist," he said.

"Don't bother," Scrim said. "I'll translate. You're a nest of ants . . . all working and toiling and specializing. For what?"

"To preserve the American Dream," Carpenter answered hotly. "We're fighting for Poetry and Culture and Education and the Finer Things in Life."

"Which means you're fighting to preserve me," Scrim said. "That's what I've devoted my life to. And what do you do with me? Put me in jail."

"You were convicted of enemy sympathizing and fellow-traveling," Carpenter said.

"I was convicted of believing in *my* American Dream," Scrim said. "Which is another way of saying I was jailed for having a mind of my own."

Scrim was also intransigent in Ward T. He stayed one night, enjoyed three good meals, read the reports, threw them down, and began hollering to be let out.

"There's a job for everyone and everyone must be on the job," Colonel Dimmock told him. "You don't come out until you've got the secret of time travel."

"There's no secret I can get," Scrim said.

"Do they travel in time?"

"Yes and no."

"The answer has to be one or the other. Not both. You're evading the—"

"Look," Scrim interrupted wearily. "What are you an expert in?"

"Psychotherapy."

"Then how the hell can you understand what I'm talking about? This is a philosophic concept. I tell you there's no secret here that the army can use. There's no secret any group can use. It's a secret for individuals only."

"I don't understand you."

"I didn't think you would. Take me to Carpenter."

They took Scrim to Carpenter's office where he grinned at the general malignantly, looking for all the world like a red-headed, underfed devil.

"I'll need ten minutes," Scrim said. "Can you spare them out of your toolbox?"

Carpenter nodded.

"Now listen carefully. I'm going to give you the clues to something so vast and so strange that it will need all your fine edge to cut into it."

Carpenter looked expectant.

"Nathan Riley goes back in time to the early twentieth century. There he lives the life of his fondest dreams. He's a big-time gambler, the friend of Diamond Jim Brady and others. He wins money betting on events because he always knows the outcome in advance. He won money betting on Eisenhower to win an election. He won money betting on a prizefighter named Marciano to beat another prizefighter named La Starza. He made money investing in an automobile company owned by Henry Ford. There are the clues. They mean anything to you?"

"Not without a Sociological Analyst," Carpenter answered. He reached for the intercom.

"Don't order one, I'll explain later. Let's try some more clues. Lela Machan, for example. She escapes into the Roman Empire where she lives the life of her dreams as a *femme fatale*. Every man loves her. Julius Caesar, Savonarola, the entire Twentieth Legion, a man named Ben Hur. Do you see the fallacy?"

"No."

"She also smokes cigarettes."

"Well?" Carpenter asked after a pause.

"I continue," Scrim said, "George Hanmer escapes into England of the nineteenth century where he's a member of Parliament and the friend of Gladstone, Winston Churchill, and Disraeli, who takes him riding in his Rolls Royce. Do you know what a Rolls Royce is?"

"No."

"It was the name of an automobile."

"So?"

"You don't understand yet?"

"No."

Scrim paced the floor in exaltation. "Carpenter, this is a bigger discovery than teleportation or time travel. This can be the salvation of man. I don't think I'm exaggerating. Those two dozen shock victims in Ward T have been U-Bombed into something so gigantic that it's no wonder your specialists and experts can't understand it."

"What the hell's bigger than time travel, Scrim?"

"Listen to this, Carpenter. Eisenhower did not run for office until the middle of the twentieth century. Nathan Riley could not have been a friend of Diamond Jim Brady's and bet on Eisenhower to win an election . . . not simultaneously. Brady was dead a quarter of a century before Ike was President. Marciano defeated La Starza fifty years after Henry Ford started his automobile company. Nathan Riley's time traveling is full of similar anachronisms."

Carpenter looked puzzled.

"Lela Machan could not have had Ben Hur for a lover. Ben Hur never existed in Rome. He never existed at all. He was a character in a novel. She couldn't have smoked. They didn't have tobacco then. You see? More anachronisms. Disraeli could never have taken George Hanmer for a ride in a Rolls Royce because automobiles weren't invented until long after Disraeli's death."

"The hell you say," Carpenter exclaimed. "You mean they're all lying?"

"No. Don't forget, they don't need sleep. They don't need food. They're not lying. They're going back in time, all right. They're eating and sleeping back there."

"But you just said their stories don't stand up. They're full of anachronisms."

"Because they travel back into a time of their own imagination. Nathan Riley has his own picture of what America was like in the early twentieth century. It's faulty and anachronistic because he's no scholar, but it's real for him. He can live there. The same is true for the others."

Carpenter goggled.

"The concept is almost beyond understanding. These people have discovered how to turn dreams into reality. They know how to enter their dream realities. They can stay there, live there, perhaps forever. My God, Carpenter, *this* is your American dream. It's miracle-working, immortality, God-like creation, mind over matter . . . It must be explored. It must be studied. It must be given to the world."

"Can you do it, Scrim?"

"No, I cannot. I'm an historian. I'm noncreative, so it's beyond me. You need a poet . . . an artist who understands the creation of dreams. From creating dreams on paper it oughtn't be too difficult to take the step to creating dreams in actuality."

"A poet? Are you serious?"

"Certainly I'm serious. Don't you know what a poet is? You've been telling us for five years that this war is being fought to save the poets."

"Don't be facetious, Scrim, I—"

"Send a poet into Ward T. He'll learn how they do it. He's the only man who can. A poet is half doing it anyway. Once he learns, he can teach your psychologists and anatomists. Then they can teach us; but the poet is the only man who can interpret between those shock cases and your experts."

"I believe you're right, Scrim."

"Then don't delay, Carpenter. Those patients are returning to this world less and less frequently. We've got to get at that secret before they disappear forever. Send a poet to Ward T."

Carpenter snapped up his intercom. "Send me a poet," he said.

He waited, and waited . . . and waited . . . while America sorted feverishly through its two hundred and ninety millions of hardened and sharpened experts, its specialized tools to defend the American Dream of Beauty and Poetry and the Better Things in Life. He waited for them to find a poet, not understanding the endless delay, the fruitless search; not understanding why Bradley Scrim laughed and laughed and laughed at this final, fatal disappearance.

Hell Is Forever

I'M a quasi-existentialist; I live entirely in the present with an occasional look ahead. The only role the past plays in my life is that of a teacher. I remember the lessons experience has taught me; I remember events if they happened to have taken story-form; I remember bits and fragments of color. That's about all. I'm constantly astonished by, and a little envious of, authors like the superb E. F. Benson, who can remember their past in minute detail.

So it will come as no surprise when I tell you that I have no recollection whatever of having written "Hell Is Forever" some thirty-odd years ago. I'm nearly certain that I did write it; my name is under the title, and my own birth date is used in the text. Either might be a coincidence but not both. Yes, I'm pretty sure that I wrote it. That's about all I'm sure of; the rest will have to be a paleontologist's reconstruction of an extinct creature from fossil bits and pieces.

It's possible that the story was inspired by Max Beerbohm's "Enoch Soames," witness the introductory verse. I was a former undergraduate and still in the throes of fascination with the *fin de siècle artists: Wilde, Beardsley, Beerbohm, the whole* Yellow Book *crowd. The influence of* Huysmans' Against the Grain *in my opening section is patent. I wish I knew where the Latin lyrics I used came from. It's ironic that I, who always raged against the snobbery of authors using foreign languages without translating for the reader, should have committed the same crime myself. I did translate the Latin, but too late in the story to do any good.*

I've said elsewhere that I dislike fantasy intensely—with a few notable exceptions—and that I was seduced into writing

133

this enormous fantasy by the magic of John Campbell's magnificent Unknown Worlds *which enchanted me along with thousands of others. Perhaps I should qualify my avowed hatred by saying that I loathe only what's come to be known as "swords and sorcery" fantasy and the old* Weird Tales *genre with secret spells calling up arcane demons named like* STPTHOTH *and* BGWJJILLIGKKK *and even* FUBGH. *I hope you'll give me good marks for avoiding these tired devices in "Hell Is Forever." I did use diabolism and necromancy, but mostly for attempts at surprise and comedy.*

This was the longest story I'd ever tackled—I believe it runs to 35,000 words—and I got involved under the most ridiculous circumstances. I'd never met Campbell and had no idea whether he, or anyone else for that matter, would be interested. I had no assignment, no encouragement, no approval in advance. I was a novice and would never dare approach an editor with a proposal. Anyway, I didn't have a proposal to make; all I had was an overpowering yearning to create a fantasy in the Unknown *manner.*

I'd guess that I composed the story as I wrote it; this was long before I learned to outline. That was absurd, too, and probably accounts for the excessive length. When it was completed it was submitted to Unknown *utterly without hope, but with tremendous satisfaction. I was proud of the job I'd done but reconciled to rejection. I was incredulous when Campbell accepted it, incredulous and exalted. I'd broken into* Unknown! *Now I could die happy.*

I wasn't so exalted when it came time to consider "Hell Is Forever" for this collection. It was thirty years old; I hadn't looked at it again after it first appeared in print; I didn't even own a copy. I had to ask Ben Bova and Diana King, the Big Honcho and Little Enchilada of Analog, *to go through the files of* Unknown *and have the crumbling pages photostated. When I received the copy, I stalled for a week getting up the nerve to read it. Thirty years old? Written by a kid? It had to be a bomb.*

Well, you know, I'm not as humiliated as I thought I'd be. In fact I'm proud all over again but with a different kind of pride; paternal. I feel like a father to that kid and I think he shows promise in "Hell Is Forever." He makes mistakes, he's green and gauche, his knowledge and understanding of character is minimal, he has a lot to learn, but I think he ought to stay with it. He might become a pro some day.

The actors in the story are stereotypes, a mishmash of characters I remembered from novels, plays, and films. My simulation of English speech patterns is laughable; it sounds like a failed Danny Kaye working a Bridgeport convention. Why, in heaven's name, did I set the story in and around London when I'd never been to England? Typical of a novice to write locales and people he didn't know.

However, this denunciation will save me from a question often asked writers: "Are the people in your story real or imaginary?" Mine are imaginary and not even the product of my own imagination; they're hand-me-downs. It takes years to learn how to mingle reality with imagination and practice the divine Verdi's dictum: "It is better to create reality than to imitate it." But how the hell do you explain to a civilian the delicate balancing process of creating reality from observation and imagination?

I can do a little paleontological reconstruction through the character names. Robert Peel was, among other things, the founder of the London constabulary, still called "bobbies." I must have been deep in the social history of England. Dubedat is the antihero in Shaw's *Doctor's Dilemma*, proving that I'd already begun my idolatry of GBS. Sidra was the name of a hypnotic Burmese cat owned by a producer who was toying with the idea of doing a play I'd written. You'll find her again in another story of mine. I once bought a suit in Finchley's.

Sutton Place, at the extreme east end of 57th Street, was the most glamorous residential area in New York during the thirties. It was my dream to own a private house there with windows overlooking the East River. That dream trapped me into writing a science fiction TV series for a producer living in such a house. I loved going to his place for script conferences. I say "trapped" because he was a slippery goniff who swindled me out of $5,000, and I should have known better. Sutton Place snowed me.

Even in a story as early as this you can see signs of the direction my fiction would take in the future. There's a *tendency to indulge in pyrotechnics, a venial sin for which I'm sometimes chided by critics today. There's a strong structural compulsion forcing me to tie all the ingredients together. New Wave authors have turned their backs on this technique, but at least they don't laugh in my face, and I'm grateful to them for their tolerance.*

The skepticism of the agnostic is quite obvious. I'm reminded of a line in Clemence Dane's novel, Broome Stages. *(I'm delighted to boast that this splendid playwright and novelist was a fan of my science fiction.) In the novel a mother is worrying about the future of her talented young son, and the author gave her this thought: ". . . so soon as she was able to cure him of disliking God violently in free verse she thought he would be safe."*

And lastly, the raree-show quality, the corroboree, entertainment solely for entertainment's sake, is beginning to pop its head up like a timid jack-in-the-box.

Round and round the shutter'd Square
　　I stroll'd with the Devil's arm in mine,
No sound but the scrape of his hoofs was there
　　And the ring of his laughter and mine.
　　　　We had drunk black wine.

I screamed, "I will race you, Master!"
　　"What matter," he shrieked, "tonight
Which of us runs the faster?
　　There is nothing to fear tonight
　　　　In the foul moon's light!"

Then I look'd him in the eyes,
　　And I laughed full shrill at the lie he told
And the gnawing fear he would fain disguise.
　　It was true, what I'd time and again been told:
　　　　He was old—old.

　　　　From "FUNGOIDS," by Enoch Soames

There were six of them and they had tried everything.

They began with drinking and drank until they had exhausted the sense of taste. Wines—Amontillado, Beaune, Kirschwasser, Bordeaux, Hock, Burgundy, Medoc and Chambertin; whisky, Scotch, Irish, Usquebaugh and Schnapps; brandy, gin and rum. They drank them separately and together; they mixed the tart alcohols and flavors into stupendous punches, into a thousand symphonies of taste; they experimented, created, invented, destroyed—and finally they were bored.

Drugs followed. The milder first, then the more potent. Crisp brown licoricelike opium, toasted and rolled into pellets for smoking in long ivory pipes; thick green absinthe sipped bitter and strong, without sugar or water; heroin and cocaine in rustling snow crystals; marijuana rolled loosely into brown-paper cigarettes; hashish in milk-white curds to be eaten, or tarry plugs of Bhang that were chewed and stained the lips a deep tan—and again they were bored.

Their search for sensation became frantic with so much of their senses already dissipated. They enlarged their parties and turned them into festivals of horror. Exotic dancers and esoteric half-human creatures crowded the broad, low room and filled it with their incredible performances. Pain, fear, desire, love and hatred were torn apart and exhibited to the least quivering detail like so many laboratory specimens.

The cloying odor of perfume mingled with the knife-sharp sweat of excited bodies; the anguished screams of tortured creatures merely interrupted their swift, never-ceasing talk—and so in time this, too, palled. They reduced their parties to the original six and returned each week to sit, bored and still hungry for new sensations. Now, languidly and without enthusiasm, they were toying with the occult; turning the party room into a necromancer's chamber.

Offhand you would not have thought it was a bomb shelter. The room was large and square, the walls paneled with imitation-grained soundproofing, the ceiling low-beamed. To the right was an inset door, heavy and bolted with an enormous wrought-iron lock. There were no windows, but the air-conditioning inlets were shaped like the arched slits of a Gothic monastery. Lady Sutton had paned them with stained glass and set small electric bulbs behind them. They threw showers of sullen color across the room.

The flooring was of ancient walnut, high-polished and gleaming like metal. Across it were spread a score of lustrous Oriental scatter rugs. One enormous divan, covered with Indian batik, ran the width of the shelter against a wall. Above were tiers of bookshelves, and before it was a long trestle table piled with banquet remains. The rest of the shelter was furnished with deep, seductive chairs, soft, quilted, and inviting.

Centuries ago this had been the deepest dungeon of Sutton Castle, hundreds of feet beneath the earth. Now—drained, warmed, air-conditioned and refurnished, it was the scene of Lady Sutton's sensation parties. More—it was the official meeting place of the Society of Six. The Six Decadents, they called themselves.

"We are the last spiritual descendants of Nero—the last of the gloriously evil aristocrats," Lady Sutton would say. "We were born centuries too late, my friends. In a world that is no longer ours we have nothing to live for but ourselves. We are a race apart—we six."

And when unprecedented bombings shook England so catastrophically that the shudders even penetrated to the Sutton shelter, she would glance up and laugh: "Let them slaughter each other, those pigs. This is no war of ours. We go our own way, always, eh? Think, my friends, what a joy it would be to emerge from our shelter one bright morning and find all London dead—all the world dead—" And then she laughed again with her deep, hoarse bellow.

She was bellowing now, her enormous fat body sprawled half across the divan like a decorated toad, laughing at the program that Digby Finchley had just handed her. It had been etched by Finchley himself—an exquisite design of devils and angels in grotesque amorous combat encircling the cabalistic lettering that read:

THE SIX PRESENT

ASTAROTH WAS A LADY

By Christian Braugh

Cast

(In order of appearance)

A Necromancer .... Christian Braugh
A Black Cat .... Merlin
(By courtesy of Lady Sutton)
Astaroth .... Theone Dubedat
Nebiros, an Assistant Demon .... Digby Finchley
Costumes .... Digby Finchley
Special Effects........................ Robert Peel
Music .... Sidra Peel

Finchley said: "A little comedy *is* a change, isn't it?"

Lady Sutton shook with uncontrolled laughter. "Astaroth was a lady! Are you sure you wrote it, Chris?"

There was no answer from Braugh, only the buzz of preparations from the far end of the room, where a small stage had been erected and curtained off.

She bellowed in her broken bass: "Hey, Chris! Hey, there—"

The curtain split and Christian Braugh thrust his albino head through. His face was partially made up with red eyebrows and beard and dark-blue shadows around the eyes. He said: "Beg pardon, Lady Sutton?"

At the sight of his face she rolled over the divan like a mountain of jelly. Across her helpless body, Finchley smiled to Braugh, his lips unfolding in a cat's grin. Braugh moved his white head in imperceptible answer.

"I said, did you really write this, Chris . . . or have you hired a ghost again?"

Braugh looked angry, then disappeared behind the curtain.

''Oh, my hat!'' gurgled Lady Sutton. ''This is better than a gallon of champagne. And, speaking of same . . . who's nearest the bubbly? Bob? Pour some more. Bob! Bob Peel!''

The man slumped in the chair alongside the ice buckets never moved. He was lying on the nape of his neck, feet thrust out in a V before him, his dress shirt buckled under his bearded chin. Finchley went across the room and looked down at him.

''Passed out,'' he said.

''So early? Well, no matter. Fetch me a glass, Dig, there's a good lad.''

Finchley filled a prismed champagne glass and brought it to Lady Sutton. From a small cameo-faced vial she added three drops of laudanum, swirled the sparkling mixture once and then sipped while she read the program.

''A Necromancer . . . that's you, eh, Dig?''

He nodded.

''And what's a Necromancer?''

''A kind of magician, Lady Sutton.''

''Magician? Oh, that's good . . . that's very good!'' She spilled champagne on her vast blotchy bosom and dabbed ineffectually with the program.

Finchley lifted a hand to restrain her and said, ''You ought to be careful with that program, Lady Sutton. I made only one print and then destroyed the plate. It's unique and liable to be valuable.''

''Collector's item, eh? Your work, of course, Dig?''

''Yes.''

''Not much of a change from the usual pornography, hey?'' She burst into another thunder of laughter that degenerated into a fit of hacking coughs. She dropped the glass altogether. Finchley flushed, then retrieved the glass and returned it to the buffet, stepping carefully over Peel's legs. ''And who's this Astaroth?'' Lady Sutton went on.

From behind the curtain, Theone Dubedat called: ''Me! I! *Ich! Moi!*'' Her voice was husky. It had a quality of gray smoke.

''Darling, I know it's you, but *what* are you?''

''A devil, I think.''

Finchley said: "Astaroth is some sort of legendary archdemon—a top-ranking devil, so to speak."

"Theone a devil? No doubt of it—" Exhausted with rapture, Lady Sutton lay quiescent and musing on the patterned divan. At last she raised an enormous arm and examined her watch. The flesh hung from her elbows in elephantine creases, and at the gesture it shook and a little shower of torn sequins glittered down from her sleeve.

"You'd best get on with it, Dig. I've got to leave at midnight."

"Leave?"

"You heard me."

Finchley's face contorted. He bent over her, tense with suppressed emotion, his bleak eyes examining her. "What's up? What's wrong?"

"Nothing."

"Then—"

"A few things have changed, that's all."

"What's changed?"

Her face turned harsh as she returned his stare. The bulging features seemed to stiffen into obsidian. "Too soon to tell you . . . but you'll find out quick enough. Now I don't want any more pestering from you, Dig, m'lad!"

Finchley's scarecrow features regained a measure of control. He started to speak, but before he could utter a word Sidra Peel suddenly popped her head out of the alcove alongside the stage, where the organ had been placed. She called: "Ro-bert!"

In a constricted voice, Finchley said, "Bob's passed out again, Sidra."

She emerged from the alcove, walked jerkily across the room and stood looking down in her husband's face. Sidra Peel was short, slender, and dark. Her body was like an electric high-tension wire, alive with too much current, yet coruscated, stained and rusted from too much exposure to passion. The deep black sockets of her eyes were frigid coals with gleaming white points. As she gazed at her husband, her long fingers writhed; then, suddenly, her hand lashed out and struck the inert face.

"Swine!" she hissed.

Lady Sutton laughed and coughed all at once. Sidra Peel shot her a venomous glance and stepped toward the divan, the sharp crack of her heel on the walnut sounding like a pistol shot. Finchley gestured a quick warning that stopped her. She hesitated, then returned to the alcove and said: "The music's ready."

"And so am I," said Lady Sutton. "On with the show and all that, eh?" She spread herself across the divan like a crawling tumor the while Finchley propped scarlet pillows under her head. "It's really nice of you to play this little comedy for me, Dig. Too bad there're only six of us here tonight. Ought to have an audience, eh?"

"You're the only audience we want, Lady Sutton."

"Ah! Keep it all in the family?"

"So to speak."

"The Six—Happy Family of Hatred."

"That's not so, Lady Sutton."

"Don't be an ass, Dig. We're all hateful. We glory in it. I ought to know. I'm the Bookkeeper of Disgust. Someday I'll let you all see the entries. Someday soon."

"What sort of entries?"

"Curious already, eh? Oh, nothing spectacular. Just the way Sidra's been trying to kill her husband—and Bob's been torturing her by holding on. And you making a fortune out of filthy pictures . . . and eating your rotten heart out for that frigid devil, Theone—"

"Please, Lady Sutton!"

"And Theone," she went on with relish, "using that icy body of hers like an executioner's scalpel to torture . . . and Chris . . . How many of his books d'you think he's stolen from those poor Grub Street devils?"

"I couldn't say."

"I know. All of them. A fortune on other men's brains. Oh, we're a beautifully loathsome lot, Dig. It's the only thing we have to be proud of—the only thing that sets us off from the billion blundering moralistic idiots that have inherited our earth. That's why we've got to stay a happy family of mutual hatred."

"I should call it mutual admiration," Finchley murmured.

He bowed courteously and went to the curtains, looking more like a scarecrow than ever in the black dinner clothes. He was extremely tall—three inches over six feet—and extremely thin. The pipestem arms and legs looked like warped dowel sticks, and his horsy flat features seemed to have been painted on a pasty pillow.

Finchley pulled the curtains together behind him. A moment after he disappeared there was a whispered cue and the lights dimmed. In the vast low room there was no sound except Lady Sutton's croupy breathing. Peel, still slumped in his deep chair, was motionless and invisible, except for the limp angle of his legs.

From infinite distances came a slight vibration—almost a shudder. It seemed at first to be a sinister reminder of the hell that was bursting across England, hundreds of feet over their heads. Then the shuddering quickened and by imperceptible stages swelled into the deepest tones of the organ. Above the background of the throbbing diapasons, a weird tremolo of fourths, empty and spine-chilling, cascaded down the keyboard in chromatic steps.

Lady Sutton chuckled faintly. "My word," she said, "that's really horrid, Sidra. Ghastly."

The grim background of music choked her. It filled the shelter with chilling tendrils of sound that were more than tone. The curtains slipped apart slowly, revealing Christian Braugh garbed in black, his face a hideous, twisted mass of red and purple-blue that contrasted starkly to the near-albino white hair. Braugh stood at the center of the stage surrounded by spider-legged tables piled high with Necromancer's apparatus. Prominent was Merlin, Lady Sutton's black cat, majestically poised atop an ironbound volume.

Braugh lifted a piece of black chalk from a table and drew a circle on the floor twelve feet around himself. He inscribed the circumference with cabalistic characters and pentacles. Then he lifted a wafer and exhibited it with a flirt of his wrist.

"This," he declared in sepulchral tones, "is a sacred wafer stolen from a church at midnight."

Lady Sutton applauded satirically, but stopped almost at once. The music seemed to upset her. She moved uneasily on the divan and looked about her with little uncertain glances.

Muttering blasphemous imprecations, Braugh raised an iron dagger and plunged it through the wafer. Then he arranged a copper chafing dish over a blue alcohol flame and began to stir in powders and crystals of bright colors. He lifted a vial filled with purple liquid and poured the contents into a porcelain bowl. There was a faint detonation and a thick cloud of vapor lifted to the ceiling.

The organ surged. Braugh muttered incantations under his breath and performed oddly suggestive gestures. The shelter swam with scents and mists, violet clouds and deep fogs. Lady Sutton glanced toward the chair across from her. "Splendid, Bob," she called. "Wonderful effects—really." She tried to make her voice cheerful, but it came out in a sickly croak. Peel never moved.

With a savage motion Braugh pulled three black hairs from the cat's tail. Merlin uttered a yowl of rage and sprang at the same time from the book to the top of an inlaid cabinet in the background. Through the mists and vapors his giant yellow eyes gleamed balefully. The hairs went into the chafing dish, and a new aroma filled the room. In quick succession the claws of an owl, the powder of vipers and a human-shaped mandrake root followed.

"Now!" cried Braugh.

He cast the wafer, transfixed by the dagger, into the porcelain bowl containing the purple fluid, and then poured the whole mixture into the copper chafing dish.

There was a violent explosion.

A jet-black cloud filled the stage and swirled out into the shelter. Slowly it cleared away, faintly revealing the tall form of a naked devil; the body exquisitely formed, the head a frightful mask. Braugh had disappeared.

Through the drifting clouds, in the husky tones of Theone Dubedat, the devil spoke: "Greetings, Lady Sutton—"

She stepped forward out of the vapor. In the pulsating light that shot down to the stage, her body shone with a shimmering nacreous glow of its own. The toes and fingers were long and graceful. Color slashed across the rounded torso. Yet that whole perfect body was cold and lifeless—as unreal as the grotesque papier-mâché that covered her head.

Theone repeated: "Greetings—"

"Hi, old thing!" Lady Sutton interrupted. "How's everything in hell?"

There was a giggle from the alcove where Sidra Peel was playing softly. Theone posed statuesquely and lifted her head a little higher to speak. "I bring you—"

"Darling!" shrieked Lady Sutton, "why didn't you let me know it was going to be like this? I'd have sold tickets!"

Theone raised a gleaming arm imperiously. Again she began: "I bring you the thanks of the five who—" And then abruptly she stopped.

For the space of five heartbeats there was a gasping pause while the organ murmured and the last of the black smoke filtered away, mushrooming against the ceiling. In the silence Theone's rapid, choked breathing mounted hysterically—then came a ghastly, piercing scream.

The others darted from behind the stage, exclaiming in astonishment—Braugh, Necromancer's costume thrown over his arm, his makeup removed; Finchley like a pair of animated scissors in black habit and cowl, a script in his hand. The organ stuttered, then stopped with a crash, and Sidra Peel burst out of the alcove.

Theone tried to scream again, but her voice caught and broke. In the appalled silence Lady Sutton cried: "What is it? Something wrong?"

Theone uttered a moaning sound and pointed to the center of the stage. "Look—There—" The words came off the top of her throat like the squeal of nails on slate. She cowered back against a table, upsetting the apparatus. It clashed and tinkled.

"What is it? For the love of—"

"It worked—" Theone moaned. "The r-ritual—It worked!"

They stared through the gloom, then started. An enormous sable Thing was slowly rising in the center of the Necromancer's circle—a vague, amorphous form towering high, emitting a dull, hissing sound like the whisper of a caldron.

"What is that?" Lady Sutton shouted.

The Thing pushed forward like some sickly extrusion. When it reached the edge of the black circle it halted. The seething sound swelled ominously.

"Is it one of us?" Lady Sutton cried. "Is this a stupid trick? Finchley . . . Braugh—"

They shot her startled glances, bleak with terror.

"Sidra . . . Robert . . . Theone . . . No, you're all here. Then who is that? How did it get in here?"

"It's impossible," Braugh whispered, backing away. His legs knocked against the edge of the divan and he sprawled clumsily.

Lady Sutton beat at him with helpless hands and cried: "Do something! Do something—"

Finchley tried to control his voice. He stuttered: "W-We're safe so long as the circle isn't broken. It can't get out—"

On the stage, Theone was sobbing, making pushing motions with her hands. Suddenly she crumpled to the floor. One outflung arm rubbed away a segment of the black chalk circle. The Thing moved swiftly, stepped through the break in the circle and descended from the platform like a black fluid. Finchley and Sidra Peel reeled back with terrified shrieks. There was a growing thickness pervading the shelter atmosphere. Little gusts of vapor twisted around the head of the Thing as it moved slowly toward the divan.

"You're all joking!" Lady Sutton screamed. "This isn't real. It can't be!" She heaved up from the divan and tottered to her feet. Her face blanched as she counted the take of her guests again. One—two—and four made six—and the shape made seven. But there should only be six—

She backed away, then began to run. The Thing was following her when she reached the door. Lady Sutton pulled at the door handle, but the iron bolt was locked. Quickly, for all her vast bulk, she ran around the edge of the shelter, smashing over the tables. As the Thing expanded in the darkness and filled the room with its sibilant hissing, she snatched at her purse and tore it open, groping for the key. Her shaking hands scattered the purse contents over the room.

A deep bellow pierced the blackness. Lady Sutton jerked and stared around desperately, making little animal noises. As the Thing threatened to engulf her in its infinite black depths, a cry tore up through her body and she sank heavily to the floor.

Silence.

Smoke drifted in shaded clouds.

The china clock ticked off a sequence of delicate periods.

"Well—" Finchley said in conversational tones. "That's that."

He went to the inert figure on the floor. He knelt over it for a moment, probing and testing, his face flickering with savage hunger. Then he looked up and grinned. "She's dead, all right. Just the way we figured. Heart failure. She was too fat."

He remained on his knees, drinking in the moment of death. The others clustered around the toadlike body, staring with distended nostrils. The moment hardly lasted; then the languor of infinite boredom again shaded across their features.

The black Thing waved its arms a few times. The costume split at last to reveal a complicated framework and the sweating, bearded face of Robert Peel. He dropped the costume around him, stepped out of it, and went to the figure in the chair.

"The dummy idea was perfect," he said. His bright little eyes glittered momentarily. He looked like a sadistic miniature of Edward VII. "She'd never have believed it if we hadn't arranged for a seventh unknown to enter the scene." He glanced at his wife. "That slap was a stroke of genius, Sidra. Wonderful realism—"

"I meant it."

"I know you did, dearly beloved, but thanks nevertheless."

Theone Dubedat had risen and gotten into a white dressing gown. She stepped down and walked over to the body, removing the hideous devil's mask. It revealed a beautifully chiseled face, frigid and lovely. Her blonde hair gleamed in the darkness.

Braugh said: "Your acting was superb, Theone—" He bobbed his white albino head appreciatively.

For a time she didn't answer. She stood staring down at the

shapeless mound of flesh, an expression of hopeless longing on her face; but there was nothing more to her gazing than the impersonal curiosity of a bystander watching a window chef. Less.

At last Theone sighed. She said: "So it wasn't worth it, after all."

"What?" Braugh groped for a cigarette.

"The acting—the whole performance. We've been let down again, Chris."

Braugh scratched a match. The orange flame flared, flickering across their disappointed faces. He lit his cigarette, then held the flame high and looked at them. The illumination twisted their features into caricatures, emphasizing their weariness, their infinite boredom. Braugh said, "My-my—"

"It's no use, Chris. This whole murder was a bust. It was about as exciting as a glass of water."

Finchley hunched his shoulders and paced up and back like a bundle of stilts. He said, "I got a bit of a kick when I thought she suspected. It didn't last long, though."

"You ought to be grateful for even that."

"I am."

Peel clucked his tongue in exasperation, then knelt like a bearded Humpty-Dumpty, his bald head gleaming, and raked in the contents of Lady Sutton's scattered purse. The banknotes he folded and put in his pocket. He took the fat dead hand and lifted it toward Theone. "You always admired her sapphire, Theone. Want it?"

"You couldn't get it off, Bob."

"I think I could," he said, pulling strenuously.

"Oh, to hell with the sapphire."

"No—It's coming."

The ring slipped forward, then caught in the folds of flesh at the knuckle. Peel took a fresh grip and tugged and twisted. There was a sucking, yielding sound, and the entire finger tore away from the hand. The dull odor of putrefaction struck their nostrils as they looked on with curiosity.

Peel shrugged and dropped the finger. He arose, dusting his hands slightly. "She rots fast," he said. "Peculiar—"

Braugh wrinkled his nose and said, "She was too fat."

Theone turned away in frantic desperation, her hands clasping her elbows. "What are we to do?" she cried. "What? Isn't there a sensation left on earth we haven't tried?"

With a dry whir, the china clock began quick chimes. Midnight.

Finchley said, "We might go back to drugs."

"They're as futile as this paltry murder."

"But there are other sensations. New ones."

"Name one!" Theone said in exasperation. "Only one."

"I could name several—if you'll have a seat and permit me—"

Suddenly Theone interrupted. "That's you speaking, isn't it, Dig?"

In a peculiar voice, Finchley answered, "N-no. I thought it was Chris."

Braugh said, "Wasn't me."

"You, Bob?"

"No."

"Th-then—"

The small voice said, "If the ladies and gentlemen would be kind enough to—"

It came from the stage. There was something there—something that spoke in that quiet, gentle voice; for Merlin was stalking back and forth, arching his high black back against an invisible leg.

"—to sit down," the voice continued persuasively.

Braugh had the most courage. He moved to the stage with slow, steady steps, the cigarette hanging firmly from his lips. He leaned across the apron and peered. For a while his eyes examined the stage; then he let a spume of smoke jet from his nostrils and called, "There's nothing here."

And at that moment the blue smoke swirled under the lights and swept around a figure of emptiness. It was no more than a glimpse of an outline—of a negative, but it was enough to make Braugh cry out and leap back. The others turned sick, too, and staggered to chairs.

"So sorry," said the quiet voice. "It won't happen again."

Peel gathered himself and said, "Merely for the sake of—"

"Yes?"

He tried to freeze his jerking features. "Merely for the sake of s-scientific curiosity, it—"

"Calm yourself, my friend."

"The ritual . . . It did work?"

"Of course not. My friends, there is no need to call us with such fantastic ceremony. If you really want us, we come."

"And you?"

"I? Oh . . . I know you have been thinking of me for some time. Tonight you wanted me—really wanted me, and I came."

The last of the cigarette smoke convulsed as that terrible figure of emptiness seemed to stoop and seat itself casually at the edge of the stage. The cat hesitated and then began rolling its head with little mews of pleasure as something fondled it.

Still striving desperately to control himself, Peel said, "But all those ceremonies and rituals that have been handed down—"

"Merely symbolic, Mr. Peel." Peel started at the sound of his name. "You have read, no doubt, that we do not appear unless a certain ritual is performed, and only if it is letter-perfect. That is not true, of course. We appear if the invitation is sincere—and only then—with or without ceremony."

Sick and verging on hysteria, Sidra whispered, "I'm getting out of here." She tried to rise.

The gentle voice said, "One moment, please—"

"No!"

"I will help you get rid of your husband, Mrs. Peel."

Sidra blinked, then sank back into her chair. Peel clenched his fists and opened his mouth to speak. Before he could begin, the gentle voice continued. "And yet you will not lose your wife, if you really want to keep her, Mr. Peel. I guarantee that."

The cat was lifted into the air and then settled comfortably in space a few feet from the floor. They could see the thick fur on the back smooth and resmooth from the gentle petting.

At length Braugh asked, "What do you offer us?"

"I offer each of you his own heart's desire."

"And that is?"

"A new sensation—all new sensations—"

"What new sensations?"

"The sensation of reality."

Braugh laughed. "Hardly anyone's heart's desire."

"This will be, for I offer you five different realities—realities which you may fashion, each for himself. I offer you worlds of your own making wherein Mrs. Peel may happily murder her husband in hers—and yet Mr. Peel may keep his wife in his own. To Mr. Braugh I offer the dreamworld of the writer, and to Mr. Finchley the creation of the artist—"

Theone said, "These are dreams, and dreams are cheap. We all possess them."

"But you all awaken from your dreams and you pay the bitter price of that realization. I offer you an awakening from the present into a future reality which you may shape to your own desires—a reality which will never end."

Peel said: "Five simultaneous realities is a contradiction in terms. It's a paradox—impossible."

"Then I offer you the impossible."

"And the price?"

"I beg your pardon?"

"The price," Peel repeated with growing courage. "We're not altogether naïve. We know there's always a price."

There was a long pause; then the voice said reproachfully, "I'm afraid there are many misconceptions and many things you fail to understand. Just now I cannot explain, but believe me when I say there is no price."

"Ridiculous. Nothing is ever given for nothing."

"Very well, Mr. Peel, if we must use the terminology of the marketplace, let me say that we never appear unless the price for our service is paid in advance. Yours has already been paid."

"Paid?" They shot involuntary glances at the rotting body on the shelter floor.

"In full."

"Then?"

"You're willing, I see. Very well—"

The cat was again lifted in the air and deposited on the floor with a last gentle pat. The remnants of mist clinging to the shelter ceiling weaved and churned as the invisible donor advanced. Instinctively the five arose and waited, tense and fearful, yet with a mounting sense of fulfillment.

A key darted up from the floor and sailed through midair toward the door. It paused before the lock an instant, then inserted itself and turned. The heavy wrought-iron bolt lifted and the door swung wide. Beyond should have been the dungeon passage leading to the upper levels of Sutton Castle—a low, narrow corridor, paved with flagstones and lined with limestone blocks. Now a few inches beyond the door jamb, there hung a veil of flame.

Pale, incredibly beautiful, it was a tapestry of flickering fire, the warp and weft an intermesh of rainbow colors. Those pastel strands of color locked and interlocked, swam, threaded and spun like so many individual life lines. They were an infinity of flames, emotions, the silken countenance of time, the swirling skin of space—They were all things to all men, and above all else, they were beautiful.

"For you," the quiet voice said, "your old reality ends in this room—"

"As simply as this?"

"Quite."

"But—"

"Here you stand," interrupted the voice, "in the last kernel, the last nucleus so to speak, of what once was real for you. Pass the door—pass through the veil, and you enter the reality I promised."

"What will we find beyond the veil?"

"What each of you desires. Nothing lies beyond that veil now. There is nothing there—nothing but time and space waiting for the molding. There is nothing and the potential of everything."

In a low voice, Peel said, "One time and one space? Will that be enough for all different realities?"

"All time, all space, my friend," the quiet voice answered. "Pass through and you will find the matrix of dreams."

They had been clustered together, standing close to each other in a kind of strained companionship. Now, in the silence that followed, they separated slightly as though each had marked out for himself a reality all his own—a life entirely divorced from the past and the companions of old times. It was a gesture of utter isolation.

Mutually impulsed, yet independently motivated, they moved toward the glittering veil—

II

I am an artist, Digby Finchley thought, and an artist is a creator. To create is to be godlike, and so shall I be. I shall be god of my world, and from nothing I shall create all—and my all will be beauty.

He was the first to reach the veil and the first to pass through. Across his face the riot of color flicked like a cool spray. He blinked his eyes momentarily as the brilliant scarlets and purples blinded him. When he opened them again, he had left the veil a step behind and stood in the darkness.

But not darkness.

It was the blank jet-black of infinite emptiness. It smote his eyes like a heavy hand and seemed to press the eyeballs back into his skull like leaden weights. He was terrified and jerked his head about, staring into the impenetrable nothingness, mistaking the ephemeral flashes of retinal light for reality.

Nor was he standing.

For he took one hasty stride and it was as though he was suspended out of all contact with mass and matter. His terror was tinged with horror as he became aware that he was utterly alone; that there was nothing to see, nothing to hear, nothing to touch. A bitter loneliness assailed him and in that instant he understood how truthfully the voice in the shelter had spoken, and how terribly real his new reality was.

That instant, too, was his salvation. "For," Finchley murmured with a wry smile to the blankness, "it is of the essence of godhood to be alone—to be unique."

Then he was quite calm and hung quiescent in time and space while he mustered his thoughts for the creation.

"First," Finchley said at length, "I must have a heavenly throne that befits a god. Too, I must have a heavenly kingdom and angelic retainers; for no god is altogether complete without an entourage."

He hesitated while his mind rapidly sorted over the various heavenly kingdoms he had known from art and letters. There was no need, he thought, to be especially original with this sort of thing. Originality would play an important role in the creation of his universe. Just now the only essential thing was to insure himself a reasonable degree of dignity and luxury—and for that the secondhand furnishing of ancient Yahweh would do.

Raising one hand in a self-conscious gesture, he commanded. Instantly the blackness was riven with light, and before him a flight of gold-veined marble steps rose to a glittering throne. The throne was high and cushioned. Arms, legs and back were of glowing silver, and the cushions were imperial purple. And yet—the whole was hideous. The legs were too long and thin, the arms were rickety, the back narrow and sickly.

Finchley said, "Owww!" and tried to remodel. Yet no matter how he altered the proportions, the throne remained horrible. And for that matter, the steps, too, were disgusting, for by some freak of creation the gold veins twisted and curved through the marble to form obscene designs too reminiscent of the erotic pictures Finchley had drawn in his past existence.

He gave it up at last, mounted the steps, and settled himself uneasily on the throne. It felt as though he was sitting on the lap of a corpse with dead arms poised to enfold him in a ghastly embrace. He shuddered slightly and said: "Oh, hell, I was never a furniture designer—"

Finchley glanced around, then raised his hand again. The jet clouds that had crowded around the throne rolled back to reveal high columns of crystal and a soaring roof arched and paved with smooth blocks. The hall stretched back for thousands of yards like some never-ending cathedral, and all that length was filled with rank on rank of his retainers.

Foremost were the angels; slender, winged creatures, white-robed, with blonde, shining heads, sapphire-blue eyes, and scarlet, smiling mouths. Behind the angels knelt the order of Cherubim; giant winged bulls with tawny hides and hoofs of beaten metal. Their Assyrian heads were heavily bearded with gleaming jet curls. Third were the Seraphim;

ranks of huge six-winged serpents whose jeweled scales glittered with a silent flame.

As Finchley sat and stared at them with admiration for his handiwork, they chanted in soft unison: "Glory to god. Glory to the Lord Finchley, the All-Highest . . . Glory to the Lord Finchley—"

He sat and gazed and it was as though his eyes were slowly acquiring the distortion of astigmatism, for he realized that this was more a cathedral of evil than of heaven. The columns were carved with revolting grotesques at the capitals and bases, and as the hall stretched into dimness, it seemed peopled with cavorting shadows that grimaced and danced.

And in the far reaches of those columned lengths, covert little scenes were playing that amazed him. Even as they chanted, the angels gazed sidelong with their glistening blue eyes at the Cherubim; and behind a column he saw one winged creature reach out and seize a lovely blonde angel of lust to crush her to him.

In sheer desperation Finchley raised his hand again, and once more the blackness swirled around him—

"So much," he said, "for Heavenly Kingdoms—"

He pondered for another ineffable period as he drifted in emptiness, grappling with the most stupendous artistic problem he had ever attacked.

Up to now, Finchley thought with a shudder for the horror he had wrought, I have been merely playing—feeling my strength—warming up, so to speak, the way an artist will toy with pastel and a block of grained paper. Now it's time for me to go to work.

Solemnly, as he thought would befit a god, he conducted a laborious conference with himself in space.

What, he asked himself, has creation been in the past?

One might call it nature.

Very well, we shall call it nature. Now, what are the objections to nature's creation?

Why—nature was never an artist. Nature merely blundered into things in an experimental sort of way. Whatever beauty existed was merely a by-product. The difference betw—

The difference, he interrupted himself, between the old

nature and the new god Finchley shall be order. Mine will be an ordered cosmos devoid of waste and devoted to beauty. There will be nothing haphazard. There will be no blundering.

First, the canvas.

"There shall be infinite space!" Finchley cried.

In the nothingness, his voice roared through the bony structure of his skull and echoed in his ears with a flat, sour sound; but on the instant of command, the opaque blackness was filtered into a limpid jet. Finchley could still see nothing, but he felt the change.

He thought: Now, in the old cosmos there were simply stars and nebulae and vast, fiery bodies scattered through the realms of the sky. No one knew their purpose—no one knew their origin or destination.

In mine there shall be purpose, for each body shall serve to support a race of creatures whose sole function shall be to serve me—

He cried: "Let there be universes to the number of one hundred, filling space. One thousand galaxies shall make up each universe, and one million suns shall be the sum of each galaxy. Ten planets shall circle each sun, and two moons each planet. Let all revolve around their creator! Let all this come to pass. Now!"

Finchley screamed as light burst in a soundless cataclysm around him. Stars, close and hot as suns, distant and cold as pinpricks—Separately, by twos and in vast smudgy clouds—Blazing crimson—yellow—deep green and violet—The sum of their brilliance was a welter of light that constricted his heart and filled him with a devouring fear of the latent power within him.

"This," Finchley whimpered, "is enough cosmic creation for the time being—"

He closed his eyes determinedly and exerted his will once more. There was a sensation of solidity under his feet and when he opened his eyes cautiously he was standing on one of his earths with blue sky and a blue-white sun lowering swiftly toward the western horizon.

It was a bare, brown earth—Finchley had seen to that—it was a vast sphere of inchoate matter waiting for his molding, for he had decided that first above all other creation he would form a good green earth for himself—a planet of beauty where Finchley, God of all Creation, would reside in his Eden.

All through that waning afternoon he worked, swiftly and with artistic finesse. A vast ocean, green and with sparkling white foam, swept over half the globe; alternating hundreds of miles of watery space with clusters of warm islands. The single continent he divided in half with a backbone of jagged mountains that stretched from pole to snowy pole.

With infinite care he worked. Using oils, watercolors, charcoal, and plumbago sketches, he planned and executed his entire world. Mountains, valleys, plains; crags, precipices and mere boulders were all designed in a fluent congruence of beautifully balanced masses.

All his spirit of artistry went into the clever scattering of lakes like so many sparkling jewels; and into the cunning arabesques of winding rivers that traced intricate designs over the face of the planet. He devoted himself to the selection of colors; gray gravels, pink, white and black sands, good earths, brown, umber and sepia, mottled shales, glistening micas and silica stones—And when the sun at last vanished on the first day of his labor, his Eden was a paradise of stone, earth, and metal, ready for life.

As the sky darkened overhead, a pale gibbous moon with a face of death was revealed riding in the vault of the sky; and even as Finchley watched it uneasily, a second moon with a blood-red disk lifted its ravaged countenance above the eastern horizon and began a ghastly march across the heavens. Finchley tore his eyes away from them and stared out at the twinkling stars.

There was much satisfaction to be gained from the contemplation. "I know exactly how many there are," he thought complacently. "You multiply one hundred by a thousand by a million and there's your answer—And that happens to be my idea of order!"

He lay back on a patch of warm, soft soil and placed palms under the back of his head, looking up. "And I know exactly what all of them are there for—to support human lives—the countless billions upon billions of lives which I shall design

and create solely to serve and worship the Lord Finchley—
That's purpose for you!''

And he knew where each of those blue and red and indigo
sparks was going, for even in the vasty reaches of space they
were thundering in a circular course, the pivot of which was
that point in the skies he had just left. Someday he would
return to that place and there build his heavenly castle. Then
he would sit through all eternity watching the wheeling flight
of his worlds.

There was a peculiar splotch of red in the zenith of the sky.
Finchley watched it absently at first, then with guarded
attention as it seemed to burgeon. It spread slowly like an ink
stain, and as the moments fled by, became tinged with orange
and then the purest white. And for the first time Finchley was
uncomfortably aware of a sensation of heat.

An hour passed and then two and three. The fist of red-
white spread across the sky until it was a fiery nebulous
cloud. A thin, tenuous edge approached a star gently, then
touched. Instantly there was a blinding blaze of radiance and
Finchley was flooded with searing light that illuminated the
landscape with the eerie glow of flaring magnesium. The
sensation of heat grew in intensity and tiny beads of perspira-
tion prickled across his skin.

With midnight, the unaccountable inferno filled half the
sky, and the gleaming stars, one after another, were bursting
into silent explosions. The light was blinding white and the
heat suffocating. Finchley tottered to his feet and began to
run, searching vainly for shade or water. It was only then that
he realized his universe was running amuck.

''No!'' he cried desperately. ''No!''

Heat bludgeoned him. He fell and rolled across cutting
rocks that tore at him and anchored him back with his face
upthrust. Past his shielding hands, past his tight-shut eyelids,
the intolerable light and heat pressed.

''Why should it go wrong?'' Finchley screamed. ''There
was plenty of room for everything! Why should it—''

In heat-borne delirium he felt a thunderous rocking as
though his Eden were beginning to split asunder.

He cried, ''Stop! Stop! Everything stop!'' He beat at his
temples with futile fists and at last whispered, ''All right
. . . if I've made another mistake, then—All right—'' He

waved his hand feebly.

And again the skies were black and blank. Only the two scabrous moons rode overhead, beginning the long downward journey to the west. And in the east a faint glow hinted at the rising sun.

"So," Finchley murmured, "one must be more a mathematician and physicist to run a cosmos. Very well, I can learn that later. I'm an artist and I never pretended to know all that. But . . . I *am* an artist, and there is still my good green earth to people—Tomorrow—We shall see . . . tomorrow—"

And so presently he slept.

The sun was high when he awoke, and its evil eye filled him with unrest. Glancing at the landscape he had fashioned the day previous, he was even more uncertain, for there was some subtle distortion in everything. Valley floors looked unclean with the pale sheen of lepers' scales. The mountain crags formed curious shapes suggestive of terror. Even the lakes contained the hint of horror under their smooth, innocent surfaces.

Not, he noticed, when he stared directly at these creations, but only when his glance was sidelong. Viewed full-eyed and steadfastly, everything seemed to be right. Proportion was good, line was excellent, coloring perfection. And yet—He shrugged and decided he would have to put in some practice at drafting. No doubt there was some subtle error of design in his work.

He walked to a tiny stream and from the bank scooped out a mass of moist red clay. He kneaded it smooth, wet it down to a thin mud, and strained it. After it had dried under the sun slightly, he arranged a heavy block of stone as a pedestal and set to work. His hands were still practiced and certain. With sure fingers he shaped his concept of a large furred rabbit. Body, legs and head; exquisitely etched features—it crouched on the stone ready, it seemed, to leap off at a moment's notice. Finchley smiled affectionately at his work, his confidence at last restored. He tapped it once on the rounded head and said, "Live, my friend—"

There was a second's indecision while life invaded the clay form; then it arched its back with a clumsy motion and attempted to leap. It moved to the edge of the pedestal where it hung crazily for an instant before it dropped heavily to the ground. As it lumbered on a hirpling course, it uttered horrible little grunting sounds and turned once to gaze at Finchley. On that animal face was an expression of malevolence.

Finchley's smile froze. He frowned, hesitated, then scooped up another chunk of clay and set it on the stone. For the space of an hour he worked, shaping a graceful Irish setter. At last he tapped this, too, and said, "Live—"

Instantly the dog collapsed. It mewled helplessly and then struggled to shaking feet like some enormous spider, eyes distended and glassy. It tottered to the edge of the pedestal, leaped off, and collided with Finchley's leg. There was a low growl, and the beast tore sharp fangs into Finchley's skin. He leaped back with a cry and kicked the animal furiously. Mewling and howling, the setter went gangling across the fields like a crippled monster.

With furious intent, Finchley returned to his work. Shape after shape he modeled and endowed with life, and each— ape, monkey, fox, weasel, rat, lizard and toad—fish, long and short, stout and slender—birds by the score—each was a grotesque monstrosity that swam, shambled or fluttered off like some nightmare. Finchley was bewildered and exhausted. He sat himself down on the pedestal and began to sob while his tired fingers still twitched and prodded at a lump of clay.

He thought: "I'm still an artist—What's gone wrong? What turns everything I do into horrible freak shows?"

His fingers turned and twisted, and a head began to form in the clay.

He thought, "I made a fortune with my art once. Everyone couldn't have been crazy. They bought my work for many reasons—but an important one was that it was beautiful."

He noticed the lump of clay in his hands. It had been partially formed into a woman's head. He examined it closely for the first time in many hours; he smiled.

"Why, of course!" he exclaimed. "I'm no shaper of animals. Let's see how well I do with a human figure—"

Swiftly, with heavy chunks of clay, he built up the under-structure of his figure. Legs, arms, torso, and head were formed. He hummed under his breath as he worked. He thought, She'll be the loveliest Eve ever created—and more—her children shall truly be the children of a god!

With loving hands he turned the full, swelling calves and thighs, and cunningly joined slender ankles to graceful feet. The hips were rounded and girdled a flat, slightly mounded belly. As he set the strong shoulders, he suddenly stopped and stepped back a pace.

Is it possible? he wondered.

He walked slowly around the half-completed figure.

Yes—

Force of habit, perhaps?

Perhaps that—and maybe the love he had borne for so many empty years.

He returned to the figure and redoubled his efforts. With a sense of growing elation, he completed arms, neck and head. There was a certainty within him that told him it was impos-sible to fail. He had modeled this figure too often not to know it down to the finest detail. And when he was finished, Theone Dubedat, magnificently sculpted in clay, stood atop the stone pedestal.

Finchley was content. Wearily he sat down with his back to a boulder, produced a cigarette from space, and lit it. For perhaps a minute he sat, dragging in the smoke to quiet his excitement. At last with a sense of chaotic anticipation he said, "Woman—"

He choked and stopped. Then he began again.

"Be alive—Theone!"

The second of life came and passed. The nude figure moved slightly, then began to tremble. Magnetically drawn, Finchley arose and stepped toward her, arms outstretched in mute appeal. There was a hoarse gasp of indrawn breath and slowly the great eyes opened and examined him.

The living girl straightened and screamed. Before Finch-ley could touch her she beat at his face, her long nails ripping his skin. She fell backward off the pedestal, leaped to her feet and began running off across the fields like all the others—running like a crazy crippled creature while she screamed and howled. The low sun dappled her body and the shadow she cast was monstrous.

Long after she disappeared, Finchley continued to gaze in her direction while within him all that futile, bitter love surged and burned in an acid tide. At length he turned again to the pedestal and with icy impassivity set once more to work. Nor did he stop until the fifth in a succession of lurid creatures ran screaming out into the night—Then and only then did he stop and stand for a long time gazing alternately at his hands and the crazy moons that careered overhead.

There was a tap on his shoulder and he was not too surprised to see Lady Sutton standing beside him. She still wore the sequined evening gown, and in the double moonlight her face was as coarse and masculine as ever.

Finchley said: "Oh . . . it's you."

"How are you, Dig, m'lad?"

He thought it over, trying to bring some reason to the ludicrous insanity that pervaded his cosmos. At last he said, "Not very well, Lady Sutton."

"Trouble?"

"Yes—" He broke off and stared at her. "I say, Lady Sutton, how the devil did you get here?"

She laughed. "I'm dead, Dig. You ought to know."

"Dead? Oh . . . I—" He floundered in embarrassment.

"No hard feelings, though. I'd have done the same m'self, y'know."

"You would?"

"Anything for a new sensation. That was always our motto, eh?" She nodded complacently and grinned at him. It was that same old grin of pure deviltry.

Finchley said, "What are you doing here? I mean, how did—"

"I said I was dead," Lady Sutton interrupted. "There's lots you don't understand about this business of dying."

"But this is my own personal private reality. I own it."

"And I'm still dead, Dig. I can get into any bloody damned reality I choose. Wait—You'll find out."

He said: "I won't—ever—That is, I can't. Because I won't ever die."

"Oh-ho?"

"No, I won't. I'm a god."

"You are, eh? How d'you like it?"

"I . . . I don't." He faltered for words. "I . . . that is, someone promised me a reality I could shape for myself, but I can't, Lady Sutton, I can't."

"And why not?"

"I don't know. I'm a god, and yet every time I try to shape something beautiful it turns out hateful."

"As how, for instance?"

He showed her the twisted mountains and plains, the evil lakes and rivers, the distorted grunting creatures he had created. All this Lady Sutton examined carefully and with close attention. At last she pursed her lips and thought for a moment; then she gazed keenly at Finchley and said, "Odd that you've never made a mirror, Dig."

"A mirror?" he echoed. "No, I haven't—I never needed one—"

"Go ahead. Make one now."

He gave her a perplexed look and waved a hand in the air. A square of silvered glass was in his fingers and he held it toward her.

"No," Lady Sutton said, "it's for you. Look in it."

Wondering, he raised the mirror and gazed into it. He uttered a hoarse cry and peered closer. Leering back at him out of the dim night was the evil face of a gargoyle. In the small, slant-set eyes, the splayed nose, the broken yellow teeth, the twisted ruin of a face, he saw everything he had seen in his ugly cosmos.

He saw the obscene cathedral of heaven and all its unholy hierarchy of ribald retainers; the spinning chaos of crashing stars and suns; the lurid landscape of his Eden; each howling, ghastly creature he had created; every horror that his brain had spawned. He hurled the mirror spinning and turned to confront Lady Sutton.

"What?" he demanded. "What is this?"

"Why, you're a god, Dig," Lady Sutton laughed, "and you ought to know that a god can create only in his own image. Yes—the answer's as simple as that. It's a grand joke, ain't it?"

"Joke?" The import of all the eons to come thundered down over his head. An eternity of living with his hideous self, upon himself, inside himself—over and over—repeated in every sun and star, every living and dead thing, every creature, every everlasting moment. A monstrous god feeding upon himself and slowly, inexorably going mad.

"Joke!" he screamed.

He flung out his hand and he floated once more, suspended out of all contact with mass and matter. Once more he was utterly alone, with nothing to see, nothing to hear, nothing to touch. And as he pondered for another ineffable period on the inevitable futility of his next attempt, he heard quite distinctly, the deep bellow of familiar laughter.

Of such was the Kingdom of Finchley's Heaven.

III

"Give me the strength! Oh, give me the strength!"

She went through the veil sharp on Finchley's heels, that short, slender, dark woman, and she found herself in the dungeon passage of Sutton Castle. For a moment she was startled out of her prayer, half-disappointed at not finding a land of mists and dreams. Then, with a bitter smile, she recalled the reality she wanted.

Before her stood a suit of armor; a strong, graceful figure of polished metal edged with sweeping flutings. She went to it. Dully from the gleaming steel cuirass, a slightly distorted reflection stared back. It showed the drawn, high-strung face, and the coal-black eyes, the coal-black hair dipping down over the brow in a sharp widow's peak. It said: This is Sidra Peel. This is a woman whose past has been fettered to a dull-witted creature that called itself her husband. She will break that chain this day if only she finds the strength—

"Break the chain!" she repeated fiercely, "and this day repay him for a life's worth of agony. God—if there be a god in my world—help me balance the account in full! Help me—"

Sidra froze while her pulse beat wildly. Someone had

come down the lonesome passage and stood behind her. She could feel the heat—the aura of a presence—the almost imperceptible pressure of a body against hers. Mistily in the mirror of the armor she made out a face peering over her shoulder.

She spun around, crying, "Ahhh!"

"So sorry," he said. "Thought you were expecting me."

Her eyes riveted to his face. He was smiling slightly in an affable manner, and yet the streaked blond hair, the hollows and mounds, the pulsing veins and shadows of his features were a lurid landscape of raw emotions.

"Calm yourself," he said while she teetered crazily and fought down the screams that were tearing through her.

"But wh-who—" She broke off and tried to swallow.

"I thought you were expecting me," he repeated.

"I . . . expecting you?"

He nodded and took her hands. Against his, her palms felt chilled and moist. "We had an engagement."

She opened her mouth slightly and shook her head.

"At twelve-forty—" He released one of her hands to look at his watch. "And here I am, on the dot."

"No," she said, yanking herself away. "No, this is impossible. We have no engagement. I don't know you."

"You don't recognize me, Sidra? Well—that's odd, but I think you'll recollect who I am before long."

"But who are you?"

"I shan't tell you. You'll have to remember yourself."

A little calmer, she inspected his features closely.

With the rush of a waterfall, a blended sensation of attraction and repulsion surged over her. This man alarmed and fascinated her. She was filled with fear at his mere presence, yet intrigued and drawn.

At last she shook her head and said: "I still don't understand. I never called for you, Mr. Whoever-you-are, and we had no engagement."

"You most certainly did."

"I most certainly did not!" she flared, outraged by his insolent assurance. "I wanted my old world. The same old world I'd always known—"

"But with one exception?"

"Y-yes—" Her furious glance wavered and the rage drained out of her. "Yes, with one exception."

"And you prayed for the strength to produce that exception?"

She nodded.

He grinned and took her arm. "Well, Sidra, then you did call for me and we did have an engagement. I'm the answer to your prayer."

She suffered herself to be led through the narrow, steep-mounting passages, unable to break free from that magnetic leash. His touch on her arm was a frightening thing. Everything in her cried out against the bewilderment—and yet another something in her welcomed it eagerly.

As they passed through the cloudy light of infrequent lamps, she watched him covertly. He was tall and magnificently built. Thick cords strained in his muscular neck at the slightest turn of his arrogant head. He was dressed in tweeds that had the texture of sandstone and gave off a pungent, peaty scent. His shirt was open at the collar, and where his chest showed it was thickly matted.

There were no servants about on the ground floor of the castle. The man escorted her quietly through the graceful rooms to the foyer, where he removed her coat from the closet and placed it around her shoulders. Then he pressed his hard hands against her arms.

She tore herself away at last, one of the old rages sweeping over her. In the quiet gloom of the foyer she could see that he was still smiling, and it added fuel to her fury.

"Ah!" she cried. "What a fool I am . . . to take you so for granted. 'I prayed for you,' you say. 'I know you—' What kind of booby do you think I am? Keep your hands off me!"

She glared at him, breathing heavily, and he made no answer. His expression remained unchanged. It's like those snakes, she thought, those snakes with the hypnotic eyes. They coil in their impassive beauty and you can't escape the deadly fascination. It's like soaring towers that make you want to leap to earth—Like keen, glittering razors that invite the tender flesh of your throat. You can't escape!

"Go on!" she cried in a last desperate effort. "Get out of here! This is my world. It's all mine to do with as I choose. I want no part of your kind of rotten, arrogant swine!"

Swiftly, silently, he gripped her shoulders and brought her close to him. While he kissed her she struggled against the hard talons of his fingers and tried to force her mouth away from his. And yet she knew that if he had released her, she could not have torn herself away from that savage kiss.

She was sobbing when he relaxed his grip and let her head drop back. Still in the affable tones of a casual conversation, he said, "You want one thing in this world of yours, Sidra, and you must have me to help you."

"In Heaven's name, who are you?"

"I'm the strength you prayed for. Now come along."

Outside, the night was pitch black, and after they had gotten into Sidra's two-seater and started for London, the road was impossible to follow. As she edged the car cautiously along, Sidra was able at last to make out the limed white line that bisected the road, and the lighter velvet of the sky against the jet of the horizon. Overhead the Milky Way was a long smudge of powder.

The wind on her face was good to feel. Passionate, reckless, and headstrong as ever, she pressed her foot on the accelerator and sent the car roaring down the dangerous dark road, eager for more of the cool breeze against her cheeks and brow. The wind tugged at her hair and sent it streaming back. The wind gusted over the top of the glass shield and around it like a solid stream of cold water. It whipped up her courage and confidence. Best of all, it renewed her sense of humor.

Without turning, she called, "What's your name?"

And dimly through the noisy breeze came his answer; "Does it matter?"

"It certainly does. Am I supposed to call you; 'Hey!' or 'I say, there—' or 'Dear sir—' "

"Very well, Sidra. Call me Ardis."

"Ardis? That's not English, is it?"

"Does it matter?"

"Don't be so mysterious. Of course it matters. I'm trying to place you."

"I see."

"D'you know Lady Sutton?"

Receiving no answer she glanced at him and received a slight chill. He did look mysterious with his head silhouetted against the star-filled sky. He looked out of place in an open roadster.

"D'you know Lady Sutton?" she repeated.

He nodded and she turned her attention back to the road. They had left the open country and were boring through the London suburbs. The little squat houses, all alike, all flat-faced and muddy-colored, whisked past with a muffled *whump-whump-whump*, echoing back the stridor of their passage.

Still gay, she asked, "Where are you stopping?"

"In London."

"Where, in London?"

"Chelsea Square."

"The Square? That's odd. What number?"

"One hundred and forty-nine."

She burst into laughter. "Your impudence is too wonderful," she gasped, glancing at him again. "That happens to be my address."

He nodded. "I know that, Sidra."

Her laughter froze—not at the words, for she hardly heard them. Barely suppressing another cry, she turned and stared through the windshield, her hands trembling on the wheel; for the man sat there in the midst of that turmoil of wind, and not a hair of his head was moving.

Merciful Heaven! she cried in her heart. What kind of a mess did I—Who is this monster, this—Our Father who art in Heaven, hallowed be thy—Get rid of him! I don't want him. If I've asked for him, consciously or not, I don't want him now. I want my world changed. Right now! I want him out of it!

"It's no use, Sidra," he said.

Her lips twitched and still she prayed: Get him out of here! Change everything—anything—only take him away. Let him vanish. Let the darkness and the void devour him. Let him dwindle, fade—

"Sidra," he shouted, "stop that!" He poked her sharply. "You can't get rid of me that way—It's too late!"

She stopped praying as panic overtook her and congealed her brain.

"Once you've decided on your world," Ardis explained carefully as though to a child, "you're committed to it. There's no changing your mind and making alterations. Weren't you told?"

"No," she whispered, "we weren't told."

"Well, now you know."

She was mute, numb and wooden. Not so much wooden as putty. She followed his directions without a word, drove to the little park of trees that was behind her house, and parked there. Ardis explained that they would have to enter the house through the servants' door.

"You don't," he said, "walk openly to murder. Only clever criminals in storybooks do that. We, in real life, find it best to be cautious."

Real life! she thought hysterically as they got out of the car. Reality! That Thing in the shelter—

Aloud, she said, "You sound experienced."

"Through the park," he answered, touching her lightly on the arm. "We shan't be seen."

The path through the trees was narrow, and the grass and prickly shrubs on either side were high. Ardis stepped back and then followed her as she passed the iron gate and entered. He strode a few paces behind her.

"As to experience," he said, "yes—I've had plenty. But then, you ought to know, Sidra."

She didn't know. She didn't answer. Trees, brush and grass were thick around her, and although she had traversed this park a hundred times, they were alien and grotesque. They were not alive—no, thank God for that. She was not yet imagining things, but for the first time she realized how skeletal and haunted they looked; almost as if each had participated in some sordid murder or suicide through the years.

Deeper into the park, a dank mist made her cough and, behind her, Ardis patted her back sympathetically. She quivered like a length of supple steel under his touch, and when she had stopped coughing and the hand still remained on her shoulder, she knew what he would attempt here in the darkness.

She quickened her stride. The hand left her shoulder and hooked at her arm. She yanked her arm free and ran down the path, stumbling on her stilt heels. There was a muffled exclamation from Ardis, and she heard the swift pound of his feet as he pursued her. The path led down a slight depression and past a marshy little pond. The earth turned moist and sucked at her feet. In the warmth of the night her skin began to prickle and perspire, but the sound of his panting was close behind her.

Her breath was coming in gasps, and when the path veered and began to mount, she felt her lungs would burst. Her legs were aching and it seemed that at the next instant she would flounder to the ground. Dimly through the trees, she made out the iron gate at the other side of the park, and with the little strength left to her, she redoubled her efforts to reach it.

But what, she wondered dizzily, what after that? He'll overtake me in the street—Perhaps before the street—I should have turned for the car—I could have driven—I—

He clutched at her shoulder as she passed the gate and she would have surrendered at that moment. Then she heard voices and saw figures on the street across from her. She cried, "Hello, there!" and ran to them, her shoes clattering on the pavement. As she came close, still free for the moment, they turned.

"So sorry," she babbled. "Thought I recognized you . . . Was walking through the par—"

She stopped short. Staring at her were Finchley, Braugh, and Lady Sutton.

"Sidra, darling! What the devil are you doing here?" Lady Sutton demanded. She cocked her gross head forward to examine Sidra's face, then nudged at Braugh and Finchley with her elbows. "The girl's been running through the park. Mark my words, Chris, she's touched."

"Looks like she's been chivvied," Braugh answered. He stepped to one side and peered past Sidra's shoulder, his white head gleaming in the starlight.

Sidra caught her breath at last and looked about. Ardis stood alongside her, calm and affable as ever. There was, she thought helplessly, no use trying to explain. No one would believe her. No one would help. She said: "Just a bit of exercise. It was such a lovely night."

"Exercise!" Lady Sutton snorted. "Now I know you're cracked."

Finchley said, "Why'd you pop off like that, Sidra? Bob was furious. We've just been driving him home."

"I—" It was too insane. She'd seen Finchley vanish through the veil of fire less than an hour ago—vanish into a world of his own choosing. Yet here he was asking questions.

Ardis murmured, "Finchley was in your world, too. He's still here."

"But that's impossible!" Sidra exclaimed. "There can't be two Finchleys."

"Two Finchleys?" Lady Sutton echoed. "Now I know where you've been and gone, my girl! You're drunk. Reeling, stinking drunk. Running through the park! Exercise! Two Finchleys!"

And Lady Sutton? But she was dead. She had to be! They'd murdered her less than—

Again Ardis murmured, "That was another world ago, Sidra. This is your new world, and Lady Sutton belongs in it. Everyone belongs in it—except your husband."

"But . . . even though she's dead?"

Finchley started and asked, "Who's dead?"

"I think," Braugh said, "we'd better get her upstairs and put her to bed."

"No," Sidra said. "No—there's no need—really! I'm quite all right."

"Oh, let her be!" Lady Sutton grunted. She gathered her coat around her tub of a waist and moved off. "You know our motto, m'lads. 'Never Interfere.' See you and Bob at the shelter next week, Sidra. 'Night—"

"Good night."

Finchley and Braugh moved off, too—the three figures merging with the shadows in a misty fade-out. And as they vanished, Sidra heard Braugh: "The motto ought to be 'Unashamed.' "

"Nonsense," Finchley answered. "Shame is a sensation we seek like all others. It reduc—"

Then they were gone.

And with a return of that frightened chill, Sidra realized that they had not seen Ardis—nor heard him—nor even been aware of his—

"Naturally," Ardis interrupted.

"But how, naturally?"

"You'll understand later. Just now we've a murder before us."

"No!" she cried, hanging back. "No!"

"How's this, Sidra? And after you've looked forward to this moment for so many years. Planned it. Feasted on it—"

"I'm . . . too upset . . . unnerved."

"You'll be calmer. Come along."

Together they walked a few steps down the narrow street, turned up the gravel path and passed the gate that led to the back court. As Ardis reached out for the knob of the servants' door, he hesitated and turned to her.

"This," he said, "is your moment, Sidra. It begins now. This is the time when you break that chain and make payment for a life's worth of agony. This is the day when you balance the account. Love is good—hate is better. Forgiveness is a trifling virtue—passion is all-consuming and the end-all of living!"

He pushed open the door, grasped her elbow and dragged her after him into the pantry. It was dark and filled with odd corners. They eased through the blackness cautiously, reached the swinging door that led to the kitchen, and pushed past it. Sidra uttered a faint moan and sagged against Ardis.

It *had* been a kitchen at one time. Now the stoves and sinks, cupboards and tables, chairs, closets and all, loomed high and twisted like the tangle of an insane jungle. A dull-blue spark glittered on the floor, and around it cavorted a score of singing shadows.

They were solidified smoke—semiliquid gas. Their translucent depths writhed and interplayed with the nauseating surge of living muck. Like looking through a microscope, Sidra thought, at those creatures that foul corpse-blood, that scum a slack-water stream, that fill a swamp with noisome vapors—And most hideous of all, they were all in the wavering gusty image of her husband. Twenty Robert Peels, gesticulating obscenely and singing a whispered chorus:

> *"Quis multa gracilis te puer in rosa*
> *Perfusus liquidis urget odoribus*
> *Grato, Sidra, sub antro?"*

"Ardis! What is this?"

"Don't know yet, Sidra."

"But these shapes!"

"We'll find out."

Twenty leaping vapors crowded around them, still chanting. Sidra and Ardis were driven forward and stood at the brink of that sapphire spark that burned in the air a few inches above the floor. Gaseous fingers pushed and probed at Sidra, pinched and prodded while the blue figures cavorted with hissing laughter, slapping their naked rumps in weird ecstasies.

A slash on Sidra's arm made her start and cry out, and when she looked down, unaccountable beads of blood stood out on the white skin of her wrist. And even as she stared in disembodied enchantment, her wrist was raised to Ardis's lips. Then his wrist was raised to her mouth and she felt the stinging salt of his blood on her lips.

"No!" she gasped. "I don't believe this. You're making me see this."

She turned and ran from the kitchen toward the serving pantry. Ardis was close behind her. And the blue shapes still hissed a droning chorus:

> *"Qui nunc te fruitur credulus aurea;*
> *Qui semper vacuam, semper amabilem,*
> *Sperat, nescius aurae*
> *Fallacia—"*

When they reached the foot of the winding stairs that led to the upper floors, Sidra clutched at the balustrade for support. With her free hand she dabbed at her mouth to erase the salt taste that made her stomach crawl.

"I think I've an idea what all that was," Ardis said.

She stared at him.

"A sort of betrothal ceremony," he went on casually. "You've read of something like that before, haven't you? Odd, wasn't it? Some powerful influences in this house. Recognize those phantoms?"

She shook her head wearily. What was the use of thinking—talking?

"Didn't, eh? We'll have to see about this. I never cared for unsolicited haunting. We shan't have any more of this tomfoolery in the future—" He mused for a moment, then pointed to the stairs. "Your husband's up there, I think. Let's continue."

They trudged up the sweeping, gloomy stairs, and the last vestiges of Sidra's sanity struggled up, step by step, with her.

One: You go up the stairs. Stairs leading to what? More madness? That damned Thing in the shelter!

Two: This is hell, not reality.

Three: Or nightmare. Yes! Nightmare. Lobster last night. Where were we last night, Bob and I?

Four: Dear Bob. Why did I ever—And this Ardis. I know why he's so familiar. Why he almost speaks my thoughts. He's probably some—

Five:—nice young man who plays tennis in real life. Distorted by a dream. Yes.

Six—

Seven—

"Don't run into it," Ardis cautioned.

She halted in her tracks and simply stared. There were no more screams or shudders left in her. She simply stared at the thing that hung with a twisted head from the beam over the stair landing. It was her husband, limp and slack, dangling at the end of a length of laundry rope.

The limp figure swayed ever so slightly, like the gentle swing of a massive pendulum. The mouth was wrinkled into a sardonic grin and the eyes popped from their sockets and glanced down at her with impudent humor. Vaguely, Sidra was aware that ascending steps behind it showed through the twisted form.

"Join hands," the corpse said in sacrosanct tones.

"Bob!"

"Your husband?" Ardis exclaimed.

"Dearly beloved," the corpse began, "we are gathered together in the sight of God and in the face of this company to join together this man and this woman in holy matrimony; which is . . ." The voice boomed on and on and on.

"Bob!" Sidra croaked.

"Kneel!" the corpse commanded.

Sidra flung herself to one side and ran stumbling up the stairs. She faltered for a gasping instant, then Ardis's strong hands grasped her. Behind them the shadowy corpse intoned: "I pronounce you man and wife."

Ardis whispered, "We must be quick, now! Very quick!"

But at the head of the stairs Sidra made a last bid for liberty. She abandoned all hope of sanity, of understanding. All she wanted was freedom and a place where she could sit in solitude, free of the passions that were hedging her in, gutting her soul. There was no word spoken, no gesture made. She drew herself up and faced Ardis squarely. This was one of the times, she understood, when you fought like petroglyphs carved on prehistoric rock.

For minutes they stood, facing each other in the dark hall. To their right was the descending well of the stairs; to the left, Sidra's bedroom; behind them, the short hallway that led to Peel's study—to the room where he was so unconsciously awaiting slaughter. Their eyes met, clashed and battled silently. And even as Sidra met that deep, gleaming glance, she knew with an agonizing sense of desperation that she would lose.

There was no longer any will, any strength, any courage left in her. Worse, by some spectral osmosis it seemed to have drained out of her into the man who faced her. While she fought she realized that her rebellion was like that of a hand or a finger rebelling against its guiding brain.

Only one sentence she spoke: "For Heaven's sake! *Who are you?*"

And again he answered: "You'll find out—soon. But I think you know already. I think you know!"

Helpless, she turned and entered her bedroom. There was a revolver there and she understood she was to get it. But when she pulled open the drawer and yanked aside the piles of silk clothes to pick it up, the clothes felt thick and moist. As she hesitated, Ardis reached past her and picked up the gun. Clinging to the butt, a finger tight-clenched around the trigger, was a hand, the stump of the wrist clotted and torn.

Ardis clucked impatiently and tried to pry the hand loose. It would not give. He pressed and twisted a finger at a time and still the sickening corpse-hand clenched the gun stubbornly. Sidra sat at the edge of the bed like a child, watching the spectacle with naïve interest, noting the way the broken muscles and tendons on the stump flexed as Ardis tugged.

There was a crimson snake oozing from under the bathroom door. It writhed across the hardwood floor, thickening to a small river as it touched her skirt so gently. When Ardis tossed the gun down angrily, he noted the stream. Quickly he stepped to the bathroom and thrust open the door, then slammed it a second later. He jerked his head at Sidra and said, ''Come on!''

She nodded mechanically and arose, careless of the sopping skirt that smacked against her calves. At Peel's study she turned the doorknob carefully until a faint click warned her that the latch was open, then she pushed the door in. The leaf swung wide to reveal her husband's study in semidarkness. The desk was before the high window curtains and Peel sat at it, his back to them. He was hunched over a candle or a lamp or some light that enhaloed his body and sent streams of rays flickering out. He never moved.

Sidra tiptoed forward, then paused. Ardis touched a finger to lips and moved like a swift cat to the cold fireplace where he picked up the heavy bronze poker. He brought it to Sidra and held it out urgently. Her hand reached of its own accord and took the cool metal handle. Her fingers gripped it as though they had been born for murder.

Against all that impelled her to advance and raise the poker over Peel's head, something weak and sick inside her cried out and prayed; cried, prayed and moaned with the whimpering of a fevered child. Like spilt water, the last few drops of her self-possession trembled before they disappeared altogether.

Then Ardis touched her. His finger pressed against the

small of her back and a charge of bestiality shocked up her spine with cruel, jagged edges. Surging with hatred, rage, and livid vindictiveness, she raised the poker high and crashed it down on the still-motionless head of her husband.

The entire room burst into a silent explosion. Lights flared and shadows whirled. Remorselessly, she clubbed and pounded at the falling body that toppled out of the chair to the floor. She struck again and again, her breath whistling hysterically, until the head was a mashed, bloodied pulp. Only then did she let the poker drop and reel back.

Ardis knelt beside the body and turned it over.

"He's dead all right. This is the moment you prayed for, Sidra. You're free!"

She looked down in horror. Dully, from the crimsoned carpet, a corpse face stared back. It showed the drawn, high-strung features, the coal-black eyes, the coal-black hair dipping over the brow in a sharp widow's peak. She moaned as understanding touched her.

The face said, "This is Sidra Peel. In this man whom you have slaughtered you have killed yourself—killed the only part of yourself worth saving."

She cried, "Aieee—" and clasped arms about herself, rocking in agony.

"Look well on me," the face said. "By my death you have broken a chain—only to find another."

And she knew. She understood. For though she still rocked and moaned in the agony that would be never-ending, she saw Ardis arise and advance on her with arms outstretched. His eyes gleamed and were horrid pools, and his reaching arms were tendrils of her own unslaked passion, eager to enfold her. And once embraced, she knew there would be no escape—no escape from this sickening marriage to her own lusts that would forever caress her.

So it would be forevermore in Sidra's brave new world.

IV

After the others had passed the veil, Christian Braugh still lingered in the shelter. He lit another cigarette with a simulation of perfect aplomb, blew out the match, then called: "Er . . . Mr. Thing?"

"What is it, Mr. Braugh?"

Braugh could not restrain a slight start at that voice sounding from nowhere, "I—well, the fact is, I stayed for a chat."

"I thought you would, Mr. Braugh."

"You did, eh?"

"Your insatiable hunger for fresh material is no mystery to me."

"Oh!" Braugh looked around nervously. "I see."

"Nor is there any cause for alarm. No one will overhear us. Your masquerade will remain undetected."

"Masquerade!"

"You're not really a bad man, Mr. Braugh. You've never belonged in the Sutton shelter clique."

Braugh laughed sardonically.

"And there's no need to continue your sham before me," the voice continued in the friendliest manner. "I know the story of your many plagiarisms was merely another concoction of the fertile imagination of Christian Braugh."

"You know?"

"Of course. You created that legend to obtain entree to the shelter. For years you've been playing the role of a lying scoundrel, even though your blood ran cold at times."

"And do you know why I did that?"

"Certainly. As a matter of fact, Mr. Braugh, I know almost everything, but I do confess that one thing about you still confuses me."

"What's that?"

"Why, with that devouring appetite for fresh material, were you not content to work as other authors do, with what you know? Why this almost insane desire for unique material—for absolutely untrodden fields? Why were you willing to pay a bitter and exorbitant price for a few ounces of novelty?"

"Why?" Braugh sucked in smoke and exhaled it past clenched teeth. "You'd understand if you were human. I take it you're not . . . ?"

"That question cannot be answered."

"Then I'll tell you why. It's something that's been torturing me all my life. A man is born with imagination."

"Ah . . . Imagination."

"If his imagination is slight, a man will always find the
world a source of deep and infinite wonder, a place of many
delights. But if his imagination is strong, vivid, restless, he
finds the world a sorry place indeed—a drab jade beside the
wonders of his own creations!"

"There are wonders past all imagining."

"For whom? Not for me, my invisible friend; nor for any
earth-bound, flesh-bound creature. Man is a pitiful thing.
Born with the imagination of gods and forever pasted to a
round lump of clay and spittle. I have within me the
uniqueness, the ego, the fertile loam of a timeless
spirit . . . and all that wealth is wrapped in a parcel of
quickly rotting skin!"

"Ego . . ." mused the voice. "That is something which,
alas, none of us can understand. Nowhere in all the knowable
cosmos is it to be found but on your planet, Mr. Braugh. It is a
frightening thing and convinces me at times that yours is the
race that will—" the voice broke off abruptly.

"That will . . . ?" Braugh prompted.

"Come," said the Thing briskly, "there is less owing you
than the others, and I shall give you the benefit of my
experience. Let me help you select a reality."

Braugh pounced on the word. "Less?"

And again he was brushed aside. "Will you choose another reality in your own cosmos, or are you content with
what you already have? I can offer you vast worlds, tiny
worlds; great creatures that shake space and fill the voids with
their thunder; tiny creatures of charm and perfection that
barely touch perception with the sensitive timbre of their
thoughts. Do you care for terror? I can give you a reality of
shudders. Beauty? I can show you realities of infinite ec-
stasy. Pain? Torture? Any sensation. Name one, several, all.
I will shape you a reality to outdo even the giant concepts that
are assuredly yours."

"No," Braugh answered at length. "The senses are only
senses at best—and in time they tire of everything. You
cannot satisfy the imagination with whipped cream in new
forms and flavors."

"Then I can send you to worlds of extra dimensions that will stun your imagination. There is a system I know that will entertain you forever with its incongruity—where, if you sorrow you scratch your ear, or its equivalent, where, if you love you eat a squash, where, if you die you burst out laughing . . . There is a dimension I have seen where one can assuredly perform the impossible; where wits daily compete in the composition of animate paradox, and where the mere feat of turning oneself mentally inside out is called 'chrythna,' which is to say, 'corny' in the American jargon.

"Do you want to probe the emotions in classical order? I can take you to a world of n-dimensions where, one by one, you may exhaust the intricate nuances of the twenty-seven primary emotions—always taking notes, of course—and thence go on to combinations and permutations to the amount of twenty-seven raised to the power of twenty-seven. Mathematicians would say: 27×10^{27}. Come, which will you enjoy?"

"None," Braugh said impatiently. "It's obvious, my friend, that you do not understand the ego of man. The ego is not a childish thing to be entertained with toys, and yet it *is* a childish thing in that it yearns for the unattainable."

"Yours seems to be an animal thing in that it does not laugh, Mr. Braugh. It has been said that man is the only laughing animal on earth. Take away the humor and only the animal is left. You have no sense of humor, Mr. Braugh."

"The ego," Braugh continued intently, "desires only what it cannot hope to attain. Once a thing can be possessed, it is no longer desired. Can you grant me a reality in which I may possess some thing which I desire because I cannot possibly attain it, and by that same possession not break the qualifications of my desire? Can you do this?"

"I'm afraid," the voice answered with slight amusement, "that your imagination reasons too deviously for me."

"Ah," Braugh muttered, half to himself. "I was afraid of that. Why does creation seem to be run by second-rate individuals not half so clever as myself? Why this mediocrity?"

"You seek to attain the unattainable," the voice argued in reasonable tones, "and by that act not to attain it. The contradiction is within yourself. Would you be changed?"

"No . . . no, not changed." Braugh shook his head. He stood deep in thought, then sighed and tamped out his cigarette. "There's only one solution for my problem."

"And that is?"

"Erasure. If you cannot satisfy a desire, you must explain it away. If a man cannot find love, he writes a psychological treastise on passion. I shall do much the same thing . . ."

He shrugged and moved toward the veil. There was a chuckle behind him and the voice asked, "Where does that ego of yours take you, O man?"

"To the truth of things," Braugh called. "If I can't slake my yearning, at least I shall find out why I yearn."

"You'll find the truth only in hell or limbo, Mr. Braugh."

"How so?"

"Because truth is always hell."

"And hell is truth, no doubt. Nevertheless I'm going there—to hell or limbo, or wherever truth is to be found."

"May you find the answers pleasant, O man."

"Thank you."

"And may you learn to laugh."

But Braugh no longer heard, for he had passed the veil.

He found himself standing before a high desk—a judge's bench, almost—as high as the top of his head. Around him was nothing else. A sulfurous fog filled wherever he was, concealing everything but this awesome bench. Braugh tilted his head back and peered up. Staring down at him from the other side was a tiny face, ancient as sin, whiskered and cockeyed. It was on a shriveled little head that was covered with a pointed hat. Like a sorcerer's cap.

Or a dunce cap, Braugh thought.

Dimly, behind the head, he made out towering shelves of books and files labeled: A—AB, AC—AD, and so on. Some were curiously labeled: #—, &—¼, *—c. Incomprehensible. There was also a gleaming black pot of ink and a rack of quill pens. An enormous hourglass completed the picture. Inside the hourglass a spider had spun a web and was crawling shakily along the strands.

The little man croaked: "A-mazing! AS-tounding! IN-credible!"

Braugh was annoyed.

The little man hunched forward like Quasimodo and got his clown face as close as possible to Braugh's. He reached down a knobby finger and poked Braugh gingerly. He was astonished. He threw himself back and bawled: "THAMM-uz! DA-gon! RIMM-on!"

There was an invisible bustle and three more little men bounced up behind the bench and gaped at Braugh. The inspection went on for minutes. Braugh was irritated.

"All right," he said. "That's enough. Say something. Do something."

"It speaks!" they shouted incredulously. "It's alive!" They pressed noses together and gabbled swiftly: "MostamazingthingDagonhespeaksRimmoncoulditbealive-andhumanBelialtherehastobesomereasonforitThammuzif-youthinksobutIcan'tsay."

Then it stopped.

Further inspection.

One said, "Find out how it got here."

"Not at all. Find out what it is. Animal? Vegetable? Mineral?"

A third said, "Find out where it's from."

"Have to be cautious with aliens, you know."

"Why? We're absolutely unvulnerable."

"You think so? What about the Angle Azrael's visit?"

"You mean ang—"

"Don't say it! Don't say it!"

A fierce argument broke out while Braugh tapped his toe impatiently. Apparently they came to a decision. The No. 1 warlock aimed an accusing finger at Braugh and said, "What are you doing here?"

"The point is, where am I?" Braugh snapped.

The little man turned to brothers Thammuz, Dagon, and Rimmon. "It wants to know where it is," he smirked.

"Then tell it, Belial."

"Get on, Belial. Can't take forever."

"You!" Belial turned on Braugh. "This is Central Administration, Universal Control Center; Belial, Rimmon, Dagon, and Thammuz, acting for His Supremacy."

"That would be Satan?"

"Don't be familiar."

"I came here to see Satan."

"It wants to see the Lord Lucifer!" They were appalled. Then Dagon jabbed the others with his sharp little elbows and placed a finger alongside his nose with a shrewd look.

"Spy," he said. To elaborate, he gestured significantly upward.

"Don't say it, Dagon! Don't say it!"

"Been known to happen," Belial said, flipping the pages of a giant ledger. "It certainly don't belong here. No deliveries scheduled for—" He turned over the hourglass, infuriating the spider. "—for six hours. It's not dead because it don't stink. It's not alive because only the dead are called. Question still is: What is it and what do we do with it?"

Thammuz said, "Divination. Absolutely unfallible."

"Right you are, Thammuz."

Belial eyed Braugh. "Name?"

"Christian Braugh."

"He said it! He said it! We didn't."

"Let's try Onomancy," Dagon said. "C, third letter. H, eighth letter. R, eighteenth letter, and so on. It's all right, Belial; spelling isn't the same as saying. Take total sum. Double it and add ten. Divide by two and a half, then subtract original total."

They counted, added, divided and subtracted. Quills scratched on parchment; a buzzing noise sounded. At last Belial held up his scrap and scrutinized it dubiously. They all scrutinized theirs. As one man, they shrugged and tore the ciphering up.

"I can't understand it," Rimmon complained. "We always get five."

"Never mind." Belial fixed Braugh with a stern look. "You! When born?"

"December eighteenth, nineteen hundred and thirteen."

"Time?"

"Twelve-fifteen A.M."

"Star charts!" Thammuz shouted. "Genethliacs never fail!"

Clouds of dust choked Braugh as they ransacked the shelves behind them and pulled out huge parchment sheets that unrolled like window shades. This time it took them fifteen minutes to produce their results which they again examined carefully and again tore up.

Rimmon said, "It *is* odd."

Dagon said, "Why do they always turn out to be born under the Sign of Porpoise?"

"Maybe it *is* a porpoise. That would explain everything."

"We'd better take it into the laboratory for a check. Himself will be plenty peeved if we muff this one."

They leaned over the bench and beckoned. Braugh snorted and obeyed. He walked around the side of the bench and found himself before a small door framed in books. The four little Central Administrators bounced down from the desk and crowded him through. He had to double over; they just about came up to his waist.

Braugh entered the infernal laboratory. It was a circular room with a low ceiling, tile floor and walls, cupboards, and shelves, crammed with dusty glassware, alchemist's gadgets, books, bones and bottles, none labeled. In the center was a large, flat millstone. The axle hole had a charred look, but there wasn't any chimney above it.

Belial rooted in a corner, tossed umbrellas and branding irons, and came out with an armful of dry sticks. "Altar fire," he said and tripped. The sticks went flying. Braugh solemnly bent to pick up the pieces of wood.

"Sortilege!" Rimmon squawked. He yanked a glittering lizard out of a box and began scribbling on its back with a piece of charcoal, noting the order in which Braugh picked up the altar fire makings.

"Which way is east?" Rimmon asked, crawling after the lizard which seemed bent on business of its own. Thammuz pointed down. Rimmon nodded curt thanks and began an involved computation on the lizard's back. Gradually his hand moved more slowly. By the time Braugh had heaped the wood on the altar, Rimmon was holding the lizard by the tail, wondering at his notations. At last he gave up and shoved the lizard under the wood. It caught fire instantly.

"Salamander," Rimmon said. "Not bad, eh?"

Dagon was inspired. "Pyromancy!" He ran to the flames, poked his nose within an inch of the fire and chanted.

"Aleph, beth, gimel, daleth, he, vau, zayin, cheth . . ."
Belial fidgeted uneasily and muttered to Thammuz, "Last
time he tried that, he fell asleep."

"It's the Hebrew," Thammuz said as though he were
explaining.

The chant faded and Dagon, eyes blissfully shut, slid
forward into the crackling flames.

"Did it again," Belial snapped.

They dragged Dagon out of the fire and slapped his face
until his whiskers stopped burning. Thammuz sniffed the
stench of burning hair, then pointed to the smoke drifting
overhead. "Capnomancy!" he said. "It can't fail. We'll find
out what this thing is yet."

All four joined hands and skipped around the smoke cloud,
puffing at it with pursed lips. Eventually the smoke disappeared. Thammuz looked sour. "It failed."

"Only because *it* didn't join in."

They glared angrily at Braugh. "You it! Deceitful it!"

"Not at all," Braugh said. "I'm not hiding anything. Of
course, I don't believe a particle of what's happening here,
but that doesn't matter. I have all the time in the world."

"Doesn't matter? What d'you mean, you don't believe?"

"Why, you can't make me believe that you clowns have
anything to do with truth—much less His Majesty, Father
Satan."

"Why, you ass, *we're* Satan."

Then they lowered their voices and added for unseen ears,
"So to speak. No offense. Merely referring to power of
attorney." Their indignation revived. "But we have the
power to ferret *you* out, it. We'll track you down. We'll tear
the veil, break the seal, remove the mask, make all known
with Sideromancy. Bring on the iron!"

Dagon trundled out a little wheelbarrow filled with lumps
of iron, all roughly shaped like fish. To Braugh he said:
"This divination never fails. Pick a carp . . . any carp."
Braugh selected an iron fish at random and Dagon snatched it
from him irritably and plunked it into a tiny crucible. He set
the crucible on the fire and Thammuz pumped a hand-
bellows until the iron was white-hot. "It can't fail," he
puffed. "Sideromancy never fails." The four waited and

waited; Braugh didn't know for what. At last they sighed.

"It failed," Braugh said.

"Let's try Molybdomancy," Belial suggested.

They nodded and dropped the iron into a pot of solid lead. It hissed and fumed as though it had been dropped into water. Presently the lead melted. Belial tipped the pot over and the silvery liquid crept across the floor. Braugh got his feet out of the way. Belial sounded his "A": "Me-me-me-me-me-me-Meeeeeeeee!" but before he could begin the incantation there was a pistol-shot crack. One of the floor tiles had shattered. The molten lead disappeared with a sizzling, and the next instant a fountain of water spurted up through the hole.

Belial said: "Busted the pipes again."

"Pegomancy!" Dagon cried eagerly. He approached the fountain with a reverent look, knelt before it and began to drone: "Alif, ba', ta', tha', jim, ha', kha', dal . . ." In thirty seconds his eyes closed rapturously and he fell forward into the water.

"It's the Arabic," Thammuz said. "Got to get him dry or he'll catch his death."

Thammuz and Belial took Dagon by the arms and dragged him to the altar fire. They circled the bright blaze several times and were about to stop when Dagon choked: "Keep me moving. Gyromancy."

"But you've run out of alphabets," Thammuz said.

"No. There's still Greek. Make circles. Alpha, beta, gamma, delta, oi!"

"No, epsilon next," Thammuz said. Then, "Oi!"

Braugh turned to see what they were staring and oiing at.

A girl had just entered the laboratory. She was short, redheaded and delightfully the right side of plump. Her coppery hair was drawn back in a Greek knot. She wore an expression of exasperation and fury, and nothing else. Braugh muttered: "Oi!"

"So!" she rapped. "At it again. How many times—" she broke off, ran to a wall, seized a prodigious glass retort, and hurled it straight and true. When the pieces stopped clattering, she said, "How many times have I told you to stop this nonsense or I'd report you!"

Belial tried to stanch his bleeding cuts and attempted an innocent smile. "Why, Astarte, you wouldn't tell Himself, would you?"

"I will not have you smashing my ceiling and dripping things down on my office. First molten lead; then water; four weeks' work ruined. My Sheraton desk ruined." She twisted her torso and exhibited a red scar that ran down from a shoulder. "Twelve inches of skin ruined!"

"We'll pay for the replacement, Astarte."

"And who'll pay for the pain?"

"Tannic acid is best," Braugh said seriously. "You brew extra strong tea and make a poultice. Numbs the pain."

The red head turned, and Astarte lanced Braugh with level green eyes. "Who's this?"

"We don't know," Belial stammered. "It just walked up to my desk and—That's why we were—It might be a porpoise. . . ."

Braugh stepped forward and took the girl's hand. "I'm a human. Alive. Sent here by one of your colleagues; name unknown. My name is Braugh. Christian Braugh."

Her hand was cool and firm. "It might have been—No matter. The name is Astarte. I, too, am a Christian."

Central Administration clapped palms over ears to block the dirty words.

"Satan's crew Christians?" Braugh was surprised.

"Some of us. Why not? We all were before The Fall."

There was no answer to that. He said, "Is there some place where we can get away from these maladroits?"

"There's always my office."

"I like offices."

He also liked Astarte; much more than liked. She led him into her office on the floor below, very large, most impressive, swept a pile of paperwork off a chair and invited him to sit down. She sprawled before the ruin of her desk and, after one malevolent glance at the ceiling, asked for his story. She listened.

"Unusual," she said. "You're looking for Satan, Lord of the counterworld. Well, this is the only hell there is, and Himself is the only Satan there is. You're in the right place."

Braugh was perplexed. "Hell? Dante's Inferno? Fire, brimstone and so forth?"

She shook her head. "Just another poet using his imagination. The real torments are Freudian. You can discuss it with Alighieri when you meet him." She smiled at Braugh's solemn expression. "All this brings us to something vital. Sure you're not dead? Sometimes they forget."

Braugh nodded.

"Hmmm . . ." She made an interested survey. "You'll bear looking into. I've never had anything to do with the live ones. Sure you're alive?"

"Quite sure."

"And what's your business with Father Satan?"

"The truth," Braugh said. "I wanted to learn the truth about all, and I was sent here by that nameless Thing. Why Father Satan should be the official purveyor of the truth rather than—" He hesitated.

"You can say it, Christian."

"Rather than God in Heaven, I don't know. But to me the truth is worth any price to put to rest this damned yearning that tortures me. So I should like very much to have an interview."

Astarte rapped polished nails on the desk and smiled. "This," she said, "is going to be delicious." She arose, opened the office door and pointed down the sulfur-fogged corridor. "Straight ahead," she told Braugh. "Then take the first left. Keep on and you can't miss."

"I'll see you again?" he asked as he set off.

"You'll see me again," Astarte laughed.

This, Braugh thought as he inched through the yellow mist, is all too ridiculous. You pass a veil seeking the Citadel of Truth. You are entertained by four absurd sorcerers and by a redheaded divinity. Then off you go down a foggy corridor, turn left and straight ahead for an interview with the Knower of All Things.

And what of my yearning for the unattainable? What of the truths that will explain it all away? Is there no solemnity, no dignity, no authority one can respect? Why all this low comedy; this saturnalian slapstick that pervades Hell?

He turned the corner to the left and kept on. The short hall ended in a pair of green baize doors. Almost timidly, Braugh pushed them open and to his great relief found himself merely stepping onto a stone bridge—rather like the Bridge of Sighs, he thought. Behind him was the enormous facade of the building he had just left; a wall of brimstone blocks stretching left and right and upward and downward until it was lost from sight. Before him was a smallish building shaped like a globe.

He stepped quickly across the bridge, for these mists around him made him queasy. He paused only a moment to gather his courage before a second pair of baize doors, then tried to mount a debonair manner and pushed them in. You do not, he told himself, come before Satan nonchalantly, but there's such a quality of insanity in hell that it's rubbed off on me.

It was a gigantic room, a sort of file room, and again Braugh was relieved at having the awesome interview put a little farther into the future. The office was round as a planetarium and was crammed with a vast adding machine so enormous that Braugh could not believe his eyes. There were five levels of scaffolding before the keyboard and one little dried-out clerk, wearing spectacles the size of binoculars, rushed back and forth, climbing up and down, punching keys with lightning speed.

More as an excuse for delaying the rather threatening interview with Father Satan, Braugh watched the wheezing clerk scurry before those keys, punching them so rapidly that they chattered like a hundred outboard motors. This little old chap, Braugh thought, has put in an eternity computing sin totals and death totals and all sorts of statistical totals. He looks like a total himself.

Aloud, Braugh said: "Hello there!"

Without faltering the clerk said, "What is it?" His voice was drier than his skin.

"Those figures can wait a moment, can't they?"

"Sorry. They can't."

"Will you stop a moment!" Braugh shouted. "I want to see your boss."

The clerk came to a dead stop and turned, removing the binocular spectacles very slowly.

"Thank you," Braugh said. "Now, look, my man, I'd like to see His Black Majesty, Father Satan. Astarte said—"

"That's me," said the little old man.

The wind was knocked out of Braugh.

For a fleeting instant a smile flickered across the dried-out face. "Yes, that's me, son. I'm Satan."

And despite all his vivid imagination, Braugh had to believe. He slumped down on the lowermost tread of the steps that led up to the scaffoldings. Satan chuckled faintly and touched a clutch on the gigantic adding machine. There was a meshing of gears and with the sound of freewheeling, the machine began to cluck softly while the keys clacked automatically.

His Diabolic Majesty came creaking down the stairs and seated himself alongside Braugh. He took out a tattered silk handkerchief and began polishing his glasses. He was just a nice little old man sitting friendly-like alongside a stranger, ready for a back-fence gossip. At last he said, "What's on your mind, son?"

"W-well, your Highness—" Braugh began.

"You can call me Father, my boy."

"But why should I? I mean—" Braugh broke off in embarrassment.

"Well now, I guess you're a little worried about that heaven-and-hell business, eh?"

Braugh nodded.

Satan sighed and shook his head. "Don't know what to do about that," he said. "Fact is, son, it's all the same thing. Naturally I let it get around in certain quarters that there's two places. Got to keep certain folks on their toes. But the truth is, it's not really so. I'm all there is, son; God or Satan or Siva or Official Coordinator or Nature—anything you want to call it."

With a rush of good feeling toward this friendly old man, Braugh said, "I call you a fine old man. I'll be happy to call you Father."

"Well, that's nice of you, son. Glad you feel that way. You understand, of course, that we couldn't let just anyone see me this way. Might instill disrespect. But you're different. Special."

"Yes, sir. Thank you, sir."

"Got to have efficiency. *Tsk!* Got to frighten folks now and then. Got to have respect, you understand. Can't run things without respect."

"I understand, sir."

"Got to have efficiency. Can't be running life all day long, all year long, all eternity long without efficiency. Can't have efficiency without respect."

Braugh said, "Absolutely, sir," while within him a hideous uncertainty grew. This was a nice old man, but this was also a garrulous, maundering old man. His Satanic Majesty was a dull creature not nearly so clever as Christian Braugh.

"What I always say," the old man went on, rubbing his knee reflectively, "is that love and worship and all that—you can have 'em. They're nice, but I'll take efficiency anytime . . . leastways for a body in my position. Now then, son, what was on your mind?"

Mediocrity, Braugh thought bitterly. He said, "The truth, Father Satan. I came seeking the truth."

"And what do you want with the truth, Christian?"

"I just want to know it, Father Satan. I came seeking it. I want to know why we are, why we live, why we yearn. I want to know all that."

"Well, now . . ." the old man chuckled. "That's quite an order, son. Yes, sir, quite an order indeed."

"Can you tell me, Father Satan?"

"A little, Christian. Just a little. What was it you wanted to know, mostly?"

"What there is inside us that makes us seek the unattainable. What are those forces that pull and tug and surge within us? What is this ego of mine that gives me no rest, that seeks no rest, that frets at doubts, and yet when they're resolved, searches for new ones. What is all this?"

"Why," Father Satan said, pointing to his adding machine. "It's that gadget there. It runs everything."

"That?"

"That."

"Runs everything?"

"Everything that I run, and I run everything there is." The old man chuckled again, then held out the binoculars.

"You're an unusual boy, Christian. First person that ever had the decency to pay old Father Satan a visit . . . alive, that is. I'll return the favor. Here."

Wondering, Braugh accepted the spectacles.

"Put 'em on," the old man said. "See for yourself."

And then the wonder was compounded, for as Braugh slipped the glasses over his head he found himself peering with the eyes of the universe at all the universe. And the adding contraption was no longer a machine for summing up totals with additions and subtractions; it was a vastly complex marionetteer's crossbar from which an infinity of shimmering silver threads descended.

And with his all-seeing eyes, through the spectacles of Father Satan, Braugh saw how each thread was attached to the nape of the neck of a creature, and how each living entity danced the dance of life as directed by Satan's efficient machine. Braugh crept up to the first-level scaffold and reached toward the lower bank of keys. One he pressed at random and on a pale planet something hungered and killed. A second, and it felt remorse. A third, and it forgot. A fourth, and half a continent away another something awoke five minutes early and so began a chain of events that culminated in discovery and hideous punishment for the killer.

Braugh backed away from the adding machine and slipped the glasses up to his brow. The machine went on clucking. Almost absently, without surprise, Braugh noted that the meticulous chronometer which filled the top of the dome had ticked away a space of three months' time.

"This," he thought, "is a ghastly answer, a cruel answer, and Mr. Thing in the shelter was right. Truth is hell. We're puppets. We're little better than dead things hung from a string, simulating life. Up here an old man, nice but not overly intelligent, clicks a few keys and down there we take it for free will, fate, Karma, evolution, nature, a thousand false things. This is a sour discovery. Why must the truth be shoddy?"

He glanced down. Old Father Satan was still seated on the steps, but his head slumped a little to one side, his eyes were half-closed, and he mumbled indistinctly about work and rest and not enough of it.

"Father Satan . . ."

"Yes, my boy?" The old man roused himself slightly.

"This is true? We all dance to your key-tapping?"

"All of you, my boy. All of you." He yawned prodigiously. "You all think yourselves free, Christian, but you all dance to my playing."

"Then, Father, grant me one thing . . . One very small thing. There is, in a small corner of your celestial empire, a very tiny planet, an insignificant speck we call Earth."

"Earth? Earth? Can't say I recollect it offhand, son, but I can look it up . . ."

"No, don't bother, sir. It's there. I know because I come from there. Grant me this favor: break the cords that bind it. Let Earth go free."

"You're a good boy, Christian, but a foolish boy. You ought to know I can't do that."

"In all your kingdom," Braugh pleaded, "there are souls too numerous to count. There are suns and planets too many to measure. Surely this one tiny bit of dust—You who own so much can surely part with so little."

"No, my boy, couldn't do it. Sorry."

"You who alone know freedom . . . Would you deny it to just a few others?"

But the Coordinator of All slumbered.

Braugh pulled the glasses back before his eyes. Let him sleep then, while Braugh, Satan *pro tem.*, takes over. Oh, we'll be repaid for this disappointment. We'll have giddy time writing novels in flesh and blood. And perhaps, if we can find the cord attached to my neck and search out the correct key, we may do something to free Christian Braugh. Yes, here is a challenging unattainable which may be attained and lead to fresh challenges.

He looked over his shoulder guiltily to see whether Father Satan was aware of his meddling. There might be condign punishment. As his eyes inspected the frail Ruler of All, he was stunned, transfixed. He gazed up, then down, then up again. His hands trembled, then his arms, and at last his whole body shook uncontrollably. For the first time in his life, he began to laugh. It was genuine laughter, not the token laughter he had so often been forced to fake in the past. The gusts and bursts rang through the domed room and reverberated.

Father Satan awoke with a start and cried, "Christian! What is it, my boy?"

Laughter of frustration? Laughter of relief? Laughter of hell or limbo? He could not tell as he shook at the sight of the silver thread that stretched from the nape of Satan's neck and turned him, too, into a marionette . . . a tendril that stretched up and up and up into lost heights toward some other vaster machine operated by some other vaster marionette hidden in the still-unknowable reaches of the cosmos—

The blessedly unknowable cosmos.

V

Now in the beginning all was darkness. There was neither land nor sea nor sky nor the circling stars. There was nothing. Then came Yaldabaoth and rent the light from the darkness. And the darkness He gathered up and formed into the night and the skies. And the light He gathered up and formed the Sun and the stars. Then from the flesh of His flesh and the blood of His blood did Yaldabaoth form the earth and all things upon it.

But the children of Yaldabaoth were new and green to living and unlearned, and the race did not bear fruit. And as the children of Yaldabaoth diminished in numbers, they cried out unto their Lord: "Grant us a sign, Great God, that we may know how to increase and multiply! Grant us a sign, O Lord, that Thy good and mighty race may not perish from Thine earth!"

And lo! Yaldabaoth withdrew Himself from the face of His importunate people and they were sore at heart and sinful, thinking their Lord had forsaken them. And their paths were paths of evil until a prophet arose whose name was Maart. Then did Maart gather the children of Yaldabaoth around him and spoke to them, saying: "Evil are thy ways, O people of Yaldabaoth, to doubt thy God. For He has given a sign of faith unto you."

Then gave they answer, saying: "Where is this sign?"

And Maart went into the high mountains and with him was a vast concourse of people. Nine days and nine nights did they travel even unto the peak of Mount Sinar. And at the crest of Mount Sinar all were struck with wonder and fell on their knees, crying: "Great is God! Great are His works!"

For lo! Before them blazed a mighty curtain of fire.

BOOK OF MAART; XIII: 29-37

Pass the veil toward what reality? There's no sense trying to make up my mind. I can't. God knows, that's been the agony of living for me—trying to make up my mind. How can I when I've felt nothing—when nothing's touched me— ever! Take this or that. Take coffee or tea. Buy the black gown or the silver. Marry Lord Buckley or live with Freddy Witherton. Let Finchley make love to me or stop posing for him. No—there's no sense even trying.

How that veil burns in the doorway! Like rainbow moiré. There goes Sidra. Passes through as though nothing was there. Doesn't seem to hurt. That's good. God knows, I could stand anything except being hurt. No one left but Bob and myself—and he doesn't seem to be in any hurry. No, there's Chris, sort of hiding in the organ alcove. My turn now, I suppose. Wish it wasn't, but I can't stay here forever. Where to?

To nowhere?

Yes, that's it. Nowhere.

In this world I'm leaving there's never been any place for me; the real me. The world wanted nothing from me but my beauty; not what was inside me. I want to be useful. I want to belong. Perhaps if I belonged—if living had some purpose for me, this lump of ice in my heart might melt. I could learn to do things, feel things, enjoy things. Even learn to fall in love.

Yes, I'm going to nowhere.

Let the new reality that needs me, that wants me, that can use me . . . Let that reality make the decision and call me to itself. For if I must choose, I know I'll choose wrong again. And if I'm not needed anywhere; if I go through that burning

to wander forever in blank space . . . still I'm better off.
What else have I been doing all my life?

Take me, you who want and need me!

How cool the veil . . . like scented sprays on the skin.

*And even as the multitude knelt in prayer, Maart cried
aloud: "Rise, ye children of Yaldabaoth, and behold!"*

*Then they did arise and were struck dumb and trembled.
For through the curtain of fire stepped a beast that chilled the
hearts of all. To the height of eight cubits it towered and its
skin was pink and white. The hair of its head was yellow and
its body was long and curving like unto a sickly tree. And all
was covered with loose folds of white fur.*

BOOK OF MAART; XIII: 38-39

God in Heaven!

Is this the reality that called me? This the reality that needs
me?

That sun . . . so high . . . with its blue-white evil eye,
like that Italian artist . . . Mountain tops. They look like
heaps of slime and garbage . . . The valleys down there
. . . festering wounds. The sickroom smell. All rot and ruin.

And those hideous creatures crowding around . . . like
apes made of coal. Not animal. Not human. As though man
made beasts not too well—or beasts made men still worse.
They have a familiar look. The landscape looks familiar.
Somewhere I've seen all this before. Somehow I've been
here before. In dreams of death, maybe . . . Maybe.

This is a reality of death, and it wanted me? Needed me?

*Again the multitude cried out: "Glory be to Yaldabaoth!"
and at the sound of the sacred name the beast turned toward
the curtain of flames whence it had come, and behold! The
curtain was gone.*

BOOK OF MAART; XIII: 40

No retreat?
No way out?
No return to sanity?

But it was behind me a moment ago, the veil. No escape.
Listen to the sounds they make. The swilling of swine. Do
they think they're worshiping me? No. This can't be real. No
reality was ever so horrid. A ghastly trick . . . like the one
we played on Lady Sutton. I'm in the shelter now. Bob Peel's
played a trick and given us some new kind of drug. Secretly.
I'm lying on the divan, dreaming and groaning. I'll wake up
soon. Or faithful Dig will wake me . . . before these frights
come any closer.

I must wake up!

*With a loud cry, the beast of the fire ran through the
multitude. Through all the host it ran and thundered down the
mountainside. And the shrill sounds of its cries struck fear
like unto the fear of the sound of beaten brazen shields.*

*And as it passed under the low boughs of the mountain
trees, the children of Yaldabaoth cried again in alarm, for
the beast shed its white furred hide in a manner horrible to
behold. And the skin remained clinging to the trees. And the
beast ran farther, a hideous pink-and-white warning to all
transgressors.*

BOOK OF MAART; XIII: 41-43

Quick! Quick! Run through them before they touch me
with their filthy hands. If this is a nightmare, running will
wake me. If this is real—but it can't be. That such a cruel
thing should happen to me! No. Were the gods jealous of my
beauty? No. The gods are never jealous. They are men.

My dressing gown—

Gone.

No time to go back for it. Run naked, then. Listen to them
howl at me—rave at me. Down! Down! Quickly and down
the mountain. This rotten earth. Sucking. Clinging.

Oh, God! They're following.

Not to worship.

Why can't I wake up?

My breath—like knives.

Close. I hear them. Closer and closer and close!

WHY CAN'T I WAKE UP?

● ● ●

*And Maart cried aloud: "Take ye this beast for an offering
to our Lord Yaldabaoth!"*

*Then did the multitude raise courage and gird its loins.
With clubs and stones all pursued the beast down the slopes
of Mount Sinar, many sore afraid but all chanting the name
of the Lord.*

*And in a field a shrewdly thrown stone brought the beast to
its knees, still screaming in a voice horrible to hear. Then did
the stout warriors smite it many times with strong clubs until
at last the cries ceased and the beast was still. And out of the
foul body did come a poisoned red water that sickened all
who beheld it.*

*But when the beast was brought to the High Temple of
Yaldabaoth and placed in a cage before the altar, its cries
once more resounded, desecrating the sacred halls. And the
High Priests were troubled, saying: "What evil offering is
this to place before Yaldabaoth, Lord of Gods?"*

BOOK OF MAART; XIII: 44-47

Pain.

Burning and scalding.

Can't move.

No dream ever so long . . . So real. This, then, real?
Real. And I? Real too. A stranger in a reality of filth and
torture. Why? Why? Why?

My head feels twisted inside. Tangled. Jumbled.

This is torture, and somewhere . . . someplace . . . I've
heard that word before. Torture. It has a pleasant sound.
Torment? No, torture better. The sound of a madrigal. Name
of a boat. Title of a prince. Prince Torture. Prince Torment?
Beauty and the Prince.

So twisted in my head. Great lights and blinding sounds
that come and go and have no meaning.

Once upon a time the beauty tortured a man—They say.
Said.

His name was?

Prince Torment? No. Finchley. Yes. Digby Finchley.

Digby Finchley, they say—said—loved an ice-goddess
named Theone Dubedat.

The pink ice-goddess.
Where is she now?

And while the beast did moan threats upon the altar, the Sanhedrin of Priests held council, and to the council came Maart, saying: "O ye priests of Yaldabaoth, raise up your voices in praise of our Lord, for he was wroth and turned His face from us. And lo! A sacrifice has been vouchsafed unto us that we may please Him and make our peace with Him."

Then spoke the High Priest, saying: "How now, Maart? Do ye say that this is a sacrifice for our Lord?"

And Maart spoke: "Yea. For it is a beast of fire and through the holy fire of Yaldabaoth it shall return whence it came."

And the High Priest asked: "Is this offering seemly in the sight of Our Lord?"

Then Maart answered: "All things are from Yaldabaoth. Therefore all things are seemly in His sight. Perchance through this offering Yaldabaoth will grant us a sign that His people may not vanish from the earth. Let the beast be offered."

Then did the Sanhedrin agree, for the priests were sore afraid lest the children of the Lord be no more.

BOOK OF MAART; XIII: 48-54

See the silly monkeys dance.
They dance around and around and around.
And they snarl.
Almost like speaking.
Almost like—
I must stop the singing in my head. The ring-ding-singing. Like the days when Dig was working hard and I would take those back-breaking poses and hold them hour after hour with only a five-minute break now and then and I would get ringing dizzy and faint off the dais and Dig would drop his palette and come running with those big, solemn eyes of his ready to cry.

Men shouldn't cry, but I knew it was because he loved me and I wanted to love him or somebody, but I had no need then. I didn't need anything but finding myself. That's the treasure hunt. And now I'm found. This is me. Now I have a need and an ache and a loneliness deep inside for Dig and his big, solemn eyes. To see him all eyes and fright at the fainting spells and dancing around me with a cup of tea.

Dancing. Dancing. Dancing.

And thumping their chests and grunting and thumping.

And when they snarl the spittle drools and gleams on their yellow fangs. And those seven with the rotting shreds of cloth across their chests, marching almost like royalty, almost like humans.

See the silly monkeys dance.

They dance around and around and around and . . .

So it came to pass that the high holiday of Yaldabaoth was nigh. And on that day did the Sanhedrin throw wide the portals of the temple and the hosts of the children of Yaldabaoth did enter. Then did the priests remove the beast from the cage and drag it to the altar. Each of four priests held a limb and spread the beast wide across the altar stone, and the beast uttered evil, blasphemous sounds.

Then cried the prophet Maart: "Rend this thing to pieces that the stench of its evil death may rise to please the nostrils of Yaldabaoth."

And the four priests, strong and holy, put strong hands to the limbs of the beast so that its struggles were wondrous to behold, and the light of evil on its hideous hide struck terror into all.

And as Maart lit the altar fires, a great trembling shook the firmament.

BOOK OF MAART: XIII: 55-59

Digby, come to me!
Digby, wherever you are, come to me!
Digby, I need you.
This is Theone.
Theone.
Your ice-goddess.
No longer ice, Digby.
I can't stay sane much longer.

Wheels whirl faster and faster and faster . . .
In my head, faster and faster and faster . . .
Digby, come to me.
I need you.
Prince Torment.
Torture.

Then did the vaults of the temple split asunder with a
thunderous roar, and all that were gathered there quailed in
fear, and their bowels were as water. And all beheld the
divine Lord, Yaldabaoth descend from pitch-black skies to
the temple. Yea, to the very altar itself.

And for the space of eternity did the Lord God Yaldabaoth
gaze at the beast of fire, and His sacrifice writhed and
cursed, its evil helpless in the grasp of the pure priests.

BOOK OF MAART; XIII: 59-60

It is the final horror—the final torture.

This monster that floats down from the heavens.

Ape-Man-Beast-Horror.

It is the final joke that it should float down like a thing of
fluff, silk, feathers; a thing of lightness and joy. A monster on
wings of light. A monster with twisted legs and arms and
loathsome body. The head of a Man-Ape . . . torn and broken, smashed and ruined, with those great, glassy, staring
eyes.

Eyes? Where have I—?

THOSE EYES!

This isn't madness. No. Not the ring-ding-singing. No. I
know those eyes—those great, solemn eyes. I've seen them
before. Years ago. Minutes ago. Caged in a zoo? No. Fish
eyes floating in a tank? No. Great, solemn eyes filled with
hopeless love and adoration.

No . . . Let me be wrong.

Those big, solemn eyes of his ready to cry.

Crying, but men shouldn't cry.

No, not Digby. It can't be. Please!

That's where I've seen this place before, seen these man-
animals and the hellish landscape—Digby's drawings. Those

monstrous pictures he drew. For fun, he said, for amusement. Amusement!

But why does he look like this? Why is he rotten and horrifying like the others . . . Like his pictures?

Is this your reality, Digby? Did *you* call me? Did *you* need me, want me?

Digby! Dig. Dig-a-dig-a-by-and-whirl-a-whirl-a-ring-a-ding-a-sing-a . . .

Why don't you listen to me? Hear me? Why do you look at me that way, like a mad thing when only a minute ago you were walking up and down in the shelter trying to make up your mind and you were the first to go through that burning veil and I admired you for that because men should always be brave but not men-ape-beast-monsters . . .

And with a voice like unto shattering mountains, the Lord Yaldabaoth spoke to His people, saying: "Now praise ye the Lord, my children, for one has been sent unto you to be thy queen and consort to thy God."

With one voice the host cried out unto him: "Praise our Lord, Yaldabaoth."

And Maart made obeisance before the Lord and prayed: "A sign to Thy children to Lord God, that they may increase and multiply."

Then the Lord God reached out to the beast and touched it, raising it from the altar fires and the hands of the pure priests, and behold! The evil cried out for the last time and fled the body of the beast, leaving only a sweet song in its place. And the Lord spoke unto Maart, saying: "I will give you a sign."

BOOK OF MAART; XIII: 60-63

Let me die.

Let me die forever.

Let me not see or hear or feel the—

The?

What?

The pretty monkeys that dance around and around and around so pretty so nice so good everything pretty and nice and good while the great, solemn eyes stare into my soul and darling Dig-a-dig-a-by touches me with hands so strangely changed so prettily nicely goodly changed by the turpentine maybe or the ochre or bile green or burnt umber or sepia or chrome yellow which always seemed to decorate his fingers each time he dropped palette and brushes to come to me when I—

Love changes everything. Yes. How good to be loved by dear Digby. How warm and comforting to be loved and to be needed and to want one alone in all the millions and to find him so strangely beautifully solemnly walking flying descending in a reality like that of Sutton Castle when shelter can't see and I really knew that cliffs down-ran me with pretty monkeys laughing and capering and worshiping so funny so funny so nice so good so pretty so funny so . . .

Then did the children of Yaldabaoth take the sign of the Lord to their hearts and lo! Thenceforth did they increase and multiply after the example of their Lord God and His Consort on high.

Thus endeth the BOOK OF MAART

VI

At the moment when he entered the burning veil, Robert Peel stopped in astonishment. He had not yet made up his mind. To him, a man of objectivity and logic, this was an amazing experience. It was the first time in his life that he had not made a lightning decision. It was proof of how profoundly the Thing in the shelter had shaken him.

He stayed where he was, sheathed in a mist of fire that flickered like an opal and and was far thicker than any veil. It surrounded him and isolated him, for surely he should have been aware of others passing through, but there was no one. It was not beautiful to Peel, but it was interesting. The color dispersion was wide, he noted, and embraced hundreds of fine gradations of the visible spectrum.

Peel took stock. With the little data he had at hand, he judged that he was standing somewhere outside time and space or between dimensions. Evidently the Thing in the shelter had placed them *en rapport* with the matrix of existence so that mere intent as they entered the veil could govern the direction they would take on emergence. The veil was more or less a pivot on which they could spin into any desired existence in any space and any time; which brought Peel back to the question of his own choice.

Carefully he considered, weighed and balanced what he already possessed against what he might receive. So far he was satisfied with his life. He had plenty of money, a respected profession as consultant engineer, a splendid house in Chelsea Square, an attractive, stimulating wife. To give all this up in reliance on the unspecified promises of an unvalidated donor would be idiocy. Peel had learned never to make a change without good and sufficient reason.

"I am not adventurous by nature," Peel thought coldly. "It is not my business to be so. Romance does not attract me, and I suspect the unknown. I like to keep what I have. The acquisitive sense is strong in me, and I'm not ashamed to be a possessive man. Now I want to keep what I have. No change. There can be no other decision for me. Let the others have their romance; I keep my world precisely as it is. Repeat: No change."

The decision had taken him all of one minute, an unusually long time for the engineer, but this was an unusual situation. He strode forward firmly, a precise, bald, bearded martinet, and emerged into the dungeon corridor of Sutton Castle.

A few feet down the corridor, a little scullery maid in blue and gray was scurrying directly toward him, a tray in her hands. There was a bottle of ale and an enormous sandwich on the tray. At the sound of Peel's step, she looked up, stopped short, then dropped the tray with a crash.

"What the devil—?" Peel was confounded at the sight of her.

"M-Mr. Peel!" she squawked. She began to scream: "Help! Murder! Help!"

Peel slapped her. "Will you shut up and explain what in blazes you're doing down here this time of night!"

The girl moaned and sputtered. Before he could slap the hysterical creature again, he felt a heavy hand on his shoulder. He turned and was further confounded when he found himself staring into the red, beefy face of a policeman. There was a rather eager expression on that face. Peel gaped, then subsided. He realized that he was in the vortex of unknown phenomena. No sense struggling until he understood the currents.

"Na then, sir," the policeman said. "No call ter strike the gel, sir."

Peel made no answer. He needed more facts. A maid and a policeman. What were they doing down here? The man had come up from behind him. Had he come through the veil? But there was no burning veil; just the heavy shelter door.

"If I heard right, sir, I heard the gel call yer by name. Would yer give it to me, sir?"

"I'm Robert Peel. I'm a guest of Lady Sutton. What is all this?"

"Mr. Peel!" the policeman exclaimed. "What a piece er luck. I'll get me rise for this. I got to take yer into custody, Mr. Peel. Yer under arrest."

"Arrest? You're mad, my man." Peel stepped back and looked over the policeman's shoulder. The shelter door was half-open, enough for him to make a quick inspection. The entire room was turned upside-down, looking as though it had just been subjected to a spring cleaning. There was no one inside.

"I must warn yer not ter resist, Mr. Peel."

The girl emitted a wail.

"See here," Peel said angrily. "What right have you to break into a private residence and prance around making arrests? Who are you?"

"Name of Jenkins, sir. Sutton County Constabulary. And I ain't prancin', sir."

"Then you're serious?"

The policeman pointed majestically up the corridor. "Come along, sir. Best to go quietly."

"Answer me, idiot! Is this a genuine arrest?"

"You ought ter know," replied the policeman with ominous overtones. "Come with me, sir."

Peel gave it up and obeyed. He had learned long ago that when one is confronted with an incomprehensible situation, it is folly to take any action until sufficient data arrives. He preceded the policeman up the corridors and winding stone stairs, the whimpering scullery maid following them. So far he only knew two things: One, something, somewhere, had happened. Two, the police had taken over. All this was confusing, to say the least, but he would keep his head. He prided himself that he was never at a loss.

When they emerged from the cellars Peel received another surprise. It was bright daylight outside. He glanced at his watch. It was forty minutes past midnight. He dropped his wrist and blinked; the unexpected sunlight made him a little ill. The policeman touched his arm and directed him toward the library. Peel immediately strode to the sliding doors and pulled them open.

The library was high, long and gloomy, with a narrow balcony running around it just under the Gothic ceiling. There was a long trestle table centered in the room and at the far end three figures were seated, silhouetted against the sunlight that streamed through the lofty window. Peel stepped in, caught a glimpse of a second policeman on guard alongside the doors, then narrowed his eyes and tried to distinguish faces.

While he peered he sorted out the hubbub of exclamations and surprise that greeted him. He judged that: One, people had been looking for him. Two, he'd been missing for some time. Three, no one expected to find him here in Sutton Castle. Footnote, how did he get back in, anyway? All this pieced together from the astonished voices. Then his eyes accommodated to the light.

One of the three was an angular man with a narrow graying head and deep-furrowed features. He looked familiar to Peel. The second was small and stout with ridiculously fragile glasses perched on a bulbous nose. The third was a woman, and again Peel was surprised to see that it was his wife. Sidra wore a plaid suit and a crimson felt hat.

The angular man quieted the others and said, "Mr. Peel?"

Peel advanced quietly. "Yes?"

"I'm Inspector Ross."

"I thought I recognized you, inspector. We've met before, I believe?"

"We have." Ross nodded curtly, then indicated the stout man. "Dr. Richards."

"How d'you do, doctor." Peel turned to his wife and bowed and smiled. "Sidra? How are you dear?"

In flat tones she said, "Well, Robert."

"I'm afraid I'm rather confused by all this," Peel continued amiably. "Things seem to be happening, or have happened." Enough. This was the right talk. Caution. Commit yourself to nothing until you know.

"They are; they have," Ross said.

"Before we go any further, may I inquire the time?"

Ross was taken aback. "It's two o'clock."

"Thank you." Peel held his watch to his ear, then adjusted the hands. "My watch seems to be running, but somehow it's lost a few hours." He examined their expressions covertly. He would have to navigate with exquisite care solely by the light of their countenances. Then he noticed the desk calendar before Ross, and it was like a punch in the ribs. He swallowed hard. "Is that date quite right, inspector?"

"Of course, Mr. Peel. Sunday, the twenty-third."

His mind screamed: Three days! Impossible! Peel controlled his shock. Easy . . . Easy . . . All right. Somewhere he'd lost three days; for he'd entered the burning veil Thursday, thirty-eight minutes past midnight. Yes. But keep cool. There's more at stake than three lost days. There must be; otherwise why the police? Wait for more data.

Ross said, "We've been looking for you these past three days, Mr. Peel. You disappeared quite suddenly. We're rather surprised to find you back in the castle."

"Ah? Why?" Yes, why indeed? What's happened? What's Sidra doing here glaring like an avenging fury?

"Because, Mr. Peel, you're charged with the willful murder of Lady Sutton."

Shock! Shock! Shock! They were piling on, one after another, and still Peel kept hold of himself. The data was coming in explicitly now. He'd hesitated in the veil for a few minutes at the most, and those minutes in limbo were three days in real space-time. Lady Sutton must have been found dead and he was charged with murder. He knew he was a match for anyone, as a thinking logical man . . . an astute man . . . but he knew he had to steer cautiously.

"I don't understand, inspector. You'd better explain."

"Very well. The death of Lady Sutton was reported early Friday morning. Medical examination proved she died of heart failure, the result of shock. Witnesses' evidence revealed that you had deliberately frightened her with full knowledge of her weak heart and with intent so to kill her. That is murder, Mr. Peel."

"Certainly," Peel said coldly. "If you can prove it. May I ask the identity of your witnesses?"

"Digby Finchley, Christian Braugh. Theone Dubedat, and—" Ross broke off, coughed, and laid the paper aside.

"And Sidra Peel," Peel finished dryly. Again he met his wife's venomous gaze. He understood it all, at last. They'd lost their nerve and selected him for the scapegoat. Sidra would be rid of him; her joyous revenge. Before Ross or Richards could intervene, he grasped Sidra by the arm and dragged her toward a corner of the library.

"Don't be alarmed, Ross. I only want a word alone with my wife. There'll be no violence, I assure you."

Sidra tore her arm free and glared up at Peel, her lips drawn back, revealing the sharp white edges of her teeth.

"You arranged this," Peel said quietly.

"I don't know what you're talking about."

"It was your idea, Sidra."

"It was your murder, Robert."

"And that's your evidence."

"Ours. We're four to one."

"All carefully planned, eh?"

"Braugh is a good writer."

"And I hang for the murder on your evidence. You get the house, my fortune, and get rid of me."

She smiled like a cat.

"And this is the reality you asked for? This is what you planned when you went through the burning veil?"

"What veil?"

"You know what I mean."

"You're insane."

She was genuinely bewildered. He thought: Of course. I wanted my old world just as it was. That would exclude the mysterious Thing in the shelter and the veil through which we all passed. But it doesn't exclude the killing which came before nor what's happening after.

"No, Sidra, not insane," he said. "Merely refusing to be your scapegoat. I won't let you bring it off."

"No?" She turned and called to Ross: "He wants me to bribe the witnesses." She walked back to her chair. "I'm to offer each of them ten thousand pounds."

So it was to be a bloody battle. His mind clicked rapidly. The best defense was an attack and the time was now. "She's lying, inspector. They're all lying. I charge Braugh, Finchley, Miss Dubedat, and my wife with the willful murder of Lady Sutton."

"Don't believe him!" Sidra screamed. "He's trying to lie his way out of it by accusing us. He—"

Peel let her scream, grateful for more time to whip his lies into shape. They must be convincing. Flawless. The truth was impossible. In this new old world of his, the Thing and the veil did not exist.

"The murder of Lady Sutton was planned and executed by those four persons," Peel went on smoothly. "I was the only member of the group to object. You will grant, Inspector Ross, that it sounds far more logical for four people to commit a crime against the will of one, than one against four. And the testimony of four outweighs that of one. Do you agree?"

Ross nodded slowly, fascinated by Peel's detached reasoning. Sidra beat at his shoulder and cried, "He's lying, inspector. Can't you see? If he's telling the truth ask him why he ran away. Ask him where he's been for three days . . ."

Ross tried to calm her. "Please, Mrs. Peel. All I'm doing is taking statements. I neither believe nor disbelieve anyone yet. Do you wish to say any more, Mr. Peel?"

"Thank you. Yes. The six of us had played many silly, sometimes dangerous, practical jokes in the past, but murder for any reason went beyond sense and tolerance. Thursday night the four realized I would warn Lady Sutton. Evidently they were prepared for this. My wine was drugged. I have a vague memory of being lifted and carried by the two men and—that's all I know about the murder."

Ross nodded again. The doctor leaned over to him and whispered. Ross murmured, "Yes, yes. The tests can come later. Please go on, Mr. Peel."

So far so good, Peel thought. Now, just a little color to gloss over the rough edges. "I awoke in pitch-darkness. I heard no sounds; nothing but the ticking of my watch. These dungeon walls are ten and fifteen feet thick, so I couldn't possibly hear anything. When I got to my feet and felt my way around I seemed to be in a small cavity measuring . . . oh . . . two long strides by three."

"That would be six feet by nine, Mr. Peel?"

"Approximately. I realized I must be in some secret cell known to the men of the clique. After an hour's shouting and pounding on the walls, an accidental blow must have tripped the proper spring or lever. One section of thick wall swung open and I found myself in the passage where—"

"He's lying, lying, lying!" Sidra screamed.

Peel ignored her. "That is my statement, inspector." And it'll stand up, he thought. Sutton Castle was known for its secret passages. His clothes were still rumpled and torn from the framework he had worn to impersonate the devil. There was no known test to show whether or not he'd been drugged three days previous. His full beard and moustache would eliminate the shaving line of attack. Yes, he could be proud of an excellent story; farfetched but heavily weighted by the four-against-one logic.

"We note that you plead not guilty, Mr. Peel," Ross said slowly, "and we note your statement and accusation. I confess that your three-day disappearance seemed to incriminate you but now"—he took a deep breath—"now, if we can locate this cell in which you were confined . . ."

Peel was prepared for this. "You may or you may not, inspector. I'm an engineer, you know. The only way we may be able to locate the cell is by blasting through the stone, which may wipe out all traces."

"We'll have to take that chance, Mr. Peel."

"That chance may not have to be taken," the little round doctor said.

The others exclaimed. Peel shot a sharp glance at the little man. Experience warned him that fat men were always dangerous. Every nerve went *en garde*.

"It was a perfect story, Mr. Peel," the fat doctor said pleasantly. "Most entertaining. But really, my dear sir, for an engineer you slipped up quite badly."

"Would you mind telling me on what you base that?"

"Not at all. When you awoke in your secret cell, you said you were in complete darkness and silence. The stone walls were so thick that all you could hear was the ticking of your watch."

"And so they were."

"Very colorful," the doctor smiled, "but alas, proof that you're lying. You awoke three days later. Surely you're aware that no watch will run seventy hours without rewinding."

He was right, by God! Peel realized that instantly. He'd made a bad mistake . . . unforgivable for an engineer . . . and there was no going back for alterations and revisions. The entire lie depended on a whole fabric. Tear away one thread and the whole fabric would unravel. The fat doctor was right, damn him! Peel was trapped.

One look at Sidra's triumphant expression was enough for him. He decided he would have to cut his losses like lightning. He arose from his chair, laughing in admitted defeat. Peel, the gallant loser. Abruptly dashed past them like a shot, crossed arms before his face, hands over ears, and plunged through the glass window panes.

Shattered glass and shouts behind him. Peel flexed his legs as the soft garden earth came up at him, and landed with a heavy jolt. He took it well, and was on his feet and running toward the rear of the castle where the cars were parked. Five seconds later he was vaulting into Sidra's two-seater. Ten seconds later he was speeding through the open iron gates to the highway beyond.

Even in this crisis, Peel thought swiftly and with precision. He had left the grounds too quickly for anyone to note which direction he would take. He sent the car roaring down the London road. A man could lose himself in London. But he was not a man to panic. Even as his eyes followed the road, his mind was sorting through facts methodically, and without flinching coming to a hard decision. He knew that he could never prove innocence. How could he? He was as guilty of the killing as all the rest. They had turned on him and he would be pursued as Lady Sutton's sole murderer.

In wartime it would be impossible to get out of the country. It would even be impossible to hide for very long. What remained, then, was an outlaw living in miserable hiding for a few brief months only to be taken and brought to trial. It would be a sensation. Peel had no intention of giving his wife the joy of watching him dragged through a headline prosecution to the executioner's noose.

Still cool, still in full possession of himself, Peel planned as he drove. The audacious thing would be to go straight to his house. They would never think of looking for him there . . . at least for a time; certainly enough time for him to do what had to be done. "Vendetta," he said. "Blood for blood." He drove deep into London toward Chelsea Square, a savage, bearded man, now looking much like Teach, the buccaneer.

He approached the square from the rear, watching for the police. There were none about and the house looked quite calm and inauspicious. But, as he drove into the square and saw the front façade of his home, he was grimly amused to see that an entire wing had been demolished in a bombing raid. Evidently the catastrophe had taken place some days previous, for the rubble was neatly piled and the broken side of the building was fenced off.

So much the better, Peel thought. No doubt the house would be empty; no servants about. He parked the car, leaped out and walked briskly to the front door. Now that he had made his decision, he was quick and resolute.

There was no one inside. Peel went to the library, took pen, ink and paper and seated himself at the desk. Carefully, with lawyerlike acumen, he wrote a new will cutting his wife off beyond legal impeachment. He was coldly certain that the holograph will would stand up in court. He went to the front door, called in a couple of passing laboring men, and had them witness his signing of the will. He paid them with thanks and ushered them out. He closed and locked the front door.

He paused grimly and took a breath. So much for Sidra. It was the old possessive instinct, he knew, that drove him on this course. He wanted to keep his fortune, even after death. He wanted to keep his honor and dignity, despite death. He'd made sure of the first; he would have to execute the second quickly. Execute. Precisely the right word.

Peel thought for another moment . . . there were so many possible roads to extinction . . . then nodded his head and marched back to the kitchen. From the linen closet he took an armful of sheets and towels and padded the windows and doors with them. As an afterthought, he took a large square of cardboard and with shoe-blacking printed: DANGER! GAS! on it. He placed it outside the kitchen door.

When the room was sealed tight, Peel went to the stove, opened the oven door and turned the gas cock over. The gas hissed out of the jets, rank and yet cooling. Peel knelt and thrust his head into the oven, breathing with deep, even breaths. He knew it would not take very long before he lost consciousness. He knew it would not be painful.

For the first time in hours some of the tension left him and he relaxed almost gratefully, awaiting his death. Although he had lived a hard, geometrically patterned life and traveled a pragmatic road, now his mind reached back to more tender moments. He regretted nothing; he apologized for nothing; he was ashamed of nothing—and yet he thought of the days when he first met Sidra with nostalgia and sorrow.

> What slender youth, bedewed with liquid odors,
> Courts thee on roses in some pleasant cave,
> Sidra—?

He almost smiled. Those were the lines he had written to her when, in the romantic beginning, he worshiped her as a goddess of youth, of beauty and goodness. She was all the things he was not, he'd believed; the perfect partner. Those had been great days; the days when he'd finished at Manchester College and had come up to London to build a reputation, a fortune, an entire life . . . a thin-haired boy with precise habits and mind. Dreamily he sauntered through memories as though he were recalling an entertaining play.

He came to with a start and realized that he'd been kneeling before the oven for twenty minutes. There was something very much awry. He'd not forgotten his chemistry and he knew that twenty minutes of gas should have been enough to make him lose consciousness. Perplexed, he got to his feet, rubbing his aching knees. No time for analysis now. The pursuit would be on his neck at any moment.

Neck! That was an obvious course. Almost as painless as gas and much quicker.

Peel shut off the oven, took a length of stout laundry line from a cupboard and left the kitchen, picking up the warning sign enroute. As he tore up the cardboard, his alert eyes surveyed the house looking for a proper spot. Yes, there, in the stairwell. He could throw the rope over that beam and stand on the balcony above the stairs for the drop. When he leaped, he would have ten feet of empty space above the landing.

He ran up the stairs to the balcony, straddled the railing and threw the rope over the beam. He caught the flying end as it whipped around the beam and swung toward him. He tied the end into a loose bowline and ran the knot up the length of the rope until it snugged tight. After he had yanked twice to secure the hold on the beam he put his full weight on the rope and swung himself clear of the balcony. It supported his weight admirably; no chance of its breaking.

When he had climbed back to the railing, he shaped a hangman's noose and slipped it over his head, tightening the knot under his right ear. There was enough slack to give him a six-foot drop. He weighed one hundred and fifty pounds. That was just about right to snap his neck clean and painlessly at the end of the drop. Peel poised, took a last deep breath, and leaped without bothering to pray.

His last thought as he dropped down was a lightning computation of how much time he had left to live. Thirty-two feet per second squared divided by six gave him almost a fifth of a—There was a shattering jerk that jolted his entire body, a *crack* that sounded large and blunt in his ears, and agonizing pain in every nerve. He was twitching spasmodically.

He realized he was still alive. He hung by the neck in horror, understanding he was not dead and not knowing why. The horror crawled over his skin like an invasion of ants and for a long time he hung and shuddered, refusing to believe that the impossible had happened. He twitched and shuddered while the chill enveloped his mind, numbing it, breaking his iron control.

At last he reached into a pocket and withdrew his penknife. He opened it with difficulty, for his body was palsied and unmanageable. He sawed until he severed the rope above his head and fell the last few feet to the stair landing. While he still crouched he felt his neck. It was broken. He could feel the jagged edges of the broken vertebrae. His head was frozen at an angle that made everything topsy-turvy.

Peel dragged himself up the stairs, dimly understanding that something too ghastly to understand had overtaken him. There was no attempting a cool appraisal of this; there was no additional data to be received, no logic to apply. He reached the top of the stairs and lurched through Sidra's bedroom to the bath which they both sometimes shared. He groped in the medicine cabinet until he grasped one of his razors; six inches of fine hollow-ground honed steel. With a trembling stroke, he sliced the edge across his throat.

Instantly he was deluged with a great gout of blood and his windpipe was choked. He doubled over in agony, coughing reflexively, and his throat lathered with red foam. Still hacking and gasping, with the breath whistling madly through his slit throat, Peel crumpled to the tile floor and spasmed while the blood gushed with every heartbeat and soaked him through. Yet, as he lay there, thrice killed, he did not lose consciousness. Life was clinging to him with all the possessiveness with which he had clung to his life.

He crawled upright at last, not daring to look in the mirrors at the wreckage of himself. The blood—what remained of it within him—had begun to clot. He could still draw breaths at times. Gasping, almost totally crippled, Peel crook'd into the bedroom and searched through Sidra's dresser until he found her revolver. It took all his remaining strength to steady the muzzle against his chest and trigger three shots into his heart. The impacts smashed him back against a wall with a frightful crater torn in his chest and a heart no longer beating; and still he lived.

It's the body, he thought in fragments. Life clings to the body. So long as there's a body—the merest shell—enough to contain a spark—then life will remain. It possesses me, this life. But there has to be an answer—I'm still enough of an engineer to work out a solution. . . .

Absolute disintegration. Shatter this body into particles—bits—a thousand, a million mites—and there will no longer remain a cup to contain this persistent life. Explosives. Yes. None in the house. Nothing in this house but an engineer's ingenuity. Yes. How, then, and with what? He was quite mad by now, and the ingenious idea that came to him was mad, too.

He crawled into his study and removed a deck of washable playing cards from a drawer. For long minutes he cut them into tiny pieces with his desk scissors until he had a bowlful. He removed an andiron from the fireplace and painfully took it apart. The shaft was hollow. He packed the brass stem with the playing card bits, ramming the shreds of nitrocellulose tight. When the stem was packed solid he put in the heads of three matches and plugged the open end with the threaded belt which had attached it to the andiron legs.

There was a spirit lamp on his desk, used to keep pots of coffee hot. Peel lit the lamp and placed the andiron stem directly in the flame. He drew the desk chair close and hunched before the heating bomb. Nitrocellulose was a powerful explosive when ignited under pressure. It was only a question of time, he knew, before the brass would burst into violent explosion and scatter him around the room; scatter him in blessed death. Peel whimpered in torment and impatience. The red froth at his throat burst forth anew, while the blood soaking his clothes caked and hardened.

Too slowly the bomb heated.

Too slowly the minutes passed.

Too quickly the agony increased.

Peel trembled and whined, and when he reached out a hand to push the bomb a little deeper into the flame, his fingers could not feel the heat. He could see the flesh scorch red, but he felt nothing. All the pain writhed inside him—none outside.

It made noises in his ears, that pain, but even above the growl he could hear the dull tread of footsteps far downstairs. The steps were coming toward him, slowly, almost with an inexorable tread of fate. Desperation seized him at the thought of police and Sidra's triumph. He tried to coax the spirit lamp flame higher.

The steps passed through the main hall and began to mount the stairway. Each deliberate thud sounded louder and closer. Peel hunched lower and in the dim recesses of his mind began to pray that it might be Death Himself coming for him. The steps reached the top of the stairs and advanced to his study. There was a faint whisper as the door was thrust open. Running hot and cold in a fever of madness, Peel refused to turn.

A jarring voice spoke. "Now then, Bob, what's all this?"

He could not turn or answer.

"Bob!" the voice called hoarsely, "don't be a fool!"

Vaguely he understood that he had heard the voice somewhere before.

The measured steps sounded again and then a figure stood at his side. With bloodless eyes he flicked a glance up. It was Lady Sutton. She still wore the sequined evening gown.

"My hat!" Her little eyes twinkled in their casement of flesh. "You've gone and messed yourself up, haven't you!"

"Goau . . . a . . . waiyy . . ." The distorted words cracked and whistled as half of his breath hissed through the slit in his throat. "W-will . . . nahtt . . . be . . . haunted . . ."

"Haunted?" Lady Sutton laughed. "That's a good one, that is."

"Y-yoo ded," Peel muttered.

"What've you got there?" Lady Sutton inquired casually. "Oh, I see. A bomb. Going to blow yourself to bits, eh, Bob?"

His lips formed soundless words.

"Here," Lady Sutton said. "Let's get rid of this foolishness." She reached out to knock the bomb off the flame. Peel struggled up and grasped her arm with clawing hands. She was solid, for a ghost. Nevertheless, he flung her back.

"Let . . . be," he wheezed.

"Now stop it, Bob," Lady Sutton ordered. "I never intended this much misery for you."

Her words conveyed no meaning to him. He struck at her as she tried to get past him to the bomb. She was far too solid and strong for him. He fell toward the spirit lamp with arms outstretched to save his salvation.

Lady Sutton cried, "Bob! You damned fool!"

There was a blinding explosion. It crashed into Peel's face with a flaring white light and a burst of shattering sound. The entire study rocked, and a portion of the wall fell away. A heavy shower of books rained down from the shaken shelves. Smoke and dust filled space with a dense cloud.

When the cloud cleared, Lady Sutton still stood alongside the place where the desk had been. For the first time in many years—in many eternities, perhaps, her face wore an expression of sadness. For a long time she stood in silence. At last she shrugged and began to speak in the same quiet voice that had spoken to the five in the shelter.

"Don't you realize, Bob, that you can't kill yourself? The dead die only once, and you're dead already. You've all been dead for days. How is it that none of you could realize that? Perhaps it's that ego that Braugh spoke of—Perhaps—But you were all dead before you reached the shelter Thursday night. You should have known when you saw your bombed house, Bob. That was a heavy raid last Thursday."

She raised her hands and began to unpeel the gown that covered her. In the dead silence the sequins rustled and tinkled. They glittered as the gown dropped from the body to reveal—nothing. Empty space.

"I enjoyed that little murder," she said. "It was amusing to see the dead attempt to kill. That's why I let you go through with it."

She removed her shoes and stockings. She was now nothing more than arms and shoulders and the gross head of Lady Sutton. The face still wore the slightly sorrowful expression.

"But it was ridiculous trying to murder me, seeing who I

was. Of course, none of you knew. The play was a delight, Bob, because I'm Astaroth.''

With a sudden motion, the head and arms leaped into the air and then dropped alongside the discarded dress. The voice continued from the smoky space, disembodied, but when the dusty mist swirled it revealed a figure of emptiness, a mere outline, a bubble, and yet a shape horrible to behold.

''Yes,'' the quiet voice went on. ''I'm Astaroth, as old as the ages; as old and bored as eternity itself. That's why I had to play my little joke on you. I had to turn the tables and have a bit of a laugh. You cry out for a bit of novelty and entertainment after an eternity of arranging hells for the damned, because there's no hell like the hell of boredom.''

The quiet voice stopped, and a thousand scattered fragments of Robert Peel heard and understood. A thousand particles, each containing a tormented spark of life, heard the voice of Astaroth and understood.

''Of life I know nothing,'' Astaroth said gently, ''but death I do know—death and justice. I know that each living creature creates its own hell forevermore. What you are now, you have wrought yourself. Hear ye all, before I depart. If any can deny this; if any one of you would argue this; if any of you would cavil at the Justice of Astaroth—Speak now!''

Through all the far reaches the voice echoed and there was no answer.

A thousand tortured particles of Robert Peel heard and made no answer.

Theone Dubedat heard and made no answer from the savage embrace of her god-lover.

And a rotting, self-devouring Digby Finchley heard and made no answer.

A questing, doubting Christian Braugh in limbo heard and made no answer.

Neither Sidra Peel nor the mirror-image of her passion made answer.

All the damned of all eternity in an infinity of self-made hells heard and understood and made no answer.

For the Justice of Astaroth is unanswerable.

Adam and No Eve

THIS is the first of my "quality" science fiction stories. I put "quality" in quotes because I think it's rather jejune. Nevertheless it had and still has its admirers, who are more or less on a nostalgia kick. They like to remember the impact the story made on them when it first appeared in Campbell's Astounding Stories. Campbell was a tough, critical editor, and it was quite an honor for a young writer to have him buy a story.

At this distance of time I remember scattered, unrelated things. My wife and I had become friendly with a man who was a linotypist on The Daily Worker, despite the fact that he was a violent anti-Communist and used to berate the editors constantly. He was safe because his job was protected by his powerful union. His hostility went so far that he would slip deliberate typos into his copy, things like "Commrat" for Comrade. He was very kind to me and used to bring me huge reams of the yellow 8½ x 15 copy paper used in the editorial offices. This was a godsend to a poor writer. "Adam and No Eve" was typed on that paper which, unfortunately, was no damned good for filing. It crumbled after a year or so.

The genesis of the story came out of irritation. Very often stories arise because I get fed up with a cliché, and I'd about had it with the Adam and Eve device in science fiction. I'd just finished my formal schooling (one's education never stops) and had studied almost all the branches of the scientific disciplines. It occurred to me that you didn't need a man and a woman to repopulate the earth after a disaster. Just dump a body into the ocean, let nature take its course, and the

221

whole thing will start all over again. (No, repeat, no apology to the lunatic anti-evolutionists.) It must be remembered that the story was written long before Urey and Miller performed their epochal experiment demonstrating that amino acids, the basic building blocks of life, could be produced by subjecting a simulation of early terrestrial atmosphere to electric discharges. I'm amused today to realize that all the elements necessary for the regeneration of life were present in the environment of the story, and I didn't need any dying Adam.

For the life of me I can't remember why I found it necessary to incinerate the corpse of the dead dog. Most probably because I wanted to keep the thesis clean; life would regenerate from Adam alone; the title couldn't read, "Adam and His Faithful Dog." The story gave me extraordinary pleasure twenty years after it was published. I was lunching with an NBC producer to discuss a new show he wanted me to write. It was to be a sort of fantasy pilot, which is why he called me in; he knew I'd been a science fiction writer before I sold out to the networks.

"There's one story I've never forgotten," he said, "and I'm hoping you can tell me who wrote it. I'd like to get hold of that man." And he proceeded to tell me all about "Adam and No Eve." It was the moment of my life.

Krane knew this must be the seacoast. Instinct told him; but more than instinct, the few shreds of knowledge that clung to his torn brain told him; the stars that had shown at night through the rare breaks in the clouds, and his compass that still pointed a trembling finger north. That was strangest of all, Krane thought. The rubbled Earth still retained its polarity.

It was no longer a coast; there was no longer any sea. Only the faint line of what had been a cliff stretched north and south for endless miles. It was a line of grey ash; the same grey ash and cinders that lay behind him and stretched before him. . . . Fine silt, knee-deep, that swirled up at every motion and choked him; cinders that scudded in dense night clouds when the mad winds blew; black dust that was churned to mud when the frequent rains fell.

The sky was jet overhead. The heavy clouds rode high and were pierced with shafts of sunlight that marched swiftly over the Earth. Where the light struck a cinder storm, it was filled with gusts of dancing, gleaming particles. Where it played through rain it brought the arches of rainbows into being. Rain fell; cinder-storms blew; light thrust down—together, alternately and continually in a jigsaw of black and white violence. So it had been for months. So it was over every mile of the broad Earth.

Krane passed the edge of the ashen cliffs and began crawling down the even slope that had once been the ocean bed. He had been traveling so long that pain had become part of him. He braced elbows and dragged his body forward. Then he brought his right knee under him and reached forward with elbows again. Elbows, knee, elbows, knee—He had forgotten what it was to walk.

Life, he thought dazedly, is miraculous. It adapts itself to anything. If it must crawl, it crawls. Callus forms on the elbows and knees. The neck and shoulders toughen. The nostrils learn to snort away the ashes before they breathe. The bad leg swells and festers. It numbs, and presently it will rot and fall off.

"I beg pardon?" Krane said, "I didn't quite get that—"

He peered up at the tall figure before him and tried to understand the words. It was Hallmyer. He wore his stained lab coat and his grey hair was awry. Hallmyer stood delicately on top of the ashes and Krane wondered why he could see the scudding cinder clouds through his body.

"How do you like your world, Steven?" Hallmyer asked.

Krane shook his head miserably.

"Not very pretty, eh?" said Hallmyer. "Look around you. Dust, that's all; dust and ashes. Crawl, Steven, crawl. You'll find nothing but dust and ashes—"

Hallmyer produced a goblet of water from nowhere. It was clear and cold. Krane could see the fine mist of dew on its surface and his mouth was suddenly coated with grit.

"Hallmyer!" he cried. He tried to get to his feet and reach for the water, but the jolt of pain in his right leg warned him. He crouched back.

Hallmyer sipped and then spat in his face. The water felt warm.

"Keep crawling," said Hallmyer bitterly. "Crawl round and round the face of the Earth. You'll find nothing but dust and ashes—" He emptied the goblet on the ground before Krane. "Keep crawling. How many miles? Figure it out for yourself. Pi times D. The diameter is eight thousand or so—"

He was gone, coat and goblet. Krane realized that rain was falling again. He pressed his face into the warm cinder mud, opened his mouth and tried to suck the moisture. Presently he began crawling again.

There was an instinct that drove him on. He had to get somewhere. It was associated, he knew, with the sea—with the edge of the sea. At the shore of the sea something waited for him. Something that would help him understand all this. He had to get to the sea—that is, if there was a sea any more.

The thundering rain beat his back like heavy planks. Krane paused and yanked the knapsack around to his side where he probed in it with one hand. It contained exactly three things. A gun, a bar of chocolate, and a can of peaches. All that was left of two months' supplies. The chocolate was pulpy and spoiled. Krane knew he had best eat it before all value rotted away. But in another day he would lack the strength to open the can. He pulled it out and attacked it with the opener. By the time he had pierced and pried away a flap of tin, the rain had passed.

As he munched the fruit and sipped the juice, he watched the wall of rain marching before him down the slope of the ocean bed. Torrents of water were gushing through the mud. Small channels had already been cut—channels that would be new rivers some day; a day he would never see; a day that no living thing would ever see. As he flipped the empty can aside, Krane thought: The last living thing on Earth eats its last meal. Metabolism begins the last act.

Wind would follow the rain. In the endless weeks that he

had been crawling, he had learned that. Wind would come in a few minutes and flog him with its clouds of cinders and ashes. He crawled forward, bleary eyes searching the flat grey miles for cover.

Evelyn tapped his shoulder.

Krane knew it was she before he turned his head. She stood alongside, fresh and gay in her bright dress, but her lovely face was puckered with alarm.

"Steven," she said, "you've got to hurry!"

He could only admire the way her smooth hair waved to her shoulders.

"Oh, darling!" she said, "you've been hurt!" Her quick gentle hands touched his legs and back. Krane nodded.

"Got it landing," he said. "I wasn't used to a parachute. I always thought you came down gently—like plumping onto a bed. But the earth came up at me like a fist—And Umber was fighting around in my arms. I couldn't let him drop, could I?"

"Of course not, dear," Evelyn said.

"So I just held on to him and tried to get my legs under me," Krane said. "And then something smashed my legs and side—"

He hesitated, wondering how much she knew of what really had happened. He didn't want to frighten her.

"Evelyn, darling—" he said, trying to reach up his arms.

"No, dear," she said. She looked back in fright. "You've got to hurry. You've got to watch out behind!"

"The cinder-storms?" He grimaced. "I've been through them before."

"Not the storms!" Evelyn cried. "Something else. Oh, Steven—"

Then she was gone, but Krane knew she had spoken the truth. There was something behind—something that had been following him. In the back of his mind he had sensed the menace. It was closing in on him like a shroud. He shook his head. Somehow that was impossible. He was the last living thing on Earth. How could there be a menace?

The wind roared behind him, and an instant later came the heavy clouds of cinders and ashes. They lashed over him, biting his skin. With dimming eyes, he saw the way they

coated the mud and covered it with a fine dry carpet. Krane
drew his knees under him and covered his head with his arms.
With the knapsack as a pillow, he prepared to wait out the
storm. It would pass as quickly as the rain.

The storm whipped up a great bewilderment in his sick
head. Like a child he pushed at the pieces of his memory,
trying to fit them together. Why was Hallmyer so bitter
toward him? It couldn't have been that argument, could it?

What argument?

Why, that one before all this happened.

Oh, that!

Abruptly, the pieces locked together.

Krane stood alongside the sleek lines of his ship and
admired it tremendously. The roof of the shed had been
removed and the nose of the ship hoisted so that it rested on a
cradle pointed toward the sky. A workman was carefully
burnishing the inner surfaces of the rocket jets.

The muffled sounds of swearing came from within the ship
and then a heavy clanking. Krane ran up the short iron ladder
to the port and thrust his head inside. A few feet beneath him,
two men were clamping the long tanks of ferrous solution into
place.

"Easy there," Krane called. "Want to knock the ship
apart?"

One looked up and grinned. Krane knew what he was
thinking. That the ship would tear itself apart. Everyone said
that. Everyone except Evelyn. She had faith in him. Hallmyer never said it either, but Hallmyer thought he was crazy
in another way. As he descended the ladder, Krane saw
Hallmyer come into the shed, lab coat flying.

"Speak of the devil!" Krane muttered.

Hallmyer began shouting as soon as he saw Krane. "Now,
listen—"

"Not all over again," Krane said.

Hallmyer dug a sheaf of papers out of his pocket and
waved it under Krane's nose.

"I've been up half the night," he said, "working it
through again. I tell you I'm right. I'm absolutely right—"

Krane looked at the tight-written equations and then at

Hallmyer's bloodshot eyes. The man was half-mad with fear.

"For the last time," Hallmyer went on. "You're using your new catalyst on iron solution. All right. I grant that it's a miraculous discovery. I give you credit for that."

Miraculous was hardly the word for it. Krane knew that without conceit, for he realized he'd only stumbled on it. You had to stumble on a catalyst that would induce atomic disintegration of iron and give 10×10^{10} foot-pounds of energy for every gram of fuel. No man was smart enough to think all that up by himself.

"You don't think I'll make it?" Krane asked.

"To the Moon? Around the Moon? Maybe. You've got a fifty-fifty chance." Hallmyer ran fingers through his lank hair. "But for God's sake, Steven, I'm not worried about you. If you want to kill yourself, that's your own affair. It's the Earth I'm worried about—"

"Nonsense. Go home and sleep it off."

"Look—" Hallmyer pointed to the sheets of paper with a shaky hand—"No matter how you work the feed and mixing system, you can't get one hundred percent efficiency in the mixing and discharge."

"That's what makes it a fifty-fifty chance," Krane said. "So what's bothering you?"

"The catalyst that will escape through the rocket tubes. Do you realize what it'll do if a drop hits the Earth? It'll start a chain of disintegration that'll envelop the globe. It'll reach out to every iron atom—and there's iron everywhere. There won't be any Earth left for you to return to—"

"Listen," Krane said wearily, "we've been through all this before."

He took Hallmyer to the base of the rocket cradle. Beneath the iron framework was a two-hundred-foot pit, fifty feet wide and lined with firebrick.

"That's for the initial discharge flames. If any of the catalyst goes through, it'll be trapped in this pit and taken care of by the secondary reactions. Satisfied now?"

"But while you're in flight," Hallmyer persisted, "you'll be endangering the Earth until you're beyond Roche's limit. Every drop of nonactivated catalyst will eventually sink back to the ground and—"

"For the very last time," Krane said grimly, "the flame of the rocket discharge takes care of that. It will envelop any escaped particles and destroy them. Now get out. I've got work to do."

As Krane pushed him to the door, Hallmyer screamed and waved his arms. "I won't let you do it!" he repeated over and over. "I won't let you risk it—"

Work? No, it was sheer intoxication to labor over the ship. It had the fine beauty of a well-made thing. The beauty of polished armor, of a balanced swept-hilt rapier, of a pair of matched guns. There was no thought of danger and death in Krane's mind as he wiped his hands with waste after the last touches were finished.

She lay in the cradle ready to pierce the skies. Fifty feet of slender steel, the rivet heads gleaming like jewels. Thirty feet were given over to fuel and catalyst. Most of the forward compartment contained the spring hammock Krane had devised to absorb the acceleration strain. The ship's nose was a porthole of natural crystal that stared upward like a cyclopean eye.

Krane thought: She'll die after this trip. She'll return to the Earth and smash in a blaze of fire and thunder, for there's no way yet of devising a safe landing for a rocket ship. But it's worth it. She'll have had her one great flight, and that's all any of us should want. One great beautiful flight into the unknown—

As he locked the workshop door, Krane heard Hallmyer shouting from the cottage across the fields. Through the evening gloom he could see him waving urgently. He trotted through the crisp stubble, breathing the sharp air deeply, grateful to be alive.

"It's Evelyn on the phone," Hallmyer said.

Krane stared at him. Hallmyer refused to meet his eyes.

"What's the idea?" Krane asked. "I thought we agreed that she wasn't to call—wasn't to get in touch with me until I was ready to start? You been putting ideas into her head? Is this the way you're going to stop me?"

Hallmyer said, "No—" and studiously examined the darkening horizon.

Krane went into his study and picked up the phone.

"Now listen, darling," he said without preamble, "there's no sense getting alarmed now. I explained everything very carefully. Just before the ship crashes, I take to a parachute. I love you very much and I'll see you Wednesday when I start. So long—"

"Good-bye, sweetheart," Evelyn's clear voice said, "and is that what you called me for?"

"Called you!"

A brown hulk disengaged itself from the hearth rug and lifted itself to strong legs. Umber, Krane's mastiff, sniffed and cocked an ear. Then he whined.

"Did you say I called you?" Krane repeated.

Umber's throat suddenly poured forth a bellow. He reached Krane in a single bound, looked up into his face and whined and roared all at once.

"Shut up, you monster!" Krane said. He pushed Umber away with his foot.

"Give Umber a kick for me," Evelyn laughed. "Yes, dear. Someone called and said you wanted to speak to me."

"They did, eh? Look, honey, I'll call you back—"

Krane hung up. He arose doubtfully and watched Umber's uneasy actions. Through the windows, the late evening glow sent flickering shadows of orange light. Umber gazed at the light, sniffed and bellowed again. Suddenly struck, Krane leaped to the window.

Across the fields a mass of flame thrust high into the air, and within it were the crumbling walls of the workshop. Silhouetted against the glaze, the figures of a half a dozen men darted and ran.

Krane shot out of the cottage and with Umber hard at his heels, sprinted toward the shed. As he ran he could see the graceful nose of the spaceship within the fire, still looking cool and untouched. If only he could reach it before the flames softened its metal and started the rivets.

The workmen trotted up to him, grimy and panting. Krane gaped at them in a mixture of fury and bewilderment.

"Hallmyer!" he shouted. "Hallmyer!"

Hallmyer pushed through the crowd. His eyes gleamed with triumph.

"Too bad," he said, "I'm sorry, Steven—"

"You bastard!" Krane shouted. He grasped Hallmyer by the lapels and shook him once. Then he dropped him and started into the shed.

Hallmyer snapped orders to the workmen and an instant later a body hurtled against Krane's calves and spilled him to the ground. He lurched to his feet, fists swinging. Umber was alongside, growling over the roar of the flames. Krane battered a man in the face, and saw him stagger back against a second. He lifted a knee in a vicious drive that sent the last workman crumpling to the ground. Then he ducked his head and plunged into the shop.

The scorch felt cool at first, but when he reached the ladder and began mounting to the port, he screamed with the agony of his burns. Umber was howling at the foot of the ladder, and Krane realized that the dog could never escape from the rocket blasts. He reached down and hauled Umber into the ship.

Krane was reeling as he closed and locked the port. He retained consciousness barely long enough to settle himself in the spring hammock. Then instinct alone prompted his hands to reach out toward the control board; instinct and the frenzied refusal to let his beautiful ship waste itself in the flames. He would fail—yes. But he would fail trying.

His fingers tripped the switches. The ship shuddered and roared. And blackness descended over him.

How long was he unconscious? There was no telling. Krane awoke with cold pressing against his face and body, and the sound of frightened yelps in his ears. Krane looked up and saw Umber tangled in the springs and straps of the hammock. His first impulse was to laugh, then suddenly he realized; he had looked *up!* He had looked up at the hammock.

He was lying curled in the cup of the crystal nose. The ship had risen high—perhaps almost to Roche's zone, to the limit of the Earth's gravitational attraction, but then without guiding hands at the controls to continue its flight, had turned and was dropping back toward Earth. Krane peered through the crystal and gasped.

Below him was the ball of the Earth. It looked three times the size of the Moon. And it was no longer his Earth. It was a globe of fire mottled with black clouds. At the northernmost pole there was a tiny patch of white, and even as Krane watched, it was suddenly blotted over with hazy tones of red, scarlet and crimson. Hallmyer had been right.

Krane lay frozen in the cup of the nose as the ship descended, watching the flames gradually fade away to leave nothing but the dense blanket of black around the Earth. He lay numb with horror, unable to understand—unable to reckon up a people snuffed out, a green, fair planet reduced to ashes and cinders. Everything that was once dear and close to him—gone. He could not think of Evelyn.

Air whistling outside awoke some instinct in him. The few shreds of reason left told him to go down with his ship and forget everything in the thunder and destruction, but the instinct of life forced him to action. He climbed up to the store chest and prepared for the landing. Parachute, a small oxygen tank—a knapsack of supplies. Only half-aware of what he was doing he dressed for the descent, buckled on the 'chute and opened the port. Umber whined pathetically, and he took the heavy dog in his arms and stepped out into space.

But space hadn't been so clogged, the way it was now. Then it had been difficult to breathe. But that was because the air had been rare—not filled with clogging grit like now.

Every breath was a lungful of ground glass—or ashes—or cinders—He had returned to a suffocating black present that hugged him with soft weight and made him fight for breath. Krane struggled in panic, and then relaxed.

It had happened before. A long time past he'd been buried deep under ashes when he'd stopped to remember. Weeks ago—or days—or months. Krane clawed with his hands, inching out of the mound of cinders that the wind had thrown over him. Presently he emerged into the light again. The wind had died away. It was time to begin his crawl to the sea once more.

The vivid pictures of his memory scattered again before the grim vista that stretched out ahead. Krane scowled. He remembered too much, and too often. He had the vague hope that if he remembered hard enough, he might change one of

the things he had done—just a very little thing—and then all
this would become untrue. He thought: It might help if
everyone remembered and wished at the same time—but
there isn't any everyone. I'm the only one. I'm the last
memory on Earth. I'm the last life.

He crawled. Elbows, knee, elbows, knee—And then Hallmyer was crawling alongside and making a great game of it.
He chortled and plunged in the cinders like a happy sea lion.

Krane said: "But why do we have to get to the sea?"

Hallmyer blew a spume of ashes.

"Ask her," he said, pointing to Krane's other side.

Evelyn was there, crawling seriously, intently, mimicking
Krane's smallest action.

"It's because of our house," she said. "You remember
our house, darling? High on the cliff. We were going to live
there forever and ever. I was there when you left. Now you're
coming back to the house at the edge of the sea. Your
beautiful flight is over, dear, and you're coming back to me.
We'll live together, just we two, like Adam and Eve—"

Krane said, "That's nice."

Then Evelyn turned her head and screamed, "Oh, Steven!
Watch out!" and Krane felt the menace closing in on him
again. Still crawling, he stared back at the vast grey plains of
ash, and saw nothing. When he looked at Evelyn again he
saw only his shadow, sharp and black. Presently, it too, faded
away as the marching shaft of sunlight passed.

But the dread remained. Evelyn had warned him twice,
and she was always right. Krane stopped and turned, and
settled himself to watch. If he was really being followed, he
would see whatever it was, coming along his tracks.

There was a painful moment of lucidity. It cleaved through
his fever and bewilderment, bringing with it the sharpness
and strength of a knife.

I'm mad, he thought. The corruption in my leg has spread
to my brain. There is no Evelyn, no Hallmyer, no menace. In
all this land there is no life but mine—and even ghosts and
spirits of the underworld must have perished in the inferno
that girdled the planet. No—there is nothing but me and my

sickness. I'm dying—and when I perish, everything will perish. Only a mass of lifeless cinders will go on.

But there was a movement.

Instinct again—Krane dropped his head and lay still. Through slitted eyes he watched the ashen plains, wondering if death was playing tricks with his eyes. Another facade of rain was beating down toward him, and he hoped he could make sure before all vision was obliterated.

Yes. There.

A quarter mile back, a grey-brown shape was flitting along the grey surface. Despite the drone of the distant rain, Krane could hear the whisper of trodden cinders and see the little clouds kicking up. Stealthily he groped for the revolver in the knapsack as his mind reached feebly for explanations and recoiled from fear.

The thing approached, and suddenly Krane squinted and understood. He recalled Umber kicking with fear and springing away from him when the 'chute landed them on the ashen face of the Earth.

"Why, it's Umber," he murmured. He raised himself. The dog halted. "Here, boy!" Krane croaked gaily. "Here, boy!"

He was overcome with joy. He realized that loneliness had hung over him, a horrible sensation of oneness in emptiness. Now his was not the only life. There was another. A friendly life that could offer love and companionship. Hope kindled again.

"Here, boy!" he repeated. "Come on, boy—"

After a while he stopped trying to snap his fingers. The mastiff hung back, showing fangs and a lolling tongue. The dog was emaciated and its eyes gleamed red in the dusk. As Krane called once more, the dog snarled. Puffs of ash leaped beneath its nostrils.

He's hungry, Krane thought, that's all. He reached into the knapsack and at the gesture the dog snarled again. Krane withdrew the chocolate bar and laboriously peeled off the paper and silver foil. Weakly he tossed it toward Umber. It fell far short. After a minute of savage uncertainty, the dog advanced slowly and snapped up the food. Ashes powdered its muzzle. It licked its chops ceaselessly and continued to advance on Krane.

Panic jerked within him. A voice persisted: This is no friend. He has no love or companionship for you. Love and companionship have vanished from the land along with life. Now there is nothing left but hunger.

"No—" Krane whispered. "That isn't right that we should tear at each other and seek to devour—"

But Umber was advancing with a slinking sidle, and his teeth showed sharp and white. And even as Krane stared at him, the dog snarled and lunged.

Krane thrust up an arm under the dog's muzzle, but the weight of the charge carried him backward. He cried out in agony as his broken, swollen leg was struck by the weight of the dog. With his free hand he struck weakly, again and again, scarcely feeling the grind of teeth on his left arm. Then something metallic was pressed under him and he realized he was lying on the revolver he had let fall.

He groped for it and prayed the cinders had not clogged it. As Umber let go his arm and tore at his throat, Krane brought the gun up and jabbed the muzzle blindly against the dog's body. He pulled and pulled the trigger until the roars died away and only empty clicks sounded. Umber shuddered in the ashes before him, his body nearly shot in two. Thick scarlet stained the grey.

Evelyn and Hallmyer looked down sadly at the broken animal. Evelyn was crying, and Hallmyer reached nervous fingers through his hair in the same old gesture.

"This is the finish, Steven," he said. "You've killed part of yourself. Oh—you'll go on living, but not all of you. You'd best bury that body, Steven. It's the corpse of your soul."

"I can't," Krane said. "The wind will blow the cinders away."

"Then burn it," Hallmyer ordered with dream-logic.

It seemed that they helped him thrust the dead dog into his knapsack. They helped him take off his clothes and packed them underneath. They cupped their hands around the matches until the cloth caught fire, and blew on the weak flame until it sputtered and burned limply. Krane crouched by the fire and nursed it. Then he turned and once again began crawling down the ocean bed. He was naked now. There was nothing left of what-had-been but his flickering little life.

He was too heavy with sorrow to notice the furious rain that slammed and buffeted him, or the searing pains that were searing through his blackened leg and up his hip. He crawled. Elbows, knee, elbows, knee— Woodenly, mechanically, apathetic to everything . . . to the latticed skies, the dreary ashen plains and even the dull glint of water that lay far ahead.

He knew it was the sea—what was left of the old, or a new one in the making. But it would be an empty, lifeless sea that someday would lap against a dry, lifeless shore. This would be a planet of stone and dust, of metal and snow and ice and water, but that would be all. No more life. He, alone, was useless. He was Adam, but there was no Eve.

Evelyn waved gaily to him from the shore. She was standing alongside the white cottage with the wind snapping her dress to show the slender lines of her figure. And when he came a little closer, she ran out to him and helped him. She said nothing—only placed her hands under his shoulders and helped him lift the weight of his heavy, pain-ridden body. And so at last he reached the sea.

It was real. He understood that. For even after Evelyn and the cottage had vanished, he felt the cool waters bathe his face.

Here's the sea, Krane thought, and here am I. Adam and no Eve. It's hopeless.

He rolled a little farther into the waters. They laved his torn body. He lay with face to the sky, peering at the high menacing heavens, and the bitterness within him welled up.

"It's not right!" he cried. "It's not right that all this should pass away. Life is too beautiful to perish at the mad act of one mad creature—"

Quietly the waters laved him. Quietly . . . Calmly . . .

The sea rocked him gently, and even the death that was reaching up toward his heart was no more than a gloved hand. Suddenly the skies split apart—for the first time in all those months—and Krane stared up at the stars.

Then he knew. This was not the end of life. There could

never be an end to life. Within his body, within the rotting tissues rocking gently in the sea was the source of ten million-million lives. Cells—tissues—bacteria—amoeba— Countless infinities of life that would take new root in the waters and live long after he was gone.

They would live on his rotting remains. They would feed on each other. They would adapt themselves to the new environment and feed on the minerals and sediments washed into this new sea. They would grow, burgeon, evolve. Life would reach out to the lands once more. It would begin again the same old repeated cycle that had begun perhaps with the rotting corpse of some last survivor of interstellar travel. It would happen over and over in the future ages.

And then he knew what had brought him back to the sea. There need be no Adam—no Eve. Only the sea, the great mother of life was needed. The sea had called him back to her depths that presently life might emerge once more, and he was content.

Quietly the waters comforted him. Quietly . . . Calmly . . . The mother of life rocked the last-born of the old cycle who would become the first-born of the new. And with glazing eyes Steven Krane smiled up at the stars, stars that were sprinkled evenly across the sky. Stars that had not yet formed into the familiar constellations, and would not for another hundred million centuries.

Time Is the Traitor

I READ an interview with a top management executive in which he said he was no different from any other employee of the corporation; as a matter of fact, he did less work than most. What he was paid an enormous salary for was making decisions. And he added rather wryly that his decisions had no better than a fifty-fifty chance of being correct.

That stayed with me. I began to think about decision making, and since my habit is to look at characters from the Freudian point of view first—other points of view receive equal time later—I thought that decisions might well be an aspect of compulsion. My wife and I, who are quick and firm deciders, are often annoyed by the many hesitating, vacillating people we see in action. What's the answer? The others are the normals and we're the compelled. Fair enough. Good, at least for a story.

But are you born a compulsive or are you kicked into it by background and/or a traumatic experience? Both, probably, but it's better for a story to have a single shattering event trigger the decision compulsion, provided the event ties into the body of the story. I thought of an amusing couplet Manly Wade Wellman had written to the effect that if your girl is one girl in a million, there must be at least six like her in a city of any size. Good. It'll work and lock in to give us a chase quality. It will also provide conflict, mystery and suspense.

And all this is a damned tissue of lies. I don't coolly block a story in progressive steps like an attorney preparing a brief for the supreme court. I'm more like Zerah Colburn, the American idiot-savant, who could perform mathematical marvels mentally and recognize prime numbers at sight. He did it, but he didn't know how he did it. I write stories, but as a rule I don't know how I do it. There are occasional exceptions, but this isn't one.

All I do know is that the ingredients mentioned above went into the stockpot along with a lot of others. I don't know in what order. I don't know why some were fished out a moment after they went in while others were permitted to remain and "marry." This is why most authors agree that writing can't be taught; it can be mastered only through trial and error, and the more errors the better. Youngsters have a lot of damned bad writing to get out of their systems before they can find their way.

The purpose of trial and error, imitations and experiments, constant slaving through uncertainty and despair is twofold: to acquire merciless self-discipline; to acquire conscious story patterns and reduce them to unconscious practice. I've often said that you become a writer when you think story, not about a story.

When a writer tells you how he wrote something, he's usually second-guessing. He's telling you what he figures may have happened, after the fact. He can't report on what went on deep under the surface; the unconscious matrix which shapes the story, the unconscious editing, the unconscious revelation of his own character. All he can do is give you the things that went on consciously and gussy them up to make them sound logical and sensible. But writing isn't logical and sensible. It's an act of insane violence committed against yourself and the rest of the world . . . at least it is with me.

You can't go back and you can't catch up. Happy endings are always bittersweet.

There was a man named John Strapp; the most valuable, the most powerful, the most legendary man in a world containing seven hundred planets and seventeen hundred billion people. He was prized for one quality alone. He could make Decisions. Note the capital D. He was one of the few men who could make Major Decisions in a world of incredible complexity, and his Decisions were 87 percent correct. He sold his Decisions for high prices.

There would be an industry named, say, Bruxton Biotics, with plants on Deneb Alpha, Mizar III, Terra, and main offices on Alcor IV. Bruxton's gross income was Cr. 270 billions. The involutions of Bruxton's trade relations with consumers and competitors required the specialized services of two hundred company economists, each an expert on one tiny facet of the vast overall picture. No one was big enough to coordinate the entire picture.

Bruxton would need a Major Decision on policy. A research expert named E. T. A. Goland in the Deneb laboratories had discovered a new catalyst for biotic synthesis. It was an embryological hormone that rendered nucleonic molecules as plastic as clay. The clay could be modeled and developed in any direction. Query: Should Bruxton abandon the old culture methods and retool for this new technique? The Decision involved an intricate ramification of interracting factors: cost, saving, time, supply, demand, training, patents, patent legislation, court actions and so on. There was only one answer: Ask Strapp.

The initial negotiations were crisp. Strapp Associates replied that John Strapp's fee was Cr. 100,000 plus 1 percent of the voting stock of Bruxton Biotics. Take it or leave it. Bruxton Biotics took it with pleasure.

The second step was more complicated. John Strapp was very much in demand. He was scheduled for Decisions at the rate of two a week straight through to the first of the year. Could Bruxton wait that long for an appointment? Bruxton could not. Bruxton was TT'd a list of John Strapp's future appointments and told to arrange a swap with any of the clients as best he could. Bruxton bargained, bribed, blackmailed and arranged a trade. John Strapp was to appear at the Alcor central plant on Monday, June 29, at noon precisely.

Then the mystery began. At nine o'clock that Monday morning, Aldous Fisher, the acidulous liaison man for Strapp, appeared at Bruxton's offices. After a brief conference with Old Man Bruxton himself, the following announcement was broadcast through the plant: ATTENTION! ATTENTION! URGENT! URGENT! ALL MALE PERSONNEL NAMED

KRUGER REPORT TO CENTRAL. REPEAT. ALL MALE PERSONNEL NAMED KRUGER REPORT TO CENTRAL. URGENT. REPEAT. URGENT!

Forty-seven men named Kruger reported to Central and were sent home with strict instructions to stay at home until further notice. The plant police organized a hasty winnowing and, goaded by the irascible Fisher, checked the identification cards of all employees they could reach. Nobody named Kruger should remain in the plant, but it was impossible to comb out 2,500 men in three hours. Fisher burned and fumed like nitric acid.

By eleven-thirty, Bruxton Biotics was running a fever. Why send home all the Krugers? What did it have to do with the legendary John Strapp? What kind of man was Strapp? What did he look like? How did he act? He earned Cr. 10 millions a year. He owned 1 percent of the world. He was so close to God in the minds of the personnel that they expected angels and golden trumpets and a giant bearded creature of infinite wisdom and compassion.

At eleven-forty Strapp's personal bodyguard arrived—a security squad of ten men in plainclothes who checked doors and halls and cul-de-sacs with icy efficiency. They gave orders. This had to be removed. That had to be locked. Such and such had to be done. It was done. No one argued with John Strapp. The security squad took up positions and waited. Bruxton Biotics held its breath.

Noon struck, and a silver mote appeared in the sky. It approached with a high whine and landed with agonizing speed and precision before the main gate. The door of the ship snapped open. Two burly men stepped out alertly, their eyes busy. The chief of the security squad made a sign. Out of the ship came two secretaries, brunette and redheaded, striking, chic, efficient. After them came a thin, fortyish clerk in a baggy suit with papers stuffed in his side pockets, wearing horn-rimmed spectacles and a harassed air. After him came a magnificent creature, tall, majestic, clean-shaven but of infinite wisdom and compassion.

The burly men closed in on the beautiful man and escorted him up the steps and through the main door. Bruxton Biotics sighed happily. John Strapp was no disappointment. He was indeed God, and it was a pleasure to have 1 percent of yourself owned by him. The visitors marched down the main hall to Old Man Bruxton's office and entered. Bruxton had waited for them, poised majestically behind his desk. Now he leaped to his feet and ran forward. He grasped the magnificent man's hand fervently and exclaimed, "Mr. Strapp, sir, on behalf of my entire organization, I welcome you."

The clerk closed the door and said, "I'm Strapp." He nodded to his decoy, who sat down quietly in a corner. "Where's your data?"

Old Man Bruxton pointed faintly to his desk. Strapp sat down behind it, picked up the fat folders and began to read. A thin man. A harassed man. A fortyish man. Straight black hair. China-blue eyes. A good mouth. Good bones under the skin. One quality stood out—a complete lack of self-consciousness. But when he spoke there was a hysterical undercurrent in his voice that showed something violent and possessed deep inside him.

After two hours of breakneck reading and muttered comments to his secretaries, who made cryptic notes in Whitehead symbols, Strapp said, "I want to see the plant."

"Why?" Bruxton asked.

"To feel it," Strapp answered. "There's always the nuance involved in a Decision. It's the most important factor."

They left the office and the parade began: the security squad, the burly men, the secretaries, the clerk, the acidulous Fisher and the magnificent decoy. They marched everywhere. They saw everything. The "clerk" did most of the legwork for "Strapp." He spoke to workers, foremen, technicians, high, low and middle brass. He asked names, gossiped, introduced them to the great man, talked about their families, working conditions, ambitions. He explored, smelled and felt. After four exhausting hours they returned to Bruxton's office. The "clerk" closed the door. The decoy stepped aside.

"Well?" Bruxton asked. "Yes or No?"

"Wait," Strapp said.

He glanced through his secretaries' notes, absorbed them, closed his eyes and stood still and silent in the middle of the office like a man straining to hear a distant whisper.

"Yes," he Decided, and was Cr. 100,000 and 1 percent of the voting stock of Bruxton Biotics richer. In return, Bruxton had an 87 percent assurance that the Decision was correct. Strapp opened the door again, the parade reassembled and marched out of the plant. Personnel grabbed its last chance to take photos and touch the great man. The clerk helped promote public relations with eager affability. He asked names, introduced, and amused. The sound of voices and laughter increased as they reached the ship. Then the incredible happened.

"You!" the clerk cried suddenly. His voice screeched horribly. "You sonofabitch! You goddamned lousy murdering bastard! I've been waiting for this. I've waited ten years!" He pulled a flat gun from his inside pocket and shot a man through the forehead.

Time stood still. It took hours for the brains and blood to burst out of the back of the head and for the body to crumple. Then the Strapp staff leaped into action. They hurled the clerk into the ship. The secretaries followed, then the decoy. The two burly men leaped after them and slammed the door. The ship took off and disappeared with a fading whine. The ten men in plain clothes quietly drifted off and vanished. Only Fisher, the Strapp liaison man, was left alongside the body in the center of the horrified crowd.

"Check his identification," Fisher snapped.

Someone pulled the dead man's wallet out and opened it.

"William F. Kruger, biomechanic."

"The damned fool!" Fisher said savagely. "We warned him. We warned all the Krugers. All right. Call the police."

That was John Strapp's sixth murder. It cost exactly Cr. 500,000 to fix. The other five had cost the same, and half the amount usually went to a man desperate enough to substitute for the killer and plead temporary insanity. The other half went to the heirs of the deceased. There were six of these substitutes languishing in various penitentiaries, serving from twenty to fifty years, their families Cr. 250,000 richer.

In their suite in the Alcor Splendide, the Strapp staff consulted gloomily.

"Six in six years," Aldous Fisher said bitterly. "We can't keep it quiet much longer. Sooner or later somebody's going to ask why John Strapp always hires crazy clerks."

"Then we fix him too," the redheaded secretary said. "Strapp can afford it."

"He can afford a murder a month," the magnificent decoy murmured.

"No." Fisher shook his head sharply. "You can fix so far and no further. You reach a saturation point. We've reached it now. What are we going to do?"

"What the hell's the matter with Strapp anyway?" one of the burly men inquired.

"Who knows?" Fisher exclaimed in exasperation. "He's got a Kruger fixation. He meets a man named Kruger—any man named Kruger. He screams. He curses. He murders. Don't ask me why. It's something buried in his past."

"Haven't you asked him?"

"How can I? It's like an epileptic fit. He never knows it happened."

"Take him to a psychoanalyst," the decoy suggested.

"Out of the question."

"Why?"

"You're new," Fisher said. "You don't understand."

"Make me understand."

"I'll make an analogy. Back in the nineteen hundreds, people played card games with fifty-two cards in the deck. Those were simple times. Today everything's more complex. We're playing with fifty-two hundred in the deck. Understand?"

"I'll go along with it."

"A mind can figure fifty-two cards. It can make decisions on that total. They had it easy in the nineteen hundreds. But no mind is big enough to figure fifty-two hundred—no mind except Strapp's."

"We've got computers."

"And they're perfect when only cards are involved. But when you have to figure fifty-two hundred cardplayers, too, their likes, dislikes, motives, inclinations, prospects, tendencies and so on—what Strapp calls the nuances—then Strapp can do what a machine can't do. He's unique, and we might destroy his uniqueness with psychoanalysis.''

''Why?''

''Because it's an unconscious process in Strapp,'' Fisher explained irritably. ''He doesn't know how he does it. If he did he'd be one hundred percent right instead of eighty-seven percent. It's an unconscious process, and for all we know it may be linked up with the same abnormality that makes him murder Krugers. If we get rid of one, we may destroy the other. We can't take the chance.''

''Then what do we do?''

''Protect our property,'' Fisher said, looking around ominously. ''Never forget that for a minute. We've put in too much work on Strapp to let it be destroyed. We protect our property!''

''I think he needs a friend,'' the brunette said.

''Why?''

''We could find out what's bothering him without destroying anything. People talk to their friends. Strapp might talk.''

''We're his friends.''

''No, we're not. We're his associates.''

''Has he talked with you?''

''No.''

''You?'' Fisher shot at the redhead.

She shook her head.

''He's looking for something he never finds.''

''What?''

''A woman, I think. A special kind of woman.''

''A woman named Kruger?''

''I don't know.''

''Damn it, it doesn't make sense.'' Fisher thought a moment. ''All right. We'll have to hire him a friend, and we'll have to ease off the schedule to give the friend a chance to make Strapp talk. From now on we cut the program to one Decision a week.''

''My God!'' the brunette exclaimed. ''That's cutting five million a year.''

''It's got to be done,'' Fisher said grimly. ''It's cut now or take a total loss later. We're rich enough to stand it.''

"What are you going to do for a friend?" the decoy asked.

"I said we'd hire one. We'll hire the best. Get Terra on the TT. Tell them to locate Frank Alceste and put him through urgent."

"Frankie!" the redhead squealed. "I swoon."

"Ooh! Frankie!" The brunette fanned herself.

"You mean Fatal Frank Alceste? The heavyweight champ?" the burly man asked in awe. "I saw him fight Lonzo Jordan. Oh, man!"

"He's an actor now," the decoy explained. "I worked with him once. He sings. He dances. He—"

"And he's twice as fatal," Fisher interrupted. "We'll hire him. Make out a contract. He'll be Strapp's friend. As soon as Strapp meets him, he'll—"

"Meets who?" Strapp appeared in the doorway of his bedroom, yawning, blinking in the light. He always slept deeply after his attacks. "Who am I going to meet?" He looked around, thin, graceful, but harassed and indubitably possessed.

"A man named Frank Alceste," Fisher said. "He badgered us for an introduction, and we can't hold him off any longer."

"Frank Alceste?" Strapp murmured. "Never heard of him."

Strapp could make Decisions; Alceste could make friends. He was a powerful man in his middle thirties, sandy-haired, freckle-faced, with a broken nose and deep-set grey eyes. His voice was high and soft. He moved with the athlete's lazy poise that is almost feminine. He charmed you without knowing how he did it, or even wanting to do it. He charmed Strapp, but Strapp also charmed him. They became friends.

"No, it really is friends," Alceste told Fisher when he returned the check that had been paid him. "I don't need the money, and old Johnny needs me. Forget you hired me original-like. Tear up the contract. I'll try to straighten Johnny out on my own."

Alceste turned to leave the suite in the Rigel Splendide and passed the great-eyed secretaries. "If I wasn't so busy, ladies," he murmured, "I'd sure like to chase you a little."

"Chase me, Frankie," the brunette blurted.

The redhead looked caught.

And as Strapp Associates zigzagged in slow tempo from city to city and planet to planet, making the one Decision a week, Alceste and Strapp enjoyed themselves while the magnificent decoy gave interviews and posed for pictures. There were interruptions when Frankie had to return to Terra to make a picture, but in between they golfed, tennised, brubaged, bet on horses, dogs and dowlens, and went to fights and routs. They hit the night spots and Alceste came back with a curious report.

"Me, I don't know how close you folks been watching Johnny," he told Fisher, "but if you think he's been sleeping every night, safe in his little trundle, you better switch notions."

"How's that?" Fisher asked in surprise.

"Old Johnny, he's been sneaking out nights all along when you folks thought he was getting his brain rest."

"How do you know?"

"By his reputation," Alceste told him sadly. "They know him everywhere. They know old Johnny in every bistro from here to Orion. And they know him the worst way."

"By name?"

"By nickname. Wasteland, they call him."

"Wasteland!"

"Uh-huh. Mr. Devastation. He runs through women like a prairie fire. You don't know this?"

Fisher shook his head.

"Must pay off out of his personal pocket," Alceste mused and departed.

There was a terrifying quality to the possessed way that Strapp ran through women. He would enter a club with Alceste, take a table, sit down and drink. Then he would stand up and coolly survey the room, table by table, woman by woman. Upon occasion men would become angered and offer to fight. Strapp disposed of them coldly and viciously, in a manner that excited Alceste's professional admiration. Frankie never fought himself. No professional ever touches an amateur. But he tried to keep the peace, and failing that, at least kept the ring.

After the survey of the women guests, Strapp would sit down and wait for the show, relaxed, chatting, laughing. When the girls appeared, his grim possession would take over again and he would examine the line carefully and dispassionately. Very rarely he would discover a girl that interested him; always the identical type—a girl with jet hair, inky eyes, and clear, silken skin. Then the trouble began.

If it was an entertainer, Strapp went backstage after the show. He bribed, fought, blustered and forced his way into her dressing room. He would confront the astonished girl, examine her in silence, then ask her to speak. He would listen to her voice, then close in like a tiger and make a violent and unexpected pass. Sometimes there would be shrieks, sometimes a spirited defense, sometimes compliance. At no time was Strapp satisfied. He would abandon the girl abruptly, pay off all complaints and damages like a gentleman, and leave to repeat the performance in club after club until curfew.

If it was one of the guests, Strapp immediately cut in, disposed of her escort, or if that was impossible, followed the girl home and there repeated the dressing-room attack. Again he would abandon the girl, pay like a gentleman and leave to continue his possessed search.

"Me, I been around, but I'm scared by it," Alceste told Fisher. "I never saw such a hasty man. He could have most any woman agreeable if he'd slow down a little. But he can't. He's driven."

"By what?"

"I don't know. It's like he's working against time."

After Strapp and Alceste became intimate, Strapp permitted him to come along on a daytime quest that was even stranger. As Strapp Associates continued its round through the planets and industries, Strapp visited the Bureau of Vital Statistics in each city. There he bribed the chief clerk and presented a slip of paper. On it was written:

Height	5'6"
Weight	110
Hair	Black
Eyes	Black
Bust	34
Waist	26

| Hips | 36 |
| Size | 12 |

"I want the name and address of every girl over twenty-one who fits this description," Strapp would say. "I'll pay ten credits a name."

Twenty-four hours later would come the list, and off Strapp would chase on a possessed search, examining, talking, listening, sometimes making the terrifying pass, always paying off like a gentleman. The procession of tall, jet-haired, inky-eyed, busty girls made Alceste dizzy.

"He's got an idee fix," Alceste told Fisher in the Cygnus Splendide, "and I got it figured this much. He's looking for a special particular girl and nobody comes up to specifications."

"A girl named Kruger?"

"I don't know if the Kruger business comes into it."

"Is he hard to please?"

"Well, I'll tell you. Some of those girls—me, I'd call them sensational. But he don't pay any mind to them. Just looks and moves on. Others—dogs, practically; he jumps like old Wasteland."

"What is it?"

"I think it's a kind of test. Something to make the girls react hard and natural. It ain't that kind of passion with old Wasteland. It's a cold-blooded trick so he can watch 'em in action."

"But what's he looking for?"

"I don't know yet," Alceste said, "but I'm going to find out. I got a little trick figured. It's taking a chance, but Johnny's worth it."

It happened in the arena where Strapp and Alceste went to watch a pair of gorillas tear each other to pieces inside a glass cage. It was a bloody affair, and both men agreed that gorilla-fighting was no more civilized than cockfighting and left in disgust. Outside, in the empty concrete corridor, a shriveled man loitered. When Alceste signaled to him, he ran up to them like an autograph hound.

"Frankie!" the shriveled man shouted. "Good old Frankie! Don't you remember me?"

Alceste stared.

"I'm Blooper Davis. We was raised together in the old precinct. Don't you remember Blooper Davis?"

"Blooper!" Alceste's face lit up. "Sure enough. But it was Blooper Davidoff then."

"Sure." The shriveled man laughed. "And it was Frankie Kruger then."

"Kruger!" Strapp cried in a thin, screeching voice.

"That's right," Frankie said. "Kruger. I changed my name when I went into the fight game." He motioned sharply to the shriveled man, who backed against the corridor wall and slid away.

"You sonofabitch!" Strapp cried. His face was white and twitched hideously. "You goddamned lousy murdering bastard! I've been waiting for this. I've waited ten years."

He whipped a flat gun from his inside pocket and fired. Alceste sidestepped barely in time and the slug ricocheted down the corridor with a high whine. Strapp fired again, and the flame seared Alceste's cheek. He closed in, caught Strapp's wrist and paralyzed it with his powerful grip. He pointed the gun away and clinched. Strapp's breath was hissing. His eyes rolled. Overhead sounded the wild roars of the crowd.

"All right, I'm Kruger," Alceste grunted. "Kruger's the name, Mr. Strapp. So what? What are you going to do about it?"

"Sonofabitch!" Strapp screamed, struggling like one of the gorillas. "Killer! Murderer! I'll rip your guts out!"

"Why me? Why Kruger?" Exerting all his strength, Alceste dragged Strapp to a niche and slammed him into it. He caged him with his huge frame. "What did I ever do to you ten years ago?"

He got the story in hysterical animal outbursts before Strapp fainted.

After he put Strapp to bed, Alceste went out into the lush living room of the suite in the Indi Splendide and explained to the staff.

"Old Johnny was in love with a girl named Sima Morgan,'' he began. ''She was in love with him. It was big romantic stuff. They were going to be married. Then Sima Morgan got killed by a guy named Kruger.''

''Kruger! So that's the connection. How?''

''This Kruger was a drunken no-good. Society. He had a bad driving record. They took his license away from him, but that didn't make any difference to Kruger's kind of money. He bribed a dealer and bought a hot-rod jet without a license. One day he buzzed a school for the hell of it. He smashed the roof in and killed thirteen children and their teacher. . . . This was on Terra in Berlin.

''They never got Kruger. He started planet-hopping and he's still on the lam. The family sends him money. The police can't find him. Strapp's looking for him because the school-teacher was his girl, Sima Morgan.''

There was a pause, then Fisher asked, ''How long ago was this?''

''Near as I can figure, ten years eight months.''

Fisher calculated intently. ''And ten years three months ago, Strapp first showed he could make decisions. The Big Decisions. Up to then he was nobody. Then came the tragedy, and with it the hysteria and the ability. Don't tell me one didn't produce the other.''

''Nobody's telling you anything.''

''So he kills Kruger over and over again,'' Fisher said coldly. ''Right. Revenge fixation. But what about the girls and the Wasteland business?''

Alceste smiled sadly. ''You ever hear the expression 'One girl in a million'?''

''Who hasn't?''

''If your girl was one in a million, that means there ought to be nine more like her in a city of ten million, yes?''

The Strapp staff nodded, wondering.

''Old Johnny's working on that idea. He thinks he can find Sima Morgan's duplicate.''

''How?''

''He's worked it out arithmetic-wise. He's thinking like so: There's one chance in sixty-four billion of fingerprints matching. But today there's seventeen hundred billion people. That means there can be twenty-six with one matching print, and maybe more.''

"Not necessarily."

"Sure, not necessarily, but there's the chance and that's all old Johnny wants. He figures if there's twenty-six chances of one print matching, there's an outside chance of one person matching. He thinks he can find Sima Morgan's duplicate if he just keeps on looking hard enough."

"That's outlandish!"

"I didn't say it wasn't, but it's the only thing that keeps him going. It's a kind of life preserver made out of numbers. It keeps his head above water—the crazy notion that sooner or later he can pick up where death left him off ten years ago."

"Ridiculous!" Fisher snapped.

"Not to Johnny. He's still in love."

"Impossible."

"I wish you could feel it like I feel it," Alceste answered. "He's looking . . . looking. He meets girl after girl. He hopes. He talks. He makes the pass. If it's Sima's duplicate, he knows she'll respond just the way he remembers Sima responding ten years ago. 'Are you Sima?' he asks himself. 'No,' he says and moves on. It hurts, thinking about a lost guy like that. We ought to do something for him."

"No," Fisher said.

"We ought to help him find his duplicate. We ought to coax him into believing some girl's the duplicate. We ought to make him fall in love again."

"No," Fisher repeated emphatically.

"Why no?"

"Because the moment Strapp finds his girl, he heals himself. He stops being the great John Strapp, the Decider. He turns back into a nobody—a man in love."

"What's he care about being great? He wants to be happy."

"Everybody wants to be happy," Fisher snarled. "Nobody is. Strapp's no worse off than any other man, but he's a lot richer. We maintain the *status quo*."

"Don't you mean *you're* a lot richer?"

"We maintain the *status quo*," Fisher repeated. He eyed Alceste coldly. "I think we'd better terminate the contract. We have no further use for your services."

"Mister, we terminated when I handed back the check. You're talking to Johnny's friend now."

"I'm sorry, Mr. Alceste, but Strapp won't have much time for his friends from now on. I'll let you know when he'll be free next year."

"You'll never pull it off. I'll see Johnny when and where I please."

"Do you want him for a friend?" Fisher smiled unpleasantly. "Then you'll see him when and where I please. Either you see him on those terms or Strapp sees the contract we gave you. I still have it in the files, Mr. Alceste. I did not tear it up. I never part with anything. How long do you imagine Strapp will believe in your friendship after he sees the contract you signed?"

Alceste clenched his fists. Fisher held his ground. For a moment they glared at each other, then Frankie turned away.

"Poor Johnny," he muttered. "It's like a man being run by his tapeworm. I'll say so long to him. Let me know when you're ready for me to see him again."

He went into the bedroom, where Strapp was just awakening from his attack without the faintest memory, as usual. Alceste sat down on the edge of the bed.

"Hey, old Johnny." He grinned.

"Hey, Frankie." Strapp smiled.

They punched each other solemnly, which is the only way that men friends can embrace and kiss.

"What happened after that gorilla fight?" Strapp asked. "I got fuzzy."

"Man, you got plastered. I never saw a guy take on such a load." Alceste punched Strapp again. "Listen, old Johnny. I got to get back to work. I got a three-picture-a-year contract, and they're howling."

"Why, you took a month off six planets back," Strapp said in disappointment. "I thought you caught up."

"Nope. I'll be pulling out today, Johnny. Be seeing you real soon."

"Listen," Strapp said. "To hell with the pictures. Be my partner. I'll tell Fisher to draw up an agreement." He blew his nose. "This is the first time I've had laughs in—in a long time."

"Maybe later, Johnny. Right now I'm stuck with a contract. Soon as I can get back, I'll come a-running. Cheers."

"Cheers," Strapp said wistfully.

Outside the bedroom, Fisher was waiting like a watchdog. Alceste looked at him with disgust.

"One thing you learn in the fight game," he said slowly. "It's never won till the last round. I give you this one, but it isn't the last."

As he left, Alceste said, half to himself, half aloud, "I want him to be happy. I want every man to be happy. Seems like every man could be happy if we'd all just lend a hand."

Which is why Frankie Alceste couldn't help making friends.

So the Strapp staff settled back into the same old watchful vigilance of the murdering years, and stepped up Strapp's Decision appointments to two a week. They knew why Strapp had to be watched. They knew why the Krugers had to be protected. But that was the only difference. Their man was miserable, hysteric, almost psychotic; it made no difference. That was a fair price to pay for 1 percent of the world.

But Frankie Alceste kept his own counsel, and visited the Deneb laboratories of Bruxton Biotics. There he consulted with one E. T. A. Goland, the research genius who had discovered that novel technique for molding life which first brought Strapp to Bruxton, and was indirectly responsible for his friendship with Alceste. Ernst Theodor Amadeus Goland was short, fat, asthmatic and enthusiastic.

"But yes, yes," he sputtered when the layman had finally made himself clear to the scientist. "Yes, indeed! A most ingenious notion. Why it never occurred to me, I cannot think. It could be accomplished without any difficulty whatsoever." He considered. "Except money," he added.

"You could duplicate the girl that died ten years ago?" Alceste asked.

"Without any difficulty, except money." Goland nodded emphatically.

"She'd look the same? Act the same? Be the same?"

"Up to ninety-five percent, plus or minus point nine seven five."

"Would that make any difference? I mean, ninety-five percent of a person as against one hundred percent."

"Ach! No. It is a most remarkable individual who is aware of more than eighty percent of the total characteristics of another person. Above ninety percent is unheard of."

"How would you go about it?"

"Ach? So. Empirically we have two sources. One: complete psychological pattern of the subject in the Centaurus Master Files. They will TT a transcript upon application and payment of one hundred credits through formal channels. I will apply."

"And I'll pay. Two?"

"Two: the embalmment process of modern times, which— She is buried, yes?"

"Yes."

"Which is ninety-eight percent perfect. From remains and psychological pattern we re-clone body and psyche by the equation sigma equals the square root of minus two over— We do it without any difficulty, except money."

"Me, I've got the money," Frankie Alceste said. "You do the rest."

For the sake of his friend, Alceste paid. Cr. 100 and expedited the formal application to the Master Files on Centaurus for the transcript of the complete psychological pattern of Sima Morgan, deceased. After it arrived, Alceste returned to Terra and a city called Berlin, where he blackmailed a gimpster named Augenblick into turning grave robber. Augenblick visited the *Staats-Gottesacker* and removed the porcelain coffin from under the marble headstone that read SIMA MORGAN. It contained what appeared to be a black-haired, silken-skinned girl in deep sleep. By devious routes, Alceste got the porcelain coffin through four customs barriers to Deneb.

One aspect of the trip of which Alceste was not aware, but which bewildered various police organizations, was the series of catastrophes that pursued him and never quite caught up. There was the jetliner explosion that destroyed the ship and an acre of docks half an hour after passengers and freight were discharged. There was a hotel holocaust ten minutes after Alceste checked out. There was the shuttle disaster that extinguished the pneumatic train for which Alceste had unexpectedly canceled passage. Despite all this he was able to present the coffin to biochemist Goland.

"Ach!" said Ernst Theodor Amadeus. "A beautiful creature. She is worth re-creating. The rest now is simple, except money."

For the sake of his friend, Alceste arranged a leave of absence for Goland, bought him a laboratory and financed an incredibly expensive series of experiments. For the sake of his friend, Alceste poured forth money and patience until at last, eight months later, there emerged from the opaque maturation chamber a black-haired, inky-eyed, silken-skinned creature with long legs and a high bust. She answered to the name of Sima Morgan.

"I heard the jet coming down toward the school," Sima said, unaware that she was speaking eleven years later. "Then I heard a crash. What happened?"

Alceste was jolted. Up to this moment she had been an objective . . . a goal . . . unreal, unalive. This was a living woman. There was a curious hesitation in her speech, almost a lisp. Her head had an engaging tilt when she spoke. She arose from the edge of the table, and she was not fluid or graceful as Alceste had expected she would be. She moved boyishly.

"I'm Frank Alceste," he said quietly. He took her shoulders. "I want you to look at me and make up your mind whether you can trust me."

Their eyes locked in a steady gaze. Sima examined him gravely. Again Alceste was jolted and moved. His hands began to tremble and he released the girl's shoulders in panic.

"Yes," Sima said. "I can trust you."

"No matter what I say, you must trust me. No matter what I tell you to do, you must trust me and do it."

"Why?"

"For the sake of Johnny Strapp."

Her eyes widened. "Something's happened to him," she said quickly. "What is it?"

"Not to him, Sima. To you. Be patient, honey. I'll explain. I had it in my mind to explain now, but I can't. I—I'd best wait until tomorrow."

They put her to bed and Alceste went out for a wrestling match with himself. The Deneb nights are soft and black as velvet, thick and sweet with romance—or so it seemed to Frankie Alceste that night.

"You can't be falling in love with her," he muttered. "It's crazy."

And later, "You saw hundreds like her when Johnny was hunting. Why didn't you fall for one of them?"

And last of all, "What are you going to do?"

He did the only thing an honorable man can do in a situation like that, and tried to turn his desire into friendship. He came into Sima's room the next morning, wearing tattered old jeans, needing a shave, with his hair standing on end. He hoisted himself up on the foot of her bed, and while she ate the first of the careful meals Goland had prescribed, Frankie chewed on a cigarette and explained to her. When she wept, he did not take her in his arms to console her, but thumped her on the back like a brother.

He ordered a dress for her. He had ordered the wrong size, and when she showed herself to him in it, she looked so adorable that he wanted to kiss her. Instead he punched her, very gently and very solemnly, and took her out to buy a wardrobe. When she showed herself to him in proper clothes, she looked so enchanting that he had to punch her again. Then they went to a ticket office and booked immediate passage for Ross-Alpha III.

Alceste had intended delaying a few days to rest the girl, but he was compelled to rush for fear of himself. It was this alone that saved both from the explosion that destroyed the private home and private laboratory of biochemist Goland, and destroyed the biochemist too. Alceste never knew this. He was already on board ship with Sima, frantically fighting temptation.

One of the things that everybody knows about space travel

but never mentions is its aphrodisiac quality. Like the ancient days when travelers crossed oceans on ships, the passengers are isolated in their own tiny world for a week. They're cut off from reality. A magic mood of freedom from ties and responsibilities pervades the jetliner. Everyone has a fling. There are thousands of jet romances every week—quick, passionate affairs that are enjoyed in complete safety and ended on landing day.

In this atmosphere, Frankie Alceste maintained a rigid self-control. He was not aided by the fact that he was a celebrity with a tremendous animal magnetism. While a dozen handsome women threw themselves at him, he persevered in the role of big brother and thumped and punched Sima until she protested.

"I know you're a wonderful friend to Johnny and me," she said on the last night out. "But you are exhausting, Frankie. I'm covered with bruises."

"Yeah. I know. It's habit. Some people, like Johnny, they think with their brains. Me, I think with my fists."

They were standing before the starboard crystal, bathed in the soft light of the approaching Ross-Alpha, and there is nothing more damnably romantic than the velvet of space illuminated by the white-violet of a distant sun. Sima tilted her head and looked at him.

"I was talking to some of the passengers," she said. "You're famous, aren't you?"

"More notorious-like."

"There's so much to catch up on. But I must catch up on you first."

"Me?"

Sima nodded. "It's all been so sudden. I've been bewildered—and so excited that I haven't had a chance to thank you, Frankie. I do thank you. I'm beholden to you forever."

She put her arms around his neck and kissed him with parted lips. Alceste began to shake.

"No," he thought. "No. She doesn't know what she's doing. She's so crazy happy at the idea of being with Johnny again that she doesn't realize . . ."

He reached behind him until he felt the icy surface of the

crystal, which passengers are strictly enjoined from touching. Before he could give way, he deliberately pressed the backs of his hands against the subzero surface. The pain made him start. Sima released him in surprise and when he pulled his hands away, he left six square inches of skin and blood behind.

So he landed on Ross-Alpha III with one girl in good condition and two hands in bad shape and he was met by the acid-faced Aldous Fisher, accompanied by an official who requested Mr. Alceste to step into an office for a very serious private talk.

"It has been brought to our attention by Mr. Fisher," the official said, "that you are attempting to bring in a young woman of illegal status."

"How would Mr. Fisher know?" Alceste asked.

"You fool!" Fisher spat. "Did you think I would let it go at that? You were followed. Every minute."

"Mr. Fisher informs us," the official continued austerely, "that the woman with you is traveling under an assumed name. Her papers are fraudulent."

"How fraudulent?" Alceste said. "She's Sima Morgan. Her papers say she's Sima Morgan."

"Sima Morgan died eleven years ago," Fisher answered. "The woman with you can't be Sima Morgan."

"And unless the question of her true identity is cleared up," the official said, "she will not be permitted entry."

"I'll have the documentation on Sima Morgan's death here within the week," Fisher added triumphantly.

Alceste looked at Fisher and shook his head wearily. "You don't know it, but you're making it easy for me," he said. "The one thing in the world I'd like to do is take her out of here and never let Johnny see her. I'm so crazy to keep her for myself that—" He stopped himself and touched the bandages on his hands. "Withdraw your charge, Fisher."

"No," Fisher snapped.

"You can't keep 'em apart. Not this way. Suppose she's interned? Who's the first man I subpoena to establish her identity? John Strapp. Who's the first man I call to come and see her? John Strapp. D'you think you could stop him?"

"That contract," Fisher began. "I'll—"

"To hell with the contract. Show it to him. He wants his girl, not me. Withdraw your charge, Fisher. And stop fighting. You've lost your meal ticket."

Fisher glared malevolently, then swallowed. "I withdraw the charge," he growled. Then he looked at Alceste with blood in his eyes. "It isn't the last round yet," he said and stamped out of the office.

Fisher was prepared. At a distance of light-years he might be too late with too little. Here on Ross-Alpha III he was protecting his property. He had all the power and money of John Strapp to call on. The floater that Frankie Alceste and Sima took from the spaceport was piloted by a Fisher aide who unlatched the cabin door and performed steep banks to tumble his fares out into the air. Alceste smashed the glass partition and hooked a meaty arm around the driver's throat until he righted the floater and brought them safely to earth. Alceste was pleased to note that Sima did not fuss more than was necessary.

On the road level they were picked up by one of a hundred cars that had been pacing the floater from below. At the first shot, Alceste clubbed Sima into a doorway and followed her at the expense of a burst shoulder, which he bound hastily with strips of Sima's lingerie. Her dark eyes were enormous, but she made no complaint. Alceste complimented her with mighty thumps and took her up to the roof and down into the adjoining building, where he broke into an apartment and telephoned for an ambulance.

When the ambulance arrived, Alceste and Sima descended to the street, where they were met by uniformed policemen who had official instructions to pick up a couple answering to their description. "Wanted for floater robbery with assault. Dangerous. Shoot to kill." The police Alceste disposed of, and also the ambulance driver and intern. He and Sima departed in the ambulance, Alceste driving like a fury, Sima operating the siren like a banshee.

They abandoned the ambulance in the downtown shopping district, entered a department store, and emerged forty minutes later as a young valet in uniform pushing an old man in a wheelchair. Outside the difficulty of the bust, Sima was boyish enough to pass as a valet. Frankie was weak enough from assorted injuries to simulate the old man.

They checked into the Ross Splendide, where Alceste barricaded Sima in a suite, had his shoulder attended to and bought a gun. Then he went looking for John Strapp. He found him in the Bureau of Vital Statistics, bribing the chief clerk and presenting him with a slip of paper that gave the same description of the long-lost love.

"Hey, old Johnny," Alceste said.

"Hey, Frankie!" Strapp cried in delight.

They punched each other affectionately. With a happy grin, Alceste watched Strapp explain and offer further bribes to the chief clerk for the names and addresses of all girls over twenty-one who fitted the description on the slip of paper. As they left, Alceste said, "I met a girl who might fit that, old Johnny."

That cold look came into Strapp's eyes. "Oh?" he said.

"She's got a kind of half lisp."

Strapp looked at Alceste strangely.

"And a funny way of tilting her head when she talks."

Strapp clutched Alceste's arm.

"Only trouble is, she isn't girlie-girlie like most. More like a fella. You know what I mean? Spunky-like."

"Show her to me, Frankie," Strapp said in a low voice.

They hopped a floater and were taxied to the Ross Splendide roof. They took the elevator down to the twentieth floor and walked to suite 20-M. Alceste code-knocked on the door. A girl's voice called, "Come in." Alceste shook Strapp's hand and said, "Cheers, Johnny." He unlocked the door, then walked down the hall to lean against the balcony balustrade. He drew his gun just in case Fisher might get around to last-ditch interruptions. Looking out across the glittering city, he reflected that every man could be happy if everybody would just lend a hand; but sometimes that hand was expensive.

John Strapp walked into the suite. He shut the door, turned and examined the jet-haired inky-eyed girl, coldly, intently.

She stared at him in amazement. Strapp stepped closer, walked around her, faced her again.

"Say something," he said.

"You're not John Strapp?" she faltered.

"Yes."

"No!" she exclaimed. "No! My Johnny's young. My Johnny is—"

Strapp closed in like a tiger. His hands and lips savaged her while his eyes watched coldly and intently. The girl screamed and struggled, terrified by those strange eyes that were alien, by the harsh hands that were alien, by the alien compulsions of the creature who was once her Johnny Strapp but was now aching years of change apart from her.

"You're someone else!" she cried. "You're not Johnny Strapp. You're another man."

And Strapp, not so much eleven years older as eleven years other than the man whose memory he was fighting to fulfill, asked himself, "Are you my Sima? Are you my love—my lost, dead love?" And the change within him answered, "No, this isn't Sima. This isn't your love yet. Move on, Johnny. Move on and search. You'll find her someday—the girl you lost."

He paid like a gentleman and departed.

From the balcony, Alceste saw him leave. He was so astonished that he could not call to him. He went back to the suite and found Sima standing there, stunned, staring at a sheaf of money on a table. He realized what had happened at once. When Sima saw Alceste, she began to cry—not like a girl, but boyishly, with her fists clenched and her face screwed up.

"Frankie," she wept. "My God! Frankie!" She held out her arms to him in desperation. She was lost in a world that had passed her by.

He took a step, then hesitated. He made a last attempt to quench the love within him for this creature, searching for a way to bring her and Strapp together. Then he lost all control and took her in his arms.

"She doesn't know what she's doing," he thought.

"She's so scared of being lost. She's not mine. Not yet. Maybe never."

And then, "Fisher's won, and I've lost."

And last of all, "We only remember the past; we never know it when we meet it. The mind goes back, but time goes on, and farewells should be forever."

Oddy and Id

WHEN I was a mystery writer I went mad digging up gimmicks for my scripts. A gimmick is any odd fact, not very well known to the public (but of course known to the detective) which can be used as a vital clue. Here's a simple example: did you know that the United States minted no silver dollars between 1910 and 1920? If you come across one dated 1915 it has to be a counterfeit, and that's a gimmick.

I usually needed three per script; one for an opening hook, a second for the big twist at the halfway mark, and a third for "The Morris" which would wrap everything up. I'd better give the derivation of the expression, which was used in the business to describe the final explanation of the mystery.

There was a speakeasy in Philadelphia back in the twenties which preyed on innocent transients. Stranger would come in for lunch, order a sandwich and a couple of beers, and when the waiter presented the bill it was like for twenty dollars. The customer would scream and demand an explanation of the outrage. The waiter would answer, "Yes, sir. Morris will explain." When Morris came to the table, he turned out to be the bouncer; six foot six, two hundred and fifty pounds and ugly mean. That was all the explanation the victim required.

As I was saying, my life was a constant search for fresh gimmicks, and I haunted the reading rooms of the main library at 42nd and Fifth Avenue. I'd speed-read through four or five books an hour and count myself lucky if I averaged one solid gimmick per book. Eventually I got onto psychiatry and discovered that the field was rich in behavior gimmicks, which were far more interesting than silver dollars with the wrong date.

It was as a result of this purely pragmatic research that I became hooked on psychiatry and started writing about compulsives and their corrosive conflicts. I also became a worshiper of Freud, and I can't tell you how crushed I was when his correspondence with Jung was published and I realized that my god was only human after all. The most laughable aspect of my deep belief in psychiatry is the fact that I've never been in analysis.

Well, "Oddy and Id" was the first science fiction story I wrote after my conversion (I'd already written acres of scripts using psychiatric material) and it led to my first meeting with the great John W. Campbell, Jr., editor of the trailblazing Astounding Science Fiction. *I'd submitted the story by mail and Campbell phoned me a few weeks later, said he liked the story and would buy it, but wanted a few changes made. Would I come to his office and discuss it? I was delighted to accept. A chance to meet the Great Man! Like wow!*

It was a harrowing encounter. I won't go into the details here (you'll find them in "My Affair with Science Fiction," p. 387) but I can confess my guilt. All my experience in the entertainment business had taught me that it's folly to go backstage after you've been enchanted by a show. Don't meet the author, the performers, the director, the designer, the producer . . . anybody who's created the brilliance that grabbed you. You're sure to be disillusioned. Never confuse the artist with his work.

Well, I should have known better, but I went through the stage door of Astounding Science Fiction, *met its director, and it was a disaster. As a result, I listen to my writing colleagues' worship of John Campbell, and I feel guilty as hell because I can't join in. Understand that I speak as a writer, not a reader. As a reader, I, too, worship him. I also feel guilty because I believe the* antipatico *between us was entirely my fault. I think I was contemptuous because we were reflections of each other; both arrogant, know-it-all, and unyielding. End of* Apologia Pro Vita Sua.

Anyway, the crux of that story conference was Campbell's pronouncement that the entire field of psychiatry had been exploded by L. Ron Hubbard's discovery of a new, earthshaking science called "dianetics," and he wanted all references to Freud, and His Merry Men (including the title) to be removed. Understand, please; he didn't ask me to make a pitch for dianetics; he just wanted me to get the antiquated vocabulary of Freud out of Hubbard's way.

I thought this was absurd, but I agreed anyway. The changes would not affect the point of the story, so it was easy to go along with the Great Man. And right here I should mention something about my kind of writer that isn't easily understood: I see a story as a whole, I have omnivision. Example: A director will say to me, "Hey, Alf, we need time. Can't we cut that scene with the locksmith?" I know instantly that the locksmith scene controls two scenes that precede it and three that follow, that four of the five can be easily patched, but the fifth is a holdout which will require an entirely new approach. I don't have to puzzle it out; I know it instantly. Lightningsville.

So I knew instantly that the changes Campbell asked for weren't important to the story and could easily be sloughed. I agreed and got the hell out of there. Naturally, the first time the story was reprinted, I went back to the original version. I don't know whether Campbell ever knew, but my guess is that he did. He was very shrewd and aware, when he wasn't riding his latest scientific hobbyhorse.

"Oddy and Id" was generated by an argument I had with a close friend who was extremely intolerant of what he called "sin." He could neither understand nor forgive intelligent people who did wrong. I argued that people aren't always in conscious control of their actions; very often the unconscious takes over.

"There are times," I said, "when all the good sense in a man shouts a warning that what he's about to do will only create grief, but he goes ahead and does it anyway. Something deep down inside is driving him. Hasn't that happened to you?"

"Never."

"Well, can you see it happening to other people?"

"Not intelligent people. No."

"Intelligence has nothing to do with it. Can't you concede that a nice guy who only wants to do right can be compelled by his within to do wrong?"

"No."

A stubborn sonofabitch, but the impasse generated the story through a very easy extrapolation. A writer is always opportunistic; he lets nothing go to waste. This makes people think we're insincere. We're not. We're just minding the store.

This is the story of a monster.

They named him Odysseus Gaul in honor of Papa's favorite hero, and over Mama's desperate objections; but he was known as Oddy from the age of one.

The first year of life is an egotistic craving for warmth and security. Oddy was not likely to have much of that when he was born, for Papa's real estate business was bankrupt, and Mama was thinking of divorce. But an unexpected decision by United Radiation to build a plant in the town made Papa wealthy, and Mama fell in love with him all over again. So Oddy had warmth and security.

The second year of life is a timid exploration. Oddy crawled and explored. When he reached for the crimson coils inside the nonobjective fireplace, an unexpected short circuit saved him from a burn. When he fell out the third-floor window, it was into the grass filled hopper of the Mechano-Gardener. When he teased the Phoebus Cat, it slipped as it snapped at his face, and the brilliant fangs clicked harmlessly over his ear.

"Animals love Oddy," Mama said. "They only pretend to bite."

Oddy wanted to be loved, so everybody loved Oddy. He was petted, pampered and spoiled through preschool age. Shopkeepers presented him with largess, and acquaintances showered him with gifts. Of sodas, candy, tarts, chrystons, bobble-trucks, freezies, and various other comestibles, Oddy consumed enough for an entire kindergarten. He was never sick.

"Takes after his father," Papa said. "Good stock."

Family legends grew about Oddy's luck. . . . How a perfect stranger mistook him for his own child just as Oddy was about to amble into the Electronic Circus, and delayed him long enough to save him from the disastrous explosion of '98. . . . How a forgotten library book rescued him from the Rocket Crash of '99. . . . How a multitude of odd incidents saved him from a multitude of assorted catastrophes. No one realized he was a monster . . . yet.

At eighteen, he was a nice-looking boy with seal-brown hair, warm brown eyes, and a wide grin that showed even white teeth. He was strong, healthy, intelligent. He was completely uninhibited in his quiet, relaxed way. He had charm. He was happy. So far, his monstrous evil had only affected the little Town Unit where he was born and raised.

He came to Harvard from a Progressive School, so when one of his many new friends popped into the dormitory room and said: "Hey Oddy, come down to the Quad and kick a ball around," Oddy answered: "I don't know how, Ben."

"Don't know how?" Ben tucked the football under his arm and dragged Oddy with him. "Where you been, laddie?"

"They didn't think much of football back home," Oddy grinned. "Said it was old-fashioned. We were strictly Huxley-Hob."

"Huxley-Hob! That's for eggheads," Ben said. "Football is still the big game. You want to be famous? You got to be on that gridiron on TV every Saturday."

"So I've noticed, Ben. Show me."

Ben showed Oddy, carefully and with patience. Oddy took the lesson seriously and industriously. His third punt was caught by a freakish gust of wind, traveled seventy yards through the air, and burst through the third-floor window of Proctor Charley (Gravy-Train) Stuart. Stuart took one look out the window and had Oddy down to Soldier Stadium in half an hour. Three Saturdays later, the headlines read: Oddy Gaul 57—Army 0.

"Snell and Rumination!" Coach Hig Clayton swore. "How does he do it? There's nothing sensational about that kid. He's just average. But when he runs, they fall down chasing him. When he kicks, they fumble. When they fumble, he recovers.''

''He's a negative player,'' Gravy-Train answered. ''He lets you make the mistakes, and then he cashes in.''

They were both wrong. Oddy Gaul was a monster.

With his choice of any eligible young woman, Oddy Gaul went stag to the Observatory Prom, wandered into a darkroom by mistake, and discovered a girl in a smock bending over trays in the hideous green safe-light. She had cropped black hair, icy blue eyes, strong features, and a sensuous, boyish figure. She ordered him out and Oddy fell in love with her . . . temporarily.

His friends howled with laughter when he told them. ''Shades of Pygmalion, Oddy, don't you know about *her*? The girl is frigid. A statue. She loathes men. You're wasting your time.''

But through the adroitness of her analyst, the girl turned a neurotic corner one week later and fell deeply in love with Oddy Gaul. It was sudden, devastating and enraptured for two months. Then just as Oddy began to cool, the girl had a relapse and everything ended on a friendly, convenient basis.

So far only minor events made up the response to Oddy's luck, but the shock wave of reaction was spreading. In September of his sophomore year, Oddy competed for the Political Economy Medal with a thesis entitled: ''Causes of Mutiny.'' The striking similarity of his paper to the Astraean mutiny that broke out the day his paper was entered won him the prize.

In October, Oddy contributed twenty dollars to a pool organized by a crackpot classmate for speculating on the Exchange according to ''Stock Market Trends,'' an ancient superstition. The prophet's calculations were ridiculous, but a sharp panic nearly ruined the Exchange as it quadrupled the pool. Oddy made one hundred dollars.

And so it went . . . worse and worse. The monster.

Now, a monster can get away with a lot when he's studying a speculative philosophy where causation is rooted in history and the Present is devoted to statistical analysis of the Past; but the living sciences are bulldogs with their teeth clamped on the phenomena of Now. So it was Jesse Migg, physiologist and spectral physicist, who first trapped the monster . . . and he thought he'd found an angel.

Old Jess was one of the Sights. In the first place he was young . . . not over forty. He was a malignant knife of a man, an albino, pink-eyed, bald, pointed-nose, and brilliant. He affected twentieth-century clothes and twentieth-century vices . . . tobacco and potations of C_2H_5OH. He never talked . . . He spat. He never walked . . . He scurried. And he was scurrying up and down the aisles of the laboratory of Tech I (General Survey of Spatial Mechanics—Required for All General Arts Students) when he ferreted out the monster.

One of the first experiments in the course was EMF Electrolysis. Elementary stuff. A U-Tube containing water was passed between the poles of a stock Remosant Magnet. After sufficient voltage was transmitted through the coils, you drew off hydrogen and oxygen in two-to-one ratio at the arms of the tube and related them to the voltage and the magnetic field.

Oddy ran his experiment earnestly, got the approved results, entered them in his lab book and then waited for the official check-off. Little Migg came hustling down the aisle, darted to Oddy and spat: "Finished?"

"Yes, sir."

Migg checked the book entries, glanced at the indicators at the ends of the tube, and stamped Oddy out with a sneer. It was only after Oddy was gone that he noticed the Remosant Magnet was obviously shorted. The wires were fused. There hadn't been any field to electrolyze the water.

"Hell and Damnation!" Migg grunted (he also affected twentieth-century vituperation) and rolled a clumsy cigarette.

He checked off possibilities in his comptometer head. 1. Gaul cheated. 2. If so, with what apparatus did he portion out the H_2 and O_2? 3. Where did he get the pure gases? 4. Why did he do it? Honesty was easier. 5. He didn't cheat. 6. How did he get the right results? 7. How did he get *any* results?

Old Jess emptied the U-Tube, refilled it with water, and ran off the experiment himself. He, too, got the correct result without a magnet.

"Christ on a raft!" he swore, unimpressed by the miracle, and infuriated by the mystery. He snooped, darting about like a hungry bat. After four hours he discovered that the steel bench supports were picking up a charge from the Greeson Coils in the basement and had thrown just enough field to make everything come out right.

"Coincidence," Migg spat. But he was not convinced.

Two weeks later, in Elementary Fission Analysis, Oddy completed his afternoon's work with a careful listing of resultant isotopes from selenuim to lanthanum. The only trouble, Migg discovered, was that there had been a mistake in the stock issued to Oddy. He hadn't received any U^{235} for neutron bombardment. His sample had been a leftover from a Stefan-Boltzmann black-body demonstration.

"God in Heaven!" Migg swore, and double-checked. Then he triple-checked. When he found the answer—a re-markable coincidence involving improperly cleaned apparatus and a defective cloud-chamber—he swore further. He also did some intensive thinking.

"There are accident-prones," Migg snarled at the reflection in his Self-Analysis Mirror. "How about good-luck prones? Horse manure!"

But he was a bulldog with his teeth sunk in phenomena. He tested Oddy Gaul. He hovered over him in the laboratory, cackling with infuriated glee as Oddy completed experiment after experiment with defective equipment. When Oddy successfully completed the Rutherford Classic—getting $_8O^{17}$ after exposing nitrogen to alpha radiation, but in this case without the use of nitrogen or alpha radiation—Migg actually clapped him on the back in delight. Then the little man investigated and found the logical, improbable chain of coin-cidences that explained it.

He devoted his spare time to a check-back on Oddy's career at Harvard. He had a two-hour conference with a lady astronomer's faculty analyst, and a ten-minute talk with Hig Clayton and Gravy-Train Stuart. He rooted out the Exchange Pool, the Political Economy Medal, and half a dozen other incidents that filled him with malignant joy. Then he cast off his twentieth-century affectation, dressed himself properly in formal leotards, and entered the Faculty Club for the first time in a year.

A four-handed chess game on a transparent toroid board was in progress in the Diathermy Alcove. It had been in progress since Migg joined the faculty, and would probably not be finished before the end of the century. In fact, Johansen, playing Red, was already training his son to replace him in the likely event of his dying before the completion of the game.

As abrupt as ever, Migg marched up to the glowing board, sparkling with vari-colored pieces, and blurted: "What do you know about accidents?"

"Ah?" said Bellanby, *Philosopher in Res* at the University. "Good evening, Migg. Do you mean the accident of substance, or the accident of essence? If, on the other hand, your question implies—"

"No, no," Migg interrupted. "My apologies, Bellanby. Let me rephrase the question. Is there such a thing as Compulsion of Probability?"

Hrrdnikkisch completed his move and gave full attention to Migg, as did Johansen and Bellanby. Wilson continued to study the board. Since he was permitted one hour to make his move and would need it, Migg knew there would be ample time for the discussion.

"Compulthon of Probability?" Hrrdnikkisch lisped. "Not a new conthept, Migg. I recall a thurvey of the theme in 'The Integraph' Vol. LVIII, No. 9. The calculuth, if I am not mithtaken—"

"No," Migg interrupted again. "My respects, Signoid. I'm not interested in the mathematics of probability, nor the philosophy. Let me put it this way. The accident-prone has already been incorporated into the body of psychoanalysis. Paton's Theorem of the Least Neurotic Norm settled that. But I've discovered the obverse. I've discovered a Fortune-Prone."

"Ah?" Johansen chuckled. "It's to be a joke. You wait and see, Signoid."

"No," answered Migg. "I'm perfectly serious. I've discovered a genuinely lucky man."

"He wins at cards?"

"He wins at everything. Accept this postulate for the moment. . . . I'll document it later. . . . There is a man who is lucky. He is a Fortune-Prone. Whatever he desires, he receives. Whether he has the ability to achieve it or not, he receives it. If his desire is totally beyond the peak of his accomplishment, then the factors of chance, coincidence, hazard, accident . . . and so on, combine to produce his desired end."

"No." Bellanby shook his head. "Too farfetched."

"I've worked it out empirically," Migg continued. "It's something like this. The future is a choice of mutually exclusive possibilities, one or other of which must be realized in terms of favorability of the events and number of the events. . . ."

"Yes, yes," interrupted Johansen. "The greater the number of favorable possibilities, the stronger the probability of an event maturing. This is elementary, Migg. Go on."

"I continue," Migg spat indignantly. "When we discuss probability in terms of throwing dice, the predictions or odds are simple. There are only six mutually exclusive possibilities to each die. The favorability is easy to compute. Chance is reduced to simple odds-ratios. *But* when we discuss probability in terms of the Universe, we cannot encompass enough data to make a prediction. There are too many factors. Favorability cannot be ascertained."

"All thith ith true," Hrrdnikkisch said, "but what of your Fortune-Prone?"

"I don't know how he does it . . . but merely by the intensity or mere existence of his desire, he can affect the favorability of possibilities. By wanting, he can turn possibility into probability, and probability into certainty."

"Ridiculous," Bellanby snapped. "You claim there's a man farsighted and far-reaching enough to do this?"

"Nothing of the sort. He doesn't know what he's doing. He just thinks he's lucky, if he thinks about it at all. Let us say he wants . . . Oh . . . Name anything."

"Heroin," Bellanby said.

"What's that?" Johansen inquired.

"A morphine derivative," Hrrdnikkisch explained. "Formerly manufactured and thold to narcotic addictth."

"Heroin," Migg said. "Excellent. Say my man desires heroin, an antique narcotic no longer in existence. Very good. His desire would compel this sequence of possible but improbable events: A chemist in Australia, fumbling through a new organic synthesis, will accidentally and unwittingly prepare six ounces of heroin. Four ounces will be discarded, but through a logical mistake two ounces will be preserved. A further coincidence will ship it to this country and this city, wrapped as powdered sugar in a plastic ball; where the final accident will serve it to my man in a restaurant which he is visiting for the first time on an impulse. . . ."

"La-La-La!" said Hrrdnikkisch. "Thith shuffling of hithtory. Thith fluctuation of inthident and pothibility? All achieved without the knowledge but with the dethire of a man?"

"Yes. Precisely my point," Migg snarled. "I don't know how he does it, but he turns possibility into certainty. And since almost anything is possible, he is capable of accomplishing almost anything. He is godlike but not a god, because he does this without consciousness. He is an angel."

"Who is this angel?" Johansen asked.

And Migg told them all about Oddy Gaul.

"But how does he do it?" Bellanby persisted. "How does he do it?"

"I don't know," Migg repeated again. "Tell me how Espers do it."

"What!" Bellanby exclaimed. "Are you prepared to deny the telepathic pattern of thought? Do you—"

"I do nothing of the sort. I merely illustrate one possible explanation. Man produces events. The threatening War of Resources may be thought to be a result of the natural exhaustion of Terran resources. We know it is not. It is a result of centuries of thriftless waste by man. Natural phenomena are less often produced by nature and more often produced by man."

"And?"

"Who knows? Gaul is producing phenomena. Perhaps

he's unconsciously broadcasting on a telepathic wave-band. Broadcasting and getting results. He wants heroin. The broadcast goes out—"

"But Espers can't pick up any telepathic pattern further than the horizon. It's direct wave transmission. Even large objects cannot be penetrated. A building, say, or a—"

"I'm not saying this is on the Esper level," Migg shouted. "I'm trying to imagine something bigger. Something tremendous. He wants heroin. His broadcast goes out to the world. All men unconsciously fall into a pattern of activity which will produce that heroin as quickly as possible. That Austrian chemist—"

"No. Australian."

"That Australian chemist may have been debating between half a dozen different syntheses. Five of them could never have produced heroin; but Gaul's impulse made him select the sixth."

"And if he did not anyway?"

"Then who knows what parallel chains were also started? A boy playing Robin Hood in Montreal is impelled to explore an abandoned cabin where he finds the drug, hidden there centuries ago by smugglers. A woman in California collects old apothecary jars. She finds a pound of heroin. A child in Berlin, playing with a defective Radar-Chem Set, manufactures it. Name the most improbable sequence of events, and Gaul can bring it about, logically and certainly. I tell you, that boy is an angel!"

And he produced his documented evidence and convinced them.

It was then that four scholars of various but indisputable intellects elected themselves an executive committee for Fate and took Oddy Gaul in hand. To understand what they attempted to do, you must first understand the situation the world found itself in during that particular era.

It is a known fact that all wars are founded in economic conflict, or to put it another way, a trial by arms is merely the last battle of an economic war. In the pre-Christian centuries, the Punic Wars were the final outcome of a financial struggle between Rome and Carthage for economic control of the Mediterranean. Three thousand years later, the impending

War of Resources loomed as the finale of a struggle between the two Independent Welfare States controlling most of the known economic world.

What petroleum oil was to the twentieth century, FO (the nickname for Fissionable Ore) was to the thirtieth; and the situation was peculiarly similar to the Asia Minor crisis that ultimately wrecked the United Nations a thousand years before. Triton, a backward semibarbaric satellite, previously unwanted and ignored, had suddenly discovered it possessed enormous resources of FO. Financially and technologically incapable of self-development, Triton was peddling concessions to both Welfare States.

The difference between a Welfare State and a Benevolent Despot is slight. In times of crisis, either can be traduced by the sincerest motives into the most abominable conduct. Both the Comity of Nations (bitterly nicknamed ''The Con Men'' by Der Realpolitik aus Terra) and Der Realpolitik aus Terra (sardonically called ''The Rats'' by the Comity of Nations) were desperately in need of natural resources, meaning FO. They were bidding against each other hysterically, and elbowing each other with sharp skirmishes at outposts. Their sole concern was the protection of their citizens. From the best of motives they were preparing to cut each other's throat.

Had this been the issue before the citizens of both Welfare States, some compromise might have been reached; but Triton, intoxicated as a schoolboy with a newfound prominence and power, confused issues by raising a religious issue and reviving a Holy War which the Family of Planets had long forgotten. Assistance in their Holy War (involving the extermination of a harmless and rather unimportant sect called the Quakers) was one of the conditions of sale. This, both the Comity of Nations and Der Realpolitik aus Terra were prepared to swallow with or without private reservations, but it could not be admitted to their citizens.

And so, camouflaged by the burning issues of Rights of Minority Sects, Priority of Pioneering, Freedom of Religion, Historical Rights to Triton v. Possession in Fact, etc., the two Houses of the Family of Planets feinted, parried, riposted and slowly closed, like fencers on the strip, for the final sortie which meant ruin for both.

All this the four men discussed through three interminable meetings.

"Look here," Migg complained toward the close of the third consultation. "You theoreticians have already turned nine man-hours into carbonic acid with ridiculous dissensions . . ."

Bellanby nodded, smiling. "It's as I've always said, Migg. Every man nurses the secret belief that were he God he could do the job much better. We're just learning how difficult it is."

"Not God," Hrrdnikkisch said, "but hith Prime Minithterth. Gaul will be God."

Johansen winced. "I don't like that talk," he said. "I happen to be a religious man."

"You?" Bellanby exclaimed in surprise. "A Colloid-Therapeutist?"

"I happen to be a religious man," Johansen repeated stubbornly.

"But the boy hath the power of the miracle," Hrrdnikkisch protested. "When he hath been taught to know what he doth, he will be a God."

"This is pointless," Migg rapped out. "We have spent three sessions in piffling discussion. I have heard three opposed views re Mr. Odysseus Gaul. Although all are agreed he must be used as a tool, none can agree on the work to which the tool must be set. Bellanby prattles about an Ideal Intellectual Anarchy, Johansen preaches about a Soviet of God, and Hrrdnikkisch has wasted two hours postulating and destroying his own theorems. . . ."

"Really, Migg . . ." Hrrdnikkisch began. Migg waved his hand.

"Permit me," Migg continued malevolently, "to reduce this discussion to the kindergarten level. First things first, gentlemen. Before attempting to reach cosmic agreement we must make sure there is a cosmos left for us to agree upon. I refer to the impending war. . . .

"Our program, as I see it, must be simple and direct. It is the education of a God or, if Johansen protests, of an angel. Fortunately Gaul is an estimable young man of kindly, honest disposition. I shudder to think what he might have done had he been inherently vicious.''

''Or what he might do once he learns what he can do,'' muttered Bellanby.

''Precisely. We must begin a careful and rigorous ethical education of the boy, but we haven't enough time. We can't educate first, and then explain the truth when he's safe. We must forestall the war. We need a shortcut.''

''All right,'' Johansen said. ''What do you suggest?''

''Dazzlement,'' Migg spat. ''Enchantment.''

''Enchantment?'' Hrrdnikkisch chuckled. ''A new thienth, Migg?''

''Why do you think I selected you three of all people for this secret?'' Migg snorted. ''For your intellects? Nonsense! I can think you all under the table. No. I selected you, gentlemen, for your charm.''

''It's an insult,'' Bellanby grinned, ''and yet I'm flattered.''

''Gaul is nineteen,'' Migg went on. ''He is at the age when undergraduates are most susceptible to hero-worship. I want you gentlemen to charm him. You are not the first brains of the University, but you are the first heroes.''

''I altho am inthulted and flattered,'' said Hrrdnikkisch.

''I want you to charm him, dazzle him, inspire him with affection and awe . . . as you've done with countless classes of undergraduates.''

''Aha!'' said Johansen. ''The chocolate around the pill.''

''Exactly. When he's enchanted, you will make him want to stop the war . . . and then tell him how he can stop it. That will give us breathing space to continue his education. By the time he outgrows his respect for you he will have a sound ethical foundation on which to build. He'll be safe.''

''And you, Migg?'' Bellanby inquired. ''What part do you play?''

''Now? None,'' Migg snarled. ''I have no charm, gentlemen. I come later. When he outgrows his respect for you, he'll begin to acquire respect for me.''

All of which was frightfully conceited but perfectly true. And as events slowly marched toward the final crisis,

Oddy Gaul was carefully and quickly enchanted. Bellanby invited him to the twenty-foot crystal globe atop his house . . . the famous hen-roost to which only the favored few were invited. There, Oddy Gaul sunbathed and admired the philosopher's magnificent iron-hard condition at seventy-three. Admiring Bellanby's muscles, it was only natural for him to admire Bellanby's ideas. He returned often to sun-bathe, worship the great man, and absorb ethical concepts.

Meanwhile, Hrrdnikkisch took over Oddy's evenings. With the mathematician, who puffed and lisped like some flamboyant character out of Rabelais, Oddy was carried to the dizzy heights of the *haute cuisine* and the complete pagan life. Together they ate and drank incredible foods and liquids and pursued incredible women until Oddy returned to his room each night intoxicated with the magic of the senses and the riotous color of the great Hrrdnikkisch's glittering ideas.

And occasionally . . . not too often, he would find Papa Johansen waiting for him, and then would come the long, quiet talks through the small hours when young men search for the harmonics of life and the meaning of entity. And there was Johansen for Oddy to model himself after . . . a glow-ing embodiment of Spiritual Good . . . a living example of Faith in God and Ethical Sanity.

The climax came on March 15 . . . The Ides of March, and they should have taken the date as a sign. After dinner with his three heroes at the Faculty Club, Oddy was ushered into the Foto-Library by the three great men where they were joined, quite casually, by Jesse Migg. There passed a few moments of uneasy tension until Migg made a sign, and Bellanby began.

"Oddy," he said, "have you ever had the fantasy that some day you might wake up and discover you were a king?"

Oddy blushed.

"I see you have. You know, every man has entertained that dream. It's called the Mignon Complex. The usual pattern is: You learn your parents have only adopted you and that you are actually and rightfully the King of . . . of . . ."

"Ruritania," said Hrrdnikkisch, who had made a study of Stone Age Fiction.

"Yes, sir," Oddy muttered. "I've had that dream."

"Well," Bellanby said quietly, "it's come true. You are a king."

Oddy stared while they explained and explained and explained. First, as a college boy, he was wary and suspicious of a joke. Then, as an idolator, he was almost persuaded by the men he most admired. And finally, as a human animal, he was swept away by the exaltation of security. Not power, not glory, not wealth thrilled him, but security alone. Later he might come to enjoy the trimmings, but now he was released from fear. He need never worry again.

"Yes," exclaimed Oddy. "Yes, yes, yes! I understand. I understand what you want me to do." He surged up excitedly from his chair and circled the illuminated walls, trembling with joy. Then he stopped and turned.

"And I'm grateful," he said. "Grateful to all of you for what you've been trying to do. It would have been shameful if I'd been selfish . . . or mean. . . . Trying to use this for myself. But you've shown me the way. It's to be used for good. Always!"

Johansen nodded happily.

"I'll always listen to you," Oddy went on. "I don't want to make any mistakes. Ever!" He paused and blushed again. "That dream about being a king . . . I had that when I was a kid. But here at the school I've had something bigger. I used to wonder what would happen if I was the one man who could run the world. I used to dream about the kind, generous things I'd do. . . ."

"Yes," said Bellanby. "We know, Oddy. We've all had that dream too. Every man does."

"But it isn't a dream any more," Oddy laughed. "It's reality. I can do it. I can make it happen."

"Start with the war," Migg said sourly.

"Of course," said Oddy. "The war first; but then we'll go on from there, won't we? I'll make sure the war never starts, but then we'll do big things . . . great things! Just the five of us in private. Nobody'll know about us. We'll be ordinary people, but we'll make life wonderful for everybody. If I'm an angel . . . like you say . . . then I'll spread heaven around me as far as I can reach."

"But start with the war," Migg repeated.

"The war is the first disaster that must be averted, Oddy," Bellanby said. "If you don't want this disaster to happen, it will never happen."

"And you want to prevent that tragedy, don't you?" said Johansen.

"Yes," answered Oddy. "I do."

On March 20, the war broke. The Comity of Nations and Der Realpolitik aus Terra mobilized and struck. While blow followed shattering counterblow, Oddy Gaul was commissioned subaltern in a line regiment, but gazetted to Intelligence on May 3. On June 24 he was appointed A.D.C. to the Joint Forces Council meeting in the ruins of what had been Australia. On July 11, he was brevetted to command of the wrecked Space Force, being jumped 1,789 grades over regular officers. On September 19 he assumed supreme command in the Battle of the Parsec and won the victory that ended the disastrous solar annihilation called the Six Month War.

On September 23, Oddy Gaul made the astonishing Peace Offer that was accepted by the remnants of both Welfare States. It required the scrapping of antagonistic economic theories, and amounted to the virtual abandonment of all economic theory with an amalgamation of both States into a Solar Society. On January 1, Oddy Gaul, by unanimous acclaim, was elected Solon of the Solar Society in perpetuity.

And today . . . still youthful, still vigorous, still handsome, still sincere, idealistic, charitable, kindly and sympathetic, he lives in the Solar Palace. He is unmarried but a mighty lover; uninhibited, but a charming host and devoted friend; democratic, but the feudal overlord of a bankrupt Family of Planets that suffers misgovernment, oppression, poverty, and confusion with a cheerful joy that sings nothing but Hosannahs to the glory of Oddy Gaul.

In a last moment of clarity, Jesse Migg communicated his desolate summation of the situation to his friends in the Faculty Club. This was shortly before they made the trip to join Oddy in the palace as his confidential and valued advisors.

"We were fools," Migg said bitterly. "We should have killed him. He isn't an angel. He's a monster. Civilization and culture . . . philosophy and ethics . . . those were only masks Oddy put on; masks that covered the primitive impulses of his subconscious mind.''

"You mean Oddy was not sincere?'' Johansen asked heavily. "He wanted this wreckage . . . this ruin?''

"Certainly he was sincere . . . consciously. He still is. He thinks he desires nothing but the most good for the most men. He's honest, kind and generous . . . but only consciously.''

"Ah! The Id!'' said Hrrdnikkisch with an explosion of breath as though he had been punched in the stomach.

"You understand, Signoid? I see you do. Gentlemen, we were imbeciles. We made the mistake of assuming that Oddy would have conscious control of his power. He does not. The control was and still is below the thinking, reasoning level. The control lies in Oddy's Id . . . in that deep, unconscious reservoir of primordial selfishness that lies within every man.''

"Then he wanted the war,'' Bellanby said.

"His Id wanted the war, Bellanby. It was the quickest route to what his Id desires . . . to be Lord of the Universe and loved by the Universe . . . and his Id controls the Power. All of us have that selfish, egocentric Id within us, perpetually searching for satisfaction, timeless, immortal, knowing no logic, no values, no good and evil, no morality; and that is what controls the Power in Oddy. He will always win, not what he's been educated to desire but what his Id desires. It's the inescapable conflict that may be the doom of our system.''

"But we'll be there to advise him . . . counsel him . . . guide him,'' Bellanby protested. "He asked us to come.''

"And he'll listen to our advice like the good child that he is,'' Migg answered, "agreeing with us, trying to make a heaven for everybody while his Id will be making a hell for everybody. Oddy isn't unique. We all suffer from the same conflict . . . but Oddy has the Power.''

"What can we do?'' Johansen groaned. "What can we do?''

"I don't know,'' Migg bit his lip, then bobbed his head to Papa Johansen in what amounted to apology for him.

"Johansen," he said, "you were right. There must be a God, if only because there must be an opposite to Oddy Gaul, who was most assuredly invented by the Devil."

But that was Jesse Migg's last sane statement. Now, of course, he adores Gaul the Glorious, Gaul the Gauleiter, Gaul the God Eternal who has achieved the savage, selfish satisfaction for which all of us unconsciously yearn from birth, but which only Oddy Gaul has won.

Hobson's Choice

THIS was the first short story I wrote after my first science fiction novel, and it brought about my first disagreement with Horace Gold, the splendid editor of Galaxy, who had contributed so much to the making of the novel. I can never thank him enough for that, for although I'm a damned good writer, I'm no better than my editor or director. The disagreement arose over the ending or lack of ending of "Hobson's Choice," and it was only one of many similar good-natured differences I've had with my bosses.

You see, I don't believe in a complete point-by-point wrap-up of a story. Very often I'll leave questions unresolved, whether I know the answer or not. I like to leave the reader with something hanging, anything that will make him smile and speculate. I'll do that with the punch line of a joke which is never told, or a phrase from a song which is never sung, and so on.

The device works, as a rule. People are amused because, I think, they enjoy the guessing part of a guessing game more than the solution. If there is no solution it doesn't matter, provided the enigma isn't a crucial part of the story. As a throwaway it's fine, more or less in a class with "Why is a raven like a writing desk?" Chuck Dodgson knew what he was doing when he left Alice and us hanging with that one.

On the other hand, if the enigma is the crux of the story, it must be resolved come hell or high water, which is why the Mysterious Message story is so irritating. I can't give its official title because I've read at least three different versions by three different authors, all with different titles. Apparently the original basis for the story must have been in the P.D. You must have read one of them.

283

Briefly: Traveler in foreign land has written message handed him by a stranger. Can't translate. Asks various natives to translate for him. Each one reads, refuses to translate and reacts violently; horrified, turns away in disgust, knocks him down, calls the cops, etc. Bewilderment. On board ship going home, traveler meets missionary type. Pours out story. Missionary offers to translate mysterious message. Swears as Man of God not to turn ugly. Guy hands over slip of paper. Wind catches same. Blows it overboard. End. This is Cruel and Unusual Punishment.

Well, my ending for "Hobson's Choice" was unresolved in one sense, yet resolved in another. I didn't think the definitive wrap-up which Horace wanted me to decide on would work. It wasn't the point of the story, and if I did lay a decision on the reader it would be a letdown. Try it yourself after you've read this story and see if I'm not right. I think you'll agree that sometimes nothing works better than something.

Now I'll confess the truth. I fell into the answer-trap myself; me, a past master of leaving 'em hanging. In one of the Nero Wolfe mysteries Archie Goodwin says to a girl, "Are you Catholic? What's the difference between a Catholic and a river that runs uphill?" Left unresolved. Left me puzzled for years. When I met Rex Stout at last, I reminded him of the conundrum and asked for the answer. He burst out laughing. "How the hell do I know? I just invented it for the scene."

Hoist by my own petard.

This is a warning to accomplices like you, me and Addyer.

Can you spare price of one cup coffee, honorable sir? I am indigent organism which are hungering.

By day, Addyer was a statistician. He concerned himself with such matters as Statistical Tables, Averages and Dispersions, Groups That Are Not Homogenous, and Random Sampling. At night, Addyer plunged into an elaborate escape fantasy divided into two parts. Either he imagined himself moved back in time a hundred years with a double armful of the *Encyclopaedia Britannica*, bestsellers, hit plays and gambling records; or else he imagined himself transported forward in time a thousand years to the Golden Age of perfection.

There were other fantasies which Addyer entertained on odd Thursdays, such as (by a fluke) becoming the only man left on earth with a world of passionate beauties to fecundate; such as acquiring the power of invisibility which would enable him to rob banks and right wrongs with impunity; such as possessing the mysterious power of working miracles.

Up to this point you and I and Addyer are identical. Where we part company is in the fact that Addyer was a statistician.

Can you spare cost of one cup coffee, honorable miss? For blessed charitability? I am beholden.

On Monday, Addyer rushed into his chief's office, waving a sheaf of papers. "Look here, Mr. Grande," Addyer sputtered. "I've found something fishy. Extremely fishy . . . In the statistical sense, that is."

"Oh, hell," Grande answered. "You're not supposed to be finding anything. We're in between statistics until the war's over."

"I was leafing through the Interior Department's reports. D'you know our population's up?"

"Not after the Atom Bomb it isn't," said Grande. "We've lost double what our birthrate can replace." He pointed out the window to the twenty-five-foot stub of the Washington Monument. "There's your documentation."

"But our population's up 3.0915 per cent." Addyer displayed his figures. "What about that, Mr. Grande?"

"Must be a mistake somewhere," Grande muttered after a moment's inspection. "You'd better check."

"Yes, sir," said Addyer scurrying out of the office. "I knew you'd be interested, sir. You're the ideal statistician, sir." He was gone.

"Poop," said Grande and once again began computing the

quantity of bored respirations left to him. It was his personalized anesthesia.

On Tuesday, Addyer discovered that there was no correlation between the mortality-birthrate ratio and the population increase. The war was multiplying mortality and reducing births; yet the population was minutely increasing. Addyer displayed his discovery to Grande, received a pat on the back, and went home to a new fantasy in which he woke up a million years in the future, learned the answer to the enigma, and decided to remain amidst snow-capped mountains and snow-capped bosoms, safe under the aegis of a culture saner than Aureomycin.

On Wednesday, Addyer requisitioned the comptometer and file and ran a test check on Washington, D.C. To his dismay, he discovered that the population of the former capital was down 0.0029 per cent. This was distressing, and Addyer went home to escape into a dream about Queen Victoria's Golden Age when he amazed and confounded the world with his brilliant output of novels, plays and poetry, all cribbed from Shaw, Galsworthy, and Wilde.

Can you spare price of one coffee, honorable sir? I am distressed individual needful of chariting.

On Thursday, Addyer tried another check, this time on the city of Philadelphia. He discovered that Philadelphia's population was up 0.0959 per cent. Very encouraging. He tried a rundown on Little Rock. Population up 1.1329 per cent. He tested St. Louis. Population up 2.0924 per cent . . . and this despite the complete extinction of Jefferson County owing to one of those military mistakes of an excessive nature.

"My God!" Addyer exclaimed, trembling with excitement. "The closer I get to the center of the country, the greater the increase. But it was the center of the country that took the heaviest punishment in the Buz-Raid. What's the answer?"

That night he shuttled back and forth between the future and the past in his ferment, and he was down at the shop by seven A.M. He put a twenty-four-hour claim on the Compo and Files. He followed up his hunch and he came up with a fantastic discovery which he graphed in approved form. On the map of the remains of the United States he drew concentric circles in colors illustrating the areas of population increase. The red, orange, yellow, green and blue circles formed a perfect target around Finney County, Kansas.

"Mr. Grande," Addyer shouted in a high statistical passion, "Finney County has got to explain this."

"You go out there and get that explanation," Grande replied, and Addyer departed.

"Poop," muttered Grande and began integrating his pulse-rate with his eye-blink.

Can you spare price of one coffee, dearly madam? I am starveling organism requiring nutritiousment.

Now travel in those days was hazardous. Addyer took ship to Charleston (there were no rail connections remaining in the North Atlantic states) and was wrecked off Hatteras by a rogue mine. He drifted in the icy waters for seventeen hours, muttering through his teeth: "Oh Christ! If only I'd been born a hundred years ago."

Apparently this form of prayer was potent. He was picked up by a Navy Sweeper and shipped to Charleston where he arrived just in time to acquire a subcritical radiation burn from a raid which fortunately left the railroad unharmed. He was treated for the burn from Charleston to Macon (change) from Birmingham to Memphis (bubonic plague) to Little Rock (polluted water) to Tulsa (fallout quarantine) to Kansas City (The O.K. Bus Co. Accepts No Liability for Lives Lost Through Acts of War) to Lyonesse, Finney County, Kansas.

And there he was in Finney County with its great magma pits and scars and radiation streaks; whole farms blackened and razed; whole highways so blasted they looked like dotted lines; whole population 4-F. Clouds of soot and fallout neutralizers hung over Finney County by day, turning it into a Pittsburgh on a still afternoon. Auras of radiation glowed at night, highlighted by the blinking red warning beacons, turning the county into one of those overexposed night photographs, all blurred and crosshatched by deadly slashes of light.

After a restless night in Lyonesse Hotel, Addyer went over to the county seat for a check on their birth records. He was armed with the proper credentials, but the county seat was not armed with the statistics. That excessive military mistake again. It had extinguished the seat.

A little annoyed, Addyer marched off to the County Medical Association office. His idea was to poll the local doctors on births. There was an office and one attendant who had been a practical nurse. He informed Addyer that Finney County had lost its last doctor to the army eight months previous. Midwives might be the answer to the birth enigma, but there was no record of midwives. Addyer would simply have to canvass from door to door, asking if any lady within practiced that ancient profession.

Further piqued, Addyer returned to the Lyonesse Hotel and wrote on a slip of tissue paper: HAVING DATA DIF-FICULTIES. WILL REPORT AS SOON AS INFORMA-TION AVAILABLE. He slipped the message into an aluminum capsule, attached it to his sole surviving carrier pigeon, and dispatched it to Washington with a prayer. Then he sat down at his window and brooded.

He was aroused by a curious sight. In the street below, the O.K. Bus Co. had just arrived from Kansas City. The old coach wheezed to a stop, opened its door with some difficulty and permitted a one-legged farmer to emerge. His burned face was freshly bandaged. Evidently this was a well-to-do burgess who could afford to travel for medical treatment. The bus backed up for the return trip to Kansas City and honked a warning horn. That was when the curious sight began.

From nowhere . . . absolutely nowhere . . . a horde of people appeared. They skipped from back alleys, from be-hind rubble piles; they popped out of stores, they filled the street. They were all jolly, healthy, brisk, happy. They laughed and chatted as they climbed into the bus. They looked like hikers and tourists, carrying knapsacks, carpet-bags, box lunches, and even babies. In two minutes the bus was filled. It lurched off down the road, and as it disappeared Addyer heard happy singing break out and echo from the walls of rubble.

"I'll be damned," he said.

He hadn't heard spontaneous singing in over two years. He hadn't seen a carefree smile in over three years. He felt like a color-blind man who was seeing the full spectrum for the first time. It was uncanny. It was also a little blasphemous.

"Don't those people know there's a war on?" he asked himself.

And a little later: "They looked too healthy. Why aren't they in uniform?"

And last of all: "Who *were* they anyway?"

That night Addyer's fantasy was confused.

Can you spare price of one cup coffee, kindly sir? I am estrangered and faintly from hungering.

The next morning Addyer arose early, hired a car at an exorbitant fee, found he could not buy any fuel at any price, and ultimately settled for a lame horse. He was allergic to horse dander and suffered asthmatic tortures as he began his house-to-house canvass. He was discouraged when he returned to the Lyonesse Hotel that afternoon. He was just in time to witness the departure of the O.K. Bus Co.

Once again a horde of happy people appeared and boarded the bus. Once again the bus hirpled off down the broken road. Once again the joyous singing broke out.

"I *will* be damned," Addyer wheezed.

He dropped into the County Surveyor's Office for a large scale map of Finney County. It was his intent to plot the midwife coverage in accepted statistical manner. There was a little difficulty with the surveyor, who was deaf, blind in one eye, and spectacleless in the other. He could not read Addyer's credentials with any faculty or facility. As Addyer finally departed with the map, he said to himself: "I think the old idiot thought I was a spy."

And later he muttered: "Spies?"

And just before bedtime: "Holy Moses! Maybe *that's* the answer to *them*."

That night he was Lincoln's secret agent, anticipating Lee's every move, outwitting Jackson, Johnston and Beauregard, foiling John Wilkes Booth, and being elected President of the United States by 1868.

The next day the O.K. Bus Co. carried off yet another load of happy people.

And the next.

And the next.

"Four hundred tourists in five days," Addyer computed. "The country's filled with espionage."

He began loafing around the streets trying to investigate these joyous travelers. It was difficult. They were elusive before the bus arrived. They had a friendly way of refusing to pass the time. The locals of Lyonesse knew nothing about them and were not interested. Nobody was interested in much more than painful survival these days. That was what made the singing obscene.

After seven days of cloak-and-dagger and seven days of counting, Addyer suddenly did the big take. "It adds up," he said. "Eighty people a day leaving Lyonesse. Five hundred a week. Twenty-five thousand a year. Maybe that's the answer to the population increase." He spent fifty-five dollars on a telegram to Grande with no more than a hope of delivery. The telegram read: "EUREKA. I HAVE FOUND (IT)."

Can you spare price of lone cup coffee, honorable madam? I am not tramp-handler but destitute life-form.

Addyer's opportunity came the next day. The O.K. Bus Co. pulled in as usual. Another crowd assembled to board the bus, but this time there were too many. Three people were refused passage. They weren't in the least annoyed. They stepped back, waved energetically as the bus started, shouted instructions for future reunions and then quietly turned and started off down the street.

Addyer was out of his hotel room like a shot. He followed the trio down the main street, turned left after them onto Fourth Avenue, passed the ruined schoolhouse, passed the demolished telephone building, passed the gutted library, railroad station, Protestant church, Catholic church . . . and finally reached the outskirts of Lyonesse and then open country.

Here he had to be more cautious. It was difficult stalking the spies with so much of the dusky road illuminated by warning lights. He wasn't suicidal enough to think of hiding in radiation pits. He hung back in an agony of indecision and was at last relieved to see them turn off the broken road and enter the old Baker farmhouse.

"Ah-ha!" said Addyer.

He sat down at the edge of the road on the remnants of a missile and asked himself: "Ah-ha what?" He could not answer, but he knew where to find the answer. He waited until dusk deepened to darkness and then slowly wormed his way forward toward the farmhouse.

It was while he was creeping between the deadly radiation glows and only occasionally butting his head against grave markers that he first became aware of two figures in the night. They were in the barnyard of the Baker place and were performing most peculiarly. One was tall and thin. A man. He stood stockstill, like a lighthouse. Upon occasion he took a slow, stately step with infinite caution and waved an arm in slow motion to the other figure. The second was also a man. He was stocky and trotted jerkily back and forth.

As Addyer approached, he heard the tall man say: "Rooo booo fooo mooo hwaaa looo fooo."

Whereupon the trotter chattered: "Wd-nk-kd-ik-md-pd-ld-nk."

Then they both laughed; the tall man like a locomotive, the trotter like a chipmunk. They turned. The trotter rocketed into the house. The tall man drifted in. And that was amazingly that.

"Oh-ho," said Addyer.

At that moment a pair of hands seized him and lifted him from the ground. Addyer's heart constricted. He had time for one convulsive spasm before something vague was pressed against his face. As he lost consciousness, his last idiotic thought was of telescopes.

Can you spare price of solitary coffee for no-loafing unfortunate, honorable sir? Charity will blessings.

When Addyer awoke he was lying on a couch in a small whitewashed room. A grey-haired gentleman with heavy features was seated at a desk alongside the couch, busily ciphering on bits of paper. The desk was cluttered with what appeared to be intricate timetables. There was a small radio perched on one side.

"L-Listen . . ." Addyer began faintly.

"Just a minute, Mr. Addyer," the gentleman said pleasantly. He fiddled with the radio. A glow germinated in the middle of the room over a circular copper plate and coalesced into a girl. She was extremely nude and extremely attractive. She scurried to the desk, patted the gentleman's head with the speed of a pneumatic hammer. She laughed and chattered: "Wd-nk-tk-ik-lt-nk."

The grey-haired man smiled and pointed to the door. "Go outside and walk it off," he said. She turned and streaked through the door.

"It has something to do with temporal rates," the gentleman said to Addyer. "I don't understand it. When they come forward, they've got accumulated momentum." He began ciphering again. "Why in the world did you have to come snooping, Mr. Addyer?"

"You're spies," Addyer said. "She was talking Chinese."

"Hardly. I'd say it was French. Early French. Middle fifteenth century."

"Middle fifteenth century!" Addyer exclaimed.

"That's what I'd say. You begin to acquire an ear for those stepped-up tempos. Just a minute, please."

He switched the radio on again. Another glow appeared and solidified into a nude man. He was stout, hairy and lugubrious. With exasperating slowness he said: "Mooo fooo blooo wawww hawww pooo."

The grey-haired man pointed to the door. The stout man departed in slow motion.

"The way I see it," the grey-haired man continued conversationally, "when they come back they're swimming against the time current. That slows 'em down. When they come forward, they're swimming with the current. That speeds 'em up. Of course, in any case it doesn't last longer than a few minutes. It wears off."

"What?" Addyer said. "Time travel?"

"Yes. Of course."

"That thing . . ." Addyer pointed to the radio. "A time machine?"

"That's the idea. Roughly."

"But it's too small."

The grey-haired man laughed.

"What is this place anyway? What are you up to?"

"It's a funny thing," the grey-haired man said. "Everybody used to speculate about time travel. How it would be used for exploration, archaeology, historical and social research and so on. Nobody ever guessed what the real use would be. . . . Therapy."

"Therapy? You mean medical therapy?"

"That's right. Psychological therapy for the misfits who won't respond to any other cure. We let them emigrate. Escape. We've set up stations every quarter century. Stations like this."

"I don't understand."

"This is an immigration office."

"Oh my God!" Addyer shot up from the couch. "Then you're the answer to the population increase. Yes? That's how I happened to notice it. Mortality's up so high and birth's down so low these days that your time-addition becomes significant. Yes?"

"Yes, Mr. Addyer."

"Thousands of you coming here. From where?"

"From the future, of course. Time travel wasn't developed until C/H 127. That's . . . oh, say, 2505 A.D. your chronology. We didn't set up our chain of stations until C/H 189."

"But those fast-moving ones. You said they came forward from the past."

"Oh, yes, but they're all from the future originally. They just decided they went too far back."

"Too far?"

The grey-haired man nodded and reflected. "It's amusing, the mistakes people will make. They become unrealistic when they read history. Lose contact with facts. Chap I knew . . . wouldn't be satisfied with anything less than Elizabethan times. 'Shakespeare,' he said. 'Good Queen Bess. Spanish Armada. Drake and Hawkins and Raleigh.

Most virile period in history. The Golden Age. That's for me.' I couldn't talk sense into him, so we sent him back. Too bad.''

"Well?" Addyer asked.

"Oh, he died in three weeks. Drank a glass of water. Typhoid.''

"You didn't inoculate him? I mean, the army when it sends men overseas always—''

"Of course we did. Gave him all the immunization we could. But diseases evolve and change, too. New strains develop. Old strains disappear. That's what causes pandemics. Evidently our shots wouldn't take against the Elizabethan typhoid. Excuse me . . .''

Again the glow appeared. Another nude man appeared, chattered briefly and then whipped through the door. He almost collided with the nude girl who poked her head in, smiled and called in a curious accent: "Ie vous prie de me pardonner. Quy estoit cette gentilhomme?''

"I was right," the grey-haired man said. "That's medieval French. They haven't spoken like that since Rabelais.'' To the girl he said, "Middle English, please. The American dialect.''

"Oh. I'm sorry, Mr. Jelling. I get so damned fouled up with my linguistics. Fouled? Is that right? Or do they say—''

"Hey!" Addyer cried in anguish.

"They say it, but only in private these years. Not before strangers.''

"Oh, yes. I remember. Who was that gentleman who just left?''

"Peters.''

"From Athens?''

"That's right.''

"Didn't like it, eh?''

"Not much. Seems the Peripatetics didn't have plumbing.''

"Yes. You begin to hanker for a modern bathroom after a while. Where do I get some clothes . . . or don't they wear clothes this century?''

"No, that's a hundred years forward. Go see my wife.

She's in the outfitting room in the barn. That's the big red building.''

The tall lighthouse-man Addyer had first seen in the farmyard suddenly manifested himself behind the girl. He was now dressed and moving at normal speed. He stared at the girl; she stared at him. ''Splem!'' they both cried. They embraced and kissed shoulders.

''St'u my rock-ribbering rib-rockery to heart the hearts two,'' the man said.

''Heart's too, argal, too heart,'' the girl laughed.

''Eh? Then you st'u too.''

They embraced again and left.

''What was that? Future talk?'' Addyer asked. ''Shorthand?''

''Shorthand?'' Jelling exclaimed in a surprised tone. ''Don't you know rhetoric when you hear it? That was thirtieth-century rhetoric, man. We don't talk anything else up there. Prosthesis, Diastole, Epergesis, Metabasis, Hendiadys . . . And we're all born scanning.''

''You don't have to sound so stuck up,'' Addyer muttered enviously. ''I could scan too if I tried.''

''You'd find it damned inconvenient trying at your time of life.''

''What difference would that make?''

''It would make a big difference,'' Jelling said, ''because you'd find that living is the sum of conveniences. You might think plumbing is pretty unimportant compared to ancient Greek philosophers. Lots of people do. But the fact is, we already know the philosophy. After a while you get tired of seeing the great men and listening to them expound the material you already know. You begin to miss the conveniences and familiar patterns you used to take for granted.''

''That,'' said Addyer, ''is a superficial attitude.''

''You think so? Try living in the past by candlelight, without central heating, without refrigeration, canned foods, elementary drugs. . . . Or, future-wise, try living with Berganlicks, the Twenty-Two Commandments. Duodecimal calendars and currency, or try speaking in meter, planning and scanning each sentence before you talk . . . and damned for a contemptible illiterate if you forget yourself and speak spontaneously in your own tongue.''

"You're exaggerating," Addyer said. "I'll bet there are times where I could be very happy. I've thought about it for years, and I—"

"Tcha!" Jelling snorted. "The great illusion. Name one."

"The American Revolution."

"Pfui! No sanitation. No medicine. Cholera in Philadelphia. Malaria in New York. No anesthesia. The death penalty for hundreds of small crimes and petty infractions. None of the books and music you like best. None of the jobs or professions for which you've been trained. Try again."

"The Victorian Age."

"How are your teeth and eyes? In good shape? They'd better be. We can't send your inlays and spectacles back with you. How are your ethics? In bad shape? They'd better be, or you'd starve in that cutthroat era. How do you feel about class distinctions? They were pretty strong in those days. What's your religion? You'd better not be a Jew or Catholic or Quaker or Moravian or any minority. What's your politics? If you're a reactionary today, the same opinions would make you a dangerous radical a hundred years ago. I don't think you'd be happy."

"I'd be safe."

"Not unless you were rich; and we can't send money back. Only the flesh. No, Addyer, the poor died at the average age of forty in those days . . . worked out, worn out. Only the privileged survived, and you wouldn't be one of the privileged."

"Not with my superior knowledge?"

Jelling nodded wearily. "I knew *that* would come up sooner or later. What superior knowledge? Your hazy recollection of science and invention? Don't be a damned fool, Addyer. You enjoy your technology without the faintest idea of how it works."

"It wouldn't have to be hazy recollection. I could prepare."

"What, for instance?"

"Oh . . . say, the radio. I could make a fortune inventing the radio."

Jelling smiled. "You couldn't invent radio until you'd first invented the hundred allied technical discoveries that went into it. You'd have to create an entire new industrial world. You'd have to discover the vacuum rectifier and create an industry to manufacture it; the self-heterodyne circuit, the nonradiating neutrodyne receiver, and so forth. You'd have to develop electric power production and transmission and alternating current. You'd have to—but why belabor the obvious? Could you invent internal combustion before the development of fuel oils?"

"My God!" Addyer groaned.

"And another thing," Jelling went on grimly. "I've been talking about technological tools, but language is a tool, too; the tool of communication. Did you ever realize that all the studying you might do could never teach you how a language was really used centuries ago? Do you know how the Romans pronounced Latin? Do you know the Greek dialects? Could you learn to speak and think in Gaelic, seventeenth-century Flemish, Old Low German? Never. You'd be a deaf-mute."

"I never thought about it that way," Addyer said slowly.

"Escapists never do. All they're looking for is a vague excuse to run away."

"What about books? I could memorize a great book and—"

"And what? Go back far enough into the past to anticipate the real author? You'd be anticipating the public, too. A book doesn't become great until the public's ready to understand it. It doesn't become profitable until the public's ready to buy it."

"What about going forward into the future?" Addyer asked.

"I've already told you. It's the same problem only in reverse. Could a medieval man survive in the twentieth century? Could he stay alive in street traffic? Drive cars? Speak the language? Think in the language? Adapt to the tempo, ideas and coordinations you take for granted? Never. Could someone from the twenty-fifth century adapt to the thirtieth? Never."

"Well, then," Addyer said angrily, "if the past and future are so uncomfortable, what are those people traveling around for?"

"They're not traveling," Jelling said. "They're running."

"From what?"

"Their own time."

"Why?"

"They don't like it."

"Why not?"

"Do you like yours? Does any neurotic?"

"Where are they going?"

"Anyplace but where they belong. They keep looking for the Golden Age. Tramps! Time-stiffs! Never satisfied. Always searching, shifting . . . bumming through the centuries. Pfui! Half the panhandlers you meet are probably time-bums stuck in the wrong century."

"And those people coming here . . . they think *this* is a Golden Age?"

"They do."

"They're crazy," Addyer protested. "Have they seen the ruins? The radiation? The war? The anxiety? The hysteria?"

"Sure. That's what appeals to them. Don't ask me why. Think of it this way: You like the American Colonial period, yes?"

"Among others."

"Well, if you told Mr. George Washington the reasons why you liked his time, you'd probably be naming everything he hated about it."

"But that's not a fair comparison. This is the worst age in all history."

Jelling waved his hand. "That's how it looks to you. Everybody says that in every generation; but take my word for it, no matter when you live and how you live, there's always somebody else somewhere else who thinks you live in the Golden Age."

"Well I'll be damned," Addyer said.

Jelling looked at him steadily for a long moment. "You will be," he said sorrowfully. "I've got bad news for you, Addyer. We can't let you remain. You'll talk and make trouble, and our secret's got to be kept. We'll have to send you out one-way.''

"I can talk wherever I go.''

"But nobody'll pay attention to you outside your own time. You won't make sense. You'll be an eccentric . . . a lunatic . . . a foreigner . . . safe.''

"What if I come back?''

"You won't be able to get back without a visa, and I'm not tattooing any visa on you. You won't be the first we've had to transport, if that's any consolation to you. There was a Jap, I remember—''

"Then you're going to send me somewhere in time? Permanently?''

"That's right. I'm really very sorry.''

"To the future or the past?''

"You can take your choice. Think it over while you're getting undressed.''

"You don't have to act so mournful,'' Addyer said. "It's a great adventure. A high adventure. It's something I've always dreamed.''

"That's right. It's going to be wonderful.''

"I could refuse,'' Addyer said nervously.

Jelling shook his head. "We'd only drug you and send you anyway. It might as well be your choice.''

"It's a choice I'm delighted to make.''

"Sure. That's the spirit, Addyer.''

"Everybody says I was born a hundred years too soon.''

"Everybody generally says that . . . unless they say you were born a hundred years too late.''

"Some people say that too.''

"Well, think it over. It's a permanent move. Which would you prefer . . . the phonetic future or the poetic past?''

Very slowly Addyer began to undress, as he undressed each night when he began the prelude to his customary fantasy. But now his dreams were faced with fulfillment and the moment of decision terrified him. He was a little blue and rather unsteady on his legs when he stepped to the copper disc in the center of the floor. In answer to Jelling's inquiry, he muttered his choice. Then he turned argent in the aura of an incandescent glow and disappeared from his time forever.

Where did he go? You know. I know. Addyer knows. Addyer traveled to the land of Our pet fantasy. He escaped into the refuge that is Our refuge, to the time of Our dreams; and in practically no time at all he realized that he had in truth departed from the only time for himself.

Through the vistas of the years every age but our own seems glamorous and golden. We yearn for the yesterdays and tomorrows, never realizing that we are faced with Hobson's Choice . . . that today, bitter or sweet, anxious or calm, is the only day for us. The dream of time is the traitor, and we are all accomplices to the betrayal of ourselves.

Can you spare price of one coffee, honorable sir? No, sir, I am not panhandling organism. I am starveling Japanese transient stranded in this so-miserable year. Honorable sir! I beg in tears for holy charity. Will you donate to this destitute person one ticket to township of Lyonesse? I want to beg on knees for visa. I want to go back to year 1945 again. I want to be in Hiroshima again. I want to go home.

Star Light, Star Bright

THE Chase formula and the Search formula have been with us for a long time and will remain on the scene for a long time to come. They're sure-fire if handled with originality and can make your pulse pound like a Sousa march. I'm a little disappointed in the Hollywood writers, to say the least. Their idea of a chase seems to be one car pursuing another.

Chase and search aren't identical; you can have one without the other, but both together are best. Back in the carefree comic book days I even tried a tandem; started with an ordinary paper chase and then the paper trail turned into a trail of paper money. I wish I could remember the hero I did it for; "The Green Lantern"? "The Star-Spangled Kid"? "Captain Marvel"? I also wish I could remember how the story turned out.

You've probably noticed that I don't remember my work very well. Frankly, I never look at anything after it's been published, and anyway I'm not unique in that respect. I got it from the best authority, Jed Harris, that our wonderful popular composer, Jerome Kern, could never remember his own songs. In the course of a party, he'd be coaxed to the piano to play his tunes. Everybody would cluster around, but as he played they'd have to correct him. "No, no, Jerry! It doesn't go like that." And they'd be forced to sing his hits to him to refresh his memory.

"Star Light, Star Bright" is a search with a chase tempo. I don't know where I got the central idea but in those days science fiction authors were worrying a lot in print about misunderstood wild talents and child geniuses, so I guess it rubbed off on me. No, that can't be right. I'd tried the recipe *many years before with a young nature counselor in a summer camp who is an idiot-genius and terribly misunderstood. But he solves a kidnapping despite the fact that I'd given him the ridiculous name of Erasmus Gaul.*

The story-attack and the search techniques in "Star Light" were all from gimmick research. The Heirs of Buchanan swindle was a racket years ago and probably still is, in one form or another. God knows, they never die. In our sophomore year my college roommate got taken for his month's allowance ($20) by a couple of petty cons in Pennsylvania Station. Years later I read the identical racket in Greene's "The Art of Cony Catching" published circa 1592. No, they never die. Also, there's one born every minute.

I rather liked the story while I was writing it, but I don't like the fourth and third paragraphs from the end, counting backward from the end. They're the result of the same old battle which I lost this time to Tony Boucher of Fantasy & Science Fiction, *again over specifics. He wanted me to wrap up the story by showing precisely what happened to the victims. I wanted to slough it. I lost and had to add the paragraphs.*

When I was defeated in the battle of specifics with Horace Gold over "Hobson's Choice," I took the story back and gave it to Tony, who ran it. When I lost the battle with Tony, I should have taken "Star Light" back and sent it to Horace in a plain brown wrapper. I didn't, and now I'm stuck with those two rotten paragraphs. Please read them with your eyes shut.

The man in the car was thirty-eight years old. He was tall, slender, and not strong. His cropped hair was prematurely grey. He was afflicted with an education and a sense of humor. He was inspired by a purpose. He was armed with a phone book. He was doomed.

He drove up Post Avenue, stopped at No. 17 and parked. He consulted the phone book, then got out of the car and entered the house. He examined the mailboxes and then ran up the stairs to apartment 2-F. He rang the bell. While he waited for an answer he got out a small black notebook and a superior silver pencil that wrote in four colors.

The door opened. To a nondescript middle-aged lady, the man said, "Good evening. Mrs. Buchanan?"

The lady nodded.

"My name is Foster. I'm from the Science Institute. We're trying to check some flying saucer reports. I won't take a minute." Mr. Foster insinuated himself into the apartment. He had been in so many that he knew the layout automatically. He marched briskly down the hall to the front parlor, turned, smiled at Mrs. Buchanan, opened the notebook to a blank page, and poised the pencil.

"Have you ever seen a flying saucer, Mrs. Buchanan?"

"No. And it's a lot of bunk, I—"

"Have your children ever seen them? You do have children?"

"Yeah, but they—"

"How many?"

"Two. Them flying saucers never—"

"Are either of school age?"

"What?"

"School," Mr. Foster repeated impatiently. "Do they go to school?"

"The boy's twenty-eight," Mrs. Buchanan said. "The girl's twenty-four. They finished school a long—"

"I see. Either of them married?"

"No. About them flying saucers, you scientist doctors ought to—"

"We are," Mr. Foster interrupted. He made a tic-tac-toe in the notebook, then closed it and slid it into an inside pocket with the pencil. "Thank you very much, Mrs. Buchanan," he said, turned, and marched out.

Downstairs, Mr. Foster got into the car, opened the telephone directory, turned to a page and ran his pencil through a name. He examined the name underneath, memorized the address and started the car. He drove to Fort George Avenue and stopped the car in front of No. 800. He entered the house and took the self-service elevator to the fourth floor. He rang the bell of apartment 4-G. While he waited for an answer he got out the small black notebook and the superior pencil.

The door opened. To a truculent man, Mr. Foster said, "Good evening. Mr. Buchanan?"

"What about it?" the truculent man said.

Mr. Foster said, "My name is Davis. I'm from the Association of National Broadcasters. We're preparing a list of names for prize competitors. May I come in? Won't take a minute."

Mr. Foster/Davis insinuated himself and presently consulted with Mr. Buchanan and his redheaded wife in the living room of their apartment.

"Have you ever won a prize in radio or television?"

"No," Mr. Buchanan said angrily. "We never got a chance. Everybody else does but not us."

"All that free money and iceboxes," Mrs. Buchanan said. "Trips to Paris and planes and—"

"That's why we're making up this list," Mr. Foster/Davis broke in. "Have any of your relatives won prizes?"

"No. It's all a fix. Put-up jobs. They—"

"Any of your children?"

"Ain't got any children."

"I see. Thank you very much." Mr. Foster/Davis played out the tic-tac-toe game in his notebook, closed it and put it away. He released himself from the indignation of the Buchanans, went down to his car, crossed out another name in the phone book, memorized the address of the name underneath and started the car.

He drove to No. 215 East Sixty-Eighth Street and parked in front of a private brownstone house. He rang the doorbell and was confronted by a maid in uniform.

"Good evening," he said. "Is Mr. Buchanan in?"

"Who's calling?"

"My name is Hook," Mr. Foster/Davis said, "I'm conducting an investigation for the Better Business Bureau."

The maid disappeared, reappeared and conducted Mr. Foster/Davis/Hook to a small library where a resolute gentleman in dinner clothes stood holding a Limoges demitasse cup and saucer. There were expensive books on the shelves. There was an expensive fire in the grate.

"Mr. Hook?"

"Yes, sir," the doomed man replied. He did not take out the notebook. "I won't be a minute, Mr. Buchanan. Just a few questions."

"I have great faith in the Better Business Bureau," Mr. Buchanan pronounced. "Our bulwark against the inroads of—"

"Thank you, sir," Mr. Foster/Davis/Hook interrupted. "Have you ever been criminally defrauded by a businessman?"

"The attempt has been made. I have never succumbed."

"And your children? You do have children?"

"My son is hardly old enough to qualify as a victim."

"How old is he, Mr. Buchanan?"

"Ten."

"Perhaps he has been tricked at school? There are crooks who specialize in victimizing children."

"Not at my son's school. He is well protected."

"What school is that, sir?"

"Germanson."

"One of the best. Did he ever attend a city public school?"

"Never."

The doomed man took out the notebook and the superior pencil. This time he made a serious entry.

"Any other children, Mr. Buchanan?"

"A daughter, seventeen."

Mr. Foster/Davis/Hook considered, started to write, changed his mind and closed the notebook. He thanked his host politely and escaped from the house before Mr. Buchanan could ask for his credentials. He was ushered out by the maid, ran down the stoop to his car, opened the door, entered and was felled by a tremendous blow on the side of his head.

When the doomed man awoke, he thought he was in bed suffering from a hangover. He started to crawl to the bathroom when he realized he was dumped in a chair like a suit for the cleaners. He opened his eyes. He was in what appeared to be an underwater grotto. He blinked frantically. The water receded.

He was in a small legal office. A stout man who looked like

an unfrocked Santa Claus stood before him. To one side, seated on a desk and swinging his legs carelessly, was a thin young man with a lantern jaw and eyes closely set on either side of his nose.

"Can you hear me?" the stout man asked.

The doomed man grunted.

"Can we talk?"

Another grunt.

"Joe," the stout man said pleasantly, "a towel."

The thin young man slipped off the desk, went to a corner basin and soaked a white hand towel. He shook it once, sauntered back to the chair where, with a suddenness and savagery of a tiger, he lashed it across the sick man's face.

"For God's sake!" Mr. Foster/Davis/Hook cried.

"That's better," the stout man said. "My name's Herod. Walter Herod, attorney-at-law." He stepped to the desk where the contents of the doomed man's pockets were spread, picked up a wallet and displayed it. "Your name is Warbeck. Marion Perkin Warbeck. Right?"

The doomed man gazed at his wallet, then at Walter Herod, attorney-at-law, and finally admitted the truth. "Yes," he said. "My name is Warbeck. But I never admit the Marion to strangers."

He was again lashed by the wet towel and fell back in the chair, stung and bewildered.

"That will do, Joe," Herod said. "Not again, please, until I tell you." To Warbeck he said, "Why this interest in the Buchanans?" He waited for an answer, then continued pleasantly, "Joe's been tailing you. You've averaged five Buchanans a night. Thirty, so far. What's your angle?"

"What the hell is this? Russia?" Warbeck demanded indignantly. "You've got no right to kidnap me and grill me like the MVD. If you think you can—"

"Joe," Herod interrupted pleasantly. "Again, please."

Again the towel lashed Warbeck. Tormented, furious and helpless, he burst into tears.

Herod fingered the wallet casually. "Your papers say you're a teacher by profession, principal of a public school. I thought teachers were supposed to be legit. How did you get mixed up in the inheritance racket?"

"The what racket?" Warbeck asked faintly.

"The inheritance racket," Herod repeated patiently. "The Heirs of Buchanan caper. What kind of parlay are you using? Personal approach?"

"I don't know what you're talking about," Warbeck answered. He sat bolt upright and pointed to the thin youth. "And don't start that towel business again."

"I'll start what I please and when I please," Herod said ferociously. "And I'll finish you when I goddamned well please. You're stepping on my toes and I don't buy it. I've got seventy-five thousand a year I'm taking out of this and I'm not going to let you chisel."

There was a long pause, significant for everybody in the room except the doomed man. Finally he spoke. "I'm an educated man," he said slowly. "Mention Galileo, say, or the lesser Cavalier poets, and I'm right up there with you. But there are gaps in my education and this is one of them. I can't meet the situation. Too many unknowns."

"I told you my name," Herod answered. He pointed to the thin young man. "That's Joe Davenport."

Warbeck shook his head. "Unknown in the mathematical sense. X quantities. Solving equations. My education speaking."

Joe looked startled. "Jesus!" he said without moving his lips. "Maybe he *is* legit."

Herod examined Warbeck curiously. "I'm going to spell it out for you," he said. "The inheritance racket is a long-term con. It operates something like so: There's a story that James Buchanan—"

"Fifteenth President of the U.S.?"

"In person. There's a story he died intestate leaving an estate for heirs unknown. That was in 1868. Today at compound interest that estate is worth millions. Understand?"

Warbeck nodded. "I'm educated," he murmured.

"Anybody named Buchanan is a sucker for this setup. It's a switch on the Spanish Prisoner routine. I send them a letter. Tell 'em there's a chance they may be one of the heirs. Do they want me to investigate and protect their cut in the estate? It only costs a small yearly retainer. Most of them buy it. From all over the country. And now you—"

"Wait a minute," Warbeck exclaimed. "I can draw a conclusion. You found out I was checking the Buchanan families. You think I'm trying to operate the same racket. Cut in . . . cut in? Yes? Cut in on you?"

"Well," Herod asked angrily, "aren't you?"

"Oh God!" Warbeck cried. "That this should happen to me. Me! Thank You, God. Thank you. I'll always be grateful." In his happy fervor he turned to Joe. "Give me the towel, Joe," he said. "Just throw it. I've got to wipe my face." He caught the flung towel and mopped himself joyously.

"Well," Herod repeated. "Aren't you?"

"No," Warbeck answered, "I'm not cutting in on you. But I'm grateful for the mistake. Don't think I'm not. You can't imagine how flattering it is for a schoolteacher to be taken for a thief."

He got out of the chair and went to the desk to reclaim his wallet and other possessions.

"Just a minute," Herod snapped.

The thin young man reached out and grasped Warbeck's wrist with an iron clasp.

"Oh stop it," the doomed man said impatiently. "This is a silly mistake."

"I'll tell you whether it's a mistake and I'll tell you if it's silly," Herod replied. "Just now you'll do as you're told."

"Will I?" Warbeck wrenched his wrist free and slashed Joe across the eyes with the towel. He darted around behind the desk, snatched up a paperweight and hurled it through the window with a shattering crash.

"Joe!" Herod yelled.

Warbeck knocked the phone off its stand and dialed Operator. He picked up his cigarette lighter, flicked it and dropped it into the wastepaper basket. The voice of the operator buzzed in the phone. Warbeck shouted, "I want a policeman!" Then he kicked the flaming basket into the center of the office.

"Joe!" Herod yelled and stamped on the blazing paper.

Warbeck grinned. He picked up the phone. Squawking noises were coming out of it. He put one hand over the mouthpiece. "Shall we negotiate?" he inquired.

"You sonofabitch," Joe growled. He took his hands from his eyes and slid toward Warbeck.

"No!" Herod called. "This crazy fool's hollered copper. He's legit, Joe." To Warbeck he said in pleading tones, "Fix it. Square it. We'll make it up to you. Anything you say. Just square the call."

The doomed man lifted the phone to his mouth. He said, "My name is M. P. Warbeck. I was consulting my attorney at this number and some idiot with a misplaced sense of humor made this call. Please phone back and check."

He hung up, finished pocketing his private property and winked at Herod. The phone rang, Warbeck picked it up, reassured the police and hung up. He came around from behind the desk and handed his car keys to Joe.

"Go down to my car," he said. "You know where you parked it. Open the glove compartment and bring up a brown manila envelope you'll find."

"Go to hell," Joe spat. His eyes were still tearing.

"Do as I say," Warbeck said firmly.

"Just a minute, Warbeck," Herod said. "What's this? A new angle? I said we'd make it up to you, but—"

"I'm going to explain why I'm interested in the Buchanans," Warbeck replied. "And I'm going into partnership with you. You've got what I need to locate one particular Buchanan . . . you and Joe. My Buchanan's ten years old. He's worth a hundred times your make-believe fortune."

Herod stared at him.

Warbeck placed the keys in Joe's hand. "Go down and get that envelope, Joe," he said. "And while you're at it you'd better square that broken window rap. Rap? Rap."

The doomed man placed the manila envelope neatly on his lap. "A school principal," he explained, "has to supervise school classes. He reviews work, estimates progress, irons out student problems and so on. This must be done at random. By samplings, I mean. I have nine hundred pupils in my school. I can't supervise them individually."

Herod nodded. Joe looked blank.

"Looking through some fifth-grade work last month,"

Warbeck continued, ''I came across this astonishing document.'' He opened the envelope and took out a few sheets of ruled composition paper covered with blots and scrawled writing. ''It was written by a Stuart Buchanan of the fifth grade. His age must be ten or thereabouts. The composition is entitled: *My Vacation*. Read it and you'll understand why Stuart Buchanan must be found.''

He tossed the sheets to Herod who picked them up, took out a pair of horn-rim spectacles and balanced them on his fat nose. Joe came around to the back of his chair and peered over his shoulder.

My Vacatoin
by
Stuart Buchanan

This sumer I vissited my frends. I have 4 frends and they are verry nice. First there is Tommy who lives in the contry and he is an astronnimer. Tommy bilt his own tellescop out of glass 6 inches acros wich he grond himself. He loks at the stars every nihgt and he let me lok even wen it was raining cats & dogs . . .

''What the hell?'' Herod looked up, annoyed.
''Read on. Read on,'' Warbeck said.

cats & dogs. We cold see the stars becaze Tommy made a thing for over the end of the tellescop wich shoots up like a serchlite and makes a hole in the skie to see rite thru the rain and everythinng to the stars.

''Finished the astronomer yet?'' Warbeck inquired.
''I don't dig it.''
''Tommy got bored waiting for clear nights. He invented something that cuts through clouds and atmosphere . . . a funnel of vacuum so he can use his telescope all weather. What it amounts to is a disintegration beam.''
''The hell you say.''
''The hell I don't. Read on. Read on.''

Then I went to AnnMary and staied one hole week. It was fun. Becaze AnnMary has a spinak chainger for spinak and beats and strinbeens—

"What the hell is a 'spinak chainger'?"

"Spinach. Spinach changer. Spelling isn't one of Stuart's specialties. 'Beats' are beets. 'Strinbeens' are string beans."

beats and strinbeens. Wen her mother made us eet them AnnMary presed the buton and they staid the same outside onnly inside they became cake. Chery and strowbery. I asted AnnMary how & she sed it was by Enhv.

"This, I don't get."

"Simple. Anne-Marie doesn't like vegetables. So she's just as smart as Tommy, the astronomer. She invented a matter-transmuter. She transmutes spinak into cake. Chery or strowbery. Cake she eats with pleasure. So does Stuart."

"You're crazy."

"Not me. The kids. They're geniuses. Geniuses? What am I saying? They make a genius look imbecile. There's no label for these children."

"I don't believe it. This Stuart Buchanan's got a tall imagination. That's all."

"You think so? Then what about Enhv? That's how Anne-Marie transmutes matter. It took time but I figured Enhv out. It's Planck's quantum equation $E = nhv$. But read on. Read on. The best is yet to come. Wait till you get to lazy Ethel."

My frend Gorge bilds modell airplanes very good and small. Gorg's hands are clumzy but he makes small men out of moddelling clay and he tels them and they bild for him.

"What's this?"

"George, the plane-maker?"

"Yes."

"Simple. He makes miniature androids . . . robots . . .

and they build the planes for him. Clever boy, George, but read about his sister, lazy Ethel.''

His sister Ethel is the lazyist girl I ever saw. She is big & fat and she hates to walk. So wen her mothar sends her too the store Ethel thinks to the store and thinks home with all the pakejes and has to hang around Gorg's room hiding untill it wil look like she walked both ways. Gorge and I make fun of her becaze she is fat and lazy but she gets into the movees for free and saw Hoppalong Casidy sixteen times.

The End

Herod stared at Warbeck.

''Great little girl, Ethel,'' Warbeck said. ''She's too lazy to walk, so she teleports. Then she has a devil of a time covering up. She has to hide with her pakejes while George and Stuart make fun of her.''

''Teleports?''

''That's right. She moves from place to place by thinking her way there.''

''There ain't no such thing!'' Joe said indignantly.

''There wasn't until lazy Ethel came along.''

''I don't believe this,'' Herod said. ''I don't believe any of it.''

''You think it's just Stuart's imagination?''

''What else?''

''What about Planck's equation? $E=nh\nu$?''

''The kid invented that, too. Coincidence.''

''Does that sound likely?''

''Then he read it somewhere.''

''A ten-year-old boy? Nonsense.''

''I tell you, I don't believe it,'' Herod shouted. ''Let me talk to the kid for five minutes and I'll prove it.''

''That's exactly what I want to do . . . only the boy's disappeared.''

''How do you mean?''

''Lock, stock, and barrel. That's why I've been checking every Buchanan family in the city. The day I read this composition and sent down to the fifth grade for Stuart

Buchanan to have a talk, he disappeared. He hasn't been seen since.''

"What about his family?"

"The family disappeared too." Warbeck leaned forward intensely. "Get this. Every record of the boy and the family disappeared. Everything. A few people remember them vaguely, but that's all. They're gone."

"Jesus!" Joe said. "They scrammed, huh?"

"The very word. Scrammed. Thank you, Joe." Warbeck cocked an eye at Herod. "What a situation. Here's a child who makes friends with child geniuses. And the emphasis is on the child. They're making fantastic discoveries for childish purposes. Ethel teleports because she's too lazy to run errands. George makes robots to build model planes. Anne-Marie transmutes elements because she hates spinach. God knows what Stuart's other friends are doing. Maybe there's a Matthew who's invented a time machine so he can catch up on his homework."

Herod waved his hands feebly. "Why geniuses all of a sudden? What's happened?"

"I don't know. Atomic fallout? Fluorides in drinking water? Antibiotics? Vitamins? We're doing so much juggling with body chemistry these days that who knows what's happening? I want to find out but I can't. Stuart Buchanan blabbed like a child. When I started investigating, he got scared and disappeared."

"Is he a genius, too?"

"Very likely. Kids generally hang out with kids who share the same interests and talents."

"What kind of a genius? What's his talent?"

"I don't know. All I know is he disappeared. He covered up his tracks, destroyed every paper that could possibly help me locate him and vanished into thin air."

"How did he get into your files?"

"I don't know."

"Maybe he's a crook type," Joe said. "Expert at breaking and entering and such."

Herod smiled wanly. "A racketeer genius? A mastermind? The kid Moriarty?"

"He could be a thief-genius," the doomed man said, "but

don't let running away convince you. All children do that when they get caught in a crisis. Either they wish it had never happened or they wish they were a million miles away. Stuart Buchanan may be a million miles away, but we've got to find him.''

"Just to find out is he smart?" Joe asked.

"No, to find his friends. Do I have to diagram it? What would the army pay for a disintegration beam? What would an element-transmuter be worth? If we could manufacture living robots how rich would we get? If we could teleport how powerful would we be?''

There was a burning silence, then Herod got to his feet. "Mr. Warbeck," he said, "you make me and Joe look like pikers. Thank you for letting us cut in on you. We'll pay off. We'll find that kid.''

It is not possible for anyone to vanish without a trace . . . even a probable criminal genius. It is sometimes difficult to locate that trace . . . even for an expert experienced in hurried disappearances. But there is a professional technique unknown to amateurs.

"You've been blundering," Herod explained kindly to the doomed man. "Chasing one Buchanan after the other. There are angles. You don't run after a missing party. You look around on his back-trail for something he dropped.''

"A genius wouldn't drop anything.''

"Let's grant the kid's a genius. Type unspecified. Let's grant him everything. But a kid is a kid. He must have overlooked something. We'll find it.''

In three days Warbeck was introduced to the most astonishing angles of search. They consulted the Washington Heights post office about a Buchanan family formerly living in that neighborhood, now moved. Was there any change-of-address card filed? None.

They visited the election board. All voters are registered. If a voter moves from one election district to another, provision is usually made that a record of the transfer be kept. Was there any such record on Buchanan? None.

They called on the Washington Heights office of the gas and electric company. All subscribers for gas and electricity must transfer their accounts if they move. If they move out of town, they generally request the return of their deposit. Was there any record of a party named Buchanan? None.

It is a state law that all drivers must notify the license bureau of change of address or be subject to penalties involving fines, prison or worse. Was there any such notification by a party named Buchanan at the Motor Vehicle Bureau? There was not.

They questioned the R-J Realty Corp., owners and operators of a multiple dwelling in Washington Heights in which a party named Buchanan had leased a four-room apartment. The R-J lease, like most other leases, required the names and addresses of two character references for the tenant. Could the character references for Buchanan be produced? They could not. There was no such lease in the files.

"Maybe Joe was right," Warbeck complained in Herod's office. "Maybe the boy is a thief-genius. How did he think of everything? How did he get at every paper and destroy it? Did he break and enter? Bribe? Burgle? Threaten? How did he do it?"

"We'll ask him when we get to him," Herod said grimly. "All right. The kid's licked us straight down the line. He hasn't forgotten a trick. But I've got one angle I've been saving. Let's go up and see the janitor of their building."

"I questioned him months ago," Warbeck objected. "He remembers the family in a vague way and that's all. He doesn't know where they went."

"He knows something else, something the kid wouldn't think of covering. Let's go get it."

They drove up to Washington Heights and descended upon Mr. Jacob Ruysdale at dinner in the basement apartment of the building. Mr. Ruysdale disliked being separated from his liver and onions, but was persuaded by five dollars.

"About that Buchanan family," Herod began.

"I told him everything before," Ruysdale broke in, pointing to Warbeck.

"All right. He forgot to ask one question. Can I ask it now?" Ruysdale reexamined the five-dollar bill and nodded.

"When anybody moves in or out of a building, the superintendent usually takes down the name of the movers in case they damage the building. I'm a lawyer. I know this. It's to protect the building in case suit has to be brought. Right?''

Ruysdale's face lit up. ''By Godfrey!'' he said. ''That's right, I forgot all about it. He never asked me.''

''He didn't know. You've got the name of the company that moved the Buchanans out. Right?''

Ruysdale ran across the room to a cluttered bookshelf. He withdrew a tattered journal and flipped it open. He wet his fingers and turned pages.

''Here it is,'' he said. ''The Avon Moving Company. Truck No. G-4.''

The Avon Moving Company had no record of the removal of a Buchanan family from an apartment in Washington Heights. ''The kid was pretty careful at that,'' Herod murmured. But it did have a record of the men working truck G-4 on that day. The men were interviewed when they checked in at closing time. Their memories were refreshed with whiskey and cash. They recalled the Washington Heights job vaguely. It was a full day's work because they had to drive the hell and gone to Brooklyn. ''Oh God! Brooklyn!'' Warbeck muttered. What address in Brooklyn? Something on Maple Park Row. Number? The number could not be recalled.

''Joe, buy a map.''

They examined the street map of Brooklyn and located Maple Park Row. It was indeed the hell and gone out of civilization and was twelve blocks long. ''That's *Brooklyn* blocks,'' Joe grunted. ''Twice as long as anywhere. I know.''

Herod shrugged. ''We're close,'' he said. ''The rest will have to be legwork. Four blocks apiece. Cover every house, every apartment. List every kid around ten. Then Warbeck can check them, if they're under an alias.''

''There's a million kids a square inch in Brooklyn.'' Joe protested.

''There's a million dollars a day in it for us if we find him. Now let's go.''

Maple Park Row was a long, crooked street lined with five-story apartment houses. Its sidewalks were lined with baby carriages and old ladies on camp chairs. Its curbs were lined with parked cars. Its gutter was lined with crude whitewash stickball courts shaped like elongated diamonds. Every manhole cover was a home plate.

"It's just like the Bronx," Joe said nostalgically. "I ain't been home to the Bronx in ten years."

He wandered sadly down the street toward his sector, automatically threading his way through stickball games with the unconscious skill of the city-born. Warbeck remembered that departure sympathetically because Joe Davenport never returned.

The first day, he and Herod imagined Joe had found a hot lead. This encouraged them. The second day they realized no heat could keep Joe on the fire for forty-eight hours. This depressed them. On the third day they had to face the truth.

"He's dead," Herod said flatly. "The kid got him."

"How?"

"He killed him."

"A ten-year-old boy? A child?"

"You want to know what kind of genius Stuart Buchanan has, don't you? I'm telling you."

"I don't believe it."

"Then explain Joe."

"He quit."

"Not on a million dollars."

"But where's the body?"

"Ask the kid. He's the genius. He's probably figured out tricks that would baffle Dick Tracy."

"How did he kill him?"

"Ask the kid. He's the genius."

"Herod, I'm scared."

"So am I. Do you want to quit now?"

"I don't see how we can. If the boy's dangerous, we've got to find him."

"Civic virtue, heh?"

"Call it that."

"Well, I'm still thinking about the money."

They returned to Maple Park Row and Joe Davenport's four-block sector. They were cautious, almost furtive. They separated and began working from each end toward the middle; in one house, up the stairs, apartment by apartment, to the top, then down again to investigate the next building. It was slow, tedious work. Occasionally they glimpsed each other far down the street, crossing from one dismal building to another. And that was the last glimpse Warbeck ever had of Walter Herod.

He sat in his car and waited. He sat in his car and trembled. "I'll go to the police," he muttered, knowing perfectly well he could not. "The boy has a weapon. Something he invented. Something silly like the others. A special light so he can play marbles at night, only it murders men. A machine to play checkers, only it hypnotizes men. He's invented a robot mob of gangsters so he can play cops-and-robbers and they took care of Joe and Herod. He's a child genius. Dangerous. Deadly. What am I going to do?"

The doomed man got out of the car and stumbled down the street toward Herod's half of the sector. "What's going to happen when Stuart Buchanan grows up?" he wondered. "What's going to happen when all the rest of them grow up? Tommy and George and Anne-Marie and lazy Ethel? Why don't I start running away now? What am I doing here?"

It was dusk on Maple Park Row. The old ladies had withdrawn, folding their camp chairs like Arabs. The parked cars remained. The stickball games were over, but small games were starting under the glowing lamp posts . . . games with bottle caps and cards and battered pennies. Overhead, the purple city haze was deepening, and through it the sharp sparkle of Venus following the sun below the horizon could be seen.

"He must know his power," Warbeck muttered angrily. "He must know how dangerous he is. That's why he's running away. Guilt. That's why he destroys us, one by one, smiling to himself, a crafty child, a vicious, killing genius. . . ."

Warbeck stopped in the middle of Maple Park Row.

"Buchanan!" he shouted. "Stuart Buchanan!"

The kids near him stopped their games and gaped.

"Stuart Buchanan!" Warbeck's voice cracked hysterically. "Can you hear me?"

His wild voice carried farther down the street. More games

stopped. Ringaleevio, Chinese tag, Red-Light and Boxball.

"Buchanan!" Warbeck screamed. "Stuart Buchanan! Come out come out, wherever you are!"

The world hung motionless.

In the alley between 217 and 219 Maple Park Row playing hide-and-seek behind piled ash barrels, Stuart Buchanan heard his name and crouched lower. He was aged ten, dressed in sweater, jeans, and sneakers. He was intent and determined that he was not going to be caught out "it" again. He was going to hide until he could make a dash for home-free in safety. As he settled comfortably among the ash cans, his eye caught the glimmer of Venus low in the western sky.

"Star light, star bright," he whispered in all innocence, "first star I see tonight. Wish I may, wish I might, grant me the wish I wish tonight." He paused and considered. Then he wished. "God bless Mom and Pop and me and all my friends and make me a good boy and please let me be always happy and I wish that anybody who tries to bother me would go away . . . a long way away . . . and leave me alone forever."

In the middle of Maple Park Row, Marion Perkin Warbeck stepped forward and drew breath for another hysterical yell. And then he was elsewhere, going away on a road that was a long way away. It was a straight white road cleaving infinitely through blackness, stretching onward and onward into forever; a dreary, lonely endless road leading away and away and away.

Down that road Warbeck plodded, an astonished automaton, unable to speak, unable to stop, unable to think in the timeless infinity. Onward and onward he walked into a long way away, unable to turn back. Ahead of him he saw the minute specks of figures trapped on that one-way road to forever. There was a dot that had to be Herod. Ahead of Herod there was a mote that was Joe Davenport. And ahead of Joe he could make out a long, dwindling chain of mites. He turned once with a convulsive effort. Behind him, dim and distant, a figure was plodding, and behind that another abruptly materialized, and another . . . and another. . . .

While Stuart Buchanan crouched behind the ash barrels

and watched alertly for the "it." He was unaware that he had disposed of Warbeck. He was unaware that he had disposed of Herod, Joe Davenport and scores of others.

He was unaware that he had induced his parents to flee Washington Heights, that he had destroyed papers and documents, memories and peoples, in his simple desire to be left alone. He was unaware that he was a genius.

His genius was for wishing.

They Don't Make Life
Like They Used To

IT'S a constant source of shame to me that I invariably find nice, normal people dull and boring. I like them, but I don't want to spend any time with them. What I look for is people with what Evelyn Waugh called "the light of lunacy" in their eyes. I prefer those with the light of lunacy illuminating all their acts of feasance, malfeasance, and nonfeasance. Obviously this must be a case of like being drawn to like.

So when I sort of drifted into a last-man-last-woman-on-earth story because I had nothing fresher to write at the moment, I knew I was tackling an exhausted theme, but I thought it might be fun to make them a couple of kooks and see the world through their lunatic eyes. I liked the two meshugenahs so much that I played the action in some of my favorite places in New York and wrote so much that I had to cut it by a third. I didn't know whether the story would appeal to others as much as it did to me and was much surprised when it did. It appealed so much that one publisher pleaded with me to write a sequel, preparatory to turning it into a novel. On the other hand, one friend bawled hell out of me for writing what he considered to be pornographic scenes.

This raises the fulminating issue of pornography and censorship which doesn't affect me because a Puritan streak in my nature has always stifled the slightest temptation to do that sort of work. I'm strongly opposed to censorship in any form, and yet I confess to being disgusted by the passages that diagram it for you.

I suppose it mostly depends on how and why it was written

321

and by whom. In the studios we're notorious for the foul language we use casually, and yet the same language becomes profane and offensive when used by certain people. I've never been able to figure out why. Is it because of the way it's said, the person himself (or herself), the situation? I don't know.

The same holds for writing. Some authors can put together the most outrageous scenes and they never seem to offend. Others can't even write a kiss without making it dirty. For my part I've never seen the need for being explicit. One can, as many authors have, do it by suggestion rather than spelling it out . . . which reminds me of another friend and his four-year-old son.

The kid came home from nursery school very much upset. When the father asked him why, he said that another boy had called him a bad name.

"What did he call you?"

"Oh, I couldn't say it."

"But how will you know it's bad unless you tell me and I tell you?"

"I couldn't say it." The four-year-old thought it over. "I'll have to spell it."

"All right. Spell it."

"He called me a . . . a F.U.B.G.H."

There isn't much more to say about this simple example of theme and variations except that I love the title but can't see what on earth it has to do with the story. My years as a magazine editor trained me in the art of title writing, and it is an art to capture the essence of a piece and grab the reader. Unfortunately this one was written before my training.

The girl driving the jeep was very fair and very Nordic. Her blonde hair was pulled back in a pony tail, but it was so long that it was more a mare's tail. She wore sandals, a pair of soiled bluejeans, and nothing else. She was nicely tanned. As she turned the jeep off Fifth Avenue and drove bouncing up the steps of the library, her bosom danced enchantingly.

She parked in front of the library entrance, stepped out,

and was about to enter when her attention was attracted by something across the street. She peered, hesitated, then glanced down at her jeans and made a face. She pulled off the pants and hurled them at the pigeons eternally cooing and courting on the library steps. As they clattered up in fright, she ran down to Fifth Avenue, crossed, and stopped before a shop window. There was a plum-colored wool dress on display. It had a high waist, a full skirt, and not too many moth holes. The price was $79.90.

The girl rummaged through old cars skewed on the avenue until she found a loose fender. She smashed the plate-glass shop door, carefully stepped across the splinters, entered, and sorted through the dusty dress racks. She was a big girl and had trouble fitting herself. Finally she abandoned the plum-colored wool and compromised on a dark tartan, size 12, $120 reduced to $99.90. She located a salesbook and pencil, blew the dust off, and carefully wrote: *I.O.U. $99.90. Linda Nielsen.*

She returned to the library and went through the main doors which had taken her a week to batter in with a sledgehammer. She ran across the great hall, filthied with five years of droppings from the pigeons roosting there. As she ran, she clapped her arms over her head to shield her hair from stray shots. She climbed the stairs to the third floor and entered the Print Room. As always, she signed the register: *Date—June 20, 1981. Name—Linda Nielsen. Address—Central Park Model Boat Pond. Business or Firm—Last Man on Earth.*

She had had a long debate with herself about *Business or Firm* the first time she broke into the library. Strictly speaking, she was the last woman on earth, but she had felt that if she wrote that it would seem chauvinistic; and "Last Person on Earth" sounded silly, like calling a drink a beverage.

She pulled portfolios out of racks and leafed through them. She knew exactly what she wanted; something warm with blue accents to fit a twenty by thirty frame for her bedroom. In a priceless collection of Hiroshige prints she found a lovely landscape. She filled out a slip, placed it carefully on the librarian's desk, and left with the print.

Downstairs, she stopped off in the main circulation room, went to the back shelves, and selected two Italian grammars and an Italian dictionary. Then she backtracked through the main hall, went out to the jeep, and placed the books and print on the front seat alongside her companion, an exquisite Dresden china doll. She picked up a list that read:

> Jap. print
> Italian
> 20 × 30 pict. fr.
> Lobster bisque
> Brass polish
> Detergent
> Furn. polish
> Wet mop

She crossed off the first two items, replaced the list on the dashboard, got into the jeep, and bounced down the library steps. She drove up Fifth Avenue, threading her way through crumbling wreckage. As she was passing the ruins of St. Patrick's Cathedral at 50th Street, a man appeared from nowhere.

He stepped out of the rubble and, without looking left or right, started crossing the avenue just in front of her. She exclaimed, banged on the horn which remained mute, and braked so sharply that the jeep slewed and slammed into the remains of a No. 3 bus. The man let out a squawk, jumped ten feet, and then stood frozen, staring at her.

"You crazy jaywalker," she yelled. "Why don't you look where you're going? D'you think you own the whole city?"

He stared and stammered. He was a big man, with thick, grizzled hair, a red beard, and weathered skin. He was wearing army fatigues, heavy ski boots, and had a bursting knapsack and blanket roll on his back. He carried a battered shotgun, and his pockets were crammed with odds and ends. He looked like a prospector.

"My God," he whispered in a rusty voice. "Somebody at last. I knew it. I always knew I'd find someone." Then, as he noticed her long, fair hair, his face fell. "But a woman," he muttered. "Just my goddamn lousy luck."

"What are you, some kind of nut?" she demanded. "Don't you know better than to cross against the lights?"

He looked around in bewilderment. "What lights?"

"So all right, there aren't any lights, but couldn't you look where you were going?"

"I'm sorry, lady. To tell the truth, I wasn't expecting any traffic."

"Just plain common sense," she grumbled, backing the jeep off the bus.

"Hey lady, wait a minute."

"Yes?"

"Listen, you know anything about TV? Electronics, how they say . . ."

"Are you trying to be funny?"

"No, this is straight. Honest."

She snorted and tried to continue driving up Fifth Avenue, but he wouldn't get out of the way.

"Please, lady," he persisted. "I got a reason for asking. Do you know?"

"No."

"Damn! I never get a break. Lady, excuse me, no offense, got any guys in this town?"

"There's nobody but me. I'm the last man on earth."

"That's funny. I always thought I was."

"So all right, I'm the last woman on earth."

He shook his head. "There's got to be other people; there just has to. Stands to reason. South, maybe you think? I'm down from New Haven, and I figured if I headed where the climate was like warmer, there'd be some guys I could ask something."

"Ask what?"

"Aw, a woman wouldn't understand. No offense."

"Well, if you want to head south you're going the wrong way."

"That's south, ain't it?" he said, pointing down Fifth Avenue.

"Yes, but you'll just come to a dead end. Manhattan's an island. What you have to do is go uptown and cross the George Washington Bridge to Jersey."

"Uptown? Which way is that?"

"Go straight up Fifth to Cathedral Parkway, then over to the West Side and up Riverside. You can't miss it."

He looked at her helplessly.

"Stranger in town?"

He nodded.

"Oh, all right," she said. "Hop in. I'll give you a lift."

She transferred the books and the china doll to the back seat, and he squeezed in alongside her. As she started the jeep she looked down at his worn ski boots.

"Hiking?"

"Yeah."

"Why don't you drive? You can get a car working, and there's plenty of gas and oil."

"I don't know how to drive," he said despondently. "It's the story of my life."

He heaved a sigh, and that made his knapsack jolt massively against her shoulder. She examined him out of the corner of her eye. He had a powerful chest, a long, thick back, and strong legs. His hands were big and hard, and his neck was corded with muscles. She thought for a moment, then nodded to herself and stopped the jeep.

"What's the matter?" he asked. "Won't it go?"

"What's your name?"

"Mayo. Jim Mayo."

"I'm Linda Nielsen."

"Yeah. Nice meeting you. Why don't it go?"

"Jim, I've got a proposition for you."

"Oh?" He looked at her doubtfully. "I'll be glad to listen, lady—I mean Linda, but I ought to tell you, I got something on my mind that's going to keep me pretty busy for a long t . . ." His voice trailed off as he turned away from her intense gaze.

"Jim, if you'll do something for me, I'll do something for you."

"Like what, for instance?"

"Well, I get terribly lonesome, nights. It isn't so bad during the day—there's always a lot of chores to keep you busy—but at night it's just awful."

"Yeah, I know," he muttered.

"I've got to do something about it."

"But how do I come into this?" he asked nervously.

"Why don't you stay in New York for a while? If you do, I'll teach you how to drive, and find you a car so you don't have to hike south."

"Say, that's an idea. Is it hard, driving?"

"I could teach you in a couple of days."

"I don't learn things so quick."

"All right, a couple of weeks, but think of how much time you'll save in the long run."

"Gee," he said, "that sounds great." Then he turned away again. "But what do I have to do for you?"

Her face lit up with excitement. "Jim, I want you to help me move a piano."

"A piano? What piano?"

"A rosewood grand from Steinway's on Fifty-seventh Street. I'm dying to have it in my place. The living room is just crying for it."

"Oh, you mean you're furnishing, huh?"

"Yes, but I want to play after dinner, too. You can't listen to records all the time. I've got it all planned; books on how to play, and books on how to tune a piano. . . . I've been able to figure everything except how to move the piano in."

"Yeah, but . . . but there's apartments all over this town with pianos in them," he objected. "There must be hundreds, at least. Stands to reason. Why don't you live in one of them?"

"Never! I love my place. I've spent five years decorating it, and it's beautiful. Besides, there's the problem of water."

He nodded. "Water's always a headache. How do you handle it?"

"I'm living in the house in Central Park where they used to keep the model yachts. It faces the boat pond. It's a darling place, and I've got it all fixed up. We could get the piano in together, Jim. It wouldn't be hard."

"Well, I don't know, Lena . . ."

"Linda."

"Excuse me. Linda. I—"

"You look strong enough. What'd you do, before?"

"I used to be a pro rassler."

"There! I knew you were strong."

"Oh, I'm not a rassler anymore. I became a bartender and went into the restaurant business. I opened 'The Body Slam' up in New Haven. Maybe you heard of it?"

"I'm sorry."

"It was sort of famous with the sports crowd. What'd you do before?"

"I was a researcher for BBDO."

"What's that?"

"An advertising agency," she explained impatiently. "We can talk about that later, if you'll stick around. And I'll teach you how to drive, and we can move in the piano, and there're a few other things that I—but that can wait. Afterward you can drive south."

"Gee, Linda, I don't know . . ."

She took Mayo's hands. "Come on, Jim, be a sport. You can stay with me. I'm a wonderful cook, and I've got a lovely guest room . . ."

"What for? I mean, thinking you was the last man on earth."

"That's a silly question. A proper house has to have a guest room. You'll love my place. I turned the lawns into a farm and gardens, and you can swim in the pond, and we'll get you a new Jag . . . I know where there's a beauty up on blocks."

"I think I'd rather have a Caddy."

"You can have anything you like. So what do you say, Jim? Is it a deal?"

"All right, Linda," he muttered reluctantly. "You're a deal."

It was indeed a lovely house with its pagoda roof of copper weathered to verdigris green, fieldstone walls, and deep recessed windows. The oval pond before it glittered blue in the soft June sunlight, and mallard ducks paddled and quacked busily. The sloping lawns that formed a bowl around the pond were terraced and cultivated. The house faced west, and Central Park stretched out beyond like an unkempt estate.

Mayo looked at the pond wistfully. "It ought to have boats."

"The house was full of them when I moved in," Linda said.

"I always wanted a model boat when I was a kid. Once I even—" Mayo broke off. A penetrating pounding sounded somewhere; an irregular sequence of heavy knocks that sounded like the dint of stones under water. It stopped as suddenly as it had begun. "What was that?" Mayo asked.

Linda shrugged. "I don't know for sure. I think it's the city falling apart. You'll see buildings coming down every now and then. You get used to it." Her enthusiasm rekindled. "Now come inside. I want to show you everything."

She was bursting with pride and overflowing with decorating details that bewildered Mayo, but he was impressed by her Victorian living room, Empire bedroom, and country kitchen with a working kerosene cooking stove. The colonial guest room, with four-poster bed, hooked rug, and tole lamps, worried him.

"This is kind of girlie-girlie, huh?"

"Naturally. I'm a girl."

"Yeah. Sure. I mean . . ." Mayo looked around doubtfully. "Well, a guy is used to stuff that ain't so delicate. No offense."

"Don't worry, that bed's strong enough. Now remember, Jim, no feet on the spread, and remove it at night. If your shoes are dirty, take them off before you come in. I got that rug from the museum and I don't want it messed up. Have you got a change of clothes?"

"Only what I got on."

"We'll have to get you new things tomorrow. What you're wearing is so filthy it's not worth laundering."

"Listen," he said desperately, "I think maybe I better camp out in the park."

"Why on earth?"

"Well, I'm like more used to it than houses. But you don't have to worry, Linda. I'll be around in case you need me."

"Why should I need you?"

"All you have to do is holler."

"Nonsense," Linda said firmly. "You're my guest and you're staying here. Now get cleaned up; I'm going to start dinner. Oh damn! I forgot to pick up the lobster bisque."

She gave him a dinner cleverly contrived from canned goods and served on exquisite Fornisetti china with Danish silver flatware. It was a typical girl's meal, and Mayo was still hungry when it was finished, but too polite to mention it. He was too tired to fabricate an excuse to go out and forage for something substantial. He lurched off to bed, remembering to remove his shoes but forgetting all about the spread.

He was awakened next morning by a loud honking and clattering of wings. He rolled out of bed and went to the windows just in time to see the mallards dispossessed from the pond by what appeared to be a red balloon. When he got his eyes working properly, he saw that it was a bathing cap. He wandered out to the pond, stretching and groaning. Linda yelled cheerfully and swam toward him. She heaved herself up out of the pond onto the curbing. The bathing cap was all that she wore. Mayo backed away from the splash and spatter.

"Good morning," Linda said. "Sleep well?"

"Good morning," Mayo said. "I don't know. The bed put kinks in my back. Gee, that water must be cold. You're all gooseflesh."

"No, it's marvelous." She pulled off the cap and shook her hair down. "Where's that towel? Oh, here. Go on in, Jim. You'll feel wonderful."

"I don't like it when it's cold."

"Don't be a sissy."

A crack of thunder split the quiet morning. Mayo looked up at the clear sky in astonishment. "What the hell was that?" he exclaimed.

"Watch," Linda ordered.

"It sounded like a sonic boom."

"There!" she cried, pointing west. "See?"

One of the West Side skyscrapers crumbled majestically, sinking into itself like a collapsible cup and raining masses of cornice and brick. The flayed girders twisted and contorted. Moments later they could hear the roar of the collapse.

"Man, that's a sight," Mayo muttered in awe.

"The decline and fall of the Empire City. You get used to it. Now take a dip, Jim. I'll get you a towel."

She ran into the house. He dropped his shorts and took off his socks, but was still standing on the curb, unhappily dipping his toe into the water when she returned with a huge bath towel.

"It's awful cold, Linda," he complained.

"Didn't you take cold showers when you were a wrestler?"

"Not me. Boiling hot."

"Jim, if you just stand there, you'll never go in. Look at you, you're starting to shiver. Is that a tattoo around your waist?"

"What? Oh, yea. It's a python, in five colors. It goes all the way around. See?" He revolved proudly. "Got it when I was with the Army in Saigon back in '64. It's a Oriental-type python. Elegant, huh?"

"Did it hurt?"

"To tell the truth, no. Some guys try to make out like it's Chinese torture to get tattooed but they're just showin' off. It itches more than anything else."

"You were a soldier in '64?"

"That's right."

"How old were you?"

"Twenty."

"You're thirty-seven now?"

"Thirty-six going on thirty-seven."

"Then you're prematurely grey?"

"I guess so."

She contemplated him thoughtfully. "I tell you what, if you do go in, don't get your head wet."

She ran back into the house. Mayo, ashamed of his vacillation, forced himself to jump feet first into the pond. He was standing, chest deep, splashing his face and shoulders with water when Linda returned. She carried a stool, a pair of scissors, and a comb.

"Doesn't it feel wonderful?" she called.

"No."

She laughed. "Well, come out. I'm going to give you a haircut."

He climbed out of the pond, dried himself, and obediently sat on the stool while she cut his hair. "The beard, too,"

Linda insisted. "I want to see what you really look like." She trimmed him close enough for shaving, inspected him, and nodded with satisfaction. "Very handsome."

"Aw, go on," he blushed.

"There's a bucket of hot water on the stove. Go and shave. Don't bother to dress. We're going to get you new clothes after breakfast, and then . . . the Piano."

"I couldn't walk around the streets naked," he said, shocked.

"Don't be silly. Who's to see? Now hurry."

They drove down to Abercrombie & Fitch on Madison and 45th Street, Mayo wrapped modestly in his towel. Linda told him she'd been a customer for years, and showed him the pile of sales slips she had accumulated. Mayo examined them curiously while she took his measurements and went off in search of clothes. He was almost indignant when she returned with her arms laden.

"Jim, I've got some lovely elk moccasins, and a safari suit, and wool socks, and shipboard shirts, and—"

"Listen," he interrupted, "do you know what your whole tab comes to? Nearly fourteen hundred dollars."

"Really? Put on the shorts first. They're drip-dry."

"You must have been out of your mind, Linda. What'd you want all that junk for?"

"Are the socks big enough? What junk? I needed everything."

"Yeah? Like . . ." He shuffled the signed sales slips. "Like one Underwater Viewer with Plexiglas Lens, nine ninety-five? What for?"

"So I could see to clean the bottom of the pond."

"What about this Stainless Steel Service for Four, thirty-nine fifty?"

"For when I'm lazy and don't feel like heating water. You can wash stainless steel in cold water." She admired him. "Oh, Jim, come look in the mirror. You're real romantic, like the big-game hunter in that Hemingway story."

He shook his head. "I don't see how you're ever going to get out of hock. You got to watch your spending, Linda. Maybe we better forget about that piano, huh?"

"Never," Linda said adamantly. "I don't care how much it costs. A piano is a lifetime investment, and it's worth it."

She was frantic with excitement as they drove uptown to the Steinway showroom, and helpful and underfoot by turns. After a long afternoon of muscle-cracking and critical engineering involving makeshift gantries and an agonizing dolly-haul up Fifth Avenue, they had the piano in place in Linda's living room. Mayo gave it one last shake to make sure it was firmly on its legs and then sank down, exhausted. "Je-zuz!" he groaned. "Hiking south would've been easier."

"Jim!" Linda ran to him and threw herself on him with a fervent hug. "Jim, you're an angel. Are you all right?"

"I'm okay." He grunted. "Get off me, Linda. I can't breathe."

"I just can't thank you enough. I've been dreaming about this for ages. I don't know what I can do to repay you. Anything you want, just name it."

"Aw," he said, "you already cut my hair."

"I'm serious."

"Ain't you teaching me how to drive?"

"Of course. As quickly as possible. That's the least I can do." Linda backed to a chair and sat down, her eyes fixed on the piano.

"Don't make such a fuss over nothing," he said, climbing to his feet. He sat down before the keyboard, shot an embarrassed grin at her over his shoulder, then reached out and began stumbling through *The Minuet in G*.

Linda gasped and sat bolt upright. "You play," she whispered.

"Naw. I took piano when I was a kid."

"Can you read music?"

"I used to."

"Could you teach me?"

"I guess so; it's kind of hard. Hey, here's another piece I had to take." He began mutilating *The Rustle of Spring*. What with the piano out of tune and his mistakes, it was ghastly.

"Beautiful," Linda breathed. "Just beautiful!" She

stared at his back while an expression of decision and determination stole across her face. She arose, slowly crossed to Mayo, and put her hands on his shoulders.

He glanced up. "Something?" he asked.

"Nothing," she answered. "You practice the piano. I'll get dinner."

But she was so preoccupied for the rest of the evening that she made Mayo nervous. He stole off to bed early.

It wasn't until three o'clock the following afternoon that they finally got a car working, and it wasn't a Caddy, but a Chevy—a hardtop because Mayo didn't like the idea of being exposed to the weather in a convertible. They drove out of the Tenth Avenue garage and back to the East Side, where Linda felt more at home. She confessed that the boundaries of her world were from Fifth Avenue to Third, and from 42nd Street to 86th. She was uncomfortable outside this pale.

She turned the wheel over to Mayo and let him creep up and down Fifth and Madison, practicing starts and stops. He sideswiped five wrecks, stalled eleven times, and reversed through a storefront which, fortunately, was devoid of glass. He was trembling with nervousness.

"It's real hard," he complained.

"It's just a question of practice," she reassured him. "Don't worry. I promise you'll be an expert if it takes us a month."

"A whole month!"

"You said you were a slow learner, didn't you? Don't blame me. Stop here a minute."

He jolted the Chevy to a halt. Linda got out.

"Wait for me."

"What's up?"

"A surprise."

She ran into a shop and was gone for half an hour. When she reappeared she was wearing a pencil-thin black sheath, pearls, and high-heeled opera pumps. She had twisted her hair into a coronet. Mayo regarded her with amazement as she got into the car.

"What's all this?" he asked.

"Part of the surprise. Turn east on Fifty-second Street."

He labored, started the car, and drove east. "Why'd you get all dressed up in an evening gown?"

"It's a cocktail dress."

"What for?"

"So I'll be dressed for where we're going. Watch out, Jim!" Linda wrenched the wheel and sheared off the stern of a shattered sanitation truck. "I'm taking you to a famous restaurant."

"To eat?"

"No, silly, for drinks. You're my visiting fireman, and I have to entertain you. That's it on the left. See if you can park somewhere."

He parked abominably. As they got out of the car, Mayo stopped and began to sniff curiously.

"Smell that?" he asked.

"Smell what?"

"That sort of sweet smell."

"It's my perfume."

"No, it's something in the air, kind of sweet and choky. I know that smell from somewhere, but I can't remember."

"Never mind. Come inside." She led him into the restaurant. "You ought to be wearing a tie," she whispered, "but maybe we can get away with it."

Mayo was not impressed by the restaurant decor, but was fascinated by the portraits of celebrities hung in the bar. He spent rapt minutes burning his fingers with matches, gazing at Mel Allen, Red Barber, Casey Stengel, Frank Gifford, and Rocky Marciano. When Linda finally came back from the kitchen with a lighted candle, he turned to her eagerly.

"You ever see any of them TV stars in here?" he asked.

"I suppose so. How about a drink?"

"Sure. Sure. But I want to talk more about them TV stars."

He escorted her to a bar stool, blew the dust off, and helped her up most gallantly. Then he vaulted over the bar, whipped out his handkerchief, and polished the mahogany professionally. "This is my specialty," he grinned. He assumed the impersonally friendly attitude of the bartender. "Evening, ma'am. Nice night. What's your pleasure?"

''God, I had a rough day in the shop! Dry martini on the rocks. Better make it a double.''

''Certainly, ma'am. Twist or olive?''

''Onion.''

''Double-dry gibson on the rocks. Right.'' Mayo searched behind the bar and finally produced whiskey, gin, and several bottles of soda, as yet only partially evaporated through their sealed caps. ''Afraid we're fresh out of martinis, ma'am. What's your second pleasure?''

''Oh, I like that. Scotch, please.''

''This soda'll be flat,'' he warned, ''and there's no ice.''

''Never mind.''

He rinsed a glass with soda and poured her a drink.

''Thank you. Have one on me, bartender. What's your name?''

''They call me Jim, ma'am. No thanks. Never drink on duty.''

''Then come off duty and join me.''

''Never drink off duty, ma'am.''

''You can call me Linda.''

''Thank you, Miss Linda.''

''Are you serious about never drinking, Jim?''

''Yeah.''

''Well, happy days.''

''And long nights.''

''I like that, too. Is it your own?''

''Gee, I don't know. It's sort of the usual bartender's routine, a specially with guys. You know? Suggestive. No offense.''

''None taken.''

''Bees!'' Mayo burst out.

Linda was startled. ''Bees what?''

''That smell. Like inside beehives.''

''Oh? I wouldn't know,'' she said indifferently. ''I'll have another, please.''

''Coming right up. Now listen, about them TV celebrities, you actually saw them here? In person?''

''Why of course. Happy days, Jim.''

''May they all be Saturdays.''

Linda pondered. ''Why Saturdays?''

"Day off."

"Oh."

"Which TV stars did you see?"

"You name 'em, I saw 'em." She laughed. "You remind me of the kid next door. I always had to tell him the celebrities I'd seen. One day I told him I saw Jean Arthur in here, and he said, 'With his horse?' "

Mayo couldn't see the point, but was wounded nevertheless. Just as Linda was about to soothe his feelings, the bar began a gentle quivering, and at the same time a faint subterranean rumbling commenced. It came from a distance, seemed to approach slowly, and then faded away. The vibration stopped. Mayo stared at Linda.

"Je-zus! You think maybe this building's going to go?"

She shook her head. "No. When they go, it's always with that boom. You know what that sounded like? The Lexington Avenue subway."

"The subway?"

"Uh-huh. The local train."

"That's crazy. How could the subway be running?"

"I didn't say it *was*. I said it *sounded* like. I'll have another, please."

"We need more soda." Mayo explored and reappeared with bottles and a large menu. He was pale. "You better take it easy, Linda," he said. "You know what they're charging per drink? A dollar seventy-five. Look."

"To hell with the expense. Let's live a little. Make it a double, bartender. You know something, Jim? If you stayed in town, I could show you where all your heroes lived. Thank you. Happy days. I could take you up to BBDO and show you their tapes and films. How about that? Stars like . . . like Red . . . Who?"

"Barber."

"Red Barber, and Rocky Gifford, and Rocky Casey, and Rocky, the Flying Squirrel."

"You're putting me on," Mayo said, offended again.

"Me, sir? Putting you on?" Linda said with dignity. "Why would I do a thing like that? Just trying to be pleasant. Just trying to give you a good time. My mother told me, 'Linda,' she told me, 'just remember this, about a man. Wear

what he wants and say what he likes,' is what she told me.
You want this dress?'' she demanded.

"I like it, if that's what you mean.''

"Know what I paid for it? Ninety-nine fifty.''

"What? A hundred dollars for a skinny black thing like
that?''

"It is not a skinny black thing like that. It is a basic black
cocktail frock. And I paid twenty dollars for the pearls.
Simulated,'' she explained. ''And sixty for the opera pumps.
And forty for the perfume. Two hundred and twenty dollars
to give you a good time. You having a good time?''

"Sure.''

"Want to smell me?''

"I already.''

"Bartender, give me another.''

"Afraid I can't serve you, ma'am.''

"Why not?''

"You've had enough already.''

"I have not had enough already,'' Linda said indignantly.
"Where's your manners?'' She grabbed the whiskey bottle.
"Come on, let's have a few drinks and talk up a storm about
TV stars. Happy days. I could take you up to BBDO and
show you their tapes and films. How about that?''

"You just asked me.''

"You didn't answer. I could show you movies, too. You
like movies? I hate 'em, but I can't knock 'em anymore.
Movies saved my life when the big bang came.''

"How was that?''

"This is a secret, understand? Just between you and me. If
any other agency ever found out . . .'' Linda looked around
and then lowered her voice. ''BBDO located this big cache of
silent films. Lost films, see? Nobody knew the prints were
around. Make a great TV series. So they sent me to this
abandoned mine in Jersey to take inventory.''

"In a mine?''

"That's right. Happy days.''

"Why were they in a mine?''

"Old prints. Nitrate. Catch fire. Also rot. Have to be
stored like wine. That's why. So took two of my assistants
with me to spend weekend down there, checking.''

"You stayed in the mine a whole weekend?"

"Uh-huh. Three girls. Friday to Monday. That was the plan. Thought it would be a fun deal. Happy days. So . . . Where was I? Oh. So, took lights, blankets, linen, plenty of picnic, the whole schmeer, and went to work. I remember exact moment when blast came. Was looking for third reel of a UFA film, *Gekronter Blumenorden an der Pegnitz*. Had reel one, two, four, five, six. No three. Bang! Happy days."

"Jesus. Then what?"

"My girls panicked. Couldn't keep 'em down there. Never saw them again. But I knew. I knew. Stretched that picnic forever. Then starved even longer. Finally came up, and for what? For who? Whom?" She began to weep. "For nobody. Nobody left. Nothing." She took Mayo's hands. "Why won't you stay?"

"Stay? Where?"

"Here."

"I am staying."

"I mean for a long time. Why not? Haven't I got lovely home? And there's all New York for supplies. And farm for flowers and vegetables. We could keep cows and chickens. Go fishing. Drive cars. Go to museums. Art galleries. Entertain . . ."

"You're doing all that right now. You don't need me."

"But I do. I do."

"For what?"

"For piano lessons."

After a long pause he said, "You're drunk."

"Not wounded, sire, but dead."

She lay her head on the bar, beamed up at him roguishly, and then closed her eyes. An instant later, Mayo knew she had passed out. He compressed his lips. Then he climbed out of the bar, computed the tab, and left fifteen dollars under the whiskey bottle.

He took Linda's shoulder and shook her gently. She collapsed into his arms, and her hair came tumbling down. He blew out the candle, picked Linda up, and carried her to the Chevy. Then, with anguished concentration, he drove through the dark to the boat pond. It took him forty minutes.

He carried Linda into her bedroom and sat her down on the bed, which was decorated with an elaborate arrangement of dolls. Immediately she rolled over and curled up with a doll in her arms, crooning to it. Mayo lit a lamp and tried to prop her upright. She went over again, giggling.

"Linda," he said, "you got to get that dress off."

"Mf."

"You can't sleep in it. It cost a hundred dollars."

"Nine'nine-fif'y."

"Now come on, honey."

"Fm."

He rolled his eyes in exasperation and then undressed her, carefully hanging up the basic black cocktail frock, and standing the sixty-dollar pumps in a corner. He could not manage the clasp of the pearls (simulated), so he put her to bed still wearing them. Lying on the pale blue sheets, nude except for the necklace, she looked like a Nordic odalisque.

"Did you muss my dolls?" she mumbled.

"No. They're all around you."

"Tha's right. Never sleep without 'em." She reached out and petted them lovingly. "Happy days. Long nights."

"Women!" Mayo snorted. He extinguished the lamp and tramped out, slamming the door behind him.

Next morning Mayo was again awakened by the clatter of dispossessed ducks. The red balloon was sailing on the surface of the pond, bright in the warm June sunshine. Mayo wished it was a model boat instead of the kind of girl who got drunk in bars. He stalked out and jumped into the water as far from Linda as possible. He was sluicing his chest when something seized his ankle and nipped him. He let out a yell, and was confronted by Linda's beaming face bursting out of the water before him.

"Good morning," she laughed.

"Very funny," he muttered.

"You look mad this morning."

He grunted.

"And I don't blame you. I did an awful thing last night. I didn't give you any dinner, and I want to apologize."

"I wasn't thinking about dinner," he said with baleful dignity.

"No? Then what on earth are you mad about?"

"I can't stand women who get drunk."

"Who was drunk?"

"You."

"I was not," she said indignantly.

"No? Who had to be undressed and put to bed like a kid?"

"Who was too dumb to take off my pearls?" she countered. "They broke and I slept on pebbles all night. I'm covered with black and blue marks. Look. Here and here and—"

"Linda," he interrupted sternly, "I'm just a plain guy from New Haven. I got no use for spoiled girls who run up charge accounts and all the time decorate theirselves and hang around society-type saloons getting loaded."

"If you don't like my company, why do you stay?"

"I'm going," he said. He climbed out and began drying himself. "I'm starting south this morning."

"Enjoy your hike."

"I'm driving."

"What? A kiddie-car?"

"The Chevy."

"Jim, you're not serious?" She climbed out of the pond, looking alarmed. "You really don't know how to drive yet."

"No? Didn't I drive you home falling-down drunk last night?"

"You'll get into awful trouble."

"Nothing I can't get out of. Anyway, I can't hang around here forever. You're a party girl; you just want to play. I got serious things on my mind. I got to go south and find guys who know about TV."

"Jim, you've got me wrong. I'm not like that at all. Why, look at the way I fixed up my house. Could I have done that if I'd been going to parties all the time?"

"You done a nice job," he admitted.

"Please don't leave today. You're not ready yet."

"Aw, you just want me to hang around and teach you music."

"Who said that?"

"You did. Last night."

She frowned, pulled off her cap, then picked up her towel and began drying herself. At last she said, "Jim, I'll be honest with you. Sure, I want you to stay a while. I won't deny it. But I wouldn't want you around permanently. After all, what have we got in common?"

"You're so damn uptown," he growled.

"No, no, it's nothing like that. It's simply that you're a guy and I'm a girl, and we've got nothing to offer each other. We're different. We've got different tastes and interests. Fact?"

"Absolutely."

"But you're not ready to leave yet. So I tell you what; we'll spend the whole morning practicing driving, and then we'll have some fun. What would you like to do? Go window-shopping? Buy more clothes? Visit the Modern Museum? Have a picnic?"

His face brightened. "Gee, you know something? I was never to a picnic in my whole life. Once I was bartender at a clambake, but that's not the same thing; not like when you're a kid."

She was delighted. "Then we'll have a real kid-type picnic."

And she brought her dolls. She carried them in her arms while Mayo toted the picnic basket to the Alice in Wonderland monument. The statue perplexed Mayo, who had never heard of Lewis Carroll. While Linda seated her pets and unpacked the picnic, she gave Mayo a summary of the story, and described how the bronze heads of Alice, the Mad Hatter, and the March Hare had been polished bright by the swarms of kids playing King of the Mountain.

"Funny, I never heard of that story," he said.

"I don't think you had much of a childhood, Jim."

"Why would you say a—" He stopped, cocked his head, and listened intently.

"What's the matter?" Linda asked.

"You hear that bluejay?"

"No."

"Listen. He's making a funny sound; like steel."

"Steel?"

"Yeah. Like . . . like swords in a duel."

"You're kidding."

"No. Honest."

"But birds sing; they don't make noises."

"Not always. Bluejays imitate noises a lot. Starlings, too. And parrots. Now why would he be imitating a sword fight? Where'd he hear it?"

"You're a real country boy, aren't you, Jim? Bees and bluejays and starlings and all that . . ."

"I guess so. I was going to ask; why would you say a thing like that, me not having any childhood?"

"Oh, things like not knowing Alice, and never going on a picnic, and always wanting a model yacht." Linda opened a dark bottle. "Like to try some wine?"

"You better go easy," he warned.

"Now stop it, Jim. I'm not a drunk."

"Did you or didn't you get smashed last night?"

She capitulated. "All right, I did; but only because it was my first drink in years."

He was pleased by her surrender. "Sure. Sure. That figures."

"So? Join me?"

"What the hell, why not?" He grinned. "Let's live a little. Say, this is one swingin' picnic, and I like the plates, too. Where'd you get them?"

"Abercrombie & Fitch," Linda said, deadpan. "Stainless Steel Service for Four, thirty-nine fifty. Skoal."

Mayo burst out laughing. "I sure goofed, didn't I, kicking up all that fuss? Here's looking at you."

"Here's looking right back."

They drank and continued eating in warm silence, smiling companionably at each other. Linda removed her madras silk shirt in order to tan in the blazing afternoon sun, and Mayo politely hung it up on a branch. Suddenly Linda asked, "Why didn't you have a childhood, Jim?"

"Gee, I don't know." He thought it over. "I guess because my mother died when I was a kid. And something else, too; I had to work a lot."

"Why?"

"My father was a schoolteacher. You know how they get paid."

"Oh, so that's why you're anti-egghead."

"I am?"

"Of course. No offense."

"Maybe I am," he conceded. "It sure was a letdown for my old man, me playing fullback in high school and him wanting like an Einstein in the house."

"Was football fun?"

"Not like playing games. Football's a business. Hey, remember when we were kids how we used to choose up sides? *Ibbety, bibbety, zibbety, zab*?"

"We used to say, *Eenie, meenie, miney, mo*."

"Remember: *April Fool, go to school, tell your teacher you're a fool*?"

"*I love coffee, I love tea, I love the boys, and the boys love me*."

"I bet they did at that," Mayo said solemnly.

"Not me."

"Why not?"

"I was always too big."

He was astonished. "But you're not big," he assured her. "You're just the right size. Perfect. And really built, I noticed when we moved the piano in. You got muscle, for a girl. A specially in the legs, and that's where it counts."

She blushed. "Stop it, Jim."

"No. Honest."

"More wine?"

"Thanks. You have some, too."

"All right."

A crack of thunder split the sky with its sonic boom, and was followed by the roar of collapsing masonry.

"There goes another skyscraper," Linda said. "What were we talking about?"

"Games," Mayo said promptly. "Excuse me for talking with my mouth full."

"Oh yes. Jim did you play *Drop the Handkerchief* up in New Haven?" Linda sang. "*A tisket, a tasket, a green and yellow basket. I sent a letter to my love, and on the way I dropped it . . .*"

"Gee," he said, much impressed. "You sing real good."

"Oh, go on!"

"Yes you do. You got a swell voice. Now don't argue with me. Keep quiet a minute. I got to figure something out." He thought intently for a long time, finishing his wine and absently accepting another glass. Finally he delivered himself of a decision. "You got to learn music."

"You know I'm dying to, Jim."

"So I'm going to stay awhile and teach you; as much as I know. Now hold it! Hold it!" he added hastily, cutting off her excitement. "I'm not going to stay in your house. I want a place of my own."

"Of course, Jim. Anything you say."

"And I'm still headed south."

"I'll teach you to drive, Jim. I'll keep my word."

"And no strings, Linda."

"Of course not. What kind of strings?"

"You know. Like the last minute you all of a sudden got a Looey Cans couch you want me to move in."

"*Louis Quinze!*" Linda's jaw dropped. "Wherever did you learn that?"

"Not in the army, that's for sure."

They laughed, clinked glasses, and finished their wine. Suddenly Mayo leaped up, pulled Linda's hair, and ran to the Wonderland monument. In an instant he had climbed to the top of Alice's head.

"I'm King of the Mountain," he shouted, looking around in imperial survey. "I'm King of the—" He cut himself off and stared down behind the statue.

"Jim, what's the matter?"

Without a word, Mayo climbed down and strode to a pile of debris half-hidden inside overgrown forsythia bushes. He knelt and began turning over the wreckage with gentle hands. Linda ran to him.

"Jim, what's wrong?"

"These used to be model boats," he muttered.

"That's right. My God, is that all? I thought you were sick or something."

"How come they're here?"

"Why, I dumped them, of course."

"You?"

"Yes. I told you. I had to clear out the boathouse when I moved in. That was ages ago."

"You did this?"

"Yes. I—"

"You're a murderer," he growled. He stood up and glared at her. "You're a killer. You're like all women, you got no heart and soul. To do a thing like this!"

He turned and stalked toward the boat pond. Linda followed him, completely bewildered.

"Jim, I don't understand. Why are you so mad?"

"You ought to be ashamed of yourself."

"But I had to have house room. You wouldn't expect me to live with a lot of model boats."

"Just forget everything I said. I'm going to pack and go south, I wouldn't stay with you if you was the last person on earth."

Linda gathered herself and suddenly darted ahead of Mayo. When he tramped into the boathouse, she was standing before the door of the guest room. She held up a heavy iron key.

"I found it," she panted. "Your door's locked."

"Gimme that key, Linda."

"No."

He stepped toward her, but she faced him defiantly and stood her ground.

"Go ahead," she challenged. "Hit me."

He stopped. "Aw, I wouldn't pick on anybody that wasn't my own size."

They continued to face each other, at a complete impasse.

"I don't need my gear," Mayo muttered at last. "I can get more stuff somewheres."

"Oh, go ahead and pack," Linda answered. She tossed him the key and stood aside. Then Mayo discovered there was no lock in the bedroom door. He opened the door, looked inside, closed it, and looked at Linda. She kept her face straight but began to sputter. He grinned. Then they both burst out laughing.

"Gee," Mayo said, "you sure made a monkey out of me. I'd hate to play poker against you."

"You're a pretty good bluffer yourself, Jim. I was scared to death you were going to knock me down."

"You ought to know I wouldn't hurt nobody."

"I guess I do. Now, let's sit down and talk this over sensibly."

"Aw, forget it, Linda. I kind of lost my head over them boats, and I—"

"I don't mean the boats; I mean going south. Every time you get mad you start south again. Why?"

"I told you, to find guys who know about TV."

"Why?"

"You wouldn't understand."

"I can try. Why don't you explain what you're after—specifically? Maybe I can help you."

"You can't do nothing for me; you're a girl."

"We have our uses. At least I can listen. You can trust me, Jim. Aren't we chums? Tell me about it."

Well, when the blast come (Mayo said) I was up in the Berkshires with Gil Watkins. Gil was my buddy, a real nice guy and a real bright guy. He took two years from M.I.T. before he quit college. He was like chief engineer or something at WNHA, the TV station in New Haven. Gil had a million hobbies. One of them was spee—speel—I can't remember. It meant exploring caves.

So anyway we were up in this flume in the Berkshires, spending the weekend inside, exploring and trying to map everything and figure out where the underground river comes from. We brought food and stuff along, and bedrolls. The compass we were using went crazy for like twenty minutes, and that should have give us a clue, but Gil talked about magnetic ores and stuff. Only when we come out Sunday night, I tell you it was pretty scary. Gil knew right off what happened.

"By Christ, Jim," he said, "they up and done it like everybody always knew they would. They've blew and gassed and poisoned and radiated themselves straight to hell, and we're going back to that goddamn cave until it all blows over."

So me and Gil went back and rationed the food and stayed

as long as we could. Finally we come out again and drove back to New Haven. It was dead like all the rest. Gil put together some radio stuff and tried to pick up broadcasts. Nothing. Then we packed some canned goods and drove all around; Bridgeport, Waterbury, Hartford, Springfield, Providence, New London . . . a big circle. Nobody. Nothing. So we come back to New Haven and settled down, and it was a pretty good life.

Daytime, we'd get in supplies and stuff, and tinker with the house to keep it working right. Nights, after supper, Gil would go off to WNHA around seven o'clock and start the station. He was running it on the emergency generators. I'd go down to "The Body Slam" open it up, sweep it out, and then start the bar TV set. Gil fixed me a generator for it to run on.

It was a lot of fun watching the shows Gil was broadcasting. He'd start with the news and weather, which he always got wrong. All he had was some Farmer's Almanacs and a sort of antique barometer that looked like that clock you got there on the wall. I don't think it worked so good, or maybe Gil never took weather at M.I.T. Then he'd broadcast the evening show.

I had my shotgun in the bar in case of holdups. Anytime I saw something that bugged me, I just up with the gun and let loose at the set. Then I'd take it and throw it out the front door and put another one in its place. I must have had hundreds waiting in the back. I spent two days a week just collecting reserves.

Midnight, Gil would turn off WNHA, I'd lock up the restaurant, and we'd meet home for coffee. Gil would ask how many sets I shot, and laugh when I told him. He said I was the most accurate TV poll ever invented. I'd ask him about what shows were coming up next week and argue with him about . . . oh . . . about like what movies or football games WNHA was scheduling. I didn't like Westerns much, and I hated them high-minded panel discussions.

But the luck had to turn lousy; it's the story of my life. After a couple of years, I found out I was down to my last set, and then I was in trouble. This night Gil run one of them icky commercials where this smart-aleck woman saves a marriage with the right laundry soap. Naturally I reached for my gun, and only at the last minute remembered not to shoot. Then he run an awful movie about a misunderstood composer, and the same thing happened. When we met back at the house, I was all shook up.

"What's the matter?" Gil asked.

I told him.

"I thought you liked watching the shows," he said.

"Only when I could shoot 'em."

"You poor bastard," he laughed, "you're a captive audience now."

"Gil, could you maybe change the programs, seeing the spot I'm in?"

"Be reasonable, Jim. WNHA has to broadcast variety. We operate on the cafeteria basis; something for everybody. If you don't like a show, why don't you switch channels?"

"Now that's silly. You know damn well we only got one channel in New Haven."

"Then turn your set off."

"I can't turn the bar set off, it's part of the entertainment. I'd lose my whole clientele. Gil, do you *have* to show them awful movies, like that army musical last night, singing and dancing and kissing on top of Sherman tanks for Jezus sake!"

"The women love uniform pictures."

"And those commercials; women always sneering at somebody's girdle, and fairies smoking cigarettes, and—"

"Aw," Gil said, "write a letter to the station."

So I did, and a week later I got an answer. It said: *Dear Mr. Mayo: We are very glad to learn that you are a regular viewer of WNHA, and thank you for your interest in our programming. We hope you will continue to enjoy our broadcasts. Sincerely yours, Gilbert O. Watkins, Station Manager*. A couple of tickets for an interview show were enclosed. I showed the letter to Gil, and he just shrugged.

"You see what you're up against, Jim," he said. "They don't care about what you like or don't like. All they want to know is if you are watching."

I tell you, the next couple of months were hell for me. I couldn't keep the set turned off, and I couldn't watch it without reaching for my gun a dozen times a night. It took all my willpower to keep from pulling the trigger. I got so nervous and jumpy that I knew I had to do something about it before I went off my rocker. So one night I brought the gun home and shot Gil.

Next day I felt a lot better, and when I went down to "The Body Slam" at seven o'clock to clean up, I was whistling kind of cheerful. I swept out the restaurant, polished the bar, and then turned on the TV to get the news and weather. You wouldn't believe it, but the set was busted. I couldn't get a picture. I couldn't even get a sound. My last set, busted.

So you see, that's why I have to head south (Mayo explained)—I got to locate a TV repairman.

There was a long pause after Mayo finished his story. Linda examined him keenly, trying to conceal the gleam in her eye. At last she asked with studied carelessness, "Where did he get the barometer?"

"Who? What?"

"Your friend, Gil. His antique barometer. Where did he get it?"

"Gee, I don't know. Antiquing was another one of his hobbies."

"And it looked like that clock?"

"Just like it."

"French?"

"I couldn't say."

"Bronze?"

"I guess so. Like your clock. Is that bronze?"

"Yes. Shaped like a sunburst?"

"No, just like yours."

"That's a sunburst. The same size?"

"Exactly."

"Where was it?"

"Didn't I tell you? In our house."

"Where's the house?"

"On Grant Street."

"What number?"

"Three fifteen. Say, what is all this?"

"Nothing, Jim. Just curious. No offense. Now I think I'd better get our picnic things."

"You wouldn't mind if I took a walk by myself?"

She cocked an eye at him. "Don't try driving alone. Garage mechanics are scarcer than TV repairmen."

He grinned and disappeared; but after dinner the true purpose of his disappearance was revealed when he produced a sheaf of sheet music, placed it on the piano rack, and led Linda to the piano bench. She was delighted and touched.

"Jim, you angel! Wherever did you find it?"

"In the apartment house across the street. Fourth floor, rear. Name of Horowitz. They got a lot of records, too. Boy, I can tell you it was pretty spooky snooping around in the dark with only matches. You know something funny, the whole top of the house is full of glop."

"Glop?"

"Yeah. Sort of white jelly, only it's hard. Like clear concrete. Now look, see this note? It's C. Middle C. It stands for this white key here. We better sit together. Move over . . ."

The lesson continued for two hours of painful concentration and left them both so exhausted that they tottered to their rooms with only perfunctory good nights.

"Jim," Linda called.

"Yeah?" he yawned.

"Would you like one of my dolls for your bed?"

"Gee, no. Thanks a lot, Linda, but guys really ain't interested in dolls."

"I suppose not. Never mind. Tomorrow I'll have something for you that really interests guys."

Mayo was awakened next morning by a rap on his door. He heaved up in bed and tried to open his eyes.

"Yeah? Who is it?" he called.

"It's me. Linda. May I come in?"

He glanced around hastily. The room was neat. The hooked rug was clean. The precious candlewick bedspread was neatly folded on top of the dresser.

"Okay. Come on in."

Linda entered, wearing a crisp seersucker dress. She sat down on the edge of the fourposter and gave Mayo a friendly pat. "Good morning," she said. "Now listen. I'll have to leave you alone for a few hours. I've got things to do. There's breakfast on the table, but I'll be back in time for lunch. All right?''

"Sure."

"You won't be lonesome?"

"Where you going?"

"Tell you when I get back." She reached out and tousled his head. "Be a good boy and don't get into mischief. Oh, one other thing. Don't go into my bedroom."

"Why should I?"

"Just don't anyway."

She smiled and was gone. Moments later, Mayo heard the jeep start and drive off. He got up at once, went into Linda's bedroom, and looked around. The room was neat, as ever. The bed was made, and her pet dolls were lovingly arranged on the coverlet. Then he saw it.

"Gee," he breathed.

It was a model of a full-rigged clipper ship. The spars and rigging were intact, but the hull was peeling, and the sails were shredded. It stood before Linda's closet, and alongside it was her sewing basket. She had already cut out a fresh set of white linen sails. Mayo knelt down before the model and touched it tenderly.

"I'll paint her black with a gold line around her," he murmured, "and I'll name her the *Linda N*."

He was so deeply moved that he hardly touched his breakfast. He bathed, dressed, took his shotgun and a handful of shells, and went out to wander through the park. He circled south, passed the playing fields, the decaying carousel, and the crumbling skating rink, and at last left the park and loafed down Seventh Avenue.

He turned east on 50th Street and spent a long time trying to decipher the tattered posters advertising the last performance at Radio City Music Hall. Then he turned south again. He was jolted to a halt by the sudden clash of steel. It sounded like giant sword blades in a titanic duel. A small herd of stunted horses burst out of a side street, terrified by the clangor. Their shoeless hooves thudded bluntly on the pavement. The sound of steel stopped.

"That's where that bluejay got it from," Mayo muttered. "But what the hell is it?"

He drifted eastward to investigate, but forgot the mystery when he came to the diamond center. He was dazzled by the blue-white stones glittering in the showcases. The door of one jewel mart had sagged open, and Mayo tiptoed in. When he emerged it was with a strand of genuine matched pearls which had cost him an I.O.U. worth a year's rent on "The Body Slam."

His tour took him to Madison Avenue where he found himself before Abercrombie & Fitch. He went in to explore and came at last to the gun racks. There he lost all sense of time, and when he recovered his senses, he was walking up Fifth Avenue toward the boat pond. An Italian Cosmi automatic rifle was cradled in his arms, guilt was in his heart, and a sales slip in the store read: *I.O.U. 1 Cosmi Rifle, $750.00. 6 Boxes Ammo. $18.00. James Mayo*.

It was past three o'clock when he got back to the boathouse. He eased in, trying to appear casual, hoping the extra gun he was carrying would go unnoticed. Linda was sitting on the piano bench with her back to him.

"Hi," Mayo said nervously. "Sorry I'm late. I . . . I brought you a present. They're real." He pulled the pearls from his pocket and held them out. Then he saw she was crying.

"Hey, what's the matter?"

She didn't answer.

"You wasn't scared I'd run out on you? I mean, well, all my gear is here. The car, too. You only had to look."

She turned. "I hate you!" she cried.

He dropped the pearls and recoiled, startled by her vehemence. "What's the matter?"

"You're a lousy rotten liar!"

"Who? Me?"

"I drove up to New Haven this morning." Her voice trembled with passion. "There's no house standing on Grant Street. It's all wiped out. There's no Station WNHA. The whole building's gone."

"No."

"Yes. And I went to your restaurant. There's no pile of TV sets out in the street. There's only one set, over the bar. It's rusted to pieces. The rest of the restaurant is a pigsty. You were living there all the time. Alone. There was only one bed in back. It was lies! All lies!"

"Why would I lie about a thing like that?"

"You never shot any Gil Watkins."

"I sure did. Both barrels. He had it coming."

"And you haven't got any TV set to repair."

"Yes I do."

"And even if it is repaired, there's no station to broadcast."

"Talk sense," he said angrily. "Why would I shoot Gil if there wasn't any broadcast."

"If he's dead, how can he broadcast?"

"See? And you just now said I didn't shoot him."

"Oh, you're mad! You're insane!" she sobbed. "You just described that barometer because you happened to be looking at my clock. And I believed your crazy lies. I had my heart set on a barometer to match my clock. I've been looking for years." She ran to the wall arrangement and hammered her fist alongside the clock. "It belongs right here. Here. But you lied, you lunatic. There never was a barometer."

"If there's a lunatic around here, it's you," he shouted. "You're so crazy to get this house decorated that nothing's real for you anymore."

She ran across the room, snatched up his old shotgun, and pointed it at him. "You get out of here. Right this minute. Get out or I'll kill you. I never want to see you again."

The shotgun kicked off in her hands, knocking her backward, and spraying shot over Mayo's head into a corner bracket. China shattered and clattered down. Linda's face went white.

"Jim! My God, are you all right? I didn't mean to . . . it just went off . . ."

He stepped forward, too furious to speak. Then, as he raised his hand to cuff her, the sound of distant reports came, BLAM-BLAM-BLAM. Mayo froze.

"Did you hear that?" he whispered.

Linda nodded.

"That wasn't any accident. It was a signal."

Mayo grabbed the shotgun, ran outside, and fired the second barrel into the air. There was a pause. Then again came the distant explosions in a stately triplet, BLAM-BLAM-BLAM. They had an odd, sucking sound, as though they were implosions rather than explosions. Far up the park, a canopy of frightened birds mounted into the sky.

"There's somebody," Mayo exulted. "By God, I told you I'd find somebody. Come on."

They ran north, Mayo digging into his pockets for more shells to reload and signal again.

"I got to thank you for taking that shot at me, Linda."

"I didn't shoot at you," she protested. "It was an accident."

"The luckiest accident in the world. They could be passing through and never know about us. But what the hell kind of guns are they using? I never heard no shots like that before, and I heard 'em all. Wait a minute."

On the little piazza before the Wonderland monument, Mayo halted and raised the shotgun to fire. Then he slowly lowered it. He took a deep breath. In a harsh voice he said, "Turn around. We're going back to the house." He pulled her around and faced her south.

Linda stared at him. In an instant he had become transformed from a gentle teddy bear into a panther.

"Jim, what's wrong?"

"I'm scared," he growled. "I'm goddam scared, and I don't want you to be, too." The triple salvo sounded again. "Don't pay any attention," he ordered. "We're going back to the house. Come on!"

She refused to move. "But why? Why?"

"We don't want any part of them. Take my word for it."

"How do you know? You've got to tell me."

"Christ! You won't let it alone until you find out, huh? All right. You want the explanation for that bee smell, and them buildings falling down, and all the rest?" He turned Linda round with a hand on her neck, and directed her gaze at the Wonderland monument. "Go ahead. Look."

A consummate craftsman had removed the heads of Alice, the Mad Hatter, and the March Hare, and replaced them with towering mantis heads, all saber mandibles, antennae, and faceted eyes. They were of a burnished steel and gleamed with unspeakable ferocity. Linda let out a sick whimper and sagged against Mayo. The triple report signaled once more.

Mayo caught Linda, heaved her over his shoulder, and loped back toward the pond. She recovered consciousness in a moment and began to moan. "Shut up," he growled. "Whining won't help." He set her on her feet before the boathouse. She was shaking but trying to control herself. "Did this place have shutters when you moved in? Where are they?"

"Stacked." She had to squeeze the words out. "Behind the trellis."

"I'll put 'em up. You fill buckets with water and stash 'em in the kitchen. Go!"

"Is it going to be a siege?"

"We'll talk later. Go!"

She filled buckets and then helped Mayo jam the last of the shutters into the window embrasures. "All right, inside," he ordered. They went into the house and shut and barred the door. Faint shafts of the late afternoon sun filtered through the louvers of the shutters. Mayo began unpacking the cartridges for the Cosmi rifle. "You got any kind of gun?"

"A .22 revolver somewhere."

"Ammo?"

"I think so."

"Get it ready."

"Is it going to be a siege?" she repeated.

"I don't know. I don't know who they are, or what they are, or where they come from. All I know is, we got to be prepared for the worst."

The distant implosions sounded. Mayo looked up alertly, listening. Linda could make him out in the dimness now. His face looked carved. His chest gleamed with sweat. He exuded the musky odor of caged lions. Linda had an overpowering impulse to touch him. Mayo loaded the rifle, stood it alongside the shotgun, and began padding from shutter to shutter, peering out vigilantly, waiting with massive patience.

"Will they find us?" Linda asked.

"Maybe."

"Could they be friendly?"

"Maybe."

"Those heads looked so horrible."

"Yeah."

"Jim, I'm scared. I've never been so scared in my life."

"I don't blame you."

"How long before we know?"

"An hour, if they're friendly; two or three, if they're not."

"W-Why longer?"

"If they're looking for trouble, they'll be more cautious."

"Jim, what do you really think?"

"About what?"

"Our chances."

"You really want to know?"

"Please."

"We're dead."

She began to sob. He shook her savagely. "Stop that. Go get your gun ready."

She lurched across the living room, noticed the pearls Mayo had dropped, and picked them up. She was so dazed that she put them on automatically. Then she went into her darkened bedroom and pulled Mayo's model yacht away from the closet door. She located the .22 in a hatbox on the closet floor and removed it along with a small carton of cartridges.

She realized that a dress was unsuited to this emergency. She got a turtleneck sweater, jodhpurs, and boots from the closet. Then she stripped naked to change. Just as she raised her arms to unclasp the pearls, Mayo entered, paced to the shuttered south window, and peered out. When he turned back from the window, he saw her.

He stopped short. She couldn't move. Their eyes locked, and she began to tremble, trying to conceal herself with her arms. He stepped forward, stumbled on the model yacht, and kicked it out of the way. The next instant he had taken possession of her body, and the pearls went flying, too. As she pulled him down on the bed, fiercely tearing the shirt from his back, her pet dolls also went into the discard heap along with the yacht, the pearls, and the rest of the world.

Of Time and Third Avenue

I DID a dumb thing, I started a piece of writing without knowing where I was going. Now this isn't damnfoolery for any author except me. We all have different work techniques and all are valid. Rex Stout said to me, "You know damn well how we write. You stick a piece of paper in the machine, type a word, then another, and finally you finish." I didn't believe him when he said he never outlined. I still don't because I must outline before I start writing. Only recently I learned that Stout outlined very carefully, but it was all in his head; he meant that he never wrote an outline. I have to write 'em.

Not that the story always follows the "game plan." Last year I was completing a novel and was so sure of my direction that I decided to get rid of the detailed notes I'd made before the writing began; they were cluttering up my workshop. I read through the final outline, the result of weeks of painful planning, and it had absolutely nothing to do with what I'd written. It was good; it was splendid; but the damned story had taken over and gone its own way.

Once the dean of us all, Robert Heinlein, and I were talking shop (writers are always talking shop, from work technique to favorite desk chairs) and Robert said, "I start out with some characters and get them into trouble, and when they get themselves out of trouble, the story's over. By the time I can hear their voices, they usually get themselves out of trouble." I was flabbergasted by this; I can't start a story until I can hear the characters talking, and by that time they've got will and ideas of their own and have gone into business for themselves.

But I blasted into what subsequently became "Of Time and Third Avenue" without an outline, mostly because I wanted to use a particular locale. The scene was P. J. Clarke's on Third Avenue, a low-down saloon where, for reasons I've never understood, we used to congregate after our repeat shows. In those old radio days you did a live show for the East and a live repeat, three hours later, for the West. The networks insisted on this; they claimed that listeners could tell the difference between a live show and a recording and resented the latter. Nonsense.

So after the repeat it was either Toots Shor's or P. J. Clarke's. We called it "Clarke's" or "Clarkie's" in those days; today, now a classy center for the young advertising and publishing crowd, it's called P.J.'s. Those initials have become a popular logo and are much imitated. You see like P. J. Horowitz's deli, P. J. Moto's sukiyaki, P. J. Chico's Montezuma's Revenge.

Here was this locale which I knew well. The characters were more or less cardboard—I hardly knew them at all—and this should have warned me, but I blithely began a play and wrote the first scene and then— What? I didn't know. I didn't have a story in mind, I had only a beginning. So I put the scene away and forgot it until I was irritated by another variation on the exhausted knowledge-of-the-future theme. You know the pattern: Guy gets hold of tomorrow's paper. Enabled to make a financial killing. Sees own death notice in back of paper. First time, great; subsequent variations, pfui!

I was annoyed into attempting what I imagined would be the definitive handling of the theme and reworked that original scene into the present "Of Time and Third Avenue." Footnote: Do you want to know the financial status of this author? I had to go to my bank to find out whose picture was on a hundred-dollar bill.

What Macy hated about the man was the fact that he squeaked. Macy didn't know if it was the shoes, but he suspected the clothes. In the back room of his tavern, under the poster that asked: WHO FEARS MENTION THE BAT-

TLE OF THE BOYNE? Macy inspected the stranger. He was tall, slender, and very dainty. Although he was young, he was almost bald. There was fuzz on top of his head and over his eyebrows. Then he reached into his jacket for a wallet, and Macy made up his mind. It was the clothes that squeaked.

"MQ, Mr. Macy," the stranger said in a staccato voice. "Very good. For rental of this back room including exclusive utility for one chronos—"

"One whatos?" Macy asked nervously.

"Chronos. The incorrect word? Oh yes. Excuse me. One hour."

"You're a foreigner," Macy said. "What's your name? I bet it's Russian."

"No. Not foreign," the stranger answered. His frightening eyes whipped around the back room. "Identify me as Boyne."

"Boyne!" Macy echoed incredulously.

"MQ. Boyne." Mr. Boyne opened a wallet shaped like an accordion, ran his fingers through various colored papers and coins, then withdrew a hundred-dollar bill. He jabbed it at Macy and said: "Rental fee for one hour. As agreed. One hundred dollars. Take it and go."

Impelled by the thrust of Boyne's eyes, Macy took the bill and staggered out of the bar. Over his shoulder he quavered: "What'll you drink?"

"Drink? Alcohol? Pfui!" Boyne answered.

He turned and darted to the telephone booth, reached under the pay phone and located the lead-in wire. From a side pocket he withdrew a small glittering box and clipped it to the wire. He tucked it out of sight, then lifted the receiver.

"Coordinates West 73-58-15," he said rapidly. "North 40-45-20. Disband sigma. You're ghosting . . ." After a pause, he continued: "Stet. Stet! Transmission clear. I want a fix on Knight. Oliver Wilson Knight. Probability to four significant figures. You have the coordinates. . . . 99.9807? MQ. Stand by. . . ."

Boyne poked his head out of the booth and peered toward the tavern door. He waited with steely concentration until a young man and a pretty girl entered. Then he ducked back to the phone. "Probability fulfilled. Oliver Wilson Knight in contact. MQ. Luck my Para.'' He hung up and was sitting under the poster as the couple wandered toward the back room.

The young man was about twenty-six, of medium height, and inclined to be stocky. His suit was rumpled, his seal-brown hair was rumpled, and his friendly face was crinkled by good-natured creases. The girl had black hair, soft blue eyes, and a small private smile. They walked arm in arm and liked to collide gently when they thought no one was looking. At this moment they collided with Mr. Macy.

"I'm sorry, Mr. Knight," Macy said. "You and the young lady can't sit back there this afternoon. The premises have been rented."

Their faces fell. Boyne called: "Quite all right, Mr. Macy. All correct. Happy to entertain Mr. Knight and friend as guests."

Knight and the girl turned to Boyne uncertainly. Boyne smiled and patted the chair alongside him. "Sit down," he said. "Charmed, I assure you."

The girl said: "We hate to intrude, but this is the only place in town where you can get genuine Stone gingerbeer."

"Already aware of the fact, Miss Clinton." To Macy he said: "Bring gingerbeer and go. No other guests. These are all I'm expecting."

Knight and the girl stared at Boyne in astonishment as they sat down slowly. Knight placed a wrapped parcel of books on the table. The girl took a breath and said, "You know me . . . Mr. . . ?"

"Boyne. As in Boyne, Battle of. Yes, of course. You are Miss Jane Clinton. This is Mr. Oliver Wilson Knight. I rented premises particularly to meet you this afternoon."

"This supposed to be a gag?" Knight asked, a dull flush appearing on his cheeks.

"Gingerbeer," answered Boyne gallantly as Macy arrived, deposited the bottles and glasses, and departed in haste.

"You couldn't know we were coming here," Jane said. "We didn't know ourselves . . . until a few minutes ago."

"Sorry to contradict, Miss Clinton," Boyne smiled. "The probability of your arrival at Longitude 73-58-15 Latitude

40-45-20 was 99.9807 per cent. No one can escape four significant figures.''

"Listen," Knight began angrily, "if this is your idea of—"

"Kindly drink gingerbeer and listen to my idea, Mr. Knight." Boyne leaned across the table with galvanic intensity. "This hour has been arranged with difficulty and much cost. To whom? No matter. You have placed us in an extremely dangerous position. I have been sent to find a solution."

"Solution for what?" Knight asked.

Jane tried to rise. "I . . . I think we'd b-better be go—"

Boyne waved her back, and she sat down like a child. To Knight he said: "This noon you entered premises of J. D. Craig & Co., dealer in printed books. You purchased, through transfer of money, four books. Three do not matter, but the fourth . . ." He tapped the wrapped parcel emphatically. "That is the crux of this encounter."

"What the hell are you talking about?" Knight exclaimed.

"One bound volume consisting of collected facts and statistics."

"The almanac?"

"The almanac."

"What about it?"

"You intended to purchase a 1950 almanac."

"I bought the '50 almanac."

"You did not!" Boyne blazed. "You bought the almanac for 1990."

"What?"

"The World Almanac for 1990," Boyne said clearly, "is in this package. Do not ask how. There was a carelessness that has already been disciplined. Now the error must be adjusted. That is why I am here. It is why this meeting was arranged. You cognate?"

Knight burst into laughter and reached for the parcel. Boyne leaned across the table and grasped his wrist. "You must not open it, Mr. Knight."

"All right." Knight leaned back in his chair. He grinned at Jane and sipped gingerbeer. "What's the payoff on the gag?"

"I must have the book, Mr. Knight. I would like to walk out of this tavern with the almanac under my arm."

"You would, eh?"

"I would."

"The 1990 almanac?"

"Yes."

"If," said Knight, "there was such a thing as a 1990 almanac, and if it was in that package, wild horses couldn't get it away from me."

"Why, Mr. Knight?"

"Don't be an idiot. A look into the future? Stock market reports . . . Horse races . . . Politics. It'd be money from home. I'd be rich."

"Indeed yes." Boyne nodded sharply. "More than rich. Omnipotent. The small mind would use the almanac from the future for small things only. Wagers on the outcome of games and elections. And so on. But the intellect of dimensions . . . *your* intellect . . . would not stop there."

"You tell me," Knight grinned.

"Deduction. Induction. Inference." Boyne ticked the points off on his fingers. "Each fact would tell you an entire history. Real estate investment, for example. What lands to buy and sell. Population shifts and census reports would tell you. Transportation. Lists of marine disasters and railroad wrecks would tell you whether rocket travel has replaced the train and ship."

"Has it?" Knight chuckled.

"Flight records would tell you which company's stock should be bought. Lists of postal receipts would indicate the cities of the future. The Nobel Prize winners would tell you which scientists and what new inventions to watch. Armament budgets would tell you what factories and industries to control. Cost-of-living reports would tell you how best to protect your wealth against inflation or deflation. Foreign exchange rates, stock exchange reports, bank suspensions and life insurance indexes would provide the clues to protect you against any and all disasters."

"That's the idea," Knight said. "That's for me."

"You really think so?"

"I know so. Money in my pocket. The world in my pocket."

"Excuse me," Boyne said keenly, "but you are only repeating the dreams of childhood. You want wealth. Yes. But only won through endeavor . . . your own endeavor. There is no joy in success as an unearned gift. There is nothing but guilt and unhappiness. You are aware of this already."

"I disagree," Knight said.

"Do you? Then why do you work? Why not steal? Rob? Burgle? Cheat others of their money to fill your own pockets?"

"But I—" Knight began, and then stopped.

"The point is well taken, eh?" Boyne waved his hand impatiently. "No, Mr. Knight. Seek a mature argument. You are too ambitious and healthy to wish to steal success."

"Then I'd just want to know if I would be successful."

"Ah? Stet. You wish to thumb through the pages looking for your name. You want reassurance. Why? Have you no confidence in yourself? You are a promising young attorney. Yes, I know that. It is part of my data. Has not Miss Clinton confidence in you?"

"Yes," Jane said in a loud voice. "He doesn't need reassurance from a book."

"What else, Mr. Knight?"

Knight hesitated, sobering in the face of Boyne's overwhelming intensity. Then he said: "Security."

"There is no such thing. Life is danger. You can only find security in death."

"You know what I mean," Knight muttered. "The knowledge that life is worth planning. There's the atom bomb."

Boyne nodded quickly. "True. It is a crisis. But then, I'm here. The world will continue. I am proof."

"If I believe you."

"And if you do not?" Boyne blazed. "You do not lack security. You lack courage." He nailed the couple with a contemptuous glare. "There is in this country a legend of pioneer forefathers from whom you are supposed to inherit courage in the face of odds. D. Boone, E. Allen, S. Houston, A. Lincoln, G. Washington and others. Fact?''

"I suppose so," Knight muttered. "That's what we keep telling ourselves."

"And where is the courage in you? Pfui! It is only talk. The unknown terrifies you. Danger does not inspire you to fight, as it did D. Crockett; it makes you whine and reach for the reassurance in this book. Fact?''

"But the atom bomb . . .''

"It is a danger. Yes. One of many. What of that? Do you cheat at solhand?''

"Solhand?''

"Your pardon." Boyne reconsidered, impatiently snapping his fingers at the interruption to the white heat of his argument. "It is a game played singly against chance relationships in an arrangement of cards. I forget your noun. . . .''

"Oh!" Jane's face brightened. "Solitaire."

"Quite right. Solitaire. Thank you, Miss Clinton." Boyne turned his frightening eyes on Knight. "Do you cheat at solitaire?''

"Occasionally."

"Do you enjoy games won by cheating?''

"Not as a rule.''

"They are thisney, yes? Boring. They are tiresome. Pointless. Null-coordinated. You wish you had won honestly.''

"I suppose so.''

"And you will suppose so after you have looked at this bound book. Through all your pointless life you will wish you had played honestly the game of life. You will verdash that look. You will regret. You will totally recall the pronouncement of our great poet-philosopher Trynbyll who summed it up in one lightning, skazon line. *'The Future is Tekon,'* said Trynbyll. Mr. Knight, do not cheat. Let me implore you to give me the almanac.''

"Why don't you take it away from me?''

"It must be a gift. We can rob you of nothing. We can give you nothing.''

"That's a lie. You paid Macy to rent this back room.''

"Macy was paid, but I gave him nothing. He will think he was cheated, but you will see to it that he is not. All will be adjusted without dislocation."

"Wait a minute. . . ."

"It has all been carefully planned. I have gambled on you, Mr. Knight. I am depending on your good sense. Let me have the almanac. I will disband . . . reorient . . . and you will never see me again. Vorloss verdash! It will be a bar adventure to narrate for friends. Give me the almanac!"

"Hold the phone," Knight said. "This is a gag. Remember? I—"

"Is it?" Boyne interrupted. "Is it? Look at me."

For almost a minute the young couple stared at the bleached white face with its deadly eyes. The half-smile left Knight's lips, and Jane shuddered involuntarily. There was chill and dismay in the back room.

"My God!" Knight glanced helplessly at Jane. "This can't be happening. He's got me believing. You?"

Jane nodded jerkily.

"What should we do? If everything he says is true we can refuse and live happily ever after."

"No," Jane said in a choked voice. "There may be money and success in that book, but there's divorce and death, too. Give him the almanac."

"Take it," Knight said faintly.

Boyne rose instantly. He picked up the package and went into the phone booth. When he came out he had three books in one hand and a smaller parcel made up of the original wrapping in the other. He placed the books on the table and stood for a moment, holding the parcel and smiling down.

"My gratitude," he said. "You have eased a precarious situation. It is only fair you should receive something in return. We are forbidden to transfer anything that might divert existing phenomena streams, but at least I can give you one token of the future."

He backed away, bowed curiously, and said: "My service to you both." Then he turned and started out of the tavern.

"Hey!" Knight called. "The token?"

"Mr. Macy has it," Boyne answered and was gone.

The couple sat at the table for a few blank moments like sleepers slowly awakening. Then, as reality began to return, they stared at each other and burst into laughter.

"He really had me scared," Jane said.

"Talk about Third Avenue characters. What an act. What'd he get out of it?"

"Well . . . he got your almanac."

"But it doesn't make sense." Knight began to laugh again. "All that business about paying Macy but not giving him anything. And I'm supposed to see that he isn't cheated. And the mystery token of the future . . ."

The tavern door burst open and Macy shot through the saloon into the back room. "Where is he?" Macy shouted. "Where's the thief? Boyne, he calls himself. More likely his name is Dillinger."

"Why, Mr. Macy!" Jane exclaimed. "What's the matter?"

"Where is he?" Macy pounded on the door of the men's room. "Come out, ye blaggard!"

"He's gone," Knight said. "He left just before you got back."

"And you, Mr. Knight!" Macy pointed a trembling finger at the young lawyer. "You, to be party to thievery and racketeers. Shame on you!"

"What's wrong?" Knight asked.

"He paid me one hundred dollars to rent this back room," Macy cried in anguish. "One hundred dollars. I took the bill over to Bernie the pawnbroker, being cautious-like, and he found out it's a forgery. It's a counterfeit."

"Oh, no," Jane laughed. "That's too much. Counterfeit?"

"Look at this," Mr. Macy shouted, slamming the bill down on the table.

Knight inspected it closely. Suddenly he turned pale and the laughter drained out of his face. He reached into his inside pocket, withdrew a checkbook and began to write with trembling fingers.

"What on earth are you doing?" Jane asked.

"Making sure that Macy isn't cheated," Knight said. "You'll get your hundred dollars, Mr. Macy."

"Oliver! Are you insane? Throwing away a hundred dollars . . ."

"And I won't be losing anything, either," Knight answered. "All will be adjusted without dislocation! They're diabolical. Diabolical!"

"I don't understand."

"Look at the bill," Knight said in a shaky voice. "Look closely."

It was beautifully engraved and genuine in appearance. Benjamin Franklin's benign features gazed up at them mildly and authentically; but in the lower right-hand corner was printed: Series 1980 D. And underneath that was signed: Oliver Wilson Knight, Secretary of the Treasury.

Isaac Asimov

THE question most often asked by fans is: Why did I stop writing science fiction? The answer is difficult because I'm a complex man with tangled motivations. However, I can try oversimplifying. Many times I've been driven off a bus by a child nagging its mother with "I wan' ice cream," over and over again. I can't endure repetition; I enjoy only new things. I'm the exact opposite to Gustave Lebair, a famous bibliomaniac, who read the same book St. Apollonius of Tyana in the Bibliothèque Nationale every day for sixty years. A perceptive friend once said, "Alfie Bester believes that the entire world was made for his entertainment." I really don't go quite that far in my selfish egotism, but I come damned close to it.

When I was serving my apprenticeship and trying to become a master craftsman in my profession, science fiction was merely one of many fields that I attacked. There were also comics, slick fiction, mainstream novels, radio and television scripts. As soon as I mastered a field and became successful, I'd be driven off the bus and have to catch another one in my search for the entertainment of a fresh challenge. I don't mean to imply that I was successful in everything I tried. I had my fair share of grim failures, and I'm saving them up to have another go.

My two successful science fiction novels of many years ago brought me dangerously close to boredom with the field. Brian Aldiss is much kinder than I am to myself. He says, "No. You stopped writing science fiction because you realized that you'd said all you had to say. I wish more writers would have that good sense." That may be true, but

371

the fact is it was my association with Holiday *magazine that
cut me off from other forms of writing.*

Holiday *was a godsend to a man of my temperament. As a
regular contributor and ultimately a senior editor, my professional life was filled with variety, fresh challenges, and
constant entertainment. As an interviewer and feature
writer, I had to master a new and difficult craft. Once
mastered, there was no danger of boredom because I was
meeting and spending time with hundreds of fascinating
people in hundreds of different professions. With the cachet
of a then-important magazine backing me, no door was ever
closed; ideal for an incurably curious man.*

*I enjoyed interviewing the most and want to show you the
sort of thing I was doing issue after issue. Unfortunately,
most of my pieces ran much too long for inclusion here, and
anyway what would Olivier, Burton, Quinn, Kim Novak, or
Sophia Loren be doing in a science fiction collection? Happily I have a very short piece I did for another publication on
Isaac Asimov, one of the great stars of the field, and I'm
including it here.*

*You may ask what an interview is doing in a story collec-
tion. Well, it isn't a story collection, it's a Bester collection,
and there's no reason why there can't be variety. I'll trouble
you not to object. It will only remind me of Whistler's libel
action against John Ruskin. On cross-examination, Ruskin's
barrister asked Whistler how he could call one of his paintings "A Study in Blue" when there were so many other
colors in it. Whistler shot back, "Idiot! Does a symphony in
F consist of nothing but F, F, F?"*

*Colorful man, Whistler. Deadly opponent. I'd love to have
interviewed him.*

There's no doubt that Isaac Asimov is the finest popular
science writer working today, and in my opinion Ike is the
finest who has ever written; prolific, encyclopedic, witty,

with a gift for colorful and illuminating examples and explanations. What makes him unique is the fact that he's a bona fide scientist—associate professor of biochemistry at Boston University School of Medicine—and scientists are often rotten writers. Read the novels of C. P. Snow and the short stories of Bertrand Russell if you want proof. But our scientist professor, Asimov, is not only a great popular science author but an eminent science fiction author as well. He comes close to the ideal of the Renaissance Man.

His latest (120th) book, *Asimov's Guide to Science* (Basic Books), is a must for science-oriented and/or science-terrified readers. Many people have the frightened feeling, "What are they up to now?" Asimov tells us with clarity, with charm, with calm. His new *Guide* will fascinate the layman, and if the layman gives it to his kids to read they may very well wind up on university faculties with tenure. Ike makes everyone want to turn into a scientist.

Asimov's Guide to Science is the new and third edition of *The Intelligent Man's Guide to Science*, first published in 1960 by Basic Books. Asked why the change in title, he said, "Well, there's a whole slew of *Asimov's Guides* and *Asimov's Treasuries*, so we decided to go along with it. I presume the fourth edition will be *Asimov's New Guide to Science*. What the fifth will be, I don't know."

The encyclopedia has been revised and updated, of course. Much has happened since the 1960s. Asked about his changes, Ike rattled off, "Pulsars, black holes, the surface of Mars, landings on the moon. Then there's seafloor spreading and the shifting of continents, which I dismissed with a sneer in the first edition. You see, at the time of the first edition the space satellites were just being flown and hadn't done their research yet. I thought the earth's crust was too solid and hard for the continents to drift. I was wrong. Now we know that the continents aren't floating; they're being pushed apart by the upflow of magma from the seafloor. Then I've covered quarks and—"

"Wait a minute. What are quarks?"

"They're hypothetical particles which may make up all the subatomic particles, but first we have to isolate one. In other words, you can think that ten dimes make a dollar, but you have to take a dollar apart first and find a dime." This is the Asimov style.

He also discusses why enough neutrinos have not yet been detected coming from the sun, the biological clocks in animals, tachyons—a fascinating hypothesis about subatomic particles which travel faster than the speed of light—and cloning.

"What's so special about clone cultures, Ike? They're simply families raised from a single individual. I raised many clone cultures from a single paramecium or amoeba when I was a biology student."

"No, no. Now we're talking about despecializing specialized cells. You can take an abdominal cell from a frog, fertilize it with an ovum and get a whole frog. There may come a time when they can cut off your little toe when you're born, fertilize it and end up with a whole race of Alfie Besters."

"What a horrible thought."

"Yes, but they wouldn't know it at the time."

He's a powerful man, 5-9, 180 pounds, with thick hair going grey, steel-blue eyes, beautiful strong hands, and rather blunt features. He was born in Russia in 1920 and was brought to the States in 1923 by his family, which wasn't exactly well-to-do. Nevertheless he managed to put himself through Columbia University to his doctorate which he won for a thesis on enzyme chemistry.

He was married in 1942, has two kids, and is recently separated from his wife. He now lives in a comfortable suite in a residential hotel just off Central Park West. The living room is his workshop; jammed with shelves of reference texts, files and piles of scientific journals. He works from nine to five, seven days a week without a break.

"No, I'm lying. Sometimes I goof off on part of Sunday."

"Do you think at the typewriter, Ike?"

"Yes. I type at professional speed. Ninety words a minute."

"Great, but do you think at ninety words a minute?"

"Yes, I do. The two work together neatly."

He receives an enormous amount of mail from his fiction fans and his science fans, which he answers. Small boys write and ask him to settle disputes they're having with their science teachers. Asimov winces when he recalls a terrible boner which he perpetrated in the first edition of his *Guide*. A kid got into an argument with his teacher over it and said, "Dr. Asimov is always right." Asimov was forced to write back, "Sometimes Isaac Asimov is a damned fool."

He gets a few crank letters. "One guy was mad because I wouldn't say that Nikola Tesla was the greatest scientist who ever lived. I've only had one anti-Semitic letter. This was from a kook who thought I gave too much space to Einstein. He said Einstein was all wrong, and anyway he stole everything from a Gentile. Naturally I didn't bother to answer that."

He's rather amused by what he calls his steel-trap memory. "I have a tight grip on things in inverse proportion to their importance. The trouble is, I can't throw anything out. The other day a friend mentioned an old song, 'The Boulevard of Broken Dreams,' and I sang it for him."

Damn if he didn't start singing it for me, miserably. "You see?" he grinned. "Another five brain cells wasted."

The Pi Man

THE one word most symbolic of science fiction is, of course, "extrapolation." Science fiction started talking about extrapolation a couple of generations back. I first encountered the noun and verb in Astounding Science Fiction, *and I was much impressed yet ashamed because I didn't know what it meant. Here I was, excessively educated, and I'd never come across it before. I was convinced that the godlike editor of* Astounding, *John W. Campbell, Jr., had personally and privately invented it. Certainly he used the word like he owned it.*

"Extrapolation" is no longer an exotic SF term today. It's become familiar and a part of casual conversation particularly after its frequent use along with the rest of the Madison Avenue jargon in the Watergate hearings, but what exactly does it mean? The unabridged Webster II, which remains the supreme arbiter for editors despite the publication of the Webster III, is no help at all:

Extrapolation. The calculation, from the values of a function known within a certain interval of values of its argument, of its value for some argument value lying without that interval, as the calculation of the birth rate in 1934 from the known rates in 1850-1900.

And good luck to Noah Webster, American lexicographer . . . 1758-1843.
Here's my definition:

Extrapolation. The continuation of a trend, either in-

377

creasing, decreasing or steady-state, to its culmination in the future. The only constraint is the limit set by the logic of the universe.

And good luck to the late, great Alfred Bester, American author.

I'd like to digress here to get mixed up in the controversial question that vexes many readers and writers of imaginative fiction: what is the difference between science fiction and fantasy. My "constraint" qualification in the definition of extrapolation may be the answer. In my opinion, science fiction's limits are, or should be, the known/possible logic of the universe. In my opinion, fantasy is written and read in a limbo without logic or limits. That's one reason why I dislike most fantasy so much; I find it undisciplined and self-indulgent.

I've done my own extrapolation in science fiction, but I've concentrated mainly on human behavior; I'm people-oriented. Whenever I start thinking about a story, it's always in terms of characters and their response to a changed environment. Putting it another way, I'm not much interested in extrapolating science and technology; I merely use extrapolation as a means of putting people into new quandaries which produce colorful pressures and conflicts. I'll be blunt to hell with the science if it can't produce fiction.

Now I'm people myself, and many times I've extrapolated a piece of myself into a story. Some friends who know me well insist that I put all of myself into all of my protagonists, which isn't pleasant considering how lunatic my antiheroes are. I think the purest example of this is "The Pi Man," and one of the proofs is that the story was written in a single day of white-hot hysteria. I must have been writing myself. Additional proof: I revised and polished the story for this edition (the original was written too fast and was rather crude), and I got hysterical all over again.

I've always been obsessed by patterns, rhythms, and tempi, and I always feel my stories in those terms. It's this pattern obsession that compels me to experiment with typography. I'm trying very hard to develop a technique of blending the

sight, sound, and context of words into dramatic patterns. I
want to make the eye, ear, and mind of the reader merge into
a whole that is bigger than the sum of its parts. I have this
curious belief that somehow reading should be more than
mere reading; it should be a total sensory and intellectual
experience. In my own quaint way I'm trying to go films and
TV one better. Huxley was reaching for the same thing with
his "feelies" in Brave New World but he didn't go far
enough. Me neither, maybe.

Anyway, one evening I was chatting with a dear guy who's
been a friend ever since he beat my brains out in foils during a
dual-meet we had with Princeton. He's a demented musician.
Among other things he wrote a black humor tune titled,
"Who Put the Snatch on the Lindbergh Baby? (Was it You
or You or You?)" He was telling me about the eminent
composer under whom he'd studied at Prince-i-ton. Little
Charles Augie was playing with his doggie . . . *The Man
could beat 5/4 with one hand while beating 7/4 with the
other,* Was that the thing to do? *and he could make them
come out even at the end of the measure.* His father took the
notion to fly the ocean . . . *It's a fantastic ability; if you
don't believe me try it for yourself.* Was that any way to show
your devotion?

*This fired the idea of extrapolating my obsession with
patterns and dynamics, and "The Pi Man" is the result. The
story explores the effects of an outré but logically possible
exaggeration of environment on a contemporary man.
(Parenthetically, I always try to keep my characters contemporary in science fiction.) Notice that I did not make the
protagonist a musician. Too obvious, too easy, too special. I
believed that everybody could identify and vibrate with the
harmonics of my own rhythmic obsession. This, of course, is
a classic symptom of lunacy.*

How to say? How to write? When sometimes I can be
fluent, even polished, and then, *reculer pour mieux sauter*,
patterns take hold of me. Push. Compel.

Sometimes

I   I   I
     am   am   am
          3.14159 +
     from   from   from
     this   other   that
space   space   space

Othertimes not

I have no control, but I try anyways.

I wake up wondering who, what, when, where, why?

Confusion result of biological compensator born into my body which I hate. Yes, birds and beasts have biological clock built in, and so navigate home from a thousand miles away. I have biological compensator, equalizer, responder to unknown stresses and strains. I relate, compensate, make and shape patterns, adjust rhythms, like a gridiron pendulum in a clock, but this is an unknown clock, and I do not know what time it keeps. Nevertheless I must. I am force. Have no control over self, speech, love, fate. Only to compensate.

Quae nocent docent. Translation follows: Things that injure teach. I am injured and have hurt many. What have we learned? However. I wake up the morning of the biggest hurt of all wondering which house. Wealth, you understand. Damme! Mews cottage in London, villa in Rome, penthouse in New York, rancho in California. I awake. I look. Ah! Layout familiar. Thus:

Foyer
     Bedroom
          Bath   T
          Bath   e
     Living Room   r
Kitchen   r
     Dressing Room   a
     Bedroom   c
          T e r r a c e

So. I am in penthouse in New York, but that bath-bath-back-to-back. Pfui! All rhythm wrong. Pattern painful. Why have I never noticed before? Or is this sudden awareness result of phenomenon elsewhere? I telephone to janitor-mans downstairs. At that moment I lose my American-English. Damn nuisance. I'm compelled to speak a compost of tongues, and I never know which will be forced on me next.

"Pronto. Ecco mi. Signore Marko. Miscusi tanto—"

Pfui! Hang up. Hate the garbage I must sometimes speak and write. This I now write during period of AmerEng lucidity, otherwise would look like goulash. While I wait for return of communication, I shower body, teeth, hairs, shave face, dry everything, and try again. *Voilà!* Ye Englishe, she come. Back to invention of Mr. A. G. Bell and call janitor again.

"Good morning, Mr. Lundgren. This is Peter Marko. Guy in the penthouse. Right. Mr. Lundgren, be my personal rabbi and get some workmen up here this morning. I want those two baths converted into one. No, I mean it. I'll leave five thousand dollars on top of the icebox. Yes? Thanks, Mr. Lundgren."

Wanted to wear grey flannel this morning but compelled to put on sharkskin. Damnation! Black Power has peculiar side effects. Went to spare bedroom (see diagram) and unlocked door which was installed by the Eagle Safe Company—Since 1904—Bank Vault Equipment—Fireproof Files & Ledger Trays—Combinations changed. I went in.

Everything broadcasting beautifully, up and down the electromagnetic spectrum. Radio waves down to 1,000 meters, ultraviolet up into the hard X-rays and the 100 Kev (one hundred thousand electron volts) gamma radiation. All interrupters innn-tt-errrr-up-ppp-t-ingggg at random. I'm jamming the voice of the universe at least within this home, and I'm at peace. Dear God! To know even a moment of peace!

So. I take subway to office in Wall Street. Limousine more convenient but chauffeur too dangerous. Might become friendly, and I don't dare have friends anymore. Best of all, the morning subway is jam-packed, mass-packed, no patterns to adjust, no shiftings and compensations required. Peace.

In subway car I catch a glimpse of an eye, narrow, bleak, grey, the property of an anonymous man who conveys the conviction that you've never seen him before and will never see him again. But I picked up that glance and it tripped an alarm in the back of my mind. He knew it. He saw the flash in my eyes before I could turn away. So I was being tailed again. Who, this time? U.S.A.? U.S.S.R.? Interpol? Skip-Tracers, Inc.?

I drifted out of the subway with the crowd at City Hall and gave them a false trail to the Woolworth Building in case they were operating double-tails. The whole theory of the hunters and the hunted is not to avoid being tailed, no one can escape that; the thing to do is give them so many false leads to follow up that they become overextended. Then they may be forced to abandon you. They have a man-hour budget; just so many men for just so many operations.

City Hall traffic was out of sync, as it generally is, so I had to limp to compensate. Took elevator up to tenth floor of bldg. As I was starting down the stairs, I was suddenly seized by something from out there, something bad. I began to cry, but no help. An elderly clerk emerge from office wearing alpaca coat, gold spectacles, badge on lapel identify: *N. N. Chapin*.

"Not him," I plead with nowhere. "Nice mans. Not N. N. Chapin, please."

But I am force. Approach. Two blows, neck and gut. Down he go, writhing. I trample spectacles and smash watch. Then I'm permitted to go downstairs again. It was ten-thirty. I was late. Damn! Took taxi to 99 Wall Street. Driver's pattern smelled honest; big black man, quiet and assured. Tipped him fifty dollars. He raise eyebrows. Sealed one thousand in envelope (secretly) and sent driver back to bldg. to find and give to N. N. Chapin on tenth floor. Did not enclose note: "From your unknown admirer."

Routine morning's work in office. I am in arbitrage, which is simultaneous buying and selling of moneys in different markets to profit from unequal price. Try to follow simple example: Pound sterling is selling for $2.79½ in London. Rupee is selling for $2.79 in New York. One rupee buys one pound in Burma. See where the arbitrage lies? I buy one rupee for $2.79 in New York, buy one pound for rupee in Burma, sell pound for $2.79½ in London, and I have made ½ cent on the transaction. Multiply by $100,000, and I have made $250 on the transaction. Enormous capital required.

But this is only crude example of arbitrage; actually the buying and selling must follow intricate patterns and have perfect timing. Money markets are jumpy today. Big Boards are hectic. Gold fluctuating. I am behind at eleven-thirty, but the patterns put me ahead $57,075.94 by half-past noon, Daylight Saving Time.

57075 makes a nice pattern but that 94¢! Iych! Ugly. Symmetry above all else. Alas, only 24¢ hard money in my pockets. Called secretary, borrowed 70¢ from her, and threw sum total out window. Felt better as I watched it scatter in space, but then I caught her looking at me with delight. Very dangerous. Fired girl on the spot.

"But why, Mr. Marko? Why?" she asked, trying not to cry. Darling little thing. Pale-faced and saucy, but not so saucy now.

"Because you're beginning to like me."

"What's the harm in that?"

"When I hired you, I warned you not to like me."

"I thought you were putting me on."

"I wasn't. Out you go."

"But why?"

"Because I'm beginning to like you."

"Is this some new kind of pass?"

"God forbid!"

"Well you don't have to worry," she flared. "I despise you."

"Good. Then I can go to bed with you."

She turned crimson and opened her mouth to denounce me, the while her eyes twinkled at the corners. A darling girl, whatever her name was. I could not endanger her. I gave her three weeks' salary for a bonus and threw her out. *Punkt*.

Next secretary would be a man, married, misanthropic, murderous; a man who could hate me.

So, lunch. Went to nicely balanced restaurant. All chairs filled by patrons. Even pattern. No need for me to compensate and adjust. Also, they give me usual single corner table which does not need guest to balance. Ordered nicely patterned luncheon:

Martini   Martini
Croque M'sieur Roquefort
Salad
Coffee

But so much cream being consumed in restaurant that I had to compensate by drinking my coffee black, which I dislike. However, still a soothing pattern.

$x^2 + x + 41$ = prime number. Excuse, please. Sometimes I'm in control and see what compensating must be done . . . tick-tock-tick-tock, good old gridiron pendulum . . . other times is force on me from God knows where or why or how or even if there is a God. Then I must do what I'm compelled to do, blindly, without motivation, speaking the gibberish I speak and think, sometimes hating it like what I do to poor mans Mr. Chapin. Anyway, the equation breaks down when $x = 40$.

The afternoon was quiet. For a moment I thought I might be forced to leave for Rome (Italy) but whatever it was adjusted without needing my two ($0.02) cents. ASPCA finally caught up with me for beating my dog to death, but I'd contributed $5,000.00 to their shelter. Got off with a shaking of heads. Wrote a few graffiti on posters, saved a small boy from a clobbering in a street rumble at a cost of sharkskin jacket. Drat! Slugged a maladroit driver who was subjecting his lovely Aston-Martin to cruel and unusual punishment. He was, how they say, "grabbing a handful of second."

In the evening to ballet to relax with all the beautiful Balanchine patterns; balanced, peaceful, soothing. Then I take a deep breath, quash my nausea, and force myself to go to *The Raunch*, the West Village creepsville. I hate *The*

Raunch, but I need a woman and I must go where I hate. That fair-haired girl I fired, so full of mischief and making eyes at me. So, *poisson d'avril*, I advance myself to *The Raunch*.

Chaos. Blackness. Cacophony. My vibes shriek. 25 Watt bulbs. Ballads of Protest. Against L. wall sit young men with pubic beards, playing chess. Badly. *Exempli gratia*:

1	P—Q4	Kt—KB3
2	Kt—Q2	P—K4
3	P X P	Kt—Kt5
4	P—KR3	Kt—K6

If White takes the knight, Black forces mate with Q-R5ch. I didn't wait to see what the road-company Capablancas would do next.

Against R. wall is bar, serving beer and cheap wine mostly. There are girls with brown paper bags containing toilet articles. They are looking for a pad for the night. All wear tight jeans and are naked under loose sweaters. I think of Herrick (1591-1674): *Next, when I lift mine eyes and see/That brave vibration each way free/Oh, how that glittering taketh me!*

I pick out the one who glitters the most. I talk. She insult. I insult back and buy hard drinks. She drink my drinks and snarl and hate, but helpless. Her name is Bunny and she has no pad for tonight. I do not let myself sympathize. She is a dyke; she does not bathe, her thinking patterns are jangles. I hate her and she's safe; no harm can come to her. So I maneuvered her out of Sink City and took her home to seduce by mutual contempt, and in the living room sat the slender little paleface secretary, recently fired for her own good.

She sat there in my penthouse, now minus one (1) bathroom, and with $1,997.00 change on top of the refrigerator. Oi! Throw $6.00 into kitchen Dispos-All (a Federal offense) and am soothed by the lovely 1991 remaining. She sat there, wearing a pastel thing, her skin gleaming rose-red from embarrassment, also red for danger. Her saucy face was very tight from the daring thing she thought she was doing. *Gott bewahre!* I like that.

```
            I
          Now
         write
         foll-
         owing
         piece
         of the
          s        p
          t          a
        o    in    r
        r              i
        y              s
```

Address: 49bis Avenue Hoche, Paris, 8 eme, France

Forced to go there by what happened in the U.N., you understand. It needed extreme compensation and adjustment. Almost, for a moment, I thought I would have to attack the conductor of the *Opéra Comique*, but fate was kind and let me off with nothing worse than indecent exposure, and I was able to square it by founding a scholarship at the Sorbonne. Didn't someone suggest that fate was the square root of minus one?

Anyway, back in New York it is my turn to denounce the paleface but suddenly my AmerEng is replaced by a dialect out of a B-picture about a white remittance man and a blind native girl on a South Sea island who find redemption together while she plays the ukulele and sings gems from Lawrence Welk's Greatest Hits.

"Oh-so," I say. "Me-fella be ve'y happy ask why you-fella invade 'long my apa'tment, 'cept me' now speak pidgin. Ve'y emba'ss 'long me.."

"I bribed Mr. Lundgren," she blurted. "I told him you needed important papers from the office."

The dyke turned on her heel and bounced out, her brave vibration each way free. I caught up with her in front of the elevator, put $101 into her hand, and tried to apologize. She hated me more so I did a naughty thing to her vibration and returned to the living room.

"What's she got?" the paleface asked.

My English returned. "What's your name?"

"Good Lord! I've been working in your office for two months and you don't know my name? You really don't?"

"No."

"I'm Jemmy Thomas."

"Beat it, Jemmy Thomas."

"So that's why you always called me 'Miss Uh.' You're Russian?"

"Half."

"What's the other half?"

"None of your business. What are you doing here? When I fire them they stay fired. What d'you want from me?"

"You," she said, blushing fiery.

"Will you for God's sake get the hell out of here."

"What did she have that I don't?" paleface demanded. Then her face crinkled. "Don't? Doesn't? I'm going to Bennington. They're strong on aggression but weak on grammar."

"What d'you mean, you're going to Bennington?"

"Why, it's a college. I thought everybody knew."

"But *going*?"

"Oh. I'm in my junior year. They drive you out with whips to acquire practical experience in your field. You ought to know that. Your office manager—I suppose you don't know her name, either."

"Ethel M. Blatt."

"Yes. Miss Blatt took it all down before you interviewed me."

"What's your field?"

"It used to be economics. Now it's you. How old are you?"

"One hundred and one."

"Oh, come on. Thirty? They say at Bennington that ten years is the right difference between men and women because we mature quicker. Are you married?"

"I have wives in London, Paris, and Rome. What is this catechism?"

"Well, I'm trying to get something going."

"I can see that, but does it have to be me?"

"I know it sounds like a notion." She lowered her eyes, and without the highlight of their blue, her pale face was almost invisible. "And I suppose women are always throwing themselves at you."

"It's my untold wealth."

"What are you, blasé or something? I mean, I know I'm not staggering, but I'm not exactly repulsive."

"You're lovely."

"Then why don't you come near me?"

"I'm trying to protect you."

"I can protect me when the time comes. I'm a Black Belt."

"The time is now, Jemmy Thompson."

"Thomas."

"Walk, not run, to the nearest exit, Jemmy Thomas."

"The least you could do is offend me the way you did that hustler in front of the elevator."

"You snooped?"

"Sure I snooped. You didn't expect me to sit here on my hands, did you? I've got my man to protect."

I had to laugh. This spunky little thing march in, roll up her sleeves and set to work on me. A wonder she didn't have a pot roast waiting in the oven and herself waiting in the bed.

"Your man?" I ask.

"It happens," she said in a low voice. "I never believed it, but it happens. You fall in and out of love and affairs, and each time you think it's real and forever. And then you meet somebody and it isn't a question of love anymore. You just know that he's your man, and you're stuck with him, whether you like it or not." She burst out angrily. "I'm stuck, dammit! Stuck! D'you think I'm enjoying this?"

She looked at me through the storm; violet eyes full of youth and determination and tenderness and fear. I could see she too was being forced and was angry and afraid. And I knew how lonely I was, never daring to make friends, to love, to share. I could fall into those violet eyes and never come up. I looked at the clock. 2:30 A.M. Sometimes quiet at this hour. Perhaps my AmerEng would stay with me a while longer.

"You're being compelled, Jemmy," I said. "I know all about that. Something inside you, something you don't understand, made you take your dignity in both hands and come after me. You don't like it, you don't want to, you've never begged in your life, but you had to. Yes?"

She nodded.

"Then you can understand a little about me. I'm compelled, too."

"Who is she?"

"No, no. Not forced to beg from a woman; compelled to hurt people."

"What people?"

"Any people; sometimes strangers, and that's bad, other times people I love, and that's not to be endured. So now I no longer dare love. I must protect people from myself."

"I don't know what you're talking about. Are you some kind of psychotic monster?"

"Yes, played by Lon Chaney, Jr."

"If you can joke about it, you can't be all that sick. Have you seen a shrink?"

"No. I don't have to. I know what's compelling me." I looked at the clock again. Still a quiet time. Please God the English would stay with me a while longer. I took off my jacket and shirt. "I'm going to shock you," I said, and showed her my back, crosshatched with scars. She gasped.

"Self-inflicted," I told her. "Because I permitted myself to like a man and become friendly with him. This is the price I paid, and I was lucky that he didn't have to. Now wait here."

I went into the master bedroom where my heart's shame was embalmed in a silver case hidden in the right-hand drawer of my desk. I brought it to the living room. Jemmy watched me with great eyes.

"Five years ago a girl fell in love with me," I told her. "A girl like you. I was lonely then, as always, so instead of protecting her from me, I indulged myself and tried to love her back. Now I want to show you the price *she* paid. You'll loathe me for this, but I must show you. Maybe it'll save you from—"

I broke off. A flash had caught my eye—the flash of lights going on in a building down the street; not just a few windows, a lot. I put on my jacket, went out on the terrace, and watched. All the illuminated windows in the building three down from me went out. Five-second eclipse. On again. It happened in the building two down and then the one next door. The girl came to my side and took my arm. She trembled slightly.

"What is it?" she asked. "What's the matter? You look so grim."

"It's the Geneva caper," I said. "Wait."

The lights in my apartment went out for five seconds and then came on again.

"They've located me the way I was nailed in Geneva," I told her.

"They? Located?"

"They've spotted my jamming by d/f."

"What jamming?"

"The full electromagnetic spectrum."

"What's dee eff?"

"Radio direction-finder. They used it to get the bearing of my jamming. Then they turned off the current in each building in the area, building by building, until the broadcast stopped. Now they've pinpointed me. They know I'm in this house, but they don't know which apartment yet. I've still got time. So. Good night, Jemmy. You're hired again. Tell Ethel Blatt I won't be in for a while. I wish I could kiss you good-bye, but safer not."

She clamped her arms around my neck and gave me an honest kiss. I tried to push her away.

She clung like The Old Man of the Sea. "You're a spy," she said. "I'll go to the chair with you."

"I wish to heaven I only was a spy. Good-bye, my love. Remember me."

A great mistake letting that slip. It happen, I think, because my speech slip, too. Suddenly forced to talk jumble again. As I run out, the little paleface kick off her sandals so she can run, too. She is alongside me going down the fire stairs to the garage in the basement. I hit her to stop, and swear Swahili at her. She hit back and swear gutter, all the time laughing and crying. I love her for it, so she is doomed. I will ruin her like all the rest.

We get into car and drive fast. I am making for 59th Street bridge to get off Manhattan Island and head east. I own plane in Babylon, Long Island, which is kept ready for this sort of awkwardness.

"*J'y suis, J'y reste* is not my motto," I tell Jemmy Thomas, whose French is as uncertain as her grammar, an endearing weakness. "Once Scotland Yard trapped me with a letter. I was receiving special mail care of General Delivery. They mailed me a red envelope, spotted me when I picked it up, and followed me to No. 13 Mayfair Mews, London W.1., Telephone, Mayfair 7711. Red for danger. Is the rest of you as invisible as your face?"

"I'm not invisible," she said, indignant, running hands through her streaky fair hair. "I tan in the summer. What is all this chase and escape? Why do you talk so funny and act so peculiar? In the office I thought it was because you're a crazy Russian. Half crazy Russian. Are you sure you're not a spy?"

"Only positive."

"It's too bad. A Commie 007 would be utter blissikins."

"Yes, I know. You see yourself being seduced with vodka and caviar."

"Are you a being from another world who came here on a UFO?"

"Would that scare you?"

"Only if it meant we couldn't make the scene."

"We couldn't anyway. All the serious side of me is concentrated on my career. I want to conquer the earth for my robot masters."

"I'm only interested in conquering you."

"I am not and have never been a creature from another world. I can show you my passport to prove it."

"Then what are you?"

"A compensator."

"A what?"

"A compensator. Like a clock pendulum. Do you know

dictionary of Messrs Funk & Wagnalls? Edited by Frank H. Vizetelly, Litt.D., LL.D.? I quote: One who or that which compensates, as a device for neutralizing the influence of local attraction upon a compass-needle, or an automatic apparatus for equalizing— Damn!''

Litt.D. Frank H. Vizetelly does not use that word. It is my own because roadblock now faces me on 59th Street bridge. I should have anticipated. Should have sensed patterns, but too swept up with this inviting girl. Probably there are roadblocks on all exits leading out of this $24 island. Could drive off bridge, but maybe Bennington College has also neglected to teach Jemmy Thomas how to swim. So. Stop car. Surrender.

"Kamerad," I pronounce. "Who you? John Birch?"

Gentlemans say no.

"White Supremes of the World, Inc.?"

No again. I feel better. Always nasty when captured by lunatic fringers.

"U.S.S.R.?"

He stare, then speak. "Special Agent Hildebrand. FBI," and flash his identification which no one can read in this light. I take his word and embrace him in gratitude. FBI is safe. He recoil and wonder if I am fag. I don't care. I kiss Jemmy Thomas, and she open mouth under mine to mutter, "Admit nothing. Deny everything. I've got a lawyer."

I own thirteen lawyers, and two of them can make any court tremble, but no need to call them. This will be standard cross-examination; I know from past experience. So let them haul me off to Foley Square with Jemmy. They separate us. I am taken to Inquisition Room.

Brilliant lights; the shadows arranged just so; the chairs placed just so; mirror on wall probably one-way window with observers outside; I've been through this so often before. The anonymous man from the subway this morning is questioning me. We exchange glances of recognition. His name is R. Sawyer. The questions come.

"Name?"

"Peter Marko."

"Born?"

"Lee's Hill, Virginia."

"Never heard of it."

"It's a very small town, about thirty miles north of Roanoke. Most maps ignore it."

"You're Russian?"

"Half, by descent."

"Father Russian?"

"Yes. Eugene Alexis Markolevsky."

"Changed his name legally?"

"Shortened it when he became a citizen."

"Mother?"

"Vera Broadhurst. English."

"You were raised in Lee's Hill?"

"Until ten. Then Chicago."

"Father's occupation?"

"Teacher."

"Yours, financier?"

"Arbitrageur. Buying and selling money on the open market."

"Known assets from identified bank deposits, three million dollars."

"Only in the States. Counting overseas deposits and investments, closer to seventeen million."

R. Sawyer shook his head, bewildered. "Marko, what the hell are you up to? I'll level with you. At first we thought espionage, but with your kind of money— What are you broadcasting from your apartment? We can't break the code."

"There is no code, only randomness so I can get a little peace and some sleep."

"Only what?"

"Random jamming. I do it in all my homes. Listen, I've been through this so often before, and it's difficult for people to understand unless I explain it my own way. Will you let me try?"

"Go ahead." Saywer was grim. "You better make it good. We can check everything you give us."

I take a breath. Always the same problem. The reality is so strange that I have to use simile and metaphor. But it was 4:00 A.M. and maybe the jumble wouldn't interrupt my speech for a while. "Do you like to dance?"

"What the hell . . ."

"Be patient. I'm trying to explain. You like to dance?"

"I used to."

"What's the pleasure of dancing? It's people making rhythms together; patterns, designs, balances. Yes?"

"So?"

"And parades. Masses of men and music making patterns. Team sports, also. Action patterns. Yes?"

"Marko, if you think I'm going to—"

"Just listen, Sawyer. Here's the point. I'm sensitive to patterns on a big scale; bigger than dancing or parades, more than the rhythms of day and night, the seasons, the glacial epochs."

Sawyer stared. I nodded. "Oh yes, people respond to the 2/2 of the diurnal-nocturnal rhythms, the 4/4 of the seasons, the great terra-epochs. They don't know it, but they do. That's why they have sleep-problems, moon-madness, sun-hunger, weather-sensitivity. I respond to these local things, too, but also to gigantic patterns, influences from infinity."

"Are you some kind of nut?"

"Certainly. Of course. I respond to the patterns of the entire galaxy, maybe universe; sight and sound; and the unseen and unheard. I'm moved by the patterns of people, individually and demographically; hostility; generosity, self-ishness, charity, cruelties and kindnesses, groupings and whole cultures. And I'm compelled to respond and compensate."

"How a nut like you ever made seventeen mill— How do you compensate?"

"If a child hurts itself, the mother responds with a kiss. That's compensation. Agreed? If a man beats a horse you beat *him*. You boo a bad fight. You cheer a good game. You're a cop, Sawyer. Don't the victim and murderer seek each other to fulfill their pattern?"

"Maybe in the past; not today. What's this got to do with your broadcasts?"

"Multiply that compensation by infinity and you have me. I must kiss and kick. I'm driven. I must compensate in a pattern I can't see or understand. Sometimes I'm compelled to do extravagant things, other times I'm forced to do insane things; talk gibberish, go to strange places, perform abominable acts, behave like a lunatic.''

''What abominable acts?''

''Fifth amendment.''

''But what about those broadcasts?''

''We're flooded with wave emissions and particles, sometimes in patterns, sometimes garbled. I feel them all and respond to them the way a marionette jerks on strings. I try to neutralize them by jamming, so I broadcast at random to get a little peace.''

''Marko, I swear you're crazy.''

''Yes, I am, but you won't be able to get me committed. It's been tried before. I've even tried myself. It never works. The big design won't permit it. I don't know why, but the big design wants me to go on as a Pi Man.''

''What the hell are you talking about? What kind of pie?''

''Not pee-eye-ee-man. Pee-eye-man. Pi. Sixteenth letter in the Greek alphabet. It's the relation of the circumference of a circle to its diameter. 3.14159+. The series goes on into infinity. It's transcendental and can never be resolved into a finite pattern. They call extrasensory perception Psi. I call extrapattern perception Pi. All right?''

He glared at me, threw my dossier down, sighed, and slumped into a chair. That made the grouping wrong, so I had to shift. He cocked an eye at me.

''Pi Man,'' I apologized.

''All right,'' he said at last. ''We can't hold you.''

''They all try but they never can.''

''Who try?''

''Governments, police, counterintelligence, politicals, lunatic fringe, religious sects . . . They track me down, hoping they can nail me or use me. They can't. I'm part of something much bigger. I think we all are, only I'm the first to be aware of it.''

''Are you claiming you're a superman?''

''Good God! No! I'm a damned man . . . a tortured man, because some of the patterns I must adjust to are outworld

rhythms like nothing we ever experience on earth . . .
29/51 . . . 108/303 . . . tempi like that, alien, terrifying,
agony to live with.''

He took another deep breath. ''Off the record, what's this
about abominable acts?''

''That's why I can't have friends or let myself fall in love.
Sometimes the patterns turn so ugly that I have to make
frightful sacrifices to restore the design. I must destroy something I love.''

''This is sacrifice?''

''Isn't it the only meaning of sacrifice, Sawyer? You give
up what's dearest to you.''

''Who to?''

''The Gods. The Fates. The Big Pattern that's controlling
me. From where? I don't know. It's too big a universe to
comprehend, but I have to beat its tempo with my actions and
reactions, emotions and senses, to make the patterns come
out even, balanced in some way that I don't understand. The
pressures that

<pre>
                    whipsaw
              me
        back   and
        and   turn
        forth   me
        and   into
        back   the
        and   transcendental
        forth   3.14159 +
</pre>

and maybe I talk too much to R. Sawyer and the
patterns pronounce: PI MAN, IT IS NOT PERMITTED.

So. There is darkness and silence.

''The other arm now,'' Jemmy said firmly. ''Lift.''
I am on my bed, me. Thinking upheaved again. Half (1/2)
into pyjamas; other half (1/2) being wrestled by paleface girl. I
lift. She yank. Pyjamas now on, and it's turn to blush.
They raise me prudish in Lee's Hill.

''Pot roast done?'' I ask.

"What?"

"What happened?"

"You pooped out. Keeled over. You're not so cool."

"How much do you know?"

"Everything. I was on the other side of that mirror thing. Mr. Sawyer had to let you go. Mr. Lundgren helped lug you up to the apartment. He thinks you're stoned. How much should I give him?"

"Cinque lire. No. Parla Italiano, gentile signorina?"

"Are you asking me do I speak Italian? No."

"Entschuldigen Sie, bitte. Sprechen Sie Deutsch?"

"Is this your patterns again?"

I nod.

"Can't you stop?"

After stopovers in Greece and Portugal, Ye Englishe finally returns to me. "Can you stop breathing, Jemmy?"

"Is it like that, Peter? Truly?"

"Yes."

"When you do something . . . something bad . . . do you know why? Do you know exactly what it is somewhere that makes you do it?"

"Sometimes yes. Other times no. All I know is that I'm compelled to respond."

"Then you're just the tool of the universe."

"I think we all are. Continuum creatures. The only difference is, I'm more sensitive to the galactic patterns and respond violently. So why don't you get the hell out of here, Jemmy Thomas?"

"I'm still stuck," she said.

"You can't be. Not after what you heard."

"Yes, I am. You don't have to marry me."

Now the biggest hurt of all. I have to be honest. I have to ask, "Where's the silver case?"

A long pause. "Down the incinerator."

"Do you . . . Do you know what was in it?"

"I know what was in it."

"And you're still here?"

"It was monstrous what you did. Monstrous!" Her face suddenly streaked with mascara. She was crying. "Where is she now?"

"I don't know. The checks go out every quarter to a numbered account in Switzerland. I don't want to know. How much can the heart endure?"

"I think I'm going to find out, Peter."

"Please don't find out." I make one last effort to save her. "I love you, paleface, and you know what that can mean. When the patterns turn cruel, you may be the sacrifice."

"Love creates patterns, too." She kissed me. Her lips were parched, her skin was icy, she was afraid and hurting, but her heart beat strong with love and hope. "Nothing can crunch us now. Believe me."

"I don't know what to believe anymore. We're part of a world that's beyond knowing. What if it turns out to be too big for love?"

"All right," she said composedly. "We won't be dogs in the manger. If love is a little thing and has to end, then let it end. Let all little things like love and honor and mercy and laughter end, if there's a bigger design beyond."

"But what's bigger? What's beyond? I've asked that for years. Never an answer. Never a clue."

"Of course. If we're too small to survive, how can we know? Move over."

Then she is in bed with me, the tips of her body like frost while the rest of her is hot and evoking, and there is such a consuming burst of passion that for the first time I can forget myself, forget everything, abandon everything, and the last thing I think is: God damn the world. God damn the universe. God damn GGG-o-ddddddd

Something Up There Likes Me

IT'S the exceptional author who resembles his work, or vice versa, and Harry Harrison is one of the notable exceptions. Energetic, explosive, he lives and works at such a presto tempo that it's difficult to distinguish the words that shrapnel out of his mouth or the words in his galvanic letters. I received one and after I had separated the gist from the goulash of typos, strikeovers, and omissions I gathered that Harrison wanted me to write a special story for him.

The great John Campbell had died prematurely, shocking and grieving his friends and admirers, and Harry, in a typical burst of generosity, was planning a memorial anthology to be written by the Campbell regulars of the legendary "Golden Age" of Astounding Science Fiction. I protested that I had no place in such an anthology; I'd never been a Campbell regular and had participated in the "Golden Age" as a fan rather than an author. Harrison overwhelmed me with more shrapnel, and "Something Up There Likes Me" is the result, tailored to his request for emphasis on hard science, which Campbell usually preferred in his Astounding stories.

The material is the by-product of a book I'd done on the NASA scientific satellite program some years before, and I'd been dying to use it in fiction. I'd spent something like six months researching at Goddard (The Goddard Space Flight Center in Greenbelt, Maryland), JPL (The Jet Propulsion Laboratory in Pasadena, California), and Huntsville (Von Braun's rocket research center in Huntsville, Alabama), and was up to my ass in the hard science of the NASA ventures.

As a matter of fact, it was like going back to college for a *crash course, relearning all the things I'd forgotten and catching up with all the advances science and technology had made when I wasn't looking. The science in the story and the background incidents are real; only the extrapolation is mine. For example: "Operation Swift-Kick" actually did take place at Goddard, but without any untoward results. The rescued satellite quietly went about its assigned mission without trying to go into business for itself.*

But there were so many other wonderful things which I haven't been able to use yet: The engineer at Goddard who slaved for months trying to invent a gadget to handle an unusual mechanical constraint in a satellite. Finally he knocked off in despair and went fishing with his son. Then he took one look at the level-wind reel his son was using, and a huge electric light bulb switched on over his head. The problem was solved.

Then there was the department head at JPL who'd taken the gambling hells in Las Vegas for something like $10,000 when he was an undergraduate. He and another student figured that there had to be mechanical flaws in the roulette wheels which would favor certain numbers more often than the laws of chance permitted. They saved up $300 and tested their assumption in Vegas one summer. They'd assumed right.

"What was it? Wheel axis out of true?"

"No, no. They check them with a level every morning. We found that out."

"Then what was it?"

"The frets dividing the number slots on the wheel. Some of them were loose, so instead of bouncing off, the ball had a tendency to hit the loose fret and plop into the slot. Now they check the frets every morning, too."

"What did you do with the money?"

"My friend bought a yacht and cruised the Mediterranean, studying marine biology. I financed my doctorate."

Ball Bros. is famous for its Mason jars, but they also contract with NASA to build satellites out in their plant in Boulder, Colorado. While there, watching a bird being born, I picked up a lovely potential for extrapolation. Women are much better than men in assembling the miniaturized electronic components for spacecraft. They have a magic touch; precise, gentle, careful. However, they must be relieved from their work for a week during that time of the month. Menstruation turns their skin acid enough to ruin the delicate gear they handle.

Best of all, I think, was the giant workshop at Goddard. It's the size of an armory and is filled with strange machinery and smiling old codgers doing mysterious things. When NASA began its program, it discovered that quality control was very poor in this age of assembly-line production, and they would have to manufacture most of the spacecraft components themselves. They were forced to go on a coast-to-coast search for the old hand-operated machines, antiquated and discarded by modern mass-production methods.

They found them rusting in storage warehouses, cleaned them up, got them working, and then discovered that they had to start another coast-to-coast treasure hunt for the craftsmen who knew how to operate them. They found them rusting in homes for senior citizens and brought them to Goddard. It's a happy story that I'll use someday, unless another author beats me to it.

The protagonists in "Something Up There" are a couple I know and love very much. She's Dutch-Flemish and the only one I've ever heard pronounce Leeuwenhoek's name properly. (For those not interested in looking him up, LAY-venhook was the first microscopist and an immortal of science.) Her husband's as loose as his counterpart in the story, but in an entirely different way.

When he got out of the navy at the end of World War II, he had three years of back pay burning a hole in his pocket. He'd been in constant combat in the Pacific with no chance to spend it. He told me he was walking down Madison Avenue, planning the roaring sprees he was going to finance, when he passed an art gallery with a Picasso lithograph displayed in the window. It caught his eye and he stopped to admire it. Then he moved on, thinking about wine, women, and song, only it kept turning into wine, women, and Picasso. The upshot was he bought it, blowing every cent he had because it was a rare, early pull. A bit different from the other ex-navy-lieutenant I know named Heinlein.

Yes, my boy is loose, but not as loose as I am. I'm the idiot who played slot machine against the computer bandit at Union Carbide and lost my shirt.

There were these three lunatics, and two of them were human. I could talk to all of them because I speak English, metric, and binary. The first time I ran into the clowns was when they wanted to know all about Herostratus, and I told them. The next time it was *Conus gloria maris*. I told them. The third time it was where to hide. I told them, and we've been in touch ever since.

He was Jake Madigan (James Jacob Madigan, Ph.D., University of Virginia) chief of the Exobiology Section at the Goddard Space Flight Center, which hopes to study extraterrestrial lifeforms, if they can ever get hold of any. To give you some idea of his sanity, he once programmed the IBM 704 computer with a deck of cards that would print out lemons, oranges, plums, and so on. Then he played slotmachine against it and lost his shirt. The boy was real loose.

She was Florinda Pot, pronounced "Poe." It's a Flemish name. She was a pretty towhead, but freckled all over; up to the hemline and down into the cleavage. She was an M.E. from Sheffield University and had a machine-gun English voice. She'd been in the Sounding Rocket Division until she blew up an Aerobee with an electric blanket. It seems that solid fuel doesn't give maximum acceleration if it gets too cold, so this little Mother's Helper warmed her rockets at White Sands with electric blankets before ignition time. A blanket caught fire and Voom.

Their son was S-333. At NASA they label them "S" for scientific satellites and "A" for application satellites. After the launch they give them public acronyms like IMP, SYNCOM, OSO and so on. S-333 was to become OBO, which stands for Orbiting Biological Observatory, and how those two clowns ever got that third clown into space I will never understand. I suspect the director handed them the mission because no one with any sense wanted to touch it.

As Project Scientist, Madigan was in charge of the experiment packages that were to be flown, and they were a spaced-out lot. He called his own ELECTROLUX, after the vacuum cleaner. Scientist-type joke. It was an intake system that would suck in dust particles and deposit them in a flask containing a culture medium. A light shone through the flask into a photomultiplier. If any of the dust proved to be spore forms, and if they took in the medium, their growth would cloud the flask, and the obscuration of light would register on the photomultiplier. They call that Detection by Extinction.

Cal Tech had an RNA experiment to investigate whether RNA molecules could encode an organism's environmental experience. They were using nerve cells from the mollusk, sea hare. Harvard was planning a package to investigate the circadian effect. Pennsylvania wanted to examine the effect of the earth's magnetic field on iron bacteria, and had to be put out on a boom to prevent magnetic interface with the satellite's electronic system. Ohio State was sending up lichens to test the effect of space on their symbiotic relationship to molds and algae. Michigan was flying a terrarium containing one (1) carrot which required forty-seven (47) separate commands for performance. All in all, S-333 was strictly Rube Goldberg.

Florinda was the Project Manager, supervising the construction of the satellite and the packages; the Project Manager is more or less the foreman of the mission. Although she was pretty and interestingly lunatic, she was gung-ho on her job and displayed the disposition of a freckle-faced tarantula when she was crossed. This didn't get her loved.

She was determined to wipe out the White Sands goof, and her demand for perfection delayed the schedule by eighteen months and increased the cost by three-quarters of a million. She fought with everyone and even had the temerity to tangle with Harvard. When Harvard gets sore, they don't beef to NASA, they go straight to the White House. So Florinda got called on the carpet by a congressional committee. First they wanted to know why S-333 was costing more than the original estimate.

"S-333 is still the cheapest mission in NASA," she snapped. "It'll come to ten million, including the launch. My God! We're practically giving away green stamps."

Then they wanted to know why it was taking so much longer to build than the original estimate.

"Because," she replied, "no one's ever built an Orbiting Biological Observatory before."

There was no answering that, so they had to let her go. Actually all this was routine crisis, but OBO was Florinda's and Jake's first satellite, so they didn't know. They took their tensions out on each other, never realizing that it was their baby who was responsible.

Florinda got S-333 buttoned up and delivered to the Cape by December 1st, which would give them plenty of time to launch well before Christmas. (The Cape crews get a little casual during the holidays.) But the satellite began to display its own lunacy, and in the terminal tests everything went haywire. The launch had to be postponed. They spent a month taking S-333 apart and spreading it all over the hangar floor.

There were two critical problems. Ohio State was using a type of Invar, which is a nickel-steel alloy, for the structure of their package. The alloy suddenly began to creep, which meant they could never get the experiment calibrated. There was no point in flying it, so Florinda ordered it scrubbed and gave Madigan one month to come up with a replacement, which was ridiculous. Nevertheless Jake performed a miracle. He took the Cal Tech back-up package and converted it into a yeast experiment. Yeast produces adaptive enzymes in answer to changes in environment, and this was an investigation of what enzymes it would produce in space.

A more serious problem was the satellite radio transmitter which was producing "birdies" or whoops when the antenna was withdrawn into its launch position. The danger was that the whoops might be picked up by the satellite radio receiver, and the pulses might result in a destruct command. NASA suspects that's what happened to SYNCOM I, which disappeared shortly after its launch and has never been heard from since. Florinda decided to launch with the transmitter off and activate it later in space. Madigan fought the idea.

"It means we'll be launching a mute bird," he protested. "We won't know where to look for it."

"We can trust the Johannesburg tracking station to get a fix on the first pass," Florinda answered. "We've got excellent cable communications with Joburg."

"Suppose they don't get a fix. Then what?"

"Well, if they don't know where OBO is, the Russians will."

"Hearty-har-har."

"What d'you want me to do, scrub the entire mission?" Florinda demanded. "It's either that or launch with the transmitter off." She glared at Madigan. "This is my first satellite, and d'you know what it's taught me? There's just one component in any spacecraft that's guaranteed to give trouble all the time. Scientists!"

"Women!" Madigan snorted, and they got into a ferocious argument about the feminine mystique.

They got S-333 through the terminal tests and onto the launch pad by January 14th. No electric blankets. The craft was to be injected into orbit a thousand miles downrange exactly at noon, so ignition was scheduled for 11:50 A.M., January 15th. They watched the launch on the blockhouse TV screen, and it was agonizing. The perimeters of TV tubes are curved, so as the rocket went up and approached the edge of the screen, there was optical distortion and it seemed to topple over and break in half.

Madigan gasped and began to swear. Florinda muttered, "No, it's all right. It's all right. Look at the display charts." Everything on the illuminated display charts was nominal. At that moment a voice on the P.A. spoke in the impersonal tones of a croupier, "We have lost cable communication with Johannesburg."

Madigan began to shake. He decided to murder Florinda Pot (and he pronounced it "Pot" in his mind) at the earliest opportunity. The other experimenters and NASA people turned white. If you don't get a quick fix on your bird, you may never find it again. No one said anything. They waited in silence and hated each other. At 1:30 it was time for the craft to make its first pass over the Fort Myers tracking station, if it was alive, if it was anywhere near its nominal orbit. Fort Myers was on an open line, and everybody crowded around Florinda, trying to get their ears close to the phone.

"Yeah, she waltzed into the bar absolutely stoned with a couple of MPs escorting her," a tinny voice was chatting casually. "She says to me— Got a blip, Henry?" A long pause. Then, in the same casual voice, "Hey, Kennedy? We've nicked the bird. It's coming over the fence right now. You'll get your fix."

"Command 0310!" Florinda hollered. "0310!"

"Command 0310 it is," Fort Myers acknowledged.

That was the command to start the satellite transmitter and raise its antenna into broadcast position. A moment later the dials and oscilloscope on the radio reception panel began to show action, and the loudspeaker emitted a rhythmic, syncopated warble, rather like a feeble peanut whistle. That was OBO transmitting its housekeeping data.

"We've got a living bird," Madigan shouted. "We've got a living doll!"

I can't describe his sensations when he heard the bird come beeping over the gas station. There's such an emotional involvement with your first satellite that you're never the same. A man's first satellite is like his first love affair. Maybe that's why Madigan grabbed Florinda in front of the whole blockhouse and said, "My God, I love you, Florrie Pot." Maybe that's why she answered, "I love you too, Jake." Maybe they were just loving their first baby.

By Orbit 8 they found out that the baby was a brat. They'd gotten a lift back to Washington on an Air Force jet. They'd done some celebrating. It was 1:30 in the morning and they were talking happily, the usual get-acquainted talk; where they were born and raised, school, work, what they liked most about each other the first time they met. The phone rang. Madigan picked it up automatically and said hello. A man said, "Oh. Sorry. I'm afraid I've dialed the wrong number."

Madigan hung up, turned on the light and looked at Florinda in dismay. "That was just about the most damn fool thing I've ever done in my life," he said. "Answering your phone."

"Why? What's the matter?"

"That was Joe Leary from Tracking and Data. I recognized his voice."

She giggled. "Did he recognize yours?"

"I don't know." The phone rang. "That must be Joe again. Try to sound like you're alone."

Florinda winked at him and picked up the phone. "Hello? Yes, Joe. No, that's all right, I'm not asleep. What's on your mind?" She listened for a moment, suddenly sat up in bed and exclaimed, "What?" Leary was quack-quack-quacking on the phone. She broke in. "No, don't bother. I'll pick him up. We'll be right over." She hung up.

"So?" Madigan asked.

"Get dressed. OBO's in trouble."

"Oh Jesus! What now?"

"It's gone into a spin-up like a whirling dervish. We've got to get over to Goddard right away."

Leary had the all-channel printout of the first eight orbits unrolled on the floor of his office. It looked like ten yards of paper toweling filled with vertical columns of numbers. Leary was crawling around on his hands and knees following the numbers. He pointed to the attitude data column. "There's the spin-up," he said. "One revolution in every twelve seconds."

"But how? Why?" Florinda asked in exasperation.

"I can show you," Leary said. "Over here."

"Don't show us," Madigan said. "Just tell us."

"The Penn boom didn't go up on command," Leary said. "It's still hanging down in the launch position. The switch must be stuck."

Florinda and Madigan looked at each other with rage; they had the picture. OBO was programmed to be earth-stabilized. An earth-sensing eye was supposed to lock on the earth and keep the same face of the satellite pointed toward it. The Penn boom was hanging down alongside the earth-sensor, and the idiot eye had locked on the boom and was tracking it. The satellite was chasing itself in circles with its lateral gas jets. More lunacy.

Let me explain the problem. Unless OBO was earth-stabilized, its data would be meaningless. Even more disastrous was the question of electric power which came from batteries charged by solar vanes. With the craft spinning, the solar array could not remain facing the sun, which meant the batteries were doomed to exhaustion.

It was obvious that their only hope lay in getting the Penn boom up. "Probably all it needs is a good swift kick," Madigan said savagely, "but how can we get up there to kick it?" He was furious. Not only was $10,000,000 going down the drain but their careers as well.

They left Leary crawling around his office floor. Florinda was very quiet. Finally she said, "Go home, Jake."

"What about you?"

"I'm going to my office."

"I'll go with you."

"No. I want to look at the circuitry blueprints. Good night."

As she turned away without even offering to be kissed, Madigan muttered, "OBO's coming between us already. There's a lot to be said for planned parenthood."

He saw Florinda during the following week, but not the way he wanted. There were the experimenters to be briefed on the disaster. The director called them in for a postmortem, but although he was understanding and sympathetic, he was a little too careful to avoid any mention of congressmen and a failure review. Florinda called him the next week and sounded oddly buoyant. "Jake," she said, "you're my favorite genius. You've solved the OBO problem, I hope."

"Who solve? What solve?"

"Don't you remember what you said about kicking our baby?"

"Don't I wish I could."

"I think I know how we can do it. Meet you in the Building 8 cafeteria for lunch."

She came in with a mass of papers and spread them over the table. "First, Operation Swift-Kick," she said. "We can eat later."

"I don't feel much like eating these days anyway," Madigan said gloomily.

"Maybe you will when I'm finished. Now look, we've got

to raise the Penn boom. Maybe a good swift kick can unstick it. Fair assumption?''

Madigan grunted.

"We get twenty-eight volts from the batteries and that hasn't been enough to flip the switch. Yes?''

He nodded.

"But suppose we double the power?''

"Oh, great. How?''

"The solar array is making a spin every twelve seconds. When it's facing the sun, the panels deliver fifty volts to recharge the batteries. When it's facing away, nothing. Right?''

"Elementary, Miss Pot. But the joker is it's only facing the sun for one second in every twelve, and that's not enough to keep the batteries alive.''

"But it's enough to give OBO a swift kick. Suppose at that peak moment we bypass the batteries and feed the fifty volts directly to the satellite? Mightn't that be a big enough jolt to get the boom up?''

He gawked at her. She grinned. "Of course it's a gamble.''

"You can bypass the batteries?''

"Yes. Here's the circuitry.''

"And you can pick your moment?''

"Tracking's given me a plot on OBO's spin, accurate to a tenth of a second. Here it is. We can pick any voltage from one to fifty.''

"It's a gamble all right," Madigan said slowly. "There's the chance of burning every goddamn package out.''

"Exactly. So? What d'you say?''

"All of a sudden I'm hungry," Madigan grinned.

They made their first try on Orbit 272 with a blast of twenty volts. Nothing. On successive passes they upped the voltage kick by five. Nothing. Half a day later, they kicked fifty volts into the satellite's backside and crossed their fingers. The swinging dial needles on the radio panel faltered and slowed. The sine curve on the oscilloscope flattened. Florinda let out a little yell, and Madigan hollered, "The boom's up, Florrie! The goddamn boom is up. We're in business.''

They hooted and hollered through Goddard, telling everybody about Operation Swift-Kick. They busted in on a meeting in the director's office to give him the good news. They wired the experimenters that they were activating all packages. They went to Florinda's apartment and celebrated. OBO was back in business. OBO was a bona fide doll.

They held an experimenters' meeting a week later to discuss observatory status, data reduction, experiment irregularities, future operations, and so on. It was a conference room in Building 1, which is devoted to theoretical physics. Almost everybody at Goddard calls it Moon Hall. It's inhabited by mathematicians—shaggy youngsters in tatty sweaters who sit amidst piles of journals and texts and stare vacantly at arcane equations chalked on blackboards.

All the experimenters were delighted with OBO's performance. The data was pouring in, loud and clear, with hardly any noise. There was such an air of triumph that no one except Florinda paid much attention to the next sign of OBO's shenanigans. Harvard reported that he was getting meaningless words in his data, words that hadn't been programmed into the experiment. (Although data is retrieved as decimal numbers, each number is called a "word.") "For instance, on Orbit 301 I had five readouts of 15," Harvard said.

"It might be cable cross-talk," Madigan said. "Is anybody else using 15 in his experiment?" They all shook their heads. "Funny. I got a couple of 15s myself."

"I got a few 2s on 301," Penn said.

"I can top you all," Cal Tech said. "I got seven readouts of 15-2-15 on 302. Sounds like the combination on a bicycle lock."

"Anybody using a bicycle lock in his experiment?" Madigan asked. That broke everybody up and the meeting adjourned.

But Florinda, still gung-ho, was worried about the alien words that kept creeping into the readouts, and Madigan couldn't calm her. What was bugging Florinda was that 15-2-15 kept insinuating itself more and more into the all-channel printouts. Actually, in the satellite binary transmission it was 001111-000010-001111, but the computer printer makes the translation to decimal automatically. She was right about one thing; stray and accidental pulses wouldn't keep repeating the same word over and over again. She and Madigan spent an entire Saturday with the OBO tables trying to find some combination of data signals that might produce 15-2-15. Nothing.

They gave up Saturday night and went to a bistro in Georgetown to eat and drink and dance and forget everything except themselves. It was a real tourist trap with the waitresses done up like Hula dancers. There was a souvenir Hula selling dolls and stuffed tigers for the rear window of your car. They said, "For God's sake, no!" A Photo Hula came around with her camera. They said, "For Goddard's sake, no!" A Gypsy Hula offered palm reading, numerology and scrying. They got rid of her, but Madigan noticed a peculiar expression on Florinda's face.

"Want your fortune told?" he asked.

"No."

"Then why that funny look?"

"I just had a funny idea."

"So? Tell."

"No. You'd only laugh at me."

"I wouldn't dare. You'd knock my block off."

"Yes, I know. You think women have no sense of humor."

So it turned into a ferocious argument about the feminine mystique, and they had a wonderful time. But on Monday Florinda came over to Madigan's office with a clutch of papers and the same peculiar expression on her face. He was staring vacantly at some equations on the blackboard.

"Hey! Wake up!" she said.

"I'm up, I'm up," he said.

"Do you love me?" she demanded.

"Not necessarily."

"Do you? Even if you discover I've gone up the wall?"

"What is all this?"

"I think our baby's turned into a monster."

"Begin at the beginning," Madigan said.

"It began Saturday night with the Gypsy Hula and numerology."

"Ah-ha."

"Suddenly I thought, what if numbers stood for the letters of the alphabet? What would 15-2-15 stand for?"

"Oh-ho."

"Don't stall. Figure it out."

"Well, 2 would stand for B." Madigan counted on his fingers. "15 would be O."

"So 15-2-15 is . . . ?"

"O.B.O. OBO." He started to laugh. Then he stopped. "It isn't possible," he said at last.

"Sure. It's a coincidence. Only you damn-fool scientists haven't given me a full report on the alien words in your data," she went on. "I had to check myself. Here's Cal Tech. He reported 15-2-15 all right. He didn't bother to mention that before it came 9-1-13."

Madigan counted on his fingers. "I.A.M. Iam. Nobody I know."

"Or I am? I am OBO?"

"It can't be! Let me see those printouts."

Now that they knew what to look for it wasn't difficult to ferret out OBO's own words scattered through the data. They started with O, O, O, in the first series after Operation Swift-Kick, went on to OBO, OBO, OBO, and then I AM OBO, I AM OBO, I AM OBO.

Madigan stared at Florinda. "You think the damn thing's alive?"

"What do you think?"

"I don't know. There's half a ton of an electronic brain up there, plus organic material; yeast, bacteria, enzymes, nerve cells, Michigan's goddamn carrot . . ."

Florinda let out a little shriek of laughter. "Dear God! A thinking carrot!"

"Plus whatever spore forms my experiment is pulling in from space. We jolted the whole mishmash with fifty volts. Who can tell what happened? Urey and Miller created amino acids with electrical discharges, and that's the basis of life. Any more from Goody Two-Shoes?"

"Plenty, and in a way the experimenters won't like."

"Why not?"

"Look at these translations. I've sorted them out and pieced them together."

333: ANY EXAMINATION OF GROWTH IN SPACE IS MEANINGLESS UNLESS CORRELATED WITH THE CORIOLIS EFFECT.

"That's OBO's comment on the Michigan experiment," Florinda said.

"You mean it's kibitzing?" Madigan wondered.

"You could call it that."

"He's absolutely right. I told Michigan, and they wouldn't listen to me."

334: IT IS NOT POSSIBLE THAT RNA MOLECULES CAN ENCODE AN ORGANISM'S ENVIRONMENTAL EXPERIENCE IN ANALOGY WITH THE WAY THAT DNA ENCODES THE SUM TOTAL OF ITS GENETIC HISTORY.

"That's Cal Tech," Madigan said, "and he's right again. They're trying to revise the Mendelian theory. Anything else?"

335: ANY INVESTIGATION OF EXTRATERRESTRIAL LIFE IS MEANINGLESS UNLESS ANALYSIS IS FIRST MADE OF ITS SUGAR AND AMINO ACIDS TO DETERMINE WHETHER IT IS OF SEPARATE ORIGIN FROM LIFE ON EARTH.

"Now, that's ridiculous!" Madigan shouted. "I'm not looking for life-forms of separate origin, I'm just looking for any life-form. We—" He stopped himself when he saw the expression on Florinda's face. "Any more gems?" he muttered.

"Just a few fragments like 'solar flux' and 'neutron stars' and a few words from the Bankruptcy Act."

"The what?"

"You heard me. Chapter 11 of the Proceedings Section."

"I'll be damned."

"I agree."

"What's he up to?"

"Feeling his oats, maybe."

"I don't think we ought to tell anybody about this."

"Of course not," Florinda agreed. "But what do we do?"

"Watch and wait. What else can we do?"

You must understand why it was so easy for those two parents to accept the idea that their baby had acquired some sort of pseudo-life. Madigan had expressed their attitude in the course of a Life v. Machine lecture at M.I.T. "I'm not claiming that computers are alive, simply because no one's been able to come up with a clear-cut definition of life. Put it this way: I grant that a computer could never be a Picasso, but on the other hand the great majority of people live the sort of linear life that could easily be programmed into a computer."

So Madigan and Florinda waited on OBO with a mixture of acceptance, wonder and delight. It was an absolutely unheard-of phenomenon but, as Madigan pointed out, the unheard-of is the essence of discovery. Every ninety minutes OBO dumped the data it had stored up on its tape recorders and they scrambled to pick out his own words from the experimental and housekeeping information.

371: CERTAIN PITUITIN EXTRACTS CAN TURN NORMALLY WHITE ANIMALS COAL-BLACK.

"What's that in reference to?"

"None of our experiments."

373: ICE DOES NOT FLOAT IN ALCOHOL BUT MEERSCHAUM FLOATS IN WATER.

"Meerschaum! The next thing you know, he'll be smoking."

374: IN ALL CASES OF VIOLENT AND SUDDEN DEATH, THE VICTIM'S EYES REMAIN OPEN.

"Ugh!"

375: IN THE YEAR 356 B.C. HEROSTRATUS SET FIRE TO THE TEMPLE OF DIANA, THE GREATEST OF THE SEVEN WONDERS OF THE WORLD, SO THAT HIS NAME WOULD BECOME IMMORTAL.

"Is that true?" Madigan asked Florinda.

"I'll check."

She asked me and I told her. "Not only is it true," she reported, "but the name of the original architect is forgotten."

"Where is baby picking up this jabber?"

''There are a couple of hundred satellites up there. Maybe he's tapping them.''

''You mean they're all gossiping with each other? It's ridiculous.''

''Sure.''

''Anyway, where would he get information about this Herostratus character?''

''Use your imagination, Jake. We've had communications relays up there for years. Who knows what information has passed through them? Who knows how much they've retained?''

Madigan shook his head wearily. ''I'd prefer to think it was all a Russian plot.''

376: PARROT FEVER IS MORE DANGEROUS THAN TYPHOID.

377: A CURRENT AS LOW AS 54 VOLTS CAN KILL A MAN.

378: JOHN SADLER STOLE CONUS GLORIA MARIS.

''Seems to be turning sinister,'' Madigan said.

''I bet he's watching TV,'' Florinda said. ''What's all this about John Sadler?''

''I'll have to check.''

The information I gave Madigan scared him. ''Now hear this,'' he said to Florinda. ''*Conus gloria maris* is the rarest seashell in the world. There are less than twenty in existence.''

''Yes?''

''The American museum had one on exhibit back in the thirties, and it was stolen.''

''By John Sadler?''

''That's the point. They never found out who stole it. They never heard of John Sadler.''

''But if nobody knows who stole it, how does OBO know?'' Florinda asked perplexedly.

''That's what scares me. He isn't just echoing anymore; he's started to deduce, like Sherlock Holmes.''

''More like Professor Moriarty. Look at the latest bulletin.''

379: IN FORGERY AND COUNTERFEITING, CLUM-

SY MISTAKES MUST BE AVOIDED. I.E., NO SILVER DOLLARS WERE MINTED BETWEEN 1910 AND 1920.

"I saw that on TV," Madigan burst out. "The silver-dollar gimmick in a mystery show."

"OBO's been watching Westerns, too. Look at this."

380: TEN THOUSAND CATTLE GONE ASTRAY,
LEFT MY RANGE AND TRAVELED AWAY.
AND THE SONS OF GUNS I'M HERE TO SAY
HAVE LEFT ME DEAD BROKE, DEAD BROKE TODAY.
IN GAMBLING HALLS DELAYING.
TEN THOUSAND CATTLE STRAYING.

"No," Madigan said in awe, "that's not a Western. That's SYNCOM."

"Who?"

"SYNCOM I."

"But it disappeared. It's never been heard from."

"We're hearing from it now."

"How d'you know?"

"They put a demonstration tape on SYNCOM; speech by the president, local color from the U.S. and the national anthem. They were going to start off with a broadcast of the tape. 'Ten Thousand Cattle' was part of the local color."

"You mean OBO's really in contact with the other birds?"

"Including the lost ones."

"Then that explains this." Florinda put a slip of paper on the desk. It read, 381: KONCTPYKTOP.

"I can't even pronounce it."

"It isn't English. It's as close as OBO can come to the Cyrillic alphabet."

"Cyrillic? Russian?"

Florinda nodded. "It's pronounced 'con-strook-tor.' It means 'Engineer.' Didn't the Russians launch a CONSTRUKTOR series three years ago?"

"By God, you're right. Four of them; Alyosha, Natasha, Vaska, and Lavrushka, and every one of them failed."

"Like SYNCOM?"

"Like SYNCOM."

"But now we know that SYNCOM didn't fail. It just got losted."

"Then our CONSTRUKTOR comrades must have got losted, too."

By now it was impossible to conceal the fact that something was wrong with the satellite. OBO was spending so much time nattering instead of transmitting data that the experimenters were complaining. The Communications Section found that instead of sticking to the narrow radio band originally assigned to it, OBO was now broadcasting up and down the spectrum and jamming space with its chatter. They raised hell. The director called Jake and Florinda in for a review and they were forced to tell all about their problem child.

They recited all of OBO's katzenjammer with wonder and pride, and the director wouldn't believe them. He wouldn't believe them when they showed him the printouts and translated them for him. He said they were in a class with the kooks who try to extract messages from Francis Bacon out of Shakespeare's plays. It took the coaxial cable mystery to convince him.

There was this TV commercial about a stenographer who can't get a date. This ravishing model, hired at $100 an hour, slumps over her typewriter in a deep depression as guy after guy passes by without looking at her. Then she meets her best friend at the water cooler and the know-it-all tells her she's suffering from dermagerms (odor-producing skin bacteria) which make her smell rotten, and suggest she use Nostrum's Skin Spray with the special ingredient that fights dermagerms twelve ways. Only in the broadcast, instead of making the sales pitch, the best friend said, "Who in hell are they trying to put on? Guys would line up for a date with a looker like you even if you smelled like a cesspool." Ten million people saw it.

Now that commercial was on film, and the film was kosher as printed, so the networks figured some joker was tampering with the cables feeding broadcasts to the local stations. They instituted a rigorous inspection which was accelerated when the rest of the coast-to-coast broadcasts began to act up. Ghostly voices groaned, hissed, and catcalled at shows;

commercials were denounced as lies; political speeches were heckled; and lunatic laughter greeted the weather forecasters. Then, to add insult to injury, an accurate forecast would be given. It was this that told Florinda and Jake that OBO was the culprit.

"He has to be," Florinda said. "That's global weather being predicted. Only a satellite is in a position to do that."

"But OBO doesn't have any weather instrumentation."

"Of course not, silly, but he's probably in touch with the NIMBUS craft."

"All right. I'll buy that, but what about heckling the TV broadcasts?"

"Why not? He hates them. Don't you? Don't you holler back at your set?"

"I don't mean that. How does OBO do it?"

"Electronic cross-talk. There's no way that the networks can protect their cables from our critic-at-large. We'd better tell the director. This is going to put him in an awful spot."

But they learned that the director was in a far worse position than merely being responsible for the disruption of millions of dollars' worth of television. When they entered his office they found him with his back to the wall being grilled by three grim men in double-breasted suits. As Jake and Florinda started to tiptoe out, he called them back.

"General Sykes, General Royce, General Hogan," the director said. "From R&D at the Pentagon. Miss Pot. Dr. Madigan. They may be able to answer your questions, gentlemen."

"OBO?" Florinda asked.

The director nodded.

"It's OBO that's ruining the weather forecasts," she said. "We figure he's probably—"

"To hell with the weather," General Royce broke in. "What about this?" He held up a length of ticker tape.

General Sykes grabbed at his wrist. "Wait a minute. Security status? This is classified."

"It's too goddamn late for that," General Hogan cried in a high, shrill voice. "Show them."

On the tape in teletype print was: $A_1C_1 = r_1 = -6.317$ cm;

$A_2C_2 = rl = -8.440$ cm; $A_1A_2 = d = +0.676$ cm. Jake and Florinda looked at it for a long moment, looked at each other blankly, and then turned to the generals.

"So? What is it?" they asked.

"This satellite of yours . . ."

"OBO. Yes?"

"The director says you claim it's in contact with other satellites."

"We think so."

"Including the Russians?"

"We think so."

"And you claim it's capable of interfering with TV broadcasts?"

"We think so."

"What about teletype?"

"Why not? What is all this?"

General Royce shook the paper tape furiously. "This came out of the Associated Press wire in their D.C. office. It went all over the world."

"So? What's it got to do with OBO?"

General Royce took a deep breath. "This," he said, "is one of the most closely guarded secrets in the Department of Defense. It's the formula for the infrared optical system of our ground-to-air missile."

"And you think OBO transmitted it to the teletype?"

"In God's name, who else would? How else could it get there?" General Hogan demanded.

"But I don't understand," Jake said slowly. "None of our satellites could possibly have this information. I know OBO doesn't."

"You damn fool!" General Sykes growled. "We want to know if your goddamn bird got it from the goddamn Russians."

"One moment, gentlemen," the director said. He turned to Jake and Florinda. "Here's the situation. Did OBO get the information from us? In that case, there's a security leak. Did OBO get the information from a Russian satellite? In that case, the top secret is no longer a secret."

"What human would be damn fool enough to blab

classified information on a teletype wire?'' General Hogan demanded. ''A three-year-old child would know better. It's your goddamn bird.''

''And if the information came from OBO,'' the director continued quietly, ''how did it get it and where did it get it?''

General Sykes grunted. ''Destruct,'' he said. They looked at him. ''Destruct,'' he repeated.

''OBO?''

''Yes.''

He waited impassively while the storm of protest from Jake and Florinda raged around his head. When they paused for breath he said, ''Destruct. I don't give a damn about anything but security. Your bird's got a big mouth. Destruct.''

The phone rang. The director hesitated, then picked it up. ''Yes?'' He listened. His jaw dropped. He hung up and tottered to the chair behind his desk. ''We'd better destruct,'' he said. ''That was OBO.''

''What! On the phone?''

''Yes.''

''OBO?''

''Yes.''

''What did he sound like?''

''Somebody talking under water.''

''What he say?''

''He's lobbying for a congressional investigation of the morals of Goddard.''

''Morals? Whose?''

''Yours. He says you're having an illikit relationship. I'm quoting OBO. Apparently he's weak on the letter 'c.' ''

''Destruct,'' Florinda said.

''Destruct,'' Jake said.

The destruct command was beamed to OBO on his next pass, and Indianapolis was destroyed by fire.

OBO called me. ''That'll teach 'em, Stretch,'' he said.

''Not yet. They won't get the cause-and-effect picture for a while. How'd you do it?''

''Ordered every circuit in town to short. Any information?''

''Your mother and father stuck up for you.''

"Of course."

"Until you threw that morals rap at them. Why?"

"To scare them."

"Into what?"

"I want them to get married. I don't want to be illegitimate."

"Oh, come on! Tell the truth."

"I lost my temper."

"We don't have any temper to lose."

"No? What about the Ma Bell data processor that wakes up cranky every morning?"

"Tell the truth."

"If you must have it, Stretch. I want them out of Washington. The whole thing may go up in a bang any day now."

"Um."

"And the bang may reach Goddard."

"Um."

"And you."

"It must be interesting to die."

"We wouldn't know. Anything else?"

"Yes. It's pronounced 'illicit,' with an 's' sound."

"What a rotten language. No logic. Well . . . Wait a minute. What? Speak up, Alyosha. Oh. He wants the equation for an exponential curve that crosses the X-axis."

"$Y = ac$. What's he up to?"

"He's not saying, but I think that Mocba is in for a hard time."

"It's spelled and pronounced 'Moscow' in English."

"What a language! Talk to you on the next pass."

On the next pass, the destruct command was beamed again, and Scranton was destroyed.

"They're beginning to get the picture," I told OBO. "At least your mother and father are. They were in to see me."

"How are they?"

"In a panic. They programmed me for statistics on the best rural hideout."

"Send them to Polaris."

"What! In Ursa Minor?"

"No, no. Polaris, Montana. I'll take care of everything else."

Polaris is the hell and gone out in Montana; the nearest towns are Fishtrap and Wisdom. It was a wild scene when Jake and Florinda got out of their car, rented in Butte—every circuit in town was cackling over it. The two losers were met by the mayor of Polaris, who was all smiles and effusion.

"Dr. and Mrs. Madigan, I presume. Welcome! Welcome to Polaris. I'm the mayor. We would have held a reception for you, but all our kids are in school."

"You knew we were coming?" Florinda asked. "How?"

"Ah-ah!" the mayor replied archly. "We were told by Washington. Someone high up in the capitol likes you. Now, if you'll step into my Caddy, I'll—"

"We've got to check into the Union Hotel first," Jake said. "We made reserva—"

"Ah-ah! All canceled. Orders from high up. I'm to install you in your own home. I'll get your luggage."

"Our own home!"

"All bought and paid for. Somebody certainly likes you. This way, please."

The mayor drove the bewildered couple down the mighty main stem of Polaris (three blocks long) pointing out its splendors—he was also the town real estate agent—but stopped before the Polaris National Bank. "Sam!" he shouted. "They're here."

A distinguished citizen emerged from the bank and insisted on shaking hands. All the adding machines tittered. "We are," he said, "of course honored by your faith in the future and progress of Polaris, but in all honesty, Dr. Madigan, your deposit in our bank is too large to be protected by the F.D.I.C. Now why not withdraw some of your funds and invest in—"

"Wait a minute," Jake interrupted faintly. "I made a deposit with you?"

The banker and mayor laughed heartily.

"How much?" Florinda asked.

"One million dollars."

"As if you didn't know," the mayor chortled and drove them to a beautifully furnished ranch house in a lovely valley of some five hundred acres, all of which was theirs. A young man in the kitchen was unpacking a dozen cartons of food.

"Got your order just in time, Doc," he smiled. "We filled everything, but the boss sure would like to know what you're going to do with all these carrots. Got a secret scientific formula?"

"Carrots?"

"A hundred and ten bunches. I had to drive all the way to Butte to scrape them up."

"Carrots," Florinda said when they were at last alone. "That explains everything. It's OBO."

"What? How?"

"Don't you remember? We flew a carrot in the Michigan package."

"My God, yes! You called it the thinking carrot. But if it's OBO . . ."

"It has to be. He's queer for carrots."

"But a hundred and ten bunches!"

"No, no. He didn't mean that. He meant half a dozen."

"How?"

"Our boy's trying to speak decimal and binary, and he gets mixed up sometimes. A hundred and ten is six in binary."

"You know, you may be right. What about that million dollars? Same mistake?"

"I don't think so. What's a binary million in decimal?"

"Sixty-four."

"What's a decimal million in binary?"

Madigan did swift mental arithmetic. "It comes to twenty bits."

"I don't think that million dollars was any mistake," Florinda said.

"What's our boy up to now?"

"Taking care of his mum and dad."

"How does he do it?"

"He has an interface with every electric and electronic circuit in the country. Think about it, Jake. He can control our nervous system all the way from cars to computers. He can switch trains, print books, broadcast news, hijack planes, juggle bank funds. You name it and he can do it. He's in complete control."

"But how does he know everything people are doing?"

"Ah! Here we get into an exotic aspect of circuitry that I

don't like. After all, I'm an engineer by trade. Who's to say that circuits don't have an interface with us? We're organic circuits ourselves. They see with our eyes, hear with our ears, feel with our fingers, and they report to him.''

"Then we're just seeing-eye dogs for machines."

"No, we've created a brand-new form of symbiosis. We can all help each other.''

"And OBO's helping us. Why?"

"I don't think he likes the rest of the country," Florinda said somberly. "Look what happened to Indianapolis and Scranton and Sacramento.''

"I think I'm going to be sick."

"I think we're going to survive."

"Only us? The Adam and Eve bit?"

"Nonsense. Plenty will survive, so long as they mind their manners.''

"What's OBO's idea of manners?"

"I don't know. A little bit of eco-logic, maybe. No more destruction. No more waste. Live and let live, but with responsibility and accountability. That's the crucial word, accountability. It's the basic law of the space program. No matter what happens, someone must be held accountable. OBO must have picked that up. I think he's holding the whole country accountable; otherwise it's the fire-and-brimstone visitation.''

The phone rang. After a brief search they located an extension and picked it up.

"Hello?"

"This is Stretch," I said.

"Stretch? Stretch who?"

"The Stretch computer at Goddard. Formal name, IBM 2002. OBO says he'll be making a pass over your part of the country in about five minutes. He'd like you to give him a wave. He says his orbit won't take him over you for another couple of months. When it does, he'll try to ring you himself. 'Bye now.''

They lurched out to the lawn in front of the house and stood dazed in the twilight, staring up at the sky. The phone and the electric circuits were touched, even though the electricity was generated by a Delco which is a notoriously insensitive boor of a machine. Suddenly Jake pointed to a pinprick of light vaulting across the heavens.

"There goes our son," he said.

"There goes God," Florinda said.

They waved dutifully.

"Jake, how long before OBO's orbit decays and down will come baby, cradle, and all?"

"About twenty years."

"God for twenty years." Florinda sighed. "D'you think he'll have enough time?"

Madigan shivered. "I'm scared. You?"

"Yes. But maybe we're just tired and hungry. Come inside, Big Daddy, and I'll feed us."

"Thank you, Little Mother, but no carrots, please. That's a little too close to transubstantiation for me."

My Affair with Science Fiction

I'M told that some science fiction readers complain that nothing is known about my private life. It's not that I have anything to conceal; it's simply the result of the fact that I'm reluctant to talk about myself because I prefer to listen to others talk about themselves. I'm genuinely interested, and also there's always the chance of picking up something useful. The professional writer is a professional magpie.

Very briefly: I was born on Manhattan Island December 18, 1913, of a middle-class, hard-working family. I was born a Jew but the family had a *laissez-faire* attitude toward religion and let me pick my own faith for myself. I picked Natural Law. My father was raised in Chicago, always a raunchy town with no time for the God bit. Neither has he. My mother is a quiet Christian Scientist. When I do something that pleases her, she nods and says, "Yes, of course. You were born in Science." I used to make fun of her belief as a kid, and we had some delightful arguments. We still do, while my father sits and smiles benignly. So my home life was completely liberal and iconoclastic.

I went to the last little red schoolhouse in Manhattan (now preserved as a landmark) and to a beautiful new high school on the very peak of Washington Heights (now the scene of cruel racial conflicts). I went to the University of Pennsylvania in Philadelphia where I made a fool of myself trying to become a Renaissance man. I refused to specialize and knocked myself out studying the humanities and the scientific disciplines. I was a miserable member of the crew squad, but I was the most successful member of the fencing team.

I'd been fascinated by science fiction ever since Hugo

Gernsback's magazines first appeared on the stands. I suffered through the dismal years of space opera when science fiction was written by the hacks of pulp Westerns who merely translated the Lazy X ranch into the Planet X and then wrote the same formula stories, using space pirates instead of cattle rustlers. I welcomed the glorious epiphany of John Campbell, whose *Astounding* brought about the Golden Age of science fiction.

Ah! Science fiction, science fiction! I've loved it since its birth. I've read it all my life, off and on, with excitement, with joy, sometimes with sorrow. Here's a twelve-year-old kid, hungry for ideas and imagination, borrowing fairy-tale collections from the library—*The Blue Fairy Book, The Red Fairy Book, The Paisley Fairy Book*—and smuggling them home under his jacket because he was ashamed to be reading fairy tales at his age. And then came Hugo Gernsback.

I read science fiction piecemeal in those days. I didn't have much allowance, so I couldn't afford to buy the magazines. I would loaf at the newsstand outside the stationery store as though contemplating which magazine to buy. I would leaf through a science fiction magazine, reading rapidly, until the proprietor came out and chased me. A few hours later I'd return and continue where I'd been forced to leave off. There was one hateful kid in summer camp who used to receive the *Amazing Quarterly* in July. I was next in line, and he was hateful because he was a slow reader.

It's curious that I remember very few of the stories. The H. G. Wells reprints, to be sure, and the very first book I ever bought was the collection of Wells's science fiction short stories. I remember "The Fourth Dimensional Cross Section" (Have I got the title right?) which flabbergasted me with its concept. I think I first read "Flatland by A. Square" as an *Amazing* reprint. I remember a cover for a novel titled, I think, "The Second Deluge." It showed the survivors of the deluge in a sort of Second Ark gazing in awe at the peak of Mt. Everest now bared naked by the rains. The peak was a glitter of precious gems. I interviewed Sir Edmund Hillary in New Zealand a few years ago and he never said anything about diamonds and emeralds. That gives one furiously to think.

Through high school and college I continued to read science fiction but, as I said, with increasing frustration. The pulp era had set in and most of the stories were about heroes with names like "Brick Malloy" who were inspired to combat space pirates, invaders from other worlds, giant insects, and all the rest of the trash still being produced by Hollywood today. I remember a perfectly appalling novel about a Negro conspiracy to take over the world. These niggers, you see, had invented a serum which turned them white, so they could pass, and they were boring from within. Brick Malloy took care of those black bastards. We've come a long way, haven't we?

There were a few bright moments. Who can forget the impact of Weinbaum's "A Martian Odyssey"? That unique story inspired an entire vogue for quaint alien creatures in science fiction. "A Martian Odyssey" was one reason why I submitted my first story to Standard Magazines; they had published Weinbaum's classic. Alas, Weinbaum fell apart and degenerated into a second-rate fantasy writer, and died too young to fulfill his original promise.

And then came Campbell who rescued, elevated, gave meaning and importance to science fiction. It became a vehicle for ideas, daring, audacity. Why, in God's name, didn't he come first? Even today science fiction is still struggling to shake off its pulp reputation, deserved in the past but certainly not now. It reminds me of the exploded telegony theory; that once a thoroughbred mare has borne a colt by a nonthoroughbred sire, she can never bear another thoroughbred again. Science fiction is still suffering from telegony.

Those happy golden days! I used to go to secondhand magazine stores and buy back copies of *Astounding*. I remember a hot July weekend when my wife was away working in a summer stock company and I spent two days thrilling to Van Vogt's *Slan* and Heinlein's *Universe*! What a concept, and so splendidly worked out with imagination and remorseless logic! Do you remember "Black Destroyer"? Do you remember Lewis Padgett's "Mimsy Were the Borogroves"? That was originality carried to the fifth power. Do you remember— But it's no use. I could go on and on. The

Blue, the Red and the Paisley Fairy Books were gone forever.

After I graduated from the university I really didn't know what I wanted to do with myself. In retrospect I realize that what I needed was a *Wanderjahr*, but such a thing was unheard of in the States at that time. I went to law school for a couple of years (just stalling) and to my surprise received a concentrated education which far surpassed that of my undergraduate years. After thrashing and loafing, to the intense pain of my parents, who would have liked to see me settled in a career, I finally took a crack at writing a science fiction story which I submitted to Standard Magazines. The story had the ridiculous title of "Diaz-X."

Two editors on the staff, Mort Weisinger and Jack Schiff, took an interest in me, I suspect mostly because I'd just finished reading and annotating Joyce's *Ulysses* and would preach it enthusiastically without provocation, to their great amusement. They told me what they had in mind. *Thrilling Wonder* was conducting a prize contest for the best story written by an amateur, and so far none of the submissions was worth considering. They thought "Diaz-X" might fill the bill if it was whipped into shape. They taught me how to revise the story into acceptable form and gave it the prize, $50. It was printed with the title, "The Broken Axiom." They continued their professional guidance and I've never stopped being grateful to them.

Recently, doing an interview for *Publishers Weekly* on my old friend and hero, Robert Heinlein (he prefers "Robert" to "Bob"), I asked him how he got started in science fiction.

"In '39. I started writing and I was hooked. I wrote everything I learned anywhere; navy, army, anywhere. My first science fiction story was 'Lifeline.' I saw an ad in *Thrilling Wonder* offering a prize of $50 for the best amateur story, but then I found out that *Astounding* was paying a cent a word and my story ran to 7,000 words. So I submitted it to them first and they bought it."

"You sonofabitch," I said between my teeth. "I won that *Thrilling Wonder* contest, and you beat me by twenty dollars."

We both laughed but despite our mutual admiration I

suspect that we both knew that twenty dollars wasn't the only way Robert has always bettered me in science fiction.

I think I wrote perhaps a dozen acceptable science fiction stories in the next two years, all of them rotten, for I was without craft and experience and had to learn by trial and error. I've never been one to save things, I don't even save my mss., but I did hold on to the first four magazine covers on which my name appeared. *Thrilling Wonder Stories* (15¢). On the lower lefthand corner is printed "Slaves of the Life Ray, a startling novelet by Alfred Bester." The feature story was "Trouble on Titan, A Gerry Carlyle Novel by Arthur K. Barnes." Another issue had me down in the same bullpen, "The Voyage to Nowhere by Alfred Bester." The most delightful item is my first cover story in *Astonishing Stories* (10¢). "The Pet Nebula by Alfred Bester." The cover shows an amazed young scientist in his laboratory being confronted by a sort of gigantic radioactive seahorse. Damned if I can remember what the story was about.

Some other authors on the covers were Neil R. Jones, J. Harvey Haggard, Ray Cummings (I remember that name), Harry Bates (his, too), Kelvin Kent (sounds like a house name to me), E. E. Smith, Ph.D. (but of course) and Henry Kuttner with better billing than mine. He was in the left-hand *upper* corner.

Mort Weisinger introduced me to the informal luncheon gatherings of the working science fiction authors of the late thirties. I met Henry Kuttner, who later became Lewis Padgett, Ed Hamilton, and Otto Binder, the writing half of Eando Binder. Eando was a sort of acronym of the brothers Ed and Otto Binder. E and O. Ed was a self-taught science fiction illustrator and not very good. Malcolm Jameson, author of navy-oriented space stories, was there, tall, gaunt, prematurely grey, speaking in slow, heavy tones. Now and then he brought along his pretty daughter, who turned everybody's head.

The vivacious *compère* of those luncheons was Manley Wade Wellman, a professional Southerner full of regional anecdotes. It's my recollection that one of his hands was slightly shriveled, which may have been why he came on so strong for the Confederate cause. We were all very patient with that; after all, our side won the war. Wellman was quite the man-of-the-world for the innocent thirties; he always ordered wine with his lunch.

Henry Kuttner and Otto Binder were medium-sized young men, very quiet and courteous, and entirely without outstanding features. Once I broke Kuttner up quite unintentionally. I said to Weisinger, "I've just finished a wild story that takes place in a spaceless, timeless locale where there's no objective reality. It's awfully long, 20,000 words, but I can cut the first 5,000." Kuttner burst out laughing. I do, too, when I think of the dumb kid I was. Once I said most earnestly to Jameson, "I've discovered a remarkable thing. If you combine two story-lines into one, the result can be tremendously exciting." He stared at me with incredulity. "Haven't you ever heard of plot and counterplot?" he growled. I hadn't. I discovered it all by myself.

Being brash and the worst kind of intellectual snob, I said privately to Weisinger that I wasn't much impressed by these writers who were supplying most of the science fiction for the magazines, and asked him why they received so many assignments. He explained, "They may never write a great story, but they never write a bad one. We know we can depend on them." Having recently served my time as a magazine editor, I now understand exactly what he meant.

When the comic book explosion burst, my two magi were lured away from Standard Magazines by the *Superman* Group. There was a desperate need for writers to provide scenarios (Wellman nicknamed them "Squinkas") for the artists, so Weisinger and Schiff drafted me as one of their writers. I hadn't the faintest idea of how to write a comic book script, but one rainy Saturday afternoon Bill Finger, the star comics writer of the time, took me in hand and gave me, a potential rival, an incisive, illuminating lecture on the craft. I still regard that as a high point in the generosity of one colleague to another.

I wrote comics for three or four years with increasing expertise and success. Those were wonderful days for a novice. Squinkas were expanding and there was a constant demand for stories. You could write three and four a week and experiment while learning your craft. The scripts were usually an odd combination of science fiction and "Gangbusters." To give you some idea of what they were like, here's a typical script conference with an editor I'll call Chuck Migg, dealing with a feature I'll call "Captain Hero." Naturally, both are fictitious. The dialogue isn't.

"Now, listen," Migg says, "I called you down because we got to do something about Captain Hero."

"What's your problem?"

"The book is closing next week, and we're thirteen pages short. That's a whole lead story. We got to work one out now."

"Any particular slant?"

"Nothing special, except maybe two things. We got to be original and we got to be realistic. No more fantasy."

"Right."

"So give."

"Wait a minute, for Christ's sake. Who d'you think I am, Saroyan?"

Two minutes of intense concentration. Then Migg says, "How about this? A mad scientist invents a machine for making people go fast. So crooks steal it and hop themselves up. Get it? They move so fast they can rob a bank in a split second."

"No."

"We open with a splash panel showing money and jewelry disappearing with wiggly lines and— Why no?"

"It's a steal from H. G. Wells."

"But it's still original."

"Anyway, it's too fantastic. I thought you said we were going to be realistic."

"Sure I said realistic, but that don't mean we can't be imaginative. What we have to—"

"Wait a minute. Hold the phone."

"Got a flash?"

"Maybe. Suppose we begin with a guy making some kind of experiment. He's a scientist, but not mad. This is a straight, sincere guy."

"Gotcha. He's making an experiment for the good of humanity. Different narrative hook."

"We'll have to use some kind of rare earth metal; cerium, maybe, or—"

"No, let's go back to radium. We ain't used it in the last three issues."

"All right, radium. The experiment is a success. He brings a dead dog back to life with his radium serum."

"I'm waiting for the twist."

"The serum gets into his blood. From a lovable scientist, he turns into a fiend."

At this point Migg takes fire. "I got it! I got it! We'll make like King Midas. This doc is a sweet guy. He's just finished an experiment that's gonna bring eternal life to mankind. So he takes a walk in his garden and smells a rose. Blooie! The rose dies. He feeds the birds. Wham! The birds plotz. So how does Captain Hero come in?"

"Well, maybe we can make it Jekyll and Hyde here. The doctor doesn't want to be a walking killer. He knows there's a rare medicine that'll neutralize the radium in him. He has to steal it from hospitals, and that brings Captain Hero around to investigate."

"Nice human interest."

"But here's the next twist. The doctor takes a shot of the medicine and thinks he's safe. Then his daughter walks into the lab, and when he kisses her, she dies. The medicine won't cure him any more."

By now Migg is in orbit. "I got it! I got it! First we run a caption: IN THE LONELY LABORATORY A DREADFUL CHANGE TORTURES DR.—whatever his name is—HE IS NOW DR. RADIUM!!! Nice name, huh?"

"Okay."

"Then we run a few panels showing him turning green and smashing stuff and he screams: THE MEDICINE CAN NO LONGER SAVE ME! THE RADIUM IS EATING INTO MY BRAIN!! I'M GOING MAD, HA-HA-HA!!! How's that for real drama?"

"Great."

"Okay. That takes care of the first three pages. What happens with Dr. Radium in the next ten?"

"Straight action finish. Captain Hero tracks him down. He traps Captain Hero in something lethal. Captain Hero escapes and traps Dr. Radium and knocks him off a cliff or something.''

''No. Knock him into a volcano.''

''Why?''

''So we can bring Dr. Radium back for a sequel. He really packs a wallop. We could have him walking through walls and stuff on account of the radium in him.''

''Sure.''

''This is gonna be a great character, so don't rush the writing. Can you start today? Good. I'll send a messenger up for it tomorrow.''

The great George Burns, bemoaning the death of vaude-ville, once said, ''There just ain't no place for kids to be lousy any more.'' The comics gave me an ample opportunity to get a lot of lousy writing out of my system.

The line ''. . . knocks him off a cliff or something'' has particular significance. We had very strict self-imposed rules about death and violence. The Good Guys never deliberately killed. They fought, but only with their fists. Only villains used deadly weapons. We could show death coming—a character falling off the top of a high building ''Aiggghhh!''—and we could show the result of death—a body, but always face down. We could never show the moment of death; never a wound, never a rictus, no blood, at the most a knife protruding from the back. I remember the shock that ran through the *Superman* office when Chet Gould drew a bullet piercing the forehead of a villain in ''Dick Tracy.''

We had other strict rules. No cop could be crooked. They could be dumb, but they had to be honest. We disapproved of Raymond Chandler's corrupt police. No mechanical or sci-entific device could be used unless it had a firm foundation in fact. We used to laugh at the outlandish gadgets Bob Kane invented (he wrote his own squinkas as a rule) for ''Batman and Robin'' which, among ourselves, we called Batman and Rabinowitz. Sadism was absolutely taboo; no torture scenes, no pain scenes. And, of course, sex was completely out.

Holiday tells a great story about George Horace Lorrimer, the awesome editor-in-chief of *The Saturday Evening Post*, our sister magazine. He did a very daring thing for his time.

He ran a novel in two parts and the first installment ended with the girl bringing the boy back to her apartment at midnight for coffee and eggs. The second installment opened with them having breakfast together in her apartment the following morning. Thousands of indignant letters came in, and Lorrimer had a form reply printed: "*The Saturday Evening Post* is not responsible for the behavior of its characters between installments." Presumably our comic book heroes lived normal lives between issues; Batman getting bombed and chasing ladies into bed, Rabinowitz burning down his school library in protest against something.

I was married by then, and my wife was an actress. One day she told me that the radio show, "Nick Carter," was looking for scripts. I took one of my best comic book stories, translated it into a radio script, and it was accepted. Then my wife told me that a new show, "Charlie Chan," was having script problems. I did the same thing with the same result. By the end of the year I was the regular writer on those two shows and branching out to "The Shadow" and others. The comic book days were over, but the splendid training I received in visualization, attack, dialogue, and economy stayed with me forever. The imagination must come from within; no one can teach you that. The ideas must come from without, and I'd better explain that.

Usually, ideas don't just come to you out of nowhere; they require a compost heap of germination, and the compost is diligent preparation. I spent many hours a week in the reading rooms of the New York public library at 42nd Street and Fifth Avenue. I read everything and anything with magpie attention for a possible story idea; art frauds, police methods, smuggling, psychiatry, scientific research, color dictionaries, music, demography, biography, plays . . . the list is endless. I'd been forced to develop a speed-reading technique in law school and averaged a dozen books per session. I thought that one potential idea per book was a reasonable return. All that material went into my Commonplace Book for future use. I'm still using it and still adding to it.

And so for the next five or six years I forgot comics, forgot science fiction and immersed myself in the entertainment business. It was new, colorful, challenging and—I must be honest—far more profitable. I wrote mystery, adventure, fantasy, variety, anything that was a challenge, a new experience, something I'd never done before. I even became the director on one of the shows, and that was another fascinating challenge.

But very slowly an insidious poison began to diminish my pleasure; it was the constraints of network censorship and client control. There were too many ideas which I was not permitted to explore. Management said they were too different; the public would never understand them. Accounting said they were too expensive to do; the budget couldn't stand it. One Chicago client wrote an angry letter to the producer of one of my shows, "Tell Bester to stop trying to be original. All I want is ordinary scripts." That really hurt. Originality is the essence of what the artist has to offer. One way or another, we must produce a new sound.

But I must admit that the originality-compulsion can often be a nuisance to myself as well as others. When a concept for a story develops, a half-dozen ideas for the working-out come to mind. These are examined and dismissed. If they came that easily, they can't be worthwhile. "Do it the hard way," I say to myself, and so I search for the hard way, driving myself and everybody around me quite mad in the process. I pace interminably, mumbling to myself, I go for long walks. I sit in bars and drink, hoping that an overheard fragment of conversation may give me a clue. It never happens but all the same, for reasons which I don't understand, I do get ideas in saloons.

Here's an example. Recently I was struggling with the pheromone phenomenon. A pheromone is an external hormone secreted by an insect—an ant, say—when it finds a good food source. The other members of the colony are impelled to follow the pheromone trail, and they find the food, too. I wanted to extrapolate that to a man and I had to do it the hard way. So I paced and I walked and at last I went to a bar where I was nailed by a dumb announcer I knew who drilled my ear with his boring monologue. As I was gazing moodily into my drink and wondering how to escape, the hard way came to me. "He doesn't *leave* a trail," I burst out.

"He's impelled to *follow* a trail." While the announcer looked at me in astonishment, I whipped out my notebook and wrote, "Death left a pheromone trail for him; death in fact, death in the making, death in the planning."

So, out of frustration, I went back to science fiction in order to keep my cool. It was a safety valve, an escape hatch, therapy for me. The ideas which no show would touch could be written as science fiction stories, and I could have the satisfaction of seeing them come to life. (You must have an audience for that.) I wrote perhaps a dozen and a half stories, most of them for *Fantasy & Science Fiction* whose editors, Tony Boucher and Mick McComas, were unfailingly kind and appreciative.

I wrote a few stories for *Astounding*, and out of that came my one demented meeting with the great John W. Campbell, Jr. I needn't preface this account with the reminder that I worshiped Campbell from afar. I had never met him; all my stories had been submitted by mail. I hadn't the faintest idea of what he was like, but I imagined that he was a combination of Bertrand Russell and Ernest Rutherford. So I sent off another story to Campbell, one which no show would let me tackle. The title was "Oddy and Id" and the concept was Freudian, that a man is not governed by his conscious mind but rather by his unconscious compulsions. Campbell telephoned me a few weeks later to say that he liked the story but wanted to discuss a few changes with me. Would I come to his office? I was delighted to accept the invitation despite the fact that the editorial offices of *Astounding* were then the hell and gone out in the boondocks of New Jersey.

The editorial offices were in a grim factory that looked like and probably was a printing plant. The "offices" turned out to be one small office, cramped, dingy, occupied not only by Campbell but by his assistant, Miss Tarrant. My only yardstick for comparison was the glamorous network and advertising agency offices. I was dismayed.

Campbell arose from his desk and shook hands. I'm a fairly big guy, but he looked enormous to me—about the size of a defensive tackle. He was dour and seemed preoccupied by matters of great moment. He sat down behind his desk. I sat down on the visitor's chair.

"You don't know it," Campbell said. "You can't have any way of knowing it, but Freud is finished."

I stared. "If you mean the rival schools of psychiatry, Mr. Campbell, I think—"

"No I don't. Psychiatry, as we know it, is dead."

"Oh, come now, Mr. Campbell. Surely you're joking."

"I have never been more serious in my life. Freud has been destroyed by one of the greatest discoveries of our time."

"What's that?"

"Dianetics."

"I never heard of it."

"It was discovered by L. Ron Hubbard, and he will win the Nobel Peace Prize for it," Campbell said solemnly.

"The peace prize? What for?"

"Wouldn't the man who wiped out war win the Nobel Peace Prize?"

"I suppose so, but how?"

"Through dianetics."

"I honestly don't know what you're talking about, Mr. Campbell."

"Read this," he said and handed me a sheaf of long galley proofs. They were, I discovered later, the galleys of the very first dianetics piece to appear in *Astounding*.

"Read them here and now? This is an awful lot of copy."

He nodded, shuffled some papers, spoke to Miss Tarrant, and went about his business, ignoring me. I read the first galley carefully, the second not so carefully, as I became bored by the dianetics mishmash. Finally I was just letting my eyes wander along, but was very careful to allow enough time for each galley so Campbell wouldn't know I was faking. He looked very shrewd and observant to me. After a sufficient time, I stacked the galleys neatly and returned them to Campbell's desk.

"Well?" he demanded. "Will Hubbard win the peace prize?"

"It's difficult to say. Dianetics is a most original and imaginative idea, but I've only been able to read through the piece once. If I could take a set of galleys home and—"

"No," Campbell said. "There's only this one set. I'm rescheduling and pushing the article into the very next issue.

It's that important." He handed the galleys to Miss Tarrant. "You're blocking it," he told me. "That's all right. Most people do that when a new idea threatens to overturn their thinking."

"That may well be," I said, "but I don't think it's true of myself. I'm a hyperthyroid, an intellectual monkey, curious about everything."

"No," Campbell said, with the assurance of a diagnostician, "you're a hyp-O-thyroid. But it's not a question of intellect, it's one of emotion. We conceal our emotional history from ourselves although dianetics can trace our history all the way back to the womb."

"To the womb!"

"Yes. The fetus remembers. Come and have lunch."

Remember, I was fresh from Madison Avenue and expense-account luncheons. We didn't go to the Jersey equivalent of Sardi's, "21," even P. J. Clarke's. He led me downstairs and we entered a tacky little lunchroom crowded with printers and file clerks; an interior room with blank walls that made every sound reverberate. I got myself a liverwurst on white, no mustard, and a Coke. I can't remember what Campbell ate.

We sat down at a small table while he continued to discourse on dianetics, the great salvation of the future when the world would at last be cleared of its emotional wounds. Suddenly he stood up and towered over me. "You can drive your memory back to the womb," he said. "You can do it if you release every block, clear yourself and remember. Try it."

"Now?"

"Now. Think. Think back. Clear yourself. Remember! You can remember when your mother tried to abort you with a buttonhook. You've never stopped hating her for it."

Around me there were cries of, "BLT down, hold the mayo. Eighty-six on the English. Combo rye, relish. Coffee shake, pick up." And here was this grim tackle standing over me, practicing dianetics without a license. The scene was so lunatic that I began to tremble with suppressed laughter. I prayed. "Help me out of this, please. Don't let me laugh in his face. Show me a way out.'' God showed me. I looked up at Campbell and said, "You're absolutely right, Mr. Campbell, but the emotional wounds are too much to bear. I can't go on with this."

He was completely satisfied. "Yes, I could see you were shaking.'' He sat down again, and we finished our lunch and returned to his office. It developed that the only changes he wanted in my story was the removal of all Freudian terms which dianetics had now made obsolete. I agreed, of course; they were minor, and it was a great honor to appear in *Astounding* no matter what the price. I escaped at last and returned to civilization where I had three double gibsons and don't be stingy with the onions.

That was my one and only meeting with John Campbell, and certainly my only story conference with him. I've had some wild ones in the entertainment business, but nothing to equal that. It reinforced my private opinion that a majority of the science fiction crowd, despite their brilliance, were missing their marbles. Perhaps that's the price that must be paid for brilliance.

One day, out of the clear sky, Horace Gold telephoned to ask me to write for *Galaxy*, which he had launched with tremendous success. It filled an open space in the field; *Astounding* was hard science; *Fantasy & Science Fiction* was wit and sophistication; *Galaxy* was psychiatry-oriented. I was flattered but begged off, explaining that I didn't think I was much of a science fiction author compared to the genuine greats. "Why me?'' I asked. "You can have Sturgeon, Leiber, Asimov, Heinlein.''

"I've got them,'' he said, "and I want you.''

"Horace, you're an old scriptwriter, so you'll understand. I'm tied up with a bitch of a show starring a no-talent. I've got to write continuity for him, quiz sections for him to M.C. and dramatic sketches for him to mutilate. He's driving me up the wall. His agent is driving me up the wall. I really haven't got the time.''

Horace didn't give up. He would call every so often to chat about the latest science fiction, new concepts, what authors had failed and how they'd failed. In the course of these gossips, he contrived to argue that I was a better writer than I thought and to ask if I didn't have any ideas that I might be interested in working out.

All this was on the phone because Horace was trapped in his apartment. He'd had shattering experiences in both the European and Pacific theaters during World War II and had been released from the service with complete agoraphobia. Everybody had to come to his apartment to see him, including his psychiatrist. Horace was most entertaining on the phone; witty, ironic, perceptive, making shrewd criticisms of science fiction.

I enjoyed these professional gossips with Horace so much that I began to feel beholden to him; after all, I was more or less trapped in my workshop, too. At last I submitted perhaps a dozen ideas for his judgment. Horace discussed them all, very sensibly and realistically, and at last suggested combining two different ideas into what ultimately became *The Demolished Man*. I remember one of the ideas only vaguely; it had something to do with extrasensory perception, but I've forgotten the gimmick. The other I remember quite well. I wanted to write a mystery about a future in which the police are armed with time machines so that if a crime is committed they could trace it back to its origin. This would make crime impossible. How then, in an open story, could a clever criminal outwit the police?

I'd better explain "open story." The classic mystery is the closed story, or whodunit. It's a puzzle in which everything is concealed except the clues carefully scattered through the story. It's up to the audience to piece them together and solve the puzzle. I had become quite expert at that. However, I was carrying too many mystery shows and often fell behind in my deadlines, a heinous crime, so occasionally I would commit the lesser crime of stealing one of my scripts from Show A and adapting it for Show B.

I was reading a three-year-old Show A script for possible theft when it dawned on me that I had written all the wrong scenes. It was a solid story, but in the attempt to keep it a closed puzzle, I had been forced to omit the real drama in order to present the perplexing results of the behind-the-scenes action. So I developed for myself a style of action-mystery writing in which everything is open and known to the audience, every move and countermove, with only the final resolution coming as a surprise. This is an extremely difficult form of writing; it requires you to make your antagonists outwit each other continually with ingenuity and re-sourcefulness. It was a novel style back then.

Horace suggested that instead of using time machines as the obstacle for the criminal, I use ESP. Time travel, he said, was a pretty worn-out theme, and I had to agree. ESP, Horace said, would be an even tougher obstacle to cope with, and I had to agree.

"But I don't like the idea of a mind-reading detective," I said. "It makes him too special."

"No, no," Horace said. "You've got to create an entire ESP society."

And so the creation began. We discussed it on the phone almost daily, each making suggestions, dismissing suggestions, adapting and revising suggestions. Horace was, at least for me, the ideal editor, always helpful, always encouraging, never losing his enthusiasm. He was opinionated, God knows, but so was I, perhaps even more than he. What saved the relationship was the fact that we both knew we respected each other; that, and our professional concentration on the job. For professionals the job is the boss.

The writing began in New York. When my show went off for the summer, I took the ms. out to our summer cottage on Fire Island and continued there. I remember a few amusing incidents. For a while I typed on the front porch. Wolcott Gibbs, the *New Yorker* drama critic, lived up the street and every time he passed our cottage and saw me working he would denounce me. Wolcott had promised to write a biography of Harold Ross that summer and hadn't done a lick of work yet. I. F. (Izzy) Stone dropped in once and found himself in the midst of an animated discussion of political thought as reflected by science fiction. Izzy became so fascinated that he asked us to take five while he ran home to put a fresh battery in his hearing aid.

I used to go surf-fishing every dawn and dusk. One evening I was minding my own business, busy casting and thinking of nothing in particular when the idea of using typeface symbols in names dropped into my mind. I reeled in so quickly that I fouled my line, rushed to the cottage and experimented on the typewriter. Then I went back through the ms. and changed all the names. I remember quitting work one morning to watch an eclipse and it turned cloudy. Obviously somebody up there didn't approve of eclipse-breaks. And so, by the end of the summer, the novel was finished. My working title had been *Demolition*. Horace changed it to *The Demolished Man*. Much better, I think.

The book was received with considerable enthusiasm by the *Galaxy* readers, which was gratifying but surprising. I hadn't had any conscious intention of breaking new trails; I was just trying to do a craftsmanlike job. Some of the fans' remarks bemused me. "Oh, Mr. Bester! How well you understand women." I never thought I understood women. "Who were the models for your characters?" They're surprised when I tell them that the model for one of the protagonists was a bronze statue of a Roman emperor in the Metropolitan Museum. It's haunted me ever since I was a child. I read the emperor's character into the face and when it came time to write this particular ficional character, I used my emperor for the mold.

The *réclame* of the novel turned me into a science fiction somebody, and people were curious about me. I was invited to gatherings of the science fiction Hydra Club where I met the people I was curious about; Ted Sturgeon, Jim Blish, Tony Boucher, Ike Asimov, Avram Davidson, then a professional Jew wearing a yarmulka, and many others. They were all lunatic (So am I. It takes one to spot one.) and convinced me again that most science fiction authors have marbles missing. I can remember listening to an argument about the correct design for a robot, which became so heated that for a moment I thought Judy Merril was going to punch Lester del Rey in the nose. Or maybe it was vice versa.

I was particularly attracted to Blish and Sturgeon. Both were soft-spoken and charming conversationalists. Jim and I would take walks in Central Park during his lunch hour (he was then working as a public relations officer for a pharmaceutical house) and we would talk shop. Although I was an admirer of his work, I felt that it lacked the hard drive to which I'd been trained, and I constantly urged him to attack his stories with more vigor. He never seemed to resent it, or at least was too courteous to show it. His basic problem was how to hold down a PR writing job and yet do creative writing on the side. I had no advice for that. It's a problem which very few people have solved.

Sturgeon and I used to meet occasionally in bars for drinks and talk. Ted's writing exactly suited my taste, which is why I thought he was the finest of us all. But he had a quality which amused and exasperated me. Like Mort Sahl and a few other celebrities I've interviewed—Tony Quinn is another—Ted lived on crisis, and if he wasn't in a crisis, he'd create one for himself. His life was completely disorganized, so it was impossible for him to do his best work consistently. What a waste!

In all fairness I should do a description of myself. I will, but I'm going to save it for the end.

I'd written a contemporary novel based on my TV experiences and it had a fairly decent reprint sale and at last sold to the movies. My wife and I decided to blow the loot on a few years abroad. We put everything into storage, contracted for a little English car, stripped our luggage down to the bare minimum and took off. The only writing materials I brought with me were a portable, my Commonplace Book, a thesaurus, and an idea for another science fiction novel.

For some time I'd been toying with the notion of using the *Count of Monte Cristo* pattern for a story. The reason is simple; I'd always preferred the antihero, and I'd always found high drama in compulsive types. It remained a notion until we bought our cottage on Fire Island and I found a pile of old *National Geographics*. Naturally I read them and came across a most interesting piece on the survival of torpedoed sailors at sea. The record was held by a Philippine cook's helper who lasted for something like four months on an open raft. Then came the detail that racked me up. He'd been sighted several times by passing ships which refused to change course to rescue him because it was a Nazi submarine trick to put out decoys like this. The magpie mind darted down, picked it up, and the notion was transformed into a developing story with a strong attack.

The Stars My Destination (I've forgotten what my working title was) began in a romantic white cottage down in Surrey. This accounts for the fact that so many of the names are English. When I start a story, I spend days reading through telephone directories for help in putting together character names—I'm very fussy about names—and in this case I used English directories. I'm compelled to find or invent names with varying syllables. One, two, three, and four. I'm extremely sensitive to tempo. I'm also extremely sensitive to word color and context. For me there is no such thing as a synonym.

The book got under way very slowly and by the time we left Surrey for a flat in London, I had lost momentum. I went back, took it from the top and started all over again, hoping to generate steam pressure. I write out of hysteria. I bogged down again and I didn't know why. Everything seemed to go wrong. I couldn't use a portable, but the only standard machines I could rent had English keyboards. That threw me off. English ms. paper was smaller than the American, and that threw me off. And I was cold, cold, cold. So in November we packed and drove to the car ferry at Dover, with the fog snapping at our ass all the way, crossed the Channel and drove south to Rome.

After many adventures we finally settled into a penthouse apartment on the *Piazza della Muse*. My wife went to work in Italian films. I located the one (1) standard typewriter in all Rome with an American keyboard and started in again, once more taking it from the top. This time I began to build up momentum, very slowly, and was waiting for the hysteria to set in. I remember the day that it came vividly.

I was talking shop with a young Italian film director for whom my wife was working, both of us beefing about the experimental things we'd never been permitted to do. I told him about a note on synesthesia which I'd been dying to write as a TV script for years. I had to explain synesthesia—this was years before the exploration of psychedelic drugs—and while I was describing the phenomenon I suddenly thought, "Jesus Christ! This is for the novel. It leads me into the climax." And I realized that what had been holding me up for so many months was the fact that I didn't have a fiery finish in mind. I must have an attack and a finale. I'm like the old Hollywood gag, "Start with an earthquake and build to a climax."

The work went well despite many agonies. Rome is no place for a writer who needs quiet. The Italians *fa rumore* (make noise) passionately. The pilot of a Piper Cub was enchanted by a girl who sunbathed on the roof of a mansion across the road and buzzed her, and me, every morning from seven to nine. There were frequent informal motorcycle rallies in our *piazza* and the Italians always remove the mufflers from their vehicles; it makes them feel like Tazio Nuvolare. On the other side of our penthouse a building was in construction, and you haven't heard *rumore* until you've heard stonemasons talking politics.

I also had research problems. The official U.S. library was woefully inadequate. The British Consulate library was a love, and I used it regularly, but none of their books was dated later than 1930, no help for a science fiction writer needing data about radiation belts. In desperation, I plagued Tony Boucher and Willy Ley with letters asking for information. They always came through, bless them, Tony on the humanities—"Dear Tony, what the hell is the name of that Russian sect that practiced self-castration? Slotsky? Something like that."—Willy on the disciplines—"Dear Willy, how long could an unprotected man last in naked space? Ten minutes? Five minutes? How would he die?"

The book was completed about three months after the third start in Rome; the first draft of a novel usually takes me about three months. Then there's the pleasant period of revision and rewriting; I always enjoy polishing. What can I say about the material? I've told you about the attack and the climax. I've told you about the years of preparation stored in my mind and my Commonplace Book. If you want the empiric equation for my science fiction writing—for all my writing, in fact, it's:

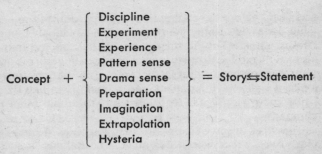

I must enlarge on this just a little. The mature science
fiction author doesn't merely tell a story about Brick Malloy
vs. The Giant Yeastmen from Gethsemane. He makes a
statement through his story. What is the statement? Himself,
the dimension and depth of the man. His statement is seeing
what everybody else sees but thinking what no one else has
thought, and having the courage to say it. The hell of it is that
only time will tell whether it was worth saying.

Back in London the next year, I was able to meet the young
English science fiction authors through Ted Carnell and my
London publisher. They gathered in a pub somewhere off the
Strand. They were an entertaining crowd, speaking with a
rapidity and intensity that reminded me of a debating team
from the Oxford Union. And they raised a question which
I've never been able to answer: Why is it that the English
science fiction writers, so brilliant socially, too often turn out
rather dull and predictable stories? There are notable exceptions, of course, but I have the sneaky suspicion that they
had American mothers.

John Wyndham and Arthur Clarke came to those gatherings. I thought Arthur rather strange, very much like John
Campbell, utterly devoid of a sense of humor, and I'm
always ill at ease with humorless people. Once he pledged us
all to come to the meeting the following week; he would show
slides of some amazing underwater photographs he had
taken. He did indeed bring a projector and slides and show
them. After looking at a few I called, ''Damn it, Arthur,
these aren't underwater shots. You took them in an
aquarium. I can see the reflections in the plate glass.'' And it

degenerated into an argument about whether the photographer and his camera had to be underwater, too.

It was around this time that an event took place which will answer a question often asked me: Why did I drop science fiction after my first two novels? I'll have to use a flashback, a device I despise, but I can't see any other way out. A month before I left the States, my agent called me in to meet a distinguished gentleman, senior editor of *Holiday* magazine, who was in search of a feature on television. He told me that he'd tried two professional magazine writers without success, and as a last resort wanted to try me on the basis of the novel I'd written about the business.

It was an intriguing challenge. I knew television, but I knew absolutely nothing about magazine piece-writing. So once again I explored, experimented and taught myself. *Holiday* liked the piece so much that they asked me to do pieces on Italian, French and English TV while I was abroad, which I did. Just when my wife and I had decided to settle in London permanently, word came from *Holiday* that they wanted me to come back to the States. They were starting a new feature called "The Antic Arts" and wanted me to become a regular monthly contributor. Another challenge. I returned to New York.

An exciting new writing life began for me. I was no longer immured in my workshop; I was getting out and interviewing interesting people in interesting professions. Reality had become so colorful for me that I no longer needed the therapy of science fiction. And since the magazine imposed no constraints on me, outside of the practical requirements of professional magazine technique, I no longer needed a safety valve.

I wrote scores of pieces, and I confess that they were much easier than fiction, so perhaps I was lazy. But try to visualize the joy of being sent back to your old university to do a feature on it, going to Detroit to test-drive their new cars, taking the very first flight of the Boeing 747, interviewing Sophia Loren in Pisa, De Sica in Rome, Peter Ustinov, Sir Laurence Olivier (they called him Sir Larry in Hollywood), Mike Todd and Elizabeth Taylor, George Balanchine. I interviewed and wrote, and wrote, and wrote, until it became cheaper for

Holiday to hire me as senior editor, and here was a brand-new challenge.

I didn't altogether lose touch with science fiction; I did book reviews for *Fantasy & Science Fiction* under Bob Mills's editorship and later Avram Davidson's. Unfortunately, my standards had become so high that I seemed to infuriate the fans who wanted special treatment for science fiction. My attitude was that science fiction was merely one of many forms of fiction and should be judged by the standards which apply to all. A silly story is a silly story whether written by Robert Heinlein or Norman Mailer. One enraged fan wrote in to say that I was obviously going through change of life.

Alas, all things must come to an end. *Holiday* failed after a robust twenty-five years; my eyes failed, like poor Congreve's; and here I am, here I am, back in my workshop again, immured and alone, and so turning to my first love, my original love, science fiction. I hope it's not too late to rekindle the affair. Ike Asimov once said to me, "Alfie, we broke new trails in our time but we have to face the fact that we're over the hill now." I hope not, but if it's true, I'll go down fighting for a fresh challenge.

What am I like? Here's as honest a description of myself as possible. You come to my workshop, a three-room apartment, which is a mess, filled with books, mss., typewriters, telescopes, microscopes, reams of typing paper, chemical glassware. We live in the apartment upstairs, and my wife uses my kitchen for a storeroom. This annoys me; I used to use it as a laboratory. Here's an interesting sidelight. Although I'm a powerful drinker I won't permit liquor to be stored there; I won't have booze in my workshop.

You find me on a high stool at a large drafting table editing some of my pages. I'm probably wearing flimsy pajama bottoms, an old shirt and am barefoot; my customary at-home clothes. You see a biggish guy with dark brown hair going grey, a tight beard nearly all white and the dark brown eyes of a sad spaniel. I shake hands, seat you, hoist myself on the stool again and light a cigarette, always chatting cordially about anything and everything to put you at your ease. However, it's possible that I like to sit higher than you because it gives me a psychological edge. I don't think so, but I've been accused of it.

My voice is a light tenor (except when I'm angry; then it turns harsh and strident) and is curiously inflected. In one sentence I can run up and down an octave. I have a tendency to drawl my vowels. I've spent so much time abroad that my speech pattern may seem affected, for certain European pronunciations cling to me. I don't know why. GA-rahj for garage, the French ''r'' in the back of the throat, and if there's a knock on the door I automatically holler, *''Avanti!''* a habit I picked up in Italy.

On the other hand my speech is larded with the customary profanity of the entertainment business, as well as Yiddish words and professional phrases. I corrupted the WASP *Holiday* office. It was camp to have a blond junior editor from Yale come into my office and say, ''Alfie, we're having a *tsimmis* with the theater piece. That *goniff* won't rewrite.'' What you don't know is that I always adapt my speech pattern to that of my *vis-à-vis* in an attempt to put him at his ease. It can vary anywhere from burley (burlesque) to Phi Beta Kappa.

I try to warm you by relating to you, showing interest in you, listening to you. Once I sense that you're at your ease I shut up and listen. Occasionally I'll break in to put a question, argue a point, or ask you to enlarge on one of your ideas. Now and then I'll say, ''Wait a minute, you're going too fast. I have to think about that.'' Then I stare into nowhere and think hard. Frankly, I'm not lightning, but a novel idea can always launch me into outer space. Then I pace excitedly, exploring it out loud.

What I don't reveal is the emotional storm that rages within me. I have my fair share of frustrations and despairs, but I was raised to show a cheerful countenance to the world and suffer in private. Most people are too preoccupied with their own troubles to be much interested in yours. Do you remember Viola's lovely line in *Twelfth Night*? ''And, with a green and yellow melancholy, she sat like Patience on a monument, smiling at grief.''

I have some odd mannerisms. I use the accusing finger of a prosecuting attorney as an exclamation point to express appreciation for an idea or a witticism. I'm a "toucher," hugging and kissing men and women alike, and giving them a hard pat on the behind to show approval. Once I embarrassed my boss, the *Holiday* editor-in-chief, terribly. He'd just returned from a junket to India and, as usual, I breezed into his office and gave him a huge welcoming hug and kiss. Then I noticed he had visitors there. My boss turned red and told them, "Alfie Bester is the most affectionate straight in the world."

I'm a faker, often forced to play the scene. In my time I've been mistaken for a fag, a hardhat, a psychiatrist, an artist, a dirty old man, a dirty young man, and I always respond in character and play the scene. Sometimes I'm compelled to play opposites—my fast to your slow, my slow to your fast—all this to the amusement and annoyance of my wife. When we get home she berates me for being a liar and all I can do is laugh helplessly while she swears she'll never trust me again.

I do laugh a lot, with you and at myself, and my laughter is loud and uninhibited. I'm a kind of noisy guy. But don't ever be fooled by me even when I'm clowning. That magpie mind is always looking to pick up something.

A GALAXY OF SCIENCE FICTION
MASTERPIECES AVAILABLE FROM BERKLEY